"Rich in accurate wartime detail and flight-line atmosphere."

Kirkus Reviews

From the Book

The German was out of accurate range, but Ham recalled his dad teaching him how to snap-shoot quail. Ignoring his computing gunsight, Ham squeezed off three quick, instinctively aimed bursts above and ahead of his quarry. The lazily arcing tracers were placed precisely where he wanted them. The ghost of his gunnery instructor had arrived to perch on his shoulder. "Given an option, fighter pilots tent to break left when in trouble. You see, torque created by that big prop makes a turn to the left easier to control. Plus, most landing patterns are to the left, so they just get into the habit."

While the enemy pilot was still deciding on a course of evasive action, Ham moved his aim slightly left and down from the path taken by his previous bursts. He clamped his thumbs to the firing trips and held them there. The startled pilot broke hard left—directly into the path of a solid hail of .50-caliber fire. Ham's continuous stream of armor-piercing projectiles arrived just in time to rake the speeding fighter from nose to tail.

FALCONS

A Novel by

RAY ROSENBAUM

LYFORD
Books

Falcons is a novel. Although many of the events portrayed in this book are based on historical fact, specific events involving characters other than historical personages are fictitious. Except for historical figures, any resemblance of characters to persons living or dead is purely coincidental.

LYFORD Books
Published by Presidio Press
505 B San Marin Dr., Suite 300
Novato, CA 94945-1340

First published in cloth by LYFORD Books in 1993
This paperbound edition published in 1995

Library of Congress Cataloging-in-Publication Data

Rosenbaum, Ray, 1923–
    Falcons : a novel / Ray Rosenbaum.
      p.   cm.
    ISBN 0-89141-476-2 (cloth)
    ISBN 0-89141-559-9 (paper)
    1. World War, 1939–1945—Fiction. l. Title.
PS3568.0777F35   1993
813'.54—dc20   92-29016
                                            CIP

Typography by ProImage
Printed in the United States of America

For Midge

FALCONS

Prologue

☆ ☆ ☆

THE HEARING

DAY ONE

28 November 1945
Hearing Room B, Building 1048, War Department
Washington, D.C.

Lieutenant General Harley Woods tapped the ebony gavel, cleared his throat, and announced in deep, rumbling tones, "By direction of the secretary of war, this board is convened to examine circumstances leading to a severe loss of life and materiel during the bombing raid of 1 August 1942 on the oil refinery complex at Ploesti, Romania. A report to be rendered to the secretary will deal with the planning and execution of the mission, command decisions involved, and a finding that the results did or did not justify the loss of ninety-six B-24 aircraft and five hundred crew members."

He paused to scowl at nothing or no one in particular before continuing. "I declare this hearing in session. Is the recorder ready to proceed?"

Janet Templeton, her patrician features bearing a pensive expression, placed purse and gloves alongside one shapely thigh and settled back in her seat. The oak bench, polished to a mirror finish by hundreds of restless bottoms over its fifty years of use, was uncomfortable. But she knew that the army was not overly concerned with spectator comfort. In fact, she considered herself fortunate just to be there. It had required personal intervention by her father-in-law, Sen. Broderick Templeton II, to gain permission to join the other dozen or so observers, all of whom were in uniform. Even with his sponsorship, she would be excluded during certain phases when the testimony would be "classified."

1

Janet touched the petite pillbox hat perched atop her deep red hair, an unconscious reflexive action, and directed her attention to the slender, ferret-faced colonel seated behind a gleaming golden-oak table.

The man unfolded his six-foot-two-inch frame to a standing position and addressed General Woods in brisk tones. "Yes, Sir. With the general's permission I will present opening remarks at this time."

"You may proceed." General Woods didn't bother to consult the four stern-faced officers flanking him on either side.

Janet knew that Woods was not happy with his role. Nor were the other board members, all displaying not less than two stars on their epaulets. The army preferred to handle problems within its ranks in time-honored fashion. Suspicious of civilians in general, officers preferred to impose disciplinary measures for incompetence without public fanfare. Formal written records were couched in official shorthand. ". . . his judgment almost always sound" spoke volumes to members of the inner circle. Such had been the case in the Ploesti affair.

Certain officers had been quietly reassigned out of command positions, their opportunity for advancement terminated—the ultimate punishment. Her father, an Army Air Corps colonel slated for retirement now that hostilities were ended, had hinted at details. The upper echelons of command considered Ploesti a closed book.

Senator Templeton thought differently. As chairman of the Military Affairs Committee he had pressed for details of the Ploesti raid— the mission on which his son, Broderick Templeton III, Janet's husband, had lost his life—to be made public. That the country's current president, Harry S. Truman, had gained political prominence as a crusading, investigative senator went unsaid. But Janet knew; Senator Templeton's aspirations transcended his present political office.

"Gentlemen, I am Col. Dexter Blankenship. I have been designated recorder for this board. As such, my task is to present evidence and initiate questioning of those having knowledge of the matter. . . ." The lanky Blankenship's intense, pompous manner of speech failed to stir Janet's interest.

She studied the setting. A random ray of sunlight, breaking through the gloomy November skies, threw the speaker's aquiline nose and salt-and-pepper crewcut into sharp outline against the dirt- and smoke-filmed window behind him. The room itself, one of the smaller meeting rooms, reflected wartime-imposed curtailment of upkeep. Under slightly grimy overhead globes, the narrow-board oak flooring revealed the need for a good waxing and buffing. Humid, Potomac air had caused small bits of the somber pale green and buff paint to separate from its base. A faint musty odor suggested that the room was seldom used.

General Woods, possessed of a bearlike physique, crouched behind the long, elevated, semicircular table. He seemed oddly entranced with the recorder's words. Woods dominated the room, and would dominate the proceedings, Janet suspected. The findings, along with recommendations for corrective action, were most likely being composed even now behind that impassive, heavy-jowled face. The deep-set, hooded eyes would take in every aspect of the proceedings with thoughtful interest, she was sure, but with absolutely no hint of any predisposition.

She sighed unobtrusively. It was all so damned futile, she thought, this search for damning or exculpatory facts. The war was over. Ploesti had joined fading names such as Schweinfurt, Regensburg, Omaha Beach, Guadalcanal, Pearl Harbor—the list was endless. Places where men, some brave, some not so brave, went out to do what they had to do. War being what it is, not all returned. It had always been that way.

The suave, sophisticated young lieutenant she married had seemed indifferent, blasé even, to the danger. Had that playboy exterior been a sham? She discovered, after receiving news of his death, that she had never really known Broderick Templeton. What had driven him to place his life in jeopardy? How had he dealt with the ultimate challenge?

And Ross. Lieutenant Ross Colyer. The serious young officer she had dated briefly during those carefree days before the war. Honolulu—gala house parties, lazy afternoons on the sparkling, manicured beaches of Waikiki. Ross the sincere, dedicated one whose ambition was to rise to the top in the Air Corps. There had been a spark of something between them. Given another time and another place, would things have gone differently?

General Woods's gravelly voice intoning, "You may call your first witness, Colonel," failed to interrupt Janet's reverie. What was war in the air *really* like? she wondered. What mysterious alchemy transformed boys into men—professional killers? What caused them to climb back into their planes, day after day, when their odds for survival would have given pause to a gambler at a Las Vegas crap table? Patriotism? Ross, maybe. "BT," as his fellow officers had dubbed her husband, no. Ambition? A need for self-aggrandizement? Perhaps it was more complicated than that, something only members of that closed, male fraternity understood. Ross had touched on it, one night when entry into war became almost certain. Laughing off a serious, philosophical question, he had told her, "We're like falcons, Janet. We don't question the moral values of what we do. We are trained, once shown the prey, to go in for the kill. That's what we do best."

So what had prompted her to pester her father-in-law for a pass to attend the hearing? Was it a search for some great truth? Or was it nothing more than morbid curiosity?

Janet settled back to wait. And listen.

Chapter One

0700 Hours, 7 December 1941
Kahuku Point, Oahu, Hawaii
Mobile Radar Site "Opana"

"Looky here, Joe," Pvt. George Elliott called to his partner. "I'm getting a return at a hundred and thirty-six miles. A big one. That's damn near a record."

Private Joseph Lockard was unimpressed. The schedule called for them to shut down the 270-B radar set at 0700. Lockard, the senior operator, was anxious to get back to quarters. Elliott was just an apprentice operator; he had probably fucked up the equipment. They were here on a Sunday morning only to keep prowlers away. The two vans, housing a portable generator and the unit's bulky electronic gear, aroused curiosity among roaming juveniles.

Arriving at 0400, Joe had stared at the shimmering oscilloscope until his eyeballs ached. There had been nothing of interest displayed. He was already on the ground, preparing to turn the fuel shutoff on the rumbling power plant. "C'mon, George, shut that damn thing off. Let's get some breakfast."

"No, wait a minute, Joe. Come look at this. It looks like something we oughta report." The skinny, freckle-faced Elliott brushed a lock of sun-bleached hair away from his squinched eyes.

"Aw, Christ." Lockard clambered back inside the darkened interior of the operations van. His eyes widened when he looked at the rangefinder screen.

"It's goin' crazy, Joe."

"It's gotta be some kind of fucking malfunction," said Lockard. But even as he watched, the pulsing return moved inside the extreme range marker, labeled 130 miles.

His hands shaking, Joe snatched a field-phone handset from its leather carrier and spun the ringer crank.

"Sir, we have a big, and I mean a really big, return from a hunnert and thirty miles out; bearing zero-two degrees true. Sir, I've never seen anything like it before."

Lieutenant Scott Tyler, disgusted with his sudden weekend duty assignment as information center duty officer, grunted. "What does it look like?" he asked for lack of anything better to say.

Private Lockard swallowed an invisible lump in his throat. "Well— it's big—and it's moving toward us."

Tyler removed his strictly nonregulation brogans from the top of his controller's console and laid aside a month-old copy of *The Sporting News*.

"Okay," said Tyler, "stand by while I have a look at the activity log. I don't know of any kind of an exercise laid on for today." Joe waited, listening to the sound of paper flapping on the other end of the phone. Tyler's voice came back on.

"The *Enterprise* and *Lexington* aren't in the harbor. It's probably some of those carrier planes up farting around. Goddamn navy never tells us what they're up to. No, wait a minute. There's a flight of B-17s from the States with an oh-eight-hundred ETA. They'd make a big echo and it's the right direction and time. Log it and I'll put it in my report. God knows there's nothing else in it this morning."

Tyler lethargically scrawled a brief log entry and returned to an analysis of why the Dodgers lost the World Series in only five games. A nagging uneasiness prevented total concentration, however. Should he call someone? Who? Naw, he'd just get his ass chewed for getting some hungover senior officer out of bed—or screwing up somebody's golf date. In the distance he could hear church bells calling the faithful to eight o'clock mass.

0700 Hours, 7 December 1941
Hickam Field
Oahu, Hawaii

A scowl marring his sun-bronzed features, 2d Lt. Ross Colyer surveyed the untidy clutter of the Airdrome Officer's cubicle. Created by an uninspired member of the base engineering office, the AO's "office" was not an impressive place—even when neat and tidy. Shoulder-high sections of brown-stained plywood, topped with glass panels, enclosed a ten-by-ten section of a remote corner in "Base Ops"—the nerve center for all flights arriving at or departing from Hickam Field.

The accommodation hardly lived up to the prestigious title of "Airdrome Officer." Infrequent visitors were treated to the sight of a battered, yellow-oak desk, its top etched with burns from long-forgotten cigarettes, a squeaky wooden swivel chair, and a coatrack painted olive drab. Because the incumbent was expected to spend twenty-four hours on duty there, an iron cot occupied one corner. Decorative accessories were limited to a single picture: Betty Grable, scantily clad and peering coyly over one shoulder. On the picture's flip side was the stern visage of Gen. Henry H. "Hap" Arnold, commanding general of the U.S. Army Air Forces. An unwritten rule admonished the AO on duty to ensure that Miss Grable was facing the wall during the base commander's weekly inspection tour.

Lieutenant Broderick Templeton III is a first-class, brass-balled horse's ass, Ross thought. Plus, Templeton, the duty officer he had just relieved, was a lazy slob. It required only five minutes to wash and return used coffee cups to their gray-painted rack above the big percolator, put sandwich remnants and their wrappers in the outside garbage receptacle, empty the butt can of its smelly accumulation, straighten blankets on the iron cot in the corner, and return tattered, dog-eared magazines to their rack. But these minor housekeeping tasks were beneath Broderick-fucking-Templeton the Third. Let some enlisted man do it was his credo.

Ross tossed his Class A uniform cap on the slightly tipsy coatrack and set about restoring order to the spartan cell he would call home for the next twenty-four hours.

Okay, Colyer, admit it; you're pissed because the bastard has a date to go riding with Janet this morning, he muttered to himself. And Ross had left her only eight hours ago. Not much of a date. Not the kind he knew Col. Edmond Richards's daughter was accustomed to. He had apologized. "AO duty tomorrow," he explained. They had walked from her parents' quarters to the post theater. Ross had no car. It was a good movie—Bob Hope and Dorothy Lamour in *Road to Morocco*. Another short walk to the officers' club for beer, then back to the VIP housing area. He had kissed her a lingering goodnight at the door, then caught the bus back to Hickam—suffering from that young lover's malaise, "stone-ache."

Templeton, damn him, knew that Ross and Janet Richards dated frequently. He had really rubbed it in that morning. Sprawled on the rumpled cot, Templeton had preened his Ronald Coleman mustache with a crooked forefinger and greeted Ross with a drawled, "Glad you're on time, son. What a shitty way to spend a weekend, huh? Well, for me it's home and a shower. I'm due for breakfast at Colonel Richards's quarters. Afterward I have a riding date with that good-looking, red-haired daughter of his. Janet—you know her, don't you?"

He then gave Ross a perfunctory and totally inadequate briefing. "Nothing much happening; you have an inbound flight of B-17s from the States. ETA about oh-eight-hundred. You won't be involved—half the brass on base will turn out to meet them." With that, the arrogant asshole had strolled to his 1939 Mercury convertible and departed, a smug smile on his darkly handsome face.

The thing that smarted, though, was that Janet hadn't mentioned her riding date last night. Oh well, he had no claim on her. She was popular, good-looking as all hell, and chased after by every horny young officer on the island. Her mop of flaming red hair could be seen on the dance floor of every major social event. On the beach, no less than a half-dozen panting swains invariably sought to bring her cold drinks and sneak a peek down the front of her skimpy bathing suit. Ross felt lucky just to have her give him the time of day. Still . . .

He tossed his two-inch-thick *Pilot's Operating Handbook for the B-17D* onto the now semicleared desktop. He would pass an otherwise boring Sunday absorbing its contents. An outstanding performance on his checkride next week was a must. Then, perhaps, he could join the long list of left-seat–qualified copilots awaiting assignment as aircraft commanders. But first the duty routine. He snapped a black felt brassard, imprinted with the letters *AO* in white, around his left biceps. Next, the ridiculous brown leather Sam Browne belt and its holstered .45-caliber automatic. Every officer wore side arms while on duty these days. "The Japs are getting ready for something" was the word. The term "sabotage" entered into every conversation. That was the ground-pounders for you. They saw menace in every one of the 170,000 Japanese living on the island.

Picking up the gun belt, Ross uncovered a sterling-silver Ronson cigarette case and lighter. It bore the letters *BT* engraved in elaborate, Spencerian script. He resisted an urge to chuck the thing into the wastebasket and, instead, tossed it into the center desk drawer. Templeton would be back for it, he knew. He displayed the ostentatious flamethrower like a badge of office.

Master Sergeant Rufus Jones, the Base Ops duty noncommissioned officer in charge, rolled a dead cigar to one side of his mouth and greeted Ross. "Morning, Lieutenant. Caught Sunday duty, huh? Whad'ya do, get caught in the sack with the general's wife?"

Ross chuckled good-naturedly. "Naw, it was his secretary—and that's worse. Anything cooking today?"

"Just a training flight of six B-18s and that inbound formation of eleven B-17s. Typical Sunday."

"Okay, I'm taking the AO vehicle for a tour of the flight line. Call the tower and tell them I'll wait for a green light to check the runways."

"I'll see to it, Lieutenant." He peered at Ross from calculating, half-closed eyes. "You got any bets down on the football game this afternoon?"

Ross laughed outright. "Don't try making book with me, Jonesy. I don't know what odds you're giving, but I don't like them already. The goddamn navy will find beating that bunch of patsies from the infantry like taking candy from a baby, though. This is navy country; they run everything, including the frigging sports program."

He turned and strolled toward the open door, nearly bumping into a wrinkled *mama-san* scrubbing the already gleaming, battleship gray linoleum floor covering. The elderly Japanese woman bowed and scuttled backward out of his path, hissing what he took to be an apology. Regarding the frail figure, gray hair done into a tidy bun, her barely visible, almond-shaped eyes twinkling, Ross wondered: This harmless old thing a spy? Was General Short expecting the likes of her to whip out a hand grenade and race toward the parked rows of warplanes? He snorted in disbelief and inserted a checkered flag into its holder at the rear of the Dodge staff car.

After a rapid tour of the runways and taxiways, Ross stopped at the nose of a B-17 bearing the tail number 39227. His airplane. Or, rather, Lieutenant Woods's airplane. He couldn't help feeling possessive about her, however. Lieutenant Woods was one of the few aircraft commanders who shared left-seat time with their copilots. Having nothing urgent facing him, Colyer swung his lean, athletic frame through the nose hatch and clambered into the left seat. He grinned like a kid. Damn, it was a big aircraft. Not as big as the brand new B-24s, but she had such a feeling of invincibility. A news reporter had dubbed the B-17 a "Flying Fortress" when the prototype was rolled out for public viewing. Boeing picked up on the designation and the name stuck.

The aircraft bristled with .50-caliber machine guns—more firepower than an entire infantry company. Four twelve-hundred-horsepower supercharged engines gave it a cruising speed of 180 miles per hour. The payoff, however, was the fact that it could fly more than a thousand miles, drop four thousand pounds of bombs, and return home without refueling. Built to fend off endless numbers of fighters en route, the B-17 was without question the best fighting machine in the air.

From his fifteen-foot aerial perch, Ross could count nineteen more of these flying dreadnoughts drawn up in a ruler-precise line to his right. He wished the goddamn Jap high command could see this array of armed might; they would back off from their cocky, sword-waving talk—in a hurry. These planes could win a war all by themselves. Pulverize that shitty little island. Only six of the Hickam-based machines were operational at the time, but spare parts were on the way. It would be only a matter of days until the entire fleet was in the air again.

Ross looked scornfully at the row of thirty-two aging B-18s parked immediately to the rear. Among other things, two squadrons of pilots assigned to fly the obsolete machines sniffed like hungry wolves at the heels of the B-17 crews, just waiting to fill in a slot vacated by a washout. The dozen Douglas-built A-20s just out of view were neat, he had to admit. Sleek and fast, the attack-bomber pilots sang their praises to all who would listen. But they couldn't touch his airplane for sheer, raw power. A beautiful sight. It seemed to Ross that the other planes huddled around the majestic B-17s for protection. It was ironic, though. Seemingly invincible in the air, the B-17s and other aircraft had been grouped together on the ground as an antisabotage measure.

Ross privately wondered about that order, recalling a conversation he'd had in the club. One of the P-40 pilots, always contemptuous of the bombers, boasted he could wipe out the entire fleet with one firing pass. Ross had stoutly refuted the braggart's claim, but it raised some disturbing questions. He shrugged off the unsettling picture.

Inhaling the heady aroma of hydraulic fluid, electrical circuitry, stale sweat, and lingering traces of Lieutenant Woods's one-an-hour chain of cigars, he couldn't visualize trading places with any man on earth.

Ross watched a navy amphibian trundle down the ramp at nearby Ford Island and depart in a sparkling halo of spume. Bordering the

asphalt parking mat, Hickam's neat white buildings, set behind a profusion
of red, blue, and gold flowers, resembled a holiday resort more than
a military installation. With a regretful sigh, Ross dropped to the ground
and settled behind the wheel of his staff car. He must get back to his
AO's cubicle. That pilot's handbook was a cruel mistress, waiting to
be appeased.

Master Sergeant Jones, slumped behind his desk, was listening to
a tabletop Philco breathe the soft strains of "Sentimental Journey."
Ross smiled as he passed. It was common knowledge that when station KGMB remained on the air all night, aircraft from the States were
inbound. The thousand-watt station could be received up to 250 miles
out. With the brand new automatic direction finders, it was a comfort
to navigators to have the ADF needle pointing directly at the station
being received.

0715 Hours, 7 December 1941
Pacific Ocean

Lieutenant Iwakichi Mifuku of the Imperial Japanese Navy was
likewise appreciative of Glenn Miller's rendition of "Sentimental Journey."
Not that he liked the music; it was unexciting and he couldn't understand the words. But the strong signal provided a double comfort: It
confirmed his dead-reckoning navigation, and, more significantly, it
told him that the element of surprise still favored his twenty-plane
formation of Mitsubishi A6M fighters. The A6M was faster, carried
more firepower in the form of 20mm cannon and 7.7mm machine guns,
and was more maneuverable than almost any warplane in the world
at the time. Its astonishing performance in China was Japan's most
closely guarded secret. No foreign observer was present as the 300-
mph craft destroyed more than 250 Russian planes without a single
loss. British and American intelligence sources were blissfully unaware
that the vaunted "Zero" existed. Allied pursuit pilots believed that,
should war come, they would face a poorly trained enemy flying
obsolescent, fabric-covered crates. Lieutenant Mifuku, the youngest
and most handsome flight leader aboard the carrier *Hiryu,* was about
to destroy that illusion.

The two-week sea journey from the fleet rendezvous in the Kurile
Islands had been fraught with anxiety and suspense. As they plowed
through the icy North Pacific waters, Mifuku watched his leaders' faces
become drawn, their dispositions turn sour and irritable. Rumors flew

like cherry blossoms in the wind. The American fleet had sortied from its anchorage. Japanese negotiators in the American capital had signed a peace treaty, so the fleet was turning around. The flagship, *Akagi,* had been sighted by an American submarine, so the American guns would be waiting and ready. Admiral Nagumo, the task-force commander, was dead, having eaten tainted fish.

Then, as they approached the critical launch point, the weather became a concern. The fleet was running like a school of thrashing porpoises through a violent storm. Would the attack be abandoned? Cloud cover over the target was forecast to be solid. Throughout the pervasive shrouds of shipboard gloom hanging from every bulkhead, hovering in the air over every man aboard, Lieutenant Mifuku remained resolute. Success was ordained—the hated American scourge would be reduced to a whimpering dog in one mighty blow. Pride swelled in his breast at the thought that the emperor himself had selected Lt. Iwakichi Mifuku as a member of this sacred trust.

Mifuku had prepared himself well for this holy crusade. He had risen early, bathed carefully, and dressed in clean clothing from the skin out. Settling himself in the familiar cockpit, he thought the light seemed brighter in the predawn gloom, sounds sharper and more distinct, thoughts crystal clear and uncluttered. The last item of his attack wardrobe was a white *hatchimaki,* given to him by Miyoko, his betrothed. Wrapped around his leather flying helmet, the silk scarf proclaimed his willingness to die for his emperor.

Now, two hours later, niggling doubt screwed into his mind like a tapeworm. He had believed that after the nerve-racking launch nothing further could stay his hand.

Weather that would have caused a training mission to be canceled was ignored. The flight deck wallowed and tilted up to twenty degrees in total darkness, and the carrier's flank speed of twenty-four knots caused giant waves to cascade like ghostly apparitions over the bow in an eerie, glowing foam. He had only two rows of dim blue lights to guide him toward an equally dim green circle at the far end of the uneasy deck. His gallant little craft lurched airborne, only to sink into the enveloping misty darkness. Mifuku had the feeling that he was disappearing into an endless smothering void, never to return.

The sturdy engine never faltered as it howled and clawed for altitude. He was certain that he had actually kissed the wave tops with flailing prop tips. Then, with only the slightest of shudders, he felt, rather than saw, the slavering whitecaps drop beneath him. Miraculously, only one pilot failed to complete takeoff.

Where were the American aircraft carriers? he wondered. Three days earlier they had been in port. This morning, only an hour ago, a scout plane launched by the cruiser *Chikuma* reported 9 battleships, 3 light cruisers, and 17 destroyers at anchor—but no carriers. Were they lurking out of sight, screened by rain showers, waiting to pounce on the attacking force at its most vulnerable moment? More worrisome, were they, at this very moment, steaming at top speed toward the helpless Japanese carriers?

The scout-plane report had been a disappointment. The carriers were Mifuku's primary target. His job was to engage their F4F Wildcat fighters in the air if the Aichi dive-bombers were unable to catch the sleeping fleet with planes still on the deck. He regarded this responsibility as a sign of respect for his keen marksmanship.

Carrier-based planes represented a major threat to the Japanese fleet. Admiral Nagumo's force would be many miles away before the lumbering battleships could sortie. He sighed. To follow the slower, lightly armed dive-bombers and strafe the facilities at Hickam Field, his secondary target, must suffice.

But even a successful attack on that objective was not assured. Less than an hour from their target, the winged armada was flying above solid cloud cover. The sparkling clear air and brilliant sunshine were a deceptive blessing. Could they hold formation down through a blinding blanket of mist and rain, then find their individual targets? What to do? To come this far and turn back? Never! An opportunity such as this would not present itself a second time. The dedicated young pilot clenched stick and throttle and peered ahead intently, as if to pierce the concealing cloud banks by sheer willpower. He would descend to wave-top level and crash his plane into a target of opportunity if necessary.

His spirits lifted. As if willed by a divine power, the heaps of cottonlike white clouds parted. Random rays of sunshine penetrated the scanty openings, revealing an effervescent blue ocean. The breaks increased in size and number. Then he saw white surf breaking on even whiter sand. They had done it! He glued his eyes on Commander Fuchida's lead ship. There it was—a single "black dragon" flare. The battle was joined.

Five heart-pounding minutes later Pearl Harbor lay before him. Mifuku, with the Japanese appreciation for serenity and beauty, caught his breath.

The huge anchorage looked like an azure sapphire nestled in a bowl of jade. Cloud shadows chased each other down dark green mountain slopes that dipped gracefully toward ivory beaches. Red and yellow rooftops dotted the emerald landscape like a handful of carelessly scattered gems. Awed, he felt as if he were intruding into a strange and lovely lady's bedchamber. Must we ravage this beautiful place? he asked himself. The mood was shattered by the sight of ugly black beetles, nose-to-tail, marring the glass-surfaced blue harbor. Battleships! The enemy.

It was time to break radio silence. Grasping his radio microphone in one gloved hand, he ordered, *"Tenkai! Tenkai!"* As he watched his sections string into trail formation he heard Commander Fuchida shout the final command, *"Tora! Tora! Tora!"* Caught up in the deep emotion of the moment, tears streaming down his cheeks, Lieutenant Mifuku tipped the warplane's nose forward and listened as its engine's deep-throated roar wound to a shrill scream.

Chapter Two

0750 Hours, 7 December 1941
Hickam Field

Ross Colyer parked the ops vehicle alongside the base commander's olive drab sedan. That damned flight of B-17s. Naturally the old man would be on hand. He removed the checkered ramp flag from its holder. Best to revise his plans and report to Colonel Burlson first. It would have been nice to walk to the officers' club for a leisurely breakfast. The finicky old fart would want to be reassured that the runways and taxiways were clear, that fuel trucks and maintenance crews were standing by, a half-dozen trifles. You'd think the president was inbound.

Ross's reaction to the situation was totally different. The flight of B-17s was on its way to Clark Field in the Philippines. At least half of them would have mechanical write-ups. That meant repairs, and repairs required parts—parts that were already in short supply. By the time the transients left, Hickam would be lucky to have even six of its twenty Fortresses in commission.

His outlook wasn't improved by the sight of Broderick Templeton's sleek convertible. It was easing into a parking slot on the street side of Base Ops. BT slid out of the driver's seat and strolled toward Ross. He was attired in whipcord riding breeches, polished boots, and a loose-knit polo shirt. Ross's lips tightened as he observed Janet Richards sitting in the convertible's right seat. "Hey, Ross," BT called. "Did you by chance find my cigarette case in there?"

"Yeah," Ross replied, "it was under that pile of crap you didn't clean up when you left. I put it in the center desk drawer. You're lucky I didn't throw it away."

"Thanks, ol' buddy." BT threw him a sardonic grin. "I was afraid you might try to sell it." He turned his head. "I'll be right back, Janet."

As BT disappeared through the open doorway, Ross crossed the manicured grass verge and walked toward the Mercury. "Hi." He greeted his date of the previous evening with a stiff effort at informality. "Didn't know you were going to play cowgirl this morning. Just as well I didn't keep you up late."

Janet adjusted the billed riding cap atop her neatly coiffed red hair and flashed a nervous half-smile. "Oh, Ross. BT asked me ages ago to ride with him some Sunday." She wrinkled her patrician nose. "I'm really not all that good. But," she shrugged, "this island gets pretty small after four years. I did enjoy last night, Ross. You're fun to be with, you know. I—I'd like to do it again sometime."

"Yeah, sure," Ross muttered. He was as uncomfortable with the triangular confrontation as Janet appeared to be. "Well, duty calls," he added lamely. Throwing her a soft, two-fingered salute, he turned to leave, adding, "Don't fall off and break something valuable." Janet's throaty chuckle followed him.

BT, as Ross knew he would be, was making brown-nose points with Colonel Burlson. Standing in front of the counter, sipping coffee, the dour, stocky base commander was listening to BT recite some witty account that involved flying motions with both hands. The colonel displayed one of his rare smiles beneath a toothbrushlike salt-and-pepper mustache.

That goddamn BT. Why did he let the man get under his skin so? It had started while they were both in flight training at Kelly Field. Come to think of it, the bastard had aced him out of a girlfriend in San Antonio. Was it because BT flaunted the fact that his father was a senator? And not just any senator, but a member of the Senate Military Affairs Committee? Although the guy lacked his own skill as a pilot, Ross was willing to bet that BT would get a crew before he did. Army brass took care not to ruffle feathers in high places.

Ross strode to where the pair chatted, came to attention, and saluted smartly. Colonel Burlson, caught with his coffee cup in his right hand, never had an opportunity to return the AO's greeting. A resounding *whump* jarred the frame-and-stucco building. The floor trembled and a rack of coffee cups set up a brittle off-key clatter. Burlson's startled "What the hell?" was drowned by the snarling sound of an aircraft passing at high speed and extremely low altitude.

The colonel's face flushed cherry red. He slammed his coffee cup on the counter and raced for the door. "That goddamn bunch of smart-aleck fighter pilots over at Wheeler. This is the last straw. Sergeant," he called over his shoulder, "call the tower. See if they got that bastard's tail number."

Ross and BT trotted after the disappearing base commander. They reached the door just in time to see him swept from his feet by an invisible hand. They stood, mouths agape, while the two-hundred-pound, five-foot-eight-inch officer executed a spread-eagled, backward somersault, crashing face down on the asphalt surface of the parking ramp.

The explosion's shock wave reached them before the sound. Both young men were thrown across the polished floor, waxed and buffed with great care less than an hour earlier. Simultaneous with the deafening detonation of four hundred pounds of TNT, 144 panes of glass fronting the runway disappeared from their frames, sweeping the big room with their deadly hail. The aging *mama-san,* returning to admire her handiwork before leaving for the day, stood transfixed. Then a piece of shattered glass, larger than the rest and spinning like a boomerang, severed her jugular vein as neatly as might a surgeon with a razor-sharp scalpel.

Ross and BT struggled to their feet. The awful rain of destruction had passed harmlessly to their left. Ross could see BT's mouth working. Ears ringing, unable to hear, Ross shook his head and ventured out through the gaping doorway. He saw a strange airplane swoop low over one of the furthermost hangars. It appeared to be dropping little sticks of some sort. Then, as the whirling disk of its propeller became visible, he realized that the sticks were flying *up* instead of down. The interior of the hangar was exploding. As the brown and green aircraft pulled up sharply, he could see its underside clearly highlighted by the early morning sun. It looked surprisingly like the AT-6 trainer he had flown at Kelly, except that it bore two flame red disks painted on each wing. Realization dawned. Those were Jap markings!

He whirled to confront BT. "Japs!" he screamed. "The bastards are dropping bombs. We're under attack!"

BT's handsome features slacked with shock; he showed a total lack of comprehension.

Ross felt his stomach lurch. Janet! Christ, she was right in the middle of this. He raced around the corner to the streetside parking lot. Janet was standing alongside the convertible, pathetically out of place in her pink riding coat and trim gray riding breeches. Ross swept one arm around the softly pliant figure and unceremoniously dumped her into the driver's seat.

"It's the Japs," he yelled. "We're being bombed. Get the hell out of here. Head for the mountains. Get away from any kind of a military target. *Go!*"

The blood of military forefathers showed; Janet's pale face was firm. She pressed the starter button, then—as the powerful engine roared to life—drove straight ahead, jumping the curb. Executing a sluing, rubber-burning turn, the gray Mercury streaked toward the open highway.

Ross raced back through the devastated Base Ops building. He stumbled and almost fell over the recumbent body of the old scrub woman. He gazed in horror at the nearly separated head and body. "Oh, God," he moaned. What should he do about her? Move the body? Cover it with something? It was hard to think. A harsh voice penetrated his jumbled thoughts.

"Looks like we got us a war on our hands, Sir." Ross turned to confront a transformed Master Sergeant Jones. The bulky NCO was headed toward the splintered door hanging uselessly by one hinge, a World War I doughboy helmet strapped to his head. He carried a Springfield Model 1903 rifle loosely in his left hand—a half-dozen clips of ammo in his right. "Ain't been shot at since the Argonne. Figured I was going to finish my last hitch without it ever happening again. They're Japs, ain't they? I saw that red meatball as the last one went past. Well, let's just go see what the hell we can do about those yellow-bellied piss-ants."

Ross, with a dazed BT stumbling after him, emerged into a confused world behind the unhurried Sergeant Jones. They stared at the flight line in disbelief. Bombs exploded like giant hammer blows. Secondary explosions erupted in never-ceasing succession. Rank cordite fumes mingled with those of burning oil, rubber, and frame buildings. To the north a swarm of aircraft silhouettes flitted in and out of billowing clouds of black smoke.

My God, they're taking out the navy over at Pearl, Ross muttered to himself. But, to his delight, small puffs of antiaircraft fire appeared in the sky like popcorn-white blossoms.

The sound of a radial aircraft engine, at full revs with its prop in fine pitch, provided a reminder that the attack was still under way. Ross and BT dove for cover without waiting to check the dive-bomber's location. Their "cover" consisted of a bed of meticulously tended hibiscus bordering the ops building. Ross saw Sergeant Jones settle his bulky form into position behind the hood of Colonel Burlson's staff car. With the same aplomb that he might exhibit on the firing range, Jones arranged the extra ammo clips on the hood to his right. Raising the Springfield to his shoulder, sling wrapped around his left arm in the approved "firing from the standing position" form, he searched for a target. It wasn't long in appearing.

The attackers had switched their attention from hangars and fuel-storage tanks to the rows of parked aircraft. By their logic, Ross figured, the larger row of B-18s was the more important target; they were thus selected for immediate destruction. The lead plane descended until it was just above the runway, streaking for the temptingly fat target. Ross saw Sergeant Jones steady his aim, then deliver an entire clip of five rounds in as many seconds, his right hand working the bolt in a blur of movement. Caught up in the fever of fighting back, Ross leaped to his feet, jerked the .45 from its holster, and emptied it at the departing airplane.

Jones watched, expressionless, then inserted a fresh clip in his Springfield and stuffed an unlit cigar in his mouth. "May as well take out your peter and piss at him as do that," he commented about Ross's .45. "This thing," Jones patted the stock of his Springfield, "ain't much more effective. Better than doing nothing, though. Best thing you two could do, Lieutenant, is maybe get a couple of them airplanes off the ground afore they get blown up. You can bet your ass there won't be a one left flyable when these bastards finish with 'em."

Ross flushed, partially because of his irrational reaction under attack, but mostly because the tone of the Base Ops NCO's words jarred him. Jones had taken control and was giving him orders. His attitude could be considered insulting, even grounds for a court-martial, by God! As suddenly as the wave of official indignation surfaced, it disappeared. Ross regarded the heavyset sergeant through newly opened eyes. Slouched against the still-undamaged staff car, searching for a new target from beneath the rim of his steel helmet, the man was a professional soldier.

Underneath, the overweight NCO had to be as scared as anyone else. Christ, the whole scene was one of chaos—bombs and bullets were flying in all directions. The aging NCO was doing what he had been trained to do: fight back.

A lesson learned, Ross stared at the smoking automatic, empty and useless, clenched in his right fist. He moved to toss it to the ground, then stopped. Dumb-ass! He fumbled for the two forgotten spare magazines attached to the leather gun belt. Reloading the still-warm pistol, he thrust it into its holster. Never discard a weapon.

Ross returned to where BT cowered among the hibiscus. "BT, get up for Christ's sake; we have to get a couple of these birds into the air before it's too late!" he yelled. "We'll swing by and pick up a couple of maintenance men to fly right seat."

BT glared back defiantly. Crouched on all fours, his immaculate riding habit smeared with dirt, he snarled, "You're out of your fucking mind, Colyer. We wouldn't last five minutes out there on that ramp. Just look."

Ross turned to follow BT's pointing finger. A fixed-gear attacker, its bomb load disposed of on a previous run, had returned to sweep the parking mat with machine-gun fire. One wing of an A-20 in its path acquired a sick droop.

"There's still time," Ross snapped. "Now get the hell out of there. We have to at least *try*. They'll get every aircraft out there if we don't. We can even taxi past the bomb dump and load up. Those Japs have to be from an aircraft carrier. Maybe we can find the son of a bitch and sink it!"

"Oh, for Christ's sake, Colyer. Don't be an idiot. It'd take a half hour to do all that. We're getting clobbered. Just get under cover; we'll get organized when this is all over. They can't get away with this. And don't try to give me orders. I rank you by almost a hundred files, remember?"

Ross's confused thoughts jelled with cold rage. He drew his pistol. With newly acquired steel in his voice, he announced, "Lieutenant Templeton, as Airdrome Officer I represent the base commander. I'm also responsible for those aircraft sitting out there. Now, by God, I am *ordering* you to get one of them in the air. So help me, I'm ready to shoot you for desertion here and now if you refuse."

Astonished, BT stared at the crazy man confronting him. Colyer's blue eyes were like chips of ice. A fine line of dried blood on one cheek marked an unnoticed scratch from a random chip of flying glass, and his hat was missing, but the deadly looking Colt in his right hand never wavered. While not exactly pointed at him, its ominous bore suddenly assumed the dimensions of a howitzer. The bastard was serious; deadly serious.

The shaken lieutenant shrugged and scrambled to his feet. "Okay, okay. We'll never make it, but I'm damned if I'm going to lie here and get shot. Let's get it over with."

The pair trotted to where Sergeant Jones was ripping off another clip in the direction of a streaking attacker. "We're taking your cover, Jonesy," Ross yelled above the awful din. The taciturn sergeant nodded and picked up his three remaining loaded clips. Ross noticed that Colonel Burlson's inert form was still sprawled, face down, some twenty feet from the parked car. "Get a medic, Jones," he yelled as he slid behind the wheel. "The colonel looks like he's hurt bad."

Sergeant Jones, in the act of taking up a new position behind the nearby Base Ops vehicle, spat tobacco juice from his unlighted cigar into the nearby grass. "He's dead. I already checked." He resumed his hawk-eyed search in the direction of the attack.

Subduing the vague feeling that someone should at least drag the exposed body inside, Ross hit the starter. BT was still closing the right-hand door when Colyer swung the protesting Chevy into a tire-screaming turn and headed toward the transient-maintenance hangar.

The shrieking passes of their destruction-bent attackers seemed to be coming with decreased frequency. A side glance showed Ross that two men readying the B-18s for a training mission had succeeded in loading the .30-caliber nose gun of one. Even as he watched, however, their return fire was shut off. A swooping Jap plane bracketed the immobile bomber with a double row of orange-red tracers, and the ungainly craft erupted in a ball of yellow flame. The pair of courageous gunners were flung into the air, their clothing trailing fire as they tumbled like broken dolls to the ramp.

There would be no help from the maintenance crew Ross had seen milling about earlier on his rounds. The transient-maintenance hangar had taken a direct hit. Its curving sheet-metal roof was now a gaping, irregular skylight. Double sliding doors lay in a twisted, smoking heap. A dozen motionless bodies littered the ramp like so many discarded toys. Ross didn't bother stopping.

"Okay, we'll both have to fly the same plane. Two-two-seven is on the far end. It's in commission; I was out there this morning."

BT, his face a mask of anger, hadn't spoken during the wild ride. Then, as Ross slid to a stop behind the hulking aircraft, BT spoke from between clenched teeth. "Tell me, Colyer, that you're not going to try and load this thing with bombs. In addition to the gross stupidity of what we're doing, consider that we won't have a bombardier. The goddamn plane doesn't even have the bombsight installed. There'll be fighters, too, and there's no ammo on board. Remember? It's safely locked away to reduce the danger of sabotage. If you persist in going ahead with this suicide stunt, please, let's just get the hell out of range and land on one of the other islands. Look out! Jesus Christ, here comes another one—right at us!"

They were saved by the ineptness of the Japanese pilot. Pumping adrenaline had made him overcontrol, and the excessive rudder pressure caused him to deliver the destructive stream of machine-gun fire in a wild zigzag pattern. He swept over the row of parked B-17s without inflicting more than minor damage.

"I suppose you're going to claim the left seat," BT yelled as they yanked parking chocks from in front of the main gear.

"Damn right," Ross grated. Then, while racing to unsnap tie-down lines, he said, "This is my show and my airplane. Grab that Pitot-head cover and let's get the hell out of here; forget about that trip to the bomb dump. Just keep your fingers crossed that this thing has a hot battery. Come on! Let's move it."

Ross boosted BT through the forward entrance hatch, then, grasping the overhead frame, swung himself feetfirst into the passageway connecting the nose compartment to the flight deck. "Start priming all four," he snapped as he pulled the hatch cover closed behind him and scrambled into the pilot's seat. No parachute. No life jacket. What the hell? he thought. He didn't even give the dangling radio headset a second look: Getting tower clearance for what they were attempting was a joke. Ingrained habit, however, made him fasten his seat belt and check that BT had done likewise. "We'll start one and four, then you hit two and three while I taxi into position. Fuck the checklist. Parking brake set; master switch and ignition on; mixture, idle cutoff; props, high RPM, throttles cracked; generators on; start number one. Battery, goddamnit, *be there!*"

The whining crescendo of the number one starter's inertial wheel was cause for a jubilant "Hot damn, we got her made; engage number one."

BT pressed the toggle switch, which coupled the spinning cast-iron wheel to the outboard engine. The prop rotated with agonizing slowness—one blade, two, three—then, with a puff of blue smoke from its exhaust, the freshly primed top cylinder fired. Ross advanced the mixture control to auto-rich and eased the throttle forward as the cold engine settled into a balky, uneven rumble. Pumping the manual primer plunger in short strokes, BT was holding the number four starter switch in the energize position even as number one was settling into idle RPM.

The ravaging dive-bombers were replaced by fighters. Ross saw one flash across the far southern end of the field, its strange markings looking out of place. He released the parking brake and gunned the right outboard engine. With no wind to speak of, he would use Runway 35 for takeoff; its approach end was a scant fifty yards away. Wheeling out of the line of parked, silent bombers, Ross surveyed the runway complex. Shit! An ugly, still-smoking bomb crater marked the intersection of Runways 35 and 06, effectively closing both. While he searched for an alternative, he heard number two come to life at his left elbow with a protesting grumble.

"The runways are closed, BT," he barked. Commencing a 180-degree turn, he added, "We'll just use the parking mat; get number three wound up and we're on our way."

"Goddamn number three isn't saying a word, Ross," BT panted. Pumping the primer furiously, he recycled the starter. The stubborn power plant groaned and labored, but the fuel-rich cylinders refused to ignite. Ross moved the throttle full forward—BT must have overprimed. "C'mon, BT!" he snarled impatiently. "Can't you even start the fucking engines?"

His reluctant copilot glared. Wiping sweat from his brow he barked, "Be my guest, Mister Hotshot. *You* start the son of a bitch."

"Look, we don't have time to jack around," Ross snapped, ignoring BT's acid-tinged rejoinder. "We're in the only airplane on the field with props turning. Who do you think is the next candidate for shoot-'em-up? Feather that stubborn bastard and set the superchargers. I'll do a three-engine takeoff from right here."

"Oh, for Christ's sake, Colyer," BT protested. "You don't have much more than half a runway length from here. Let me have one more shot at starting her."

"Forget it, guy. We're living on borrowed time as it is. Here we go; call my airspeed after fifty and give me about fifteen degrees of flaps at seventy. We'll probably have to hang her by the props to clear those palm trees."

The big Boeing quivered to life as Ross crammed the outboard throttles to their stops. Boosted to forty-seven inches of manifold pressure by turbosuperchargers, the engines bellowed in protest. As they started to roll, Ross added power to number two in small increments, using rudder to compensate for the asymmetrical thrust.

"You got fifty-five," BT chanted.

"Sixty." Ross shoved number two's throttle to its forward stop. The empty airplane was gaining speed with gratifying quickness. "Sixty-five and I'm giving you fifteen flaps." The lumbering bomber was growing light on the controls as they left the asphalt-paved parking mat and skipped across sandy turf. They would make it easily, Ross exulted.

"Gear up!" he snapped as the nose rose and the shuddering vibration of the takeoff roll ceased.

Sergeant Jones watched the fleeing B-17 struggle into the air, muttering, "Go—go—go, damnit. Oh, go you beautiful bastard. Get the hell out of here." His heart sank, "Oh, shit." He slapped his last full clip into the Springfield and rested it atop the vehicle's concealing hood. A short distance to the south, two of the speedy Jap fighters were rolling into vertical turns—their objective was never in doubt. They would cross from right to left, directly in front of him. It was a full-deflection shot. He didn't have a prayer of bringing even one of them down with his puny weapon, but he'd try. Please, dear God; just gimme one lucky hit, he thought.

The laboring bomber cleared a row of royal palm trees with only inches to spare. Ross felt as though he could have reached out and touched them. He relaxed the mushy control wheel slightly to build up a safe climb speed. He would hug the shoreline and stay as low as possible. They just might sneak around the relatively safe north shoreline undetected.

He was scanning the best route when they seemed to fly into a sea of molasses. What the hell? Ross thought as he jerked his glance to the instrument panel. BT yelled the dreaded words: "We've been hit! We just lost number two."

Even as BT's heartbreaking message penetrated Ross's jumbled thoughts, he could hear the faint, rhythmic *toc—toc—toc* of 7.7mm slugs stitching parallel rows of neat punctures across the left wing root. Peripheral vision revealed that the number two cowling was vibrating madly; oily black smoke poured from beneath the cowl flaps. "Feather number two!" Goddamnit, they weren't finished yet. The B-17 could fly on two engines—he'd seen Lieutenant Woods do it on a checkride. He felt, as much as heard, the moaning sound of the source of their disaster as it flashed overhead.

Gallant lady that she was, B-17 serial number 39227 could not survive this combination of flight-crippling blows. The aircraft staggered just above stall speed, its efficiency diminished by flaps still at takeoff setting. Ross knew he had to bring the nose down to maintain flying speed. Flight control pressures communicated the complex computations that entered into this mathematical certainty. It would require more than the hundred feet of precious altitude beneath her to recover. Even with her number one and four engines straining at full throttle, the stricken craft settled earthward. Ross scanned the terrain ahead, searching for a suitable area of obstruction-free real estate. A stretch of white sand beach caught his eye.

It was a perfect touchdown. Chopping power at the last moment, Ross held the nose off—hold it, hold it—until he felt the underbelly contact loose sand. Deceleration after that was rapid as the prop blades, digging into the unstable surface, bent and gouged deep furrows. Ross and BT were thrown against the restraining pressure of their seat belts.

"Out! Get the hell out before number two blows!" Ross yelled. BT required no urging. Sliding his side window back, he squeezed his lithe figure through the narrow opening; Ross lunged across the cockpit to follow him. They recovered from sprawled positions and scrambled across the exposed expanse of white sand toward covering undergrowth.

Ross found himself face down in choking, gritty sand. At first he thought it was number two fuel tank's fiery eruption that had decked him. The feeling resembled having one's legs struck from behind with a ten-pound sledgehammer. He scrabbled in the shifting, loose footing, trying to stand. His right leg was numb—useless.

The growling roar of what he knew must be a Jap fighter passing overhead drummed in his ears. He gritted his teeth and started pulling himself, crablike, toward a beckoning palmetto.

BT had already reached concealment. He turned and, after a wary glance skyward, dashed back to where Ross was thrashing his arms and left leg in an effort to reach shelter. Placing both hands beneath the injured pilot's armpits, BT dragged Ross toward a line of palmetto shrubs. Panting from exertion, he squatted on his heels and said, "Okay, Superman. Now what? Do we don capes and zoom off to the rescue? I told you it was a stupid thing to do."

Ross stared back, pain starting to blur his vision. "BT—oh, just shut the fuck up, will you? I got hit somewhere in my back. Take a look; see if there's anything you can do."

The subdued copilot moved to where Ross lay face down in the sand. "You got a knife I can use to cut away your pants?"

"In my left pocket, one of those combination things. Nail clippers and a little blade. I'll get it."

BT pried open the inch-long blade and slit the pants between the crotch seam and right hip pocket. "Well," he forced back nausea at the sight of Ross's bloody right buttock, "looks like you have a gash in your right hip. There's a lot of blood, but I don't think it hit anything vital. Here," he whipped a handkerchief from his pocket, "hold this over it. The pressure will slow down the bleeding; I'll go for some help. I saw houses off to our right just before we bellied in."

Ross heard BT depart, noisily thrashing his way through dead palmetto fronds. Other sounds commenced to register: Explosions of varying size and frequency seemed to come from every direction. The blazing inferno that was B-17 39227 roared and crackled—he could feel heat from the conflagration extending into his shady lair. From the direction of Honolulu, a belated air-raid siren moaned to life. After less than a minute he heard it wind down, as if embarrassed to be a redundant reminder of impending danger.

Snarling aircraft engines provided a steady background, rising and falling as planes swooped upward to turn and dive toward already blazing targets. He couldn't keep track of numbers. My God, there must be a couple of hundred at least, he thought. Where the hell are ours? The P-40s from Wheeler? Other than scattered black puffs of smoke marking antiaircraft fire over Pearl Harbor, the attackers had no visible opposition. Then he recalled the chaos at Hickam. Of course: The closely parked fighters at Wheeler would not have escaped, either—bunched in the center of the field, ammo belts locked away to prevent sabotage. The Jap gunners would have had a field day. But the missing aircraft carriers—surely the *Enterprise* and *Lexington* were within fighter range of Oahu.

What was taking so long? He moved his left wrist to where he could see the stainless-steel aviator's chronometer. He stared in disbelief, then shook his hand. The damn thing must have stopped. But no, the sweep hand was ticking off seconds, same as always. It wasn't even nine o'clock yet! It had been less than an hour since he had spoken to Colonel Burlson in Base Ops. Shit! It seemed like he'd been here, hiding under the palm trees, for hours.

The wound on Ross's hip changed from burning pain to a duller ache, no less uncomfortable but easier to tolerate. He twisted in an attempt to see the damn thing. BT's handkerchief was saturated with blood, and his right hand was dripping. He held the piece of cloth in place, however; a swarm of buzzing, green-backed flies were doing their best to obtain a meal. But lying on his stomach, chin propped on forearm, was getting damned uncomfortable. He resumed trying to follow the savage attack.

He badly wanted a cigarette, but the effort to extract one from his breast pocket, then fish his lighter from a pants pocket, was too great. To hell with it.

An aircraft, silhouetted against the clouds, caught his eye. Larger than the swirling attack planes, it had landing gear dangling underneath and was gliding, nose down, toward Hickam. Christ, it was a B-17! Must be part of that inbound flight from the States, he realized. What was the crazy bastard doing? Surely he knew the field was under attack. Hickam tower—Ross had a mental picture of windows without glass, snapped during a brief glance as he had started his takeoff roll—Hickam tower was off the air.

As he watched, three of the darting shapes circling overhead detached themselves from the melee. Forming into a loose, fingertip-like formation, they descended on the unsuspecting bomber like crows after a hawk. The tableau passed from sight behind the overhanging palmetto. Ross imagined that he could hear the stutter of cannon and machine-gun fire.

What he saw next made his heart leap: the unmistakable sharknoses of P-40s. Four of them. Probably from one of the small auxiliary fields where detachments were rotated for gunnery practice. The thrill of seeing American planes on the scene was throat constricting. He croaked encouragement as the formation executed a graceful split-S and dove into the gaggle of Jap planes, orange tracers spewing from their guns.

This audaciously courageous act was to be in vain, however. With unbelievable swiftness a half-dozen red ball–marked planes rose to meet them. A brief, rolling dogfight ensued. One of the valiant P-40s entered a smoke-trailing spin—never to recover. The other three broke off the engagement to escape into familiar mountain valleys at ground-hugging altitude. The sounds of destruction grew mind numbing. Ross watched through a pain-induced haze as the once proud outpost of American military might was systematically reduced to smoking rubble.

Then, as suddenly as it had appeared, the boiling cloud of warplanes evaporated. Removal of their noise from the scene only served to emphasize the magnitude of the havoc they had wreaked. Sirens screamed as emergency vehicles rushed from one scene of devastation to another. Secondary explosions erupted when raging fires found stores of combustibles. Panicked shouts formed a faint background.

Ross concluded that BT, the bastard, had abandoned him. It was time to seek help on his own. He struggled to his knees; standing erect was impossible, he discovered. His right leg would not carry his weight. Just moving it caused excruciating pain. If only he had a crutch. While he searched for a solution, an ancient Model T Ford clattered into view. It was not a reassuring sight. Topless, weathered, fenders bent or missing, the vehicle appeared to have started life as a touring sedan. A modification, chopping the body behind the front seat and adding a wooden platform, had transformed it into a truck. A weary, disgusted BT sat on the dilapidated right seat, holding onto a windshield post that had no windshield to support. He waved in Ross's direction as the apparition changed course.

The driver, an elderly native, brought his machine to a shuddering halt alongside Ross's overhanging palmetto. Black eyes, set deep in his smooth brown face, darted nervous looks skyward from under the wide brim of a sweat-stained straw hat. He didn't shut off the rattling engine, simply motioned for Ross to mount the rear platform.

BT dropped to the sand, eyeing Ross's kneeling position. "Looks like you're ready to go. Didn't think I'd ever find a set of wheels. You're not gonna believe that mess back there," he jerked a thumb inland. "This old fart wouldn't venture out until after the shooting was over. You owe me five bucks, by the way. He wouldn't make the trip for a dime less. Okay now, put your right arm around my neck and I'll help you aboard."

Ross almost passed out as his movement engulfed him in waves of pain. Gritting his teeth, he allowed BT to help him hobble toward the quivering, wheezing vehicle. Climbing onto the splintered planks was a major ordeal. He collapsed, face down, gasping for air with agonizing breaths. BT swung himself alongside.

"Don't think you're going to enjoy the ride, fella," said BT. "If Mister Ford put springs on this thing, they've been replaced with concrete. I'll ride back here and keep you from jolting off." BT removed the saturated handkerchief and examined Ross's wound. "You're still losing blood like a busted garden hose. You feeling okay?"

"Oh, sure," Ross replied through clenched jaws. "Just shut up and get me to a hospital."

"Well now, that's something else I was going to talk to you about." BT had stripped off his polo shirt and was fashioning a compress. Pressing it firmly in place on Ross's hip, he continued, "There's no way this rig is going to get near a hospital. Traffic is snarled in every direction I could see. Best we can hope for is to flag an army ambulance. We'll just have to take our chances. Okay," he reached over the tattered front seat and slapped their reluctant driver on the shoulder, "home, James."

Weak from loss of blood, Ross fainted as they jounced over the first bump. Fading in and out of awareness, he heard BT arguing with an MP. The words "Fort Shafter gymnasium" registered. Sometime later, a figure swam before him—a man wearing a stethoscope over a blood-stained sport shirt and golfing knickers. "Superficial flesh wound," he heard the man tell a hovering corpsman. "If we still have an antiseptic solution, irrigate and suture."

Ross roused in anger at the word "superficial." "I lost a lot of blood out there," he mumbled.

"I'm sure you did," was the weary-voiced response. "But there's nothing to replace it with. You'll be weak but your pulse and blood pressure are above the critical point. I'll give you a shot to ease the discomfort; that's the best I can do for now." The scene faded, then went dark.

1018 Hours, 7 December 1941
123 Miles North of Koko Head, Hawaii

Lieutenant Iwakichi Mifuku peered at the broadly grinning face of his wingman, Irikami. Raising a clenched fist above his head, Mifuku gave the classic sign of victory. To break radio silence was an awful temptation. Orders were orders, however: Give the Americans no means

of tracking their return route. The carriers would be at their most vulnerable while their returning warbirds—ammunition and bombs expended—were recovered. He wanted to shout the news to the entire
world: The arrogant Americans have been defeated! Their mighty fleet
lies shattered at the bottom of Pearl Harbor. Japan, Land of the Rising Sun, rules the Pacific Ocean!

Additional cause for jubilation was the string of seventeen craft formed
up behind him. They had lost only three of the original twenty; the
planners had feared as many as half might be downed. Mifuku was
not aware of a single shot being fired at his marauding fighters. Over
the harbor, where the big ships were moored, it had been a different
story. At least a dozen of the slower bombers, the Nakajima B5Ns and
the flimsily constructed Aichi D3A dive-bombers, had fallen, trailing
flame and smoke.

He patted the receiver mechanisms of the two 7.7mm machine guns
extending from the instrument panel; they had done their work well,
shooting down the lone B-17 attempting to escape from Hickam. His
20mm cannon magazines empty, he had spotted the big craft making
its takeoff run. With Irikami trailing off his left wing, Mifuku had
pounced. When the bomber's left inboard engine was clearly in the
cross hairs of his reflective gunsight, he tripped continuous short bursts
until the last round aboard was fired. Pulling up in a spiraling turn,
he saw his wingman raising spurts of sand at the feet of two figures
scuttling toward cover.

Mifuku thought he saw one stumble and fall. More gratifying, however,
was the sight of the dark green bomber. It lay sprawled on the contrasting white sand, flames licking from one engine.

His thoughts turned to their present situation. Anxious to see his
flight safely aboard the *Hiryu,* he closed slightly on the leading bomber
formation, which navigated for the single-seat fighters. He silently urged
them to greater speed. Ample daylight remained to refuel, rearm, and
return for a final, crippling blow.

He glanced at his instrument-panel clock. He would be above the
carrier in less than an hour. It was time to switch to his reserve fuel
tank. Mifuku rotated the control clockwise with his left hand without
looking. He had scarcely returned his hand to the throttle when the
deep, even roar of his engine faltered. There was a brief surge, then
silence enveloped the tiny cockpit. At the same time, the rank, pun-
gent odor of raw gasoline filled his instrument-cluttered enclosure.

Dropping the nose to maintain flying speed, he instinctively returned the fuel tank selector to its original position. The engine hesitated, then returned to life with a gratifying roar. Lieutenant Irikami closed to within less than twenty feet, gave him an inquiring look, then settled back into formation.

Mifuku scanned his instruments. He could see nothing amiss. The reserve-tank fuel gauge registered full. Closer examination, however, revealed fuel trickling from a small hole, no larger than a pencil, beneath the fuel tank selector panel. The edges of the hole protruded in jagged points, like a tiny flower. A bullet hole. A random hit, unnoticed in the heat of battle. Mifuku decided that the line leading from the reserve tank to the main supply line was severed. The engine-driven fuel pump was receiving only air instead of fuel. A cupful of the suddenly precious liquid now sloshed on the bare metal floor between his feet. Clearly his endurance in the air was limited to the amount of fuel remaining in the main tank, whose white indicator hand rested alarmingly close to empty.

Should he stretch his flight to the utmost and perhaps ditch alongside an escort ship? Break radio silence and request assistance? No, he couldn't risk endangering the entire fleet. He hand signaled to Irikami to assume the lead position. Ignoring his wingman's look of startled concern, he dropped down and left to clear the formation.

He swiftly carried out emergency procedures rehearsed over and over in training: Reduce speed to 115 knots—just above stall speed—retard the air control valve until the engine spluttered with fuel starvation, and reduce engine RPM to seventeen hundred. After that, he adjusted the trim tabs to permit the slightest of glides. All that remained was to sit, and hope.

Overcome with frustrated rage, Mifuku pounded his thigh with a clenched fist. A perfect mission. Every objective destroyed with consummate skill and daring. A performance worthy of praise by Premier Tojo himself. And to end so ignominiously—defeated by a pinprick wound.

The trailing formation of victorious fighters flashed overhead, dwindled in size, then disappeared. The sturdy little machine drifted lower, engine ticking over with no more than a murmur of exhaust; the fuel tank indicator hand would move no lower. The sea ahead remained empty and placid. He was low enough to make out individual whitecaps when the thirsty cylinders consumed the last drop of available fuel. The gentle glide steepened.

Lieutenant Iwakichi Mifuku decided to die in the finest samurai tradition. A warrior's place in the afterlife could be determined by the manner in which he accepted death. He calmly slid the overhead canopy open. Then the young pilot stood erect, helmeted head thrust into the slipstream, loose ends of the symbolic white *hatchimaki* fluttering madly. Standing straight, arms folded, his expression devoid of fear, Mifuku faced straight ahead. The plane struck the top of a swell, skipped once, then nosed over. A defiant *"Banzai! Banzai! Banzai!"* trailed into the wind. Only a splash and trail of bubbles, insignificant in the vast reaches of the Pacific, marked the disappearance of plane and pilot.

2133 Hours, 7 December 1941
Post Gymnasium
Fort Shafter, Hawaii

Ross opened bleary eyes, wincing as they were assailed by bright light. He looked to one side from where he lay face down on a steel cot. Close enough to touch was another cot, its occupant immobile beneath a white sheet. Low voices, interspersed with groans, buzzed in the background. Where the hell am I? he wondered. Memory returned with a rush. He tried to roll over and sit up, almost screaming at the effort. Flopping back to his original position, he contemplated a highly polished hardwood floor. A gymnasium. Lights. It had to be nighttime. That wild, nightmare flight had taken place that morning. He'd been out of it all day. Oddly he didn't feel that bad—except when he moved.

A soft, familiar voice intruded. "Ross, are you awake?"

It was Janet. He hardly recognized her. Red hair, normally arranged in perfect symmetry, hung in random wisps. Her face, devoid of makeup, sagged with fatigue. He rolled his head to one side and replied, "Yeah, sort of. What are you doing here?"

"I'm a Red Cross volunteer." Her voice was near breaking with strain. "The hospitals are full and there aren't enough nurses; I'm helping out where I can. You hungry? I can bring you something."

"Not really. I'm thirsty as hell, though."

"All right. Some orange juice?"

At his nod she continued, "Okay, I'll be right back. BT is around somewhere. He's been using his car to bring drugs and supplies. He'll want to talk with you."

Ross wasn't sure he wanted to talk with BT, but remained silent. Minutes later he heard quick, light footsteps and Janet telling him dully, "Here's your juice and a pitcher of water. BT's here too; say 'hi.' I'll be back shortly."

Ross propped himself on an elbow and surveyed BT's disheveled condition. The young pilot was clad in a blood-smeared undershirt and stained, wrinkled riding breeches; his face sagged with shock and weariness.

Taking a long drink of the cold, tangy juice, Ross gave him a weak smile. "Guess I owe you, BT. Not only a new shirt, but it would seem that you sort of saved my ass, damaged as it is."

BT's grim expression didn't change. "Don't let it prey on your mind, Colyer. I probably won't see you again soon. But I will, someday. Rumor has it they plan to give you 'walking wounded' a Purple Heart and get you out of here on the first ship."

Ross interrupted him. "What the hell do you mean, ship me out? I'll be back in the cockpit within a month. I'm going to get even with those bastards."

"Well, short and to the point, there aren't going to be any cockpits for you, or anyone else, to get into within a month. Not even *six* months, probably. We lost damn near every bomber on the island. Worse than that, the Japs hit the Philippines this afternoon. We lost both of the groups at Clark. On the ground, would you believe? After they had word of what happened here? Far East Air Force is flat on its ass.

"But I didn't want you to get away before I was able to tell you this, so listen good: You pointed a gun at me today and called me a coward—humiliated me in front of an enlisted man. *Nobody* does that to me, Colyer. Nobody, understand? This is a small Air Corps and it's going to be a long war. Our paths will cross again someday, and when they do, Ross Colyer, I'm going to hang your ass out to dry—remember that." The wooden-faced BT turned on his heel and stalked out of sight.

Taken aback by the vehemence in Templeton's voice, Ross settled back to his chin-on-forearms position. Conflicting thoughts raced through his mind. BT's threat was unsettling, but Ross knew that what he had done was right, damnit! That son of a bitch!

Ross laughed bitterly, closed his eyes, and let the encroaching weariness and depression take over.

Chapter Three

21 January 1942
Thunderbird Field
Phoenix, Arizona

Ross counted five one-dollar bills into the grinning Mexican cabdriver's outstretched hand. In return he received a bright red business card that read "RED TOP TAXI" along with a bit of advice: "Anytime you need ride to town, you call José, okay? I show you all the hot spots where cute babes hang out, okay?"

Ross gravely assured José that he would do that, then stood and surveyed his surroundings. This was an army airfield? He had sharply questioned the cabbie in that respect. Reached after a one-hour drive from Phoenix, mostly along a gravel road running between groves of citrus trees, there hadn't even been an MP at the gate to check his ID.

Spread out before his eyes in every direction lay acres of desert. Only the barren folds of mountains on the horizon, a single adobe shack about a mile distant, and occasional gaunt arms of a giant cactus reassured him that he wasn't perhaps on the moon. There wasn't a cloud in the sky, and from the amount of dust stirring, he was sure there hadn't been for several weeks.

From not far behind him, Ross heard the whine of power saws and the racket of exhaust from heavy construction equipment. Shrill, shouted orders provided the first hard evidence that the place was actually inhabited. He turned to regard the bare frames and rafters of more than a dozen buildings swarming with dark figures. The dust-laden air was filled with the resinous smell of freshly sawed pine boards.

One complete building existed. José had deposited Ross near its main entrance. A neatly lettered sign proclaimed that it housed the "HEAD-QUARTERS, 1337th Flight Training Detachment." Ross resisted an urge to loosen his tie. His freshly pressed green wool uniform was a bit too much for the eighty-degree day, but the book said to always report to a new station wearing Class A's. He squared his cap and approached the unpainted door.

In the act of reaching for its handle, he was almost knocked off his feet. A man dressed in dark slacks and a short-sleeved white shirt emerged abruptly and brushed past Ross without apology. His sun-darkened face was set in a dark scowl. "Well, excuse the hell out of me," Ross muttered after him. Shaking his head, he decided to try the reporting-in sequence once more.

A tousle-haired corporal dressed in shapeless OD fatigues regarded Ross's immaculate presence through heavy-framed GI glasses. "Can I help you, Lieutenant?"

"Lieutenant Colyer, Corporal—reporting in."

"Lieutenant Colyer? Let's see, Sir." The serious young man consulted a clipboard. "It shows here you ain't due to report for another week."

"That's right, I'm reporting early. Here's a copy of my orders—where's the sign-in book?"

"Well, I ain't got around to making up a regular sign-in-and-out register. You see, there's only eight of us here for now." He gave Ross a friendly grin and stuck out a hand. "I'm Corporal Washington, Sir. I'm acting first sergeant, company clerk, supply sergeant, you name it. I just sort of make notes and fill in the morning report from memory."

"I see." Ross smiled in return. "Well, if you'll tell me where to find the adjutant, I'll report in and get to work."

"We don't rightly have an adjutant, Lieutenant. There's just me and Major Wilson here in headquarters. Captain Ashley is the engineering officer. He's out there someplace." He made a vague wave toward the door. "Only other officers on board now are Lieutenant Koonz and Lieutenant Tibbs. They're up in Van Nuys today, ferrying a couple more airplanes in from the factory." He cocked an ear toward a closed door. "Sounds like the major's on the phone. Soon as he's finished, you can report to him."

Ross found a chair next to Corporal Washington's desk and sat down to wait. The room and its contents had that raw, unfinished appearance of new occupancy. In the far corner a silent, brown-complected man brushed mustard yellow paint on beaverboard walls. The floor, made of six-inch-wide pine boards, was still without paint or covering. The furniture, desks, file cabinets, and chairs were obviously only recently uncrated.

"Who was the human tornado that damn near knocked me down as I came in?" Ross queried.

"Oh, that was Mister Anderson. He's superintendent for Air West, the contractor. He and Major Wilson had kind of an argument, I guess."

Before Ross could pursue the matter, a connecting door swung open to admit a stocky, beetle-browed man wearing gold major's leaves on the collar of his khaki shirt. Reddish brown hair cropped in a close crewcut topped what looked like a recently sunburned face. He tossed a handful of papers into an already overflowing file box marked "PENDING."

"Wash, see to this damn stuff, will you?" the major said wearily. Then, suddenly aware of Ross's presence, he stopped and raised his eyebrows.

Ross sprang to his feet and rendered his best salute. "Second Lieutenant Colyer, Ross F., reporting for duty, Sir."

"Colyer—Colyer," the major's brows furrowed as he returned the salute with a movement that resembled brushing away an annoying gnat. "Oh, yeah." An enigmatic grin made a brief appearance. "Another instructor pilot. You're early, aren't you?"

"Yes, Sir. A week early. Ran out of things to do on leave."

"Huh, you'll wish you hadn't been in such a hurry in a few weeks," Wilson grunted. "Well, come on in. I'll fill you in on this screwed-up operation, get you settled in, and find you something to do."

Waving Ross to a facing chair, the major settled himself behind another new desk. A nameplate, fashioned from a piece of aluminum bar stock, displayed a pair of pilot's wings and the words "THEODORE WILSON, Major, USA" engraved beneath them. The "Major" was a recent, glued-on addition; the word "Captain" was still visible underneath. Otherwise, the office was a carbon copy of the orderly room: An American flag, fold creases still showing, and a bulletin board, labeled "READY STATUS," were the only additions.

"Okay, let me see your Form-5 and your Sixty-Six."

Retrieving the requested documents from the fiberboard folder he carried, Ross placed his official log of flying time and his master personnel record on the cluttered desktop. The major reached for the Form-5 first. Flipping to the front, he nodded in satisfaction. "Took your primary in the Stearman. Good. Saves time for a checkout." He turned to the last entries. "B-17, huh?" he raised his eyebrows. "Hickam, 19th Bomb Group. I'll be damned. You there when the Japs attacked?"

"Yes, Sir, very much so. I was AO that Sunday."

"The hell you say!" Wilson leaned back in his chair. "Was it as bad as they say it was?"

Ross hesitated. The full extent of losses suffered on that black Sunday was not public knowledge. Everyone departing the island had received explicit instructions regarding the importance of keeping it that way. What the hell? The major was army too, wasn't he? "Worse," he said softly.

"I gathered that." Ross's new commanding officer didn't press him. As he scanned the salmon-colored Form-66, he added casually, "My wife's cousin was there. Probably still out there someplace, I guess. His name's Templeton—Broderick Templeton the Third, no less. Ever happen to run across him?"

Ross felt slightly sick. "Yes, Sir. I knew him quite well. As a matter of fact, he was flying right seat when we tried to get a '17 into the air that day—before the Japs got them all."

"I'll be damned." The major was skimming his record and appeared not to have heard him. "Purple Heart, eh? You get that during the raid?"

"Yes, Sir. We were hit before we could get the airplane out of there. I set it down on a beach and got this," he pointed sheepishly at his buttock, "as I was trying to reach cover. It's nothing much. As soon as I can see a flight surgeon, I'll be cleared to get back on flying status."

"Nothing or not, it was enough to put you on convalescent leave for six weeks." He glanced at Ross's uniform and frowned. "I see you aren't wearing the ribbon."

"No, Sir." Ross squirmed. "Look, Major, it's really sort of embarrassing."

Wilson regarded him without expression for a moment. Then he grinned. A tentative chuckle rippled from his throat. Finally, unable to contain himself, he whooped with laughter. Wiping tears from his eyes, he sobered and said, "I'm sorry. I know it isn't funny to you,

Colyer, but, damnit, you'll have to admit. . . . Oh, well. I know a few things *you* don't. Anyway, about the ribbon. You'll *have* to wear it. We'll be having an inspection before too long, and we got us a colonel, Thurston, who's death about things like that. I even have a memo from him somewhere in this mess about the wearing of decorations.

"About the setup here. Thunderbird Field is a contract operation. The army has a helluva job ahead of it turning out new pilots. There just aren't enough of us in uniform to do the actual instructing, so Western Army Flight Training Command is setting up civilian-run fields all over. An outfit named Air West has the contract to construct the facilities here and handle the training with civilian pilots. We'll have six army pilots to give checkrides and generally ride herd on the civilian instructors."

Ross frowned. "Civilians? Teaching army pilots?"

"Yep. And don't knock it. Some of these guys have logbooks two inches thick. The army will still run advanced training, but primary and basic will be done by civilians for the most part. We have to give them the standards we want and kick butts to get them to do things our way. That'll be your job. You're going to be senior check pilot." He paused as he saw Ross's jaw drop.

"Look here, Colyer. We aren't set up to make a big production out of it, but, effective last week, you're a first lieutenant." The major grinned. "I've got your orders and a set of silver bars here. Congratulations." He walked around the desk, handed Ross a sheet of paper and the new rank insignia, then pumped Ross's hand. Then he turned back to the desk to pick up a rectangular box and another sheet of paper. He handed them to Ross without comment.

Major Wilson took a step back and watched as Ross first glanced at the orders and then, with shaking hands, opened the box.

Ross couldn't believe what he saw. Inside the box were a Silver Star ribbon and medal. The nation's third-highest award for valor! He forgot all about Major Wilson as he sank back into the chair next to the desk and, through misty eyes, read the citation accompanying the official orders:

. . . for conspicuous gallantry on the morning of 7 December 1941. Lieutenant Colyer, serving as Hickam Army Airfield's Airdrome Officer, at the risk of his life, attempted to fly a B-17 aircraft to safety during the surprise Japanese attack on the Pearl

Harbor Navy Base and neighboring Army and Marine Corps installations, and thus preserve the aircraft from almost certain destruction. His was the only bomber to get airborne from Hickam, and, unarmed and crewed only by Lieutenant Colyer and his copilot, was seriously damaged by Japanese fighters. Rather than abandon his stricken aircraft, Lieutenant Colyer crash-landed on a beach and was wounded while seeking cover from strafing fighters. His actions are in keeping with the highest traditions of the military service and reflect great credit upon himself, his unit, and the Army Air Corps.

Ross shook his head in disbelief. Who could have recommended him for the award? Surely not that bastard BT. Maybe it was Master Sergeant Jones. Or Janet's father. It didn't matter. Seeing the words on paper helped erase the bitter memory of BT's diatribe and served to reinforce his own belief that his actions had been right all along. He wiped at his cheeks, then looked up when the major harrumphed.

"It's like I said before, Colyer, we aren't set up to make a big production of it." The major walked over and put his hand on Ross's shoulder, giving it a slight squeeze. "But I was serious about the old man. He's a stickler for this shit. Those ribbons and silver bars make you the head honcho—the other pilots are all second johns."

Wilson returned to his seat. "Okay," the major was once more all business, "we're to get our first class of sixty cadets in three weeks. Air West is dragging its feet—I just had an ass-chewing session with their superintendent. We'll be operating out of tents for a while, but we're going to put those kids in the air by the first of March if I have to ride front seat myself.

"Your first job is to ferry airplanes from the factory. Soon as you get medical clearance from the flight surgeon over at Luke Field, I'll give you a checkride. Then you can join Koonz and Tibbs on the ferry run. We have nine birds so far, with a dozen to go. Now, Washington will get you cleared in. You'll get off-base subsistence. The rest of the officers are living in a motel in Phoenix, the Desert Inn. Not the best, but it's affordable." He stood and extended his hand. "Glad to have you aboard, Colyer. My wife will want to meet you—hear how her cousin made out during the Jap attack. And I'd like to hear about that takeoff and belly landing," he grinned. "How about this weekend? Can you come by the apartment for Saturday dinner?"

Ross stood also. "Thank you, Sir, but there is one thing I must tell you: I intend to apply for immediate return to a combat flying assignment."

Wilson chuckled. "You'll have to get in line, Colyer. I have to endorse it, but I'll recommend disapproval—and it *will* be disapproved, I can guarantee that. The plain fact of the matter is, there aren't enough combat airplanes to go around. This is classified, of course, but it will be close to a year before the aircraft factories can start turning out airplanes in any numbers. Until then, top priority goes to aircrew training." He walked with Ross to the office door.

"Corporal Washington," he called, "Lieutenant Colyer wishes to apply for a combat assignment. Would you type up a request for him first thing tomorrow? You can use mine for proper format and so forth. After he signs it and you add my endorsement recommending disapproval, we'll get it on its way." He slapped Ross's shoulder.

"Doris and I'll look for you Saturday. Is five-ish okay?"

Ross watched the major return to his desk. "Shit," Ross muttered under his breath.

Corporal Washington tried hard not to smirk.

The Desert Inn was neither in the desert nor an "inn." It was a shabby collection of imitation adobe huts. They featured fake roof beams protruding from the flat tops and were badly in need of paint. No blade of grass marred the brown sand through which a blacktop drive and white-graveled paths wandered. A dust-covered prickly pear cactus constituted the sole pathetic effort to provide landscaping.

Perhaps the location had been considered scenic desert when an ill-advised retired farmer from Iowa built it, but the main highway to Flagstaff had been shifted three miles west. The motel's nearest neighbors were an odoriferous paper mill and a gravel-surfaced parking lot for heavy equipment.

"I'm giving you number seven," the sad-faced proprietress advised. "The other officers are in five and six. I'll keep you all close together like. And you're right next to the swimming pool. If you want ice, it's in the lobby, but the office closes at nine. Phone's around the corner. Just let me know if you need anything."

Ross dumped his bags on the double bed, opened a window, and switched on the overhead Casablanca fan. The interior reflected a midwesterner's concept of Southwest Indian motif. A faded Mexican serape hung on off-white walls, and turquoise-painted trim framed windows and doors. The drapes and bedspread were from Sears & Roebuck. The place more resembled one of those roadside motels one would expect to find in Dubuque displaying a neon sombrero and called something like *La Casa Grande*.

After a brief inspection of the bath—the shower worked and the stool flushed—he slumped into a worn, plush armchair and propped his feet on the bed. He wished he'd thought to ask how he could get a cold beer.

The idea of the promotion and the medal lifted his spirits briefly, but was soon replaced by the depression that had dogged him during the three-day train ride from Justin Falls, Michigan. A damn flight instructor—not only that, but in a lowly primary flying school. It was humiliating. He had believed that he would be returning to his old outfit after convalescent leave. The orders had been forwarded to his father's house in Justin Falls between Christmas and New Year's. He'd called WAFTC headquarters in Denver and screamed his head off. A Major Ames had told him in icy tones that he would report as ordered.

Coming home wasn't all it was cracked up to be in the sad songs and movies, Ross decided. He was a guest in the house he grew up in. Welcome, but still a guest. And going downtown was an ordeal. Small talk was out of the question. How could he discuss the merits of the current crop of basketball players? The bowling league? The deer season—had it been a good one or a bad one? Who had the fanciest fish house on the lake? So, the talk was all of the war. What had it *really* been like at Pearl Harbor? Were we going to win the war? How long would it take? So, you're a pilot, huh? You sure look good in that uniform—you're an officer? Do you think my Lenny could get into the Air Corps?

Two days after war was declared, the order came down that members of the armed forces would wear the uniform at all times, on or off duty. He felt conspicuous. His butt hurt, but he clenched his teeth rather than limp; that *really* collected a crowd. There had been an interview with the *Justin Falls Journal*—twisted into an embarrassing editorial. He was guest of honor at the Rotary luncheon; he'd been offered the pledge of a lifetime of free drinks at the Veterans of Foreign Wars club. After being coerced into addressing an assembly at the high school,

Ross fled to the sanctuary of home, hearth, and a steady diet of war news on the radio.

A conversation with Dad's housekeeper, Bea, made him decide to report to Phoenix a week early. His hip wound was healed and he was restless. Bea was an angel, really. But, like all civilians, she seemed to think the war should be fought only by people she didn't know and love. He had joined her for lunch in the cozy, plank-floored kitchen. He sat in the breakfast nook in brooding introspection. Bea placed a steaming bowl of split-pea soup and cheese sandwiches made with thick slices of her home-baked bread before him, then, pouring herself a mug of coffee, sat down opposite him.

Ross smiled to himself. It had been a scene right out of his high school days when he came home for lunch. The garrulous housekeeper would seat herself across from him and provide the day's ration of neighborhood gossip. And drink coffee. Bea's coffee was the worst he had ever tasted. A stained, blue granite–enameled percolator was a permanent fixture on a back burner of the circa 1929 gas range. Supposedly she emptied the pot on occasion, but Ross had never caught her in the act; he'd only seen her add more coffee and water. His father would drink no other, however. The pair of them drank at least a dozen cups during the day and Doctor Colyer's frequent long, sleepless nights.

Bea had propped her generous bosom on the oak tabletop and fixed Ross with a piercing glare. "You giving that nice Rhoda Clarkson a ring before you go?"

"You mean on the phone?" Ross asked, his expression innocent. "Yeah, I thought I would call and give her the news."

Bea snorted. "You know what I mean. Don't talk smart-alecky to me. You let that girl get away and you'll regret it the rest of your life."

Ross allowed his teasing grin to fade. "It isn't that simple, Bea. Rhoda deserves a guy who'll be around, a seven-day-a-week husband. I can't give her that. Until this war is over, marriage wouldn't be fair for her; army pilots make lousy husbands."

"You tell her that?"

Ross laughed and shook his finger at his inquisitor. "Bea, my love life and the things I tell or don't tell my girlfriends are none of your business—I've told you before and I'm telling you again."

"Well," the elderly housekeeper grumbled, "you hurt that girl's feelings and I'll skin you alive, hear?"

Rhoda had threatened eternal severance of their relationship if he didn't at least put in an appearance at her New Year's Eve party. Uncomfortable—it hurt to stand for very long and, at that time, hurt worse to sit—he ended up drinking too much. "It's the war" was the sage observation. "He must have gone through hell during the attack on Pearl Harbor. Clyde Hostetter was like that after the last war—had to drink to forget."

Civilians. Ross realized that he no longer had anything in common with civilians. They didn't understand war. The Rotary meeting. Asking people to register for duty as air-raid wardens. Talking about blackout procedures. An air raid on Michigan's upper peninsula—Jesus Christ! If you ever told them that you had seen people you knew blown to bloody, motionless pulp and not been overcome with grief, you would be regarded as a monster.

Now he spoke a different language. Bea's surprising insight and blunt directness had shaken him more than he cared to admit. Then there was the profanity. Bea hadn't mentioned it, but he noticed her wince a couple of times. He had never used words like that before when he lived at home. Priorities—what difference did a thousand dollars' annual earnings make? Lives, professionalism in job performance, honor, duty, loyalty—those were the standards by which men were measured.

What the hell was he even doing here? he thought. Acting on an impulse, he decided to report early. Even if the flight surgeon wouldn't immediately restore him to flying status, he could find something to do. The next day he would take the bus to Lansing, catch a train, and keep going.

Rhoda had insisted on driving him to Lansing—the buses were impossible to get on. She would spend the night with her cousin and return the next day. Ross detected Bea's fine hand. It snowed during the drive and by the time the outskirts of Lansing appeared, Ross's watch read four o'clock.

"I need a drink," Ross said, making no effort to conceal the effects of the drive. "We'll drop off your bag at your cousin's apartment and head for the station. They have a bar and a pretty good restaurant there. We'll have a few drinks, dinner, and I'll catch the next train I can get on. I might even luck out and get a Pullman berth. I'll flash my convalescent-leave orders—play on their sympathy a bit."

Rhoda extracted a cigarette from a crumpled pack. As Ross held
his lighter for her, she asked, "Don't the trains run tomorrow?"

"Well—yeah. But never in hell could I find a hotel room this late
in the day."

"Eileen has a big apartment."

"Oh, I couldn't barge in on a perfect stranger. . . ."

"She isn't there. She's visiting her parents in Madison."

"Huh?"

"She left the key with a friend. If you'll pick up a bottle on the
way, we'll have that drink while I fix dinner for you." Rhoda's gaze
was direct and without embarrassment.

Ross poured a drink at the kitchen counter and returned to the
darkened living room. Rhoda slept soundly behind the closed door to
the apartment's single bedroom. She hadn't stirred as he'd eased from
between the satin sheets. He located the sofa and sat down, propping
his bare feet on the coffee table. The luminous dial of his watch showed
2:00 A.M. His cigarette pack was empty. He fished a long butt from
the overflowing ashtray and managed to light it without singeing the
hairs in his nose.

Guess I'm not the only person changed by this war, he mused. A
year ago, heavy breathing, wet kisses, and a hand stopped halfway up
a silken thigh had marked the zenith of their relationship. As for tonight, Rhoda's performance in bed bore the stamp of experience. He
hadn't been the first one, he realized. What was it? Did war cause people
to behave differently? Sweet, shy Rhoda now said and did things "nice"
girls weren't even supposed to know about. He smiled into the darkness. The word "marriage" hadn't surfaced once during the entire evening
of abandoned lovemaking.

Home. Its meaning had changed. It was no longer the same. He had
wanted only to get the obligatory visit over with and get the hell away.
Dad had understood; Ross could see that now. The aging doctor made
a few efforts to engage in small talk, but father and son no longer had
common interests. Parkinson's disease was slowly eroding Willard
Colyer's motor nerves. He was embarrassed when he explained to Ross
that he couldn't examine his hip wound—he no longer maintained an
office. A bitterly cold wind was blowing the day they were to visit
Mom's grave, so Ross had gone by himself. It occurred to him that
unconsciously he had always used "home" as a crutch. If everything

went to hell, he could always "go back home." But he couldn't. The realization made him faintly sad.

So, what the hell did he want out of life? Get out of the army after the war, finish school, and settle down in Justin Falls? That was out of the question. The taste of excitement and danger during the past few months made him realize that his future would always revolve around airplanes and the army. Ross drained his drink, rinsed the glass, and reentered the dark bedroom, now rank with the musk of hours-old sex.

Chapter Four

3 May 1942
Thunderbird Field

Pilot Class 43-E arrived in two chartered buses during the last phases of construction. Ross had watched the cadets disembark with wonderment in his eyes. Was *he* ever that young? That green? His own cadet days seemed years in the past. After two days of orientation followed by a rigorous schedule of ground school and physical training, the kids were flying. Three weeks later, an even dozen of the fledgling aviators were driven into Phoenix and placed aboard trains. Their destination: infantry basic training. The "washing machine" was merciless as far as the inept were concerned.

The installation known as Thunderbird Field sprang from the desert like an ugly mushroom. Buildings that had looked like skeletons on Ross's arrival became a series of living quarters, classrooms, and offices. Two corrugated steel hangars went up almost overnight. The flying field, a mile-square area of packed, sandy soil, was the source of a constant background of snarling Continental engines from first light to dusk. A small, self-contained community now existed where only weeks before jackrabbits and lizards had held territorial rights.

A double row of stubby, fabric-covered biplanes, now numbering twenty, squatted in front of the two hangars. Built by the Boeing Aircraft Company for utility rather than beauty, the Stearman Kaydet did little to inspire poetic discourse. Painting the fuselage blue and the wings a brilliant yellow did little to camouflage an awkward arrangement of wires, spars, and fixed landing gear.

Ross had little that was good to recall from his own experience with the legendary PT-13. He had first flown the thing at Kelly during the winter. Even suited up in leather flying helmet, sheepskin-lined jacket and boots, and with goggles the size of saucers in place, he had frozen his ass. The student flew from the rear cockpit. The instructor pilot, seated directly in front, and the nose and engine rearing up ahead, made forward visibility possible only by sticking one's head out in the slipstream.

Instrumentation in the dual cockpits was little more sophisticated than that in a Model A Ford. One could determine airspeed, altitude, and direction. A turn needle and ball in the exact center of the cluster supposedly made it possible to fly "blind" in clouds. Ross had never known a pilot who actually did, however. A throttle, an on/off magneto switch, and individual wheel brakes on the rudder pedals completed the array of controls available to the fledgling aviator. The instructor was provided one additional refinement. A Mister Gosport had devised a simple method of communication in lieu of radio equipment. A hard-rubber funnel in front was affixed to a tube that ran to the rear cockpit. The tube forked and was inserted into earpieces built into the student's helmet. The device worked surprisingly well. The student couldn't talk back to the instructor, a feature of no great concern; in addition, the arrangement could be used to express displeasure by the more sadistic: By holding the mouthpiece outside the cockpit, an angry instructor could funnel the slipstream directly into a wayward student's ears.

Despite the Stearman's lack of charm and helpful accessories, pilots soon developed love affairs with the machine. It was virtually indestructible in the air. Its response to the slightest touch made possible an endless number of acrobatic maneuvers. It was unbelievably stable; students were told that if they lost control in the air, they should simply remove their hands and feet from the stick and rudder; the craft would return to normal flight unassisted. The plane reserved one nasty little surprise for the unwary, however. Its relatively high and close-set landing gear required a deft touch on landing rollout. A sickening turn, known as a ground loop, was almost impossible to recover from. Once it was started, the pilot found himself executing a full circle, with the outer, fabric-covered wingtip dragging the ground. Not only was it highly embarrassing, a ground loop was cause for receiving punishment "tours." A tour consisted of an hour of marching around the parade ground wearing a parachute pack.

Ross strode across the parking area toward the row of planes waiting silently for their daily workout. Most still reflected factory newness—smelling of fabric dope, new leather, and only faintly of engine oil and sweat—their paint jobs still unbleached by the desert sun. Aviation Cadet Willis Ackerman waited in front of Stearman number 37921. He came to attention and saluted as Ross approached.

"At ease, Mister Ackerman. Let's talk a bit before we leap off, okay?"

"Yes, Sir!" It was more an exclamation than a reply. The young man twanged to parade rest—eyes still focused straight ahead.

Ross sighed. Cadet Ackerman was washout material. After twelve hours of dual, his instructor had given up. "Lacks coordination and manual dexterity. Becomes confused easily," Roger Gibbs had recorded. This was to be Ackerman's elimination ride, a term that cadets used in the same hushed tone as that reserved for death. It was up to Ross either to confirm the instructor's diagnosis or give the aspiring candidate another chance to earn those coveted silver wings. Historically, elimination rides offered little hope for optimism.

Cadet Ackerman didn't even look like a pilot—not the ones that posed for recruiting posters, at least. The product of a North Dakota wheat farm, he was a tall—six-foot-two—country-looking boy. No issue flight suit could completely cover his dangling, rawboned wrists and the last six inches of skinny calf and ankle. When he walked, it was with a graceless, slow lope. But if flying skill resulted entirely from effort, Ackerman would have aced the course. His lumpy, unhandsome features wore a chronic frown of concentration. Ground school hardly presented a challenge.

"Ackerman," Ross said as he swung his chute into the front cockpit, "Mister Gibbs says you have some problems. What do you think?"

"Yessir, I suppose I do. I haven't soloed yet."

"Why not? Is it your landings? Takeoffs? Air work?"

The lanky cadet's face assumed a worried expression. "I don't know that it's any *one* thing, Sir. Mister Gibbs," he paused and his face reddened, "he says I'm just a natural-born fuckup, Sir."

"Well, let's see what we can see," Ross replied easily. "Just relax and don't try too hard; that sometimes causes mistakes. You checked the Form-1?"

"Yessir, no write-ups."

"Okay, let's do a walk-around inspection, then crank 'er up and get airborne."

Ackerman removed a bulky, two-handled crank from the rear cockpit and fitted it over a stubby shaft protruding from the engine fairing. "Switch off," he called.

"Switch off," Ross responded from the front cockpit. "Parking brake set."

While the lanky Ackerman wound the inertial wheel starter to moaning life, Ross gave the engine primer three short strokes. When the sound of the starter reached a high-pitched whine, the cadet removed the crank and called, "Contact."

Ross turned the mag switch to "both" and echoed, "Contact." Ackerman pulled a small T-handle, engaging inertial wheel and engine. The prop kicked over twice and sputtered to life as Ross advanced the throttle slightly.

Cadet Ackerman, a profusion of arms and legs, scrambled into the rear cockpit. Chute harness buckled, seat belt fastened, Gosport tubes in place over his helmet earpieces, Ackerman gave a thumbs-up signal.

Ross saw the gesture in the rearview mirror. Grasping the Gosport's speaking tube, Ross gave a cheery, "Okay, she's all yours. Make the takeoff and climb out northeast to five thousand." Ackerman nodded and nudged the throttle forward.

Ross placed both hands in plain view on the rim of his cockpit—a move that supposedly inspired confidence in a student pilot. Ackerman proceeded toward the takeoff position, using big S turns to see ahead around the whirling prop. Stopping in a corner of the mile-square airfield, he checked the oversized wooden wind-tee set in the exact center of the field. Turning into the wind, he made a careful engine run-up and magneto check. A steady green light in the control tower indicated Cadet Willis Ackerman's elimination ride was under way.

The little Stearman's 220-horsepower Continental emitted a steady, reassuring thunder from its seven unmuffled exhaust stacks. Ross grinned to himself. This was flying. His anger at being relegated to a primary trainer had disappeared with that first orientation ride with Major Wilson. Big planes spoiled you. You lost that sense of being a *part* of the machine —the delicate touch, the sound of wind passing through rigging wires, the rush of a ninety-mile-per-hour slipstream past the little windshield that protected your open cockpit. The leather A-2 jacket felt good in the early morning air as they climbed through three thousand feet.

A half hour later, Ross reached for the Gosport mouthpiece. Raising his voice above the engine noise he called, "All right, let's go to auxiliary number one and shoot a couple of landings." Two acceptable—not great—demonstrations later, he told the sweat-soaked Ackerman, "Taxi over there by the wind-tee. I have to take a piss. Leave the engine running."

Standing on the wing, he removed his parachute from the front cockpit and fastened the empty seat belt. Ackerman, at least that portion of his face visible beneath the large aviator goggles, looked puzzled. Ross leaned close and yelled. "You've been screwing off long enough, Mister. You can fly this airplane as well as I can; you're just too goddamn lazy to solo. Now, while I'm over here taking a leak, you make three takeoffs and landings. And, goddamnit, don't forget to come back here for me, you understand?"

The normally constant background noise of aircraft engines ended as the last flight of the day taxied to the parking area and shut down. Ross met a red-faced Roger Gibbs in the empty student ready room. "I don't appreciate your interference, Lieutenant," said Gibbs. "Ackerman is a menace when he's in an airplane. You had no authority to solo him and I refuse to sign off on the ride," the stocky, dark-haired civilian raged.

Ross's response was icy. "Gibbs, sit down here and listen. You can protest this if you want to. Go ahead, get Major Wilson and your boss, Andy Anderson, together; I'd love for them to hear Ackerman tell them what he told me about your instruction methods. They'll have an unsatisfactory report from me to read at the same time. In it I'll recommend that *you* be given a checkride."

The angry instructor ignored Ross's invitation to sit. He paced, muttering, "You army flyboys act like you own this fucking place. I have more flying time than all of you put together."

"Gibbs, I concede that you're a top-notch flyer. As an instructor, however, you stink. You play favorites. I've overheard some of your comments to students. You're a snob. You hadn't lived out of sight of the L.A. streetcar tracks until you got this job. Ackerman, to you, is a dumb farm kid. You harassed him. Things like telling him he'd spent too much time behind a walking plow, sighting down the ass of a mule—that's why he couldn't pick up wind drift on final approach. Now, you can pursue this thing if you like, but I suggest you drop it."

Gibbs sneered. "I thought the idea around here was to see how your precious cadets held up under pressure."

"Pressure, yes." Ross was growing weary of the conversation. "Personal slurs and insults don't fall under that heading, however. Now, I've already arranged for Ackerman to be assigned to another instructor. You sleep on it, okay?"

That same evening Ross recounted the day's confrontation to Lieutenants Tibbs, Koonz, and their most recently assigned check pilot, 2d Lt. Eddie Brown. Lounging poolside at the Desert Inn, the foursome drank cold beer and swapped flight-line gossip. "Buster" Tibbs propped his stocky figure on one elbow and squinted in Ross's direction. A product of Maine's fishing coast, his observations were invariably as laconic as they were direct. "What if Mister Ackerman busts his ass next week, Ross?"

"I'll just have to take the flak," Ross replied with a shrug. "Maybe I'll get reassigned overseas as punishment."

His words prompted a concerted hooting. "You're dreaming, Colyer," Lieutenant Koonz responded. He took a long pull from his beer and belched with satisfaction. "Major Wilson has told anyone who'll listen that he's gonna be the first Indian off this reservation. More'n likely you'll end up with his job." After a round of derisive laughter, talk drifted to other topics. The war, as always, dominated their conversations.

"Those goddamn Japs; if we don't get off our ass they're going to chase us all the way back to San Francisco," Ross lamented bitterly. "I should be out there instead of here."

"Better you than me, old buddy." Koonz set his beer aside and prepared to enter the water. "That goddamn Jap Zero must be something else. I'm basically a fighter pilot. I'm willing to wait until we have something hotter than P-40s before I tangle with them." His monkeylike features crinkled into a grin. "In the meantime I'll just concentrate on keeping the girls down at the Biltmore entertained—which, by the way, I'm scheduled to do in exactly three hours. Anybody else coming?" No one answered. He dove cleanly into the tepid water.

Loathe to stir from his comfortable surroundings, Ross idly considered Koonz's conjecture. *Could* he replace Wilson, if necessary? That confrontation with Gibbs, and the order, at gunpoint, for BT to

accompany him that wild Sunday—they had occurred without conscious effort. Yes, damnit, he could take over as detachment commander.
A slightly guilty feeling pervaded his thoughts. He actually enjoyed
directing other, less competent men. Did this make him a despot? A
dictator? He recalled a long-ago comment by his father: "Don't ever
forget that humility is an essential ingredient in a man's makeup. . . ."
The circumstances escaped him, but the words remained.

Chapter Five

0447 Hours, 4 June 1942
Midway Island
Pacific Ocean

"Lieutenant Templeton?"

"Yeah, Smitty?" BT responded without interest. A tinge of false dawn in the east marked the end of a second night without restful sleep. Strip alert. It meant sleeping in or under one's airplane, eating lukewarm chow delivered by truck, relieving oneself in a stinking slit trench, and being ready to take off on fifteen minutes' notice. And the sand— Christ, it was in his eyes, his ears, his mouth. The thought of a shower assumed divine proportions.

"Sir," said the fuzzy-cheeked private, squatted between the B-17's landing gear, "you think the Japs are really headed this way?"

"I sincerely hope so, Smitty, I sincerely hope so. I can't think of a more fitting punishment for those little yellow bastards than to make them live on this goddamn pile of sand for the next hundred years. They'll all die of boredom, dysentery, and insanity, and we'll be back at Hickam sleeping between clean sheets and taking hot showers."

"You're making a joke," the nineteen-year-old GI replied in a reproving voice. "Corporal Woodley says the Japs are nowhere near here; he says they're all busy down south around the Philippines."

"Corporal Woodley gets my vote for general." BT closed his burning, grit-filled eyes. "Please tell him to enlighten Admiral Nimitz so we can go home."

He wished the kid would shut up. Smith's nasal whine got on his nerves. And the little waist gunner talked constantly. BT sought a more comfortable position and feigned sleep.

A jeep, driven by a helmeted sailor, clattered to a halt less than six feet from BT's position. "This Lieutenant Woods's airplane?" the driver bellowed.

"Yeah," BT replied disgustedly. "I'm Lieutenant Templeton, the copilot. Whatta you need?"

"Word is the B-17s sortie at oh-eight-hunnert. Officers' briefing in the main hangar in fifteen minutes."

"Oh, shit! What about chow?"

"Dunno, Sir. You'll have to ask your CO about that. I'm just passing the word." The vehicle departed, leaving the stink of exhaust fumes hanging in the humid island stillness.

BT slipped his feet into clammy, sandy boots and plodded to the bomber's rear entrance. Sticking his head inside, he called, "Lieutenant Woods? Officers' briefing in fifteen minutes." He withdrew immediately. Bad as it was sleeping outside on a strip of canvas, it was better than sharing the waist and radio compartments with eight snoring, farting fellow crew members.

Three hours later, nine of the squadron's fourteen heavy bombers sat, nose to tail, awaiting takeoff. The island airfield now teemed with activity. Engines coughed to life as more than fifty assorted warplanes prepared to repel a threatening Jap fleet. And the Japs were coming. It was a sobering thought. It had all seemed so unreal at first. Standing in one corner of the echoing metal cavern of a hangar, Lt. Col. J. J. Sweeney, the task-force commander, made it sound like a training exercise.

"This is a search and destroy mission, men. A large Jap force is some five hundred miles to the northwest. Battleships, carriers—the works. They're headed this way; Midway Island is about to catch hell."

The unshaven, sleepy-eyed aircrews facing him straightened as one man. Canteen cups filled with coffee paused in midair. The faint background of murmured complaints faded into absolute silence.

BT heard only snippets of the ensuing pep talk: ". . . this is our chance to start striking back. . . . I know I can count on every man to do his best. . . ." The dark-haired copilot's attention was focused on the other officers making up the B-17 contingent. Woods was the only pro among them. A stolid, sallow-complected Texan, Jack Woods was a comforting guy to fly with. The rest, including BT, constituted "pickup" crews. Experienced crew members had been rushed to the Philippines in an effort to stem the yellow tide rolling over Southeast Asia. Critical spare parts had gone with them. Hickam was left with a few replacement planes, ferried from the States, and those rebuilt from the wrecks surviving Black Sunday. None were manned by trained crews.

BT wished that he could share his leader's confidence. The grumbling crews seemed oblivious of the sphincter-tightening experience they faced. They talked as if the B-17 was invincible. One would cruise through untroubled skies at will, drop impersonal destruction upon impersonal targets, then return home to a clean bed and a hot meal. BT knew otherwise. He recalled with vivid clarity the deadly, slashing fighter attack that had forced Ross to crash-land their B-17, the flaming destruction caused by harmless-appearing puffs of black smoke left by antiaircraft fire, the bright red blood spewing from the old *mama-san*'s severed neck. He stifled an urge to join Colonel Sweeney up front and tell them how it was: The Flying Fortress *wasn't* indestructible; the Japs *weren't* a bunch of mindless yellow monkeys.

Orders to deploy to Midway had created chaos at Hickam. Of the fourteen B-17s making the trip, only about half could honestly be called combat ready. After raiding barracks, maintenance hangars, and supply rooms for able bodies, only three B-17s had a full complement of ten crew members. The whining gunner whom BT knew as Smitty, for example, had gone to cook-and-baker's school and never fired a .50-caliber waist gun. Their flight engineer, a kid just out of school himself, showed Private Smith how to mount and arm the weapon during the flight from Hickam.

Lieutenant Woods, one of the few experienced aircraft commanders, was assigned to lead the second box of six ships. As section lead, he drew one of the better bombardiers, 2d Lt. Leroy Bristow. A recent transfer from a stateside bombardier school, Bristow had been a simulator instructor. Now the boasting confidence that Bristow displayed during the flight up was gone. His pale, sweating countenance did little to inspire BT.

BT had heard Colonel Sweeney's frustrated rage grow to towering proportions as, one by one, five pilots reported crippling mechanical problems. The navy, which ran the installation at Midway, knew nothing about maintaining or repairing an army B-17. Support consisted of parking a fuel truck close enough for aircrews to refuel their own planes and dumping five-hundred-pound bombs in the sand for sweating aircrews to load. Even Lieutenant Woods's normally taciturn composure had been replaced by a disposition infused with snarling irritation. His six-plane box was reduced to three. Their number three engine had a 100-RPM mag drop on run-up. The intercom to the tail section was out. Bristow was mumbling about a bombsight gyro that refused to come on speed. Private Smith's plaintive query—"Did anyone get us some box lunches?"—could easily have cost him his head if he had been within Woods's reach.

Engines ticked over with a muted rumble as they waited. Woods and BT gazed outside without speaking. Just off their taxiway, the Midway Island gooney birds, unconcerned by the hectic activity, went about their daily affairs like a gaggle of gossiping washerwomen. These ungainly feathered creatures, roughly the size of a full-grown snow goose, were the source of hilarity to newcomers. Their awkward, bobbing mating dance alone brought tears of laughter. The birds' awkward attempts to become airborne reduced the aviation fraternity to speechless astonishment. The shambling run, wings beating madly, would often consume a half-block. Their ensuing graceful, soaring flight elicited little comment.

The humorous novelty of the gooney birds dissipated after the first day. They presented a hazard to aircraft taking off and landing. The obscene piles of droppings they left required care in selecting where one placed one's feet. They seemed never to sleep, and their naked, featherless offspring were repulsive. Nevertheless, BT was forced to chuckle at a particularly inept display of airmanship. A lumbering male, having mastered the seemingly impossible task of overcoming gravity, flew into a cul-de-sac formed by three palm trees. Without room to maneuver, its flight path blocked, the bird collapsed its wings and folded them neatly. The twenty-pound fowl crashed to the ground, bounced, tumbled, then regained its feet and waddled along as if nothing untoward had happened.

"You know," Woods observed, "that's what this whole affair reminds me of: trying to launch a flight of goddamn gooney birds."

Two hours of eyeball-aching search passed with monotonous slowness. Nothing disturbed the featureless ocean beneath them. Then Bristow stammered into the intercom, "There—up there—off to the right—there they are—Christ, it looks like the whole Jap navy!"

BT swiveled his gaze to the right. The benign appearance of their target was a surprise. Twenty thousand feet of altitude made warships the size of two football fields look like toys a child might launch in a bathtub. Jesus Christ, that ass Bristow can never hit one of those dinky little things, he thought.

He was jolted back to reality by Woods's voice. "Look for carriers; they're our first priority."

BT strained his eyes. Hell, from up here they all look alike to me, he thought.

Woods led his three-ship attack force in a descending turn to the right. "Pilot to bombardier. They've spotted us. I'm going down to twelve thousand. See those two carriers in the center? We'll make our run on an axis of three-hundred-twenty degrees. Okay, gunners, look alive; that one in front is launching planes. BT, you get on the radio. Report the contact and request fighter cover."

BT punched channel D on the VHF panel. The call signs and code words provided at the briefing fled his memory. To hell with it. "Navy, navy, this is B-17 Eight-Eight-Four. We have the enemy fleet in sight. We are starting our bomb run. Request fighter cover. Repeat, request fighter cover." He released his mike button and waited. Silence. He repeated the message, this time with a note of urgency in his voice. Switching to intercom he called, "Radio, do we have the right crystals installed to talk with the navy?"

"Gosh, I don't know, Sir. What frequency do they use?"

"Oh, for Christ's sake," BT exploded. "Didn't you get any kind of a briefing?"

"Uh—no, Sir. Was I supposed to?"

Lieutenant Woods interrupted. "Forget it, BT. We're on our own. It's too late anyway. Bombardier, I'm turning to three-twenty—I see targets at twelve o'clock. Take over anytime you're ready." There was no response. "Pilot to bombardier, over." Again, no response. Bristow's head suddenly popped up through the hatch leading from the flight deck to the nose compartment. He yelled into Woods's ear, "I think my fucking intercom is out."

Lieutenant Woods said something BT couldn't hear. Then he thumbed the radio mike button. "Orange Leader to Orange Two and Three. I have intercom malfunction. Break formation and drop at your discretion. Stay close, though. We got fighters on the way up. Remember, carriers first."

BT watched the wingmen slide from view. Woods was on the intercom again. "Pilot to navigator. You relay for the bombardier. We'll do a three-sixty and make another pass."

The enemy armada scattered, trailing foamy wakes. Dreaded blobs of black smoke from antiaircraft guns appeared. The fire wasn't directed toward them, thank heaven. Tiny dots were visible at wave-top altitude—the torpedo bombers. Some of the puffs of smoke appeared larger than others—good God, they were coming from exploding aircraft! BT counted a dozen—almost all of the torpedo-launching task force. None had scored a visible hit.

Below, madly zigzagging ships covered an area of ten to twelve square miles. Except the carriers. BT could see the flattops steaming straight into the wind while spitting fighters into the air. Then a bone-rattling jar and sharp concussion announced that the Jap antiaircraft guns had found their range. BT flinched and ducked reflexively as the Plexiglas astrodome in front of the windshield disappeared. Why the hell didn't Woods take some evasive action?

But Woods's jaw hardened. He plowed straight ahead, eyes fixed on the direction indicator. He aligned his ship, steadied on the bomb run. Bristow's bombsight fed course corrections to the pilot via the PDI.

"Bandits, four o'clock high," an unidentified voice, close to panic, called over the intercom. Then, "Bandits, six o'clock, coming in!" And the goddamn intercom to the tail section isn't working! BT thought. How can we warn the gunners?

BT sat frozen, unable to remember what his duties were during an attack. He made himself as small as possible, unwilling even to look outside. Instead he focused mindlessly on the instrument panel.

The navigator's excited voice burst from his throat just as a blinking light indicated bomb release. "Bombardier says bombs away!"

"Bombs? How many bombs, for Christ's sake?" Woods snapped. "He didn't salvo the entire load, did he?"

Silence. Then, "I—I think so, Lieutenant."

"Oh, shit," the furious pilot muttered. "What a fucked-up mess. Okay, Nav, I guess that's it. Give me a heading back to Midway. Maybe we can reload and have another go at the bastards. I'm taking her down on the deck. Where are those fucking fighters? Smith, watch for our bomb hits. Where is our goddamn fighter escort, damnit? BT, can't you raise *anyone?* Where are our wingmen?"

As the frustrated pilot stood the ungainly B-17 on one wing in a diving turn, the only response to his questions was the shuddering chatter of machine guns in the rear.

BT tried vainly to break into the excited conversations filling channel D, the interplane frequency. He was thrown against his seat belt by a bone-jarring explosion. A panicked glance to his right revealed that the number four engine was spewing flame and smoke. At least six feet of the right wing had disappeared. From some inner resource he summoned enough presence of mind to shout, "Feathering number four." Disgustedly, he heard his voice come through the headset as an adolescent squeak. "We have a fire! I'm punching the fire extinguisher." Lieutenant Woods, jaws clenched as he fought to right the stricken plane, could only nod.

They almost made it. But as they limped away from the battle at wave-top altitude, smoke from the shattered right wing gave them away. Two streaking Zeroes raked the left wing with 20mm cannon fire. BT watched number one's manifold pressure and oil pressure drop to the peg as the straining engine took a succession of direct hits. Mercifully, their attackers broke off to engage another victim, leaving them to struggle toward sanctuary more than two hundred miles away.

An hour later Woods announced calmly, "We've had it. She just won't maintain altitude. Pilot to crew. Take ditching positions. Remember to wait 'til we stop moving before you leave your positions. Engineer, go back to the waist and get both of those life rafts out and inflated first thing."

Aligning his mortally wounded bomber parallel to the ocean swell, Lieutenant Woods did a masterful job of touching down precisely on the crest of one. Deceleration was deceptively gentle. Then a giant hand seemed to push them forward as the ship settled to a stop in a blinding spray of green seawater.

Listening to instructors describing ditching drill, BT had often conjectured that the cockpit window was not wide enough to crawl through. It became amazingly easy once the flight deck was ankle-deep with cold, swirling water. Reaching overhead he grasped a gun barrel and popped himself out as though uncorking a wine bottle. Laden with full flying gear, he sank like a rock until he had the presence of mind to jerk the CO_2 lanyard to his life vest. He shot to the surface, spewing out a strangling mouthful of salty seawater. The crippled bomber, already half-submerged, emitted gurgling bubbles as it began to settle like a scuttled and broken bird toward a watery burial.

Private Smith had managed to shove a life raft out the right waist window and was floundering alongside. BT yelled garbled instructions for pulling the inflation lanyard. Then he saw Bristow, who had followed him out the copilot's window, clinging to a blade of the number three prop. His life vest was uninflated—the young bombardier was frozen with fright. Get to the life raft. Inflate it, then rescue Bristow, BT thought. Shoving Smitty to one side, BT snatched the cord dangling from the CO_2 bottle and was rewarded by a gratifying *swoosh*.

The ocean swell that had looked so gentle at altitude now took on the appearance of towering surf. It made clambering aboard the bobbing raft a major, exhausting undertaking.

At last, sprawled flat, gasping for air, BT pulled the thrashing, weakening waist gunner aboard. Dismayed, he saw that they had drifted several yards from the barely visible airplane. The second raft, with two floundering crewmen clinging to it, bobbed on the airplane's left side. Ignoring the paddle clipped to the side of the raft, BT flailed at the water with his hands as he struggled to get to where Bristow's head remained in view alongside the number three engine. He watched in horror as the bomber slid from sight, the screaming bombardier still clutching the useless prop blade.

Twelve anxious hours later a vigilant destroyer hove into view out of the darkness. In a matter of minutes, navy seamen snatched the exhausted, dejected, and seasick crew from their fragile yellow rafts. Lieutenant Woods, tears in his eyes, voice choked with emotion, told the destroyer captain, "Goddamn a war you have to fight with green, untrained kids. Four of them went down with the plane."

BT collapsed after attempting to kiss the steel deck. He covered his mouth with a clenched fist to keep from screaming the thought that had hounded him through the long, terror-ridden night: I could have saved Bristow! I could have gone to him first!

Chapter Six

12 July 1942
Thunderbird Field

Class 43-F reported in and the upper/lower class caste system surfaced. The Arizona sun turned the flight line into an oven. Routine replaced the enthusiasm of first-time accomplishment. Once bright, shiny new trainers acquired dirt-grimed streaks of oil; 110-degree heat made tempers short. The formerly close-knit group of pilots calling the Desert Inn home quarreled and sulked.

Ross, stripped to his undershorts, lay reading his mail. He picked up a square, heavy envelope of expensive parchment. Sipping from a moisture-beaded can of Blue Ribbon, he scanned the envelope's contents.

COLONEL AND MRS. EDMOND RICHARDS
ANNOUNCE
THE MARRIAGE OF THEIR DAUGHTER
JANET ELIZABETH
TO
FIRST LIEUTENANT BRODERICK TEMPLETON III

Ross read on, a wry grin on his face. The wedding would be next week in the Hickam Field base chapel. A single sheet of lavender notepaper was tucked inside.

Dear Ross,

I'm sorry I didn't reply to your letter. I didn't really know how. This is the way things have worked out. Given another time and place, maybe . . . Oh, well, please, please understand and give me your best wishes.

> I'll always remember you,
> Janet

Ross showered, dressed, and called a cab. "The Biltmore," he instructed the cabby. There being no officers' club at Thunderbird, the bar at the Biltmore Hotel became the informal haunt of the handful of officers assigned to the base.

Ross went alone. Over the first scotch and water, he recalled the night at Major Wilson's quarters. They had spent a lazy evening partaking of his commanding officer's special chili, drinking beer, and becoming acquainted. Major Wilson's wife, Doris, chattered on about army life. Every time her cousin, Broderick, was mentioned, Ross evaded direct answers.

Then, one day in early June, the major had asked him to stop by his office. "Ross," he asked through a cloud of cigar smoke, "what gives with you and Doris's cousin?"

"Oh, it was a stupid thing, really," Ross had replied. "You saw the citation for my Silver Star. But there was more to it than what you read. BT argued with me. I was AO that day and I'm afraid I pulled a gun and ordered him to go." Ross shrugged. "He was pretty mad about it."

"The hell you say!" The major grinned and slapped his thigh. "Don't tell Doris I said this, but I've always felt that the guy was a stuck-up little shit. But surely you know who 'Big Daddy' is."

"Oh, yes. BT the Second is a U.S. senator. Believe me, everyone who knows BT the Third for more than five minutes knows that."

"Well, let me tell you a little secret," Major Wilson said conspiratorially. "After Doris wrote and told the little bastard that you were assigned here, I got a call from General Smithers, at Headquarters, WAFTC. In a nutshell, he hinted that I should watch you, that you were trouble. You sure made yourself a dangerous enemy, my boy."

Ross ordered a refill and brooded. Women. He had felt something special with Janet, but dragged his feet because of Rhoda. Now Rhoda had made it clear that she preferred playing the field. And to lose Janet to that asshole Templeton. . . .

He awoke that morning scarcely remembering what went on after he took Lola, the cocktail waitress, home after her shift.

Major Wilson, attired in his flight suit, met Ross in the ready room. "Morning, Major," Ross said in greeting. "You taking a cross-country?"

"Nope. Thought I'd give one of the new bunch his orientation ride. I don't get to see enough of the students."

"Great," Ross grinned. "Don't get lost now." He stalked gingerly to a cubicle shared by the check pilots and spent the next hour nursing his hangover and catching up on paperwork. His only scheduled activity was a final checkride at 0900 with one of the graduating class.

His precheckride briefing was interrupted by a wide-eyed student clattering into the ready room. "Sir," the panting cadet called, "I think there's a plane in trouble out there."

Ross frowned. "What kind of trouble?"

"Well, it's just wandering around, sort of. Over by Camelback Mountain. I watched them for quite a while, and it looks like nobody's flying it."

"Them?"

"Yes, Sir. There's two people in it."

"You get the tail number?"

"Yes, Sir. Seven-two-four."

Ross spun around and scanned the flight-scheduling board. There it was: 724—orientation ride—Major Wilson. He bit his lower lip. What the hell? Was the major just letting the new student try his hand? Probably, but an uneasy feeling persisted.

"How close did you get?" Ross snapped.

"Not closer than five hundred feet, Sir" came the defensive response. "We're not to get any closer than that to another ship, you know."

"Yeah, yeah," Ross replied absently. "Did they make any kind of signal? Wave their arms or something?"

"Well, the one in the back—maybe. I couldn't see all that well."

"Okay." Ross turned to the student he was scheduled to ride with. "Mister Evans, let's go take a look. I don't like the sound of this. We'll talk about your checkride later."

Ross stopped at the door, then returned to snatch from the wall a small chalkboard used to diagram flight maneuvers. Tucking it under one arm, he led the way to the waiting plane at a brisk trot.

Ross set up a circling search at five thousand feet, straining his eyes in an effort to locate Major Wilson's blue and yellow trainer. He ignored two ships, each with only one pilot visible. Then he spotted Wilson's plane.

Skirting dangerously close to the barren mountaintop, a lone Stearman wandered aimlessly in a sloppy turn. Dropping the nose of his plane and adding throttle, Ross was soon alongside, a scant wingtip's length away.

"Oh shit." Ross sucked in his breath. The helmeted figure in the rear seat was frantically waving one arm. The pilot in front was slumped forward, barely visible. "Okay, Mister Evans," he spoke into the Gosport, "can you hold her in position?"

The student behind him nodded vigorously. Ross could see his eyes, wide with excitement, through the oversized goggles. Then Ross scrawled "YOU OK?" on the chalkboard and held it broadside to the errant plane.

The student responded with an urgent negative headshake, his free hand pointing toward the front cockpit. Major Wilson was apparently unconscious. It was the student's first ride in a PT-13. Even having had the standard ten hours of Cub time in preflight, he would have his hands full trying to land the sometimes tricky Stearman.

Ross briefly considered the situation, then called to the rear cockpit. "Here's what we're going to do, Evans. Pull just a little bit ahead of him and I'll try to get him to follow us back to the field and land. Make all your moves—turns especially—slow and easy."

He then wrote a new message: "CAN FOLLOW?" and held it up. The young trainee nodded without any sign of conviction. Ross placed both hands into the slipstream indicating an echelon formation, then drew them back in and wrote: "ALL OKAY—RELAX." He followed that message with: "LOTS TIME" and "HANG CLOSE."

The kid almost blew it on the first turn. He dropped below, out of sight, then reappeared well ahead of the lead plane. Ross groaned. Slowly the two planes maneuvered back into a semblance of formation. The young student pilot learned quickly, though. After a few minutes' practice he was at least staying in sight.

Ross's mind raced. The landing. It was apt to be messy. The Stearman was a sturdy little job, but it had that tendency to ground-loop if the pilot didn't stay on the rudders during rollout, and it would bounce if not completely stalled at touchdown.

"Ease back on the throttle and set up a shallow glide," Ross said into the Gosport tube, then held his breath.

Again, near disaster. The unwary student shot ahead, confused by the change in attitude and airspeed. He made three valiant tries before he was able to adapt to the changes made by his leader. Then it was time. The kid was as ready as he would ever be.

Ross wrote: "WE GO LAND." Unable to detect a reaction, he added: "MAG OFF ON TOUCHDOWN." A weak nod from the student told Ross that the youth understood.

Approaching the field, Ross considered his next moves. It was a normal day's flying schedule, so other planes would be landing and taking off. They would have no clue that an emergency was in progress—oooh boy!

Then there was the goddamn wind. No way was he going to lead the kid into a crosswind landing. And the wind-tee was pointing directly at the hangars and parking ramp. Oh, well—the kid would probably ground-loop before he rolled that far anyway.

Ross turned and forced a grin at the intense young man behind him. "You're doing great," he called. "We won't land on the first pass. As soon as you cross the fence, pour the coal to 'er and we'll go around. You pull this off, Evans, and you've passed your checkride, okay?" He was rewarded by a big grin.

Evans commenced a gentle glide from two miles out and watched his wingman, who was wobbly but holding position. Their airspeed slowly decreased. As Ross watched the indicator drop from seventy to sixty, what he had feared the most happened: A student, entering final from a normal, power-off pattern, couldn't see them and was descending from directly above. "Easy, Evans, easy," Ross told his student pilot in calm, reassuring tones. "Add some power and pull off to the right. We have to climb back out and try again."

It was a near miss. Evans was forced to leave traffic with a turn into the wingman; the anxious neophyte pilot in Wilson's aircraft almost didn't make the turn. Ross wiped sweat from his brow as a shaky join-up was finally completed. He printed an encouraging "DOING GREAT!" on the chalkboard.

An alert control-tower operator detected that something was wrong. Ross noticed that aircraft on final approach were being waved off with red lights. Ross had Evans try the same gentle glide, going lower and slower. When the airfield boundary flashed beneath, Evans added full power and they began climbing away, leaving Wilson's plane behind.

Ross could stand it no longer; he took over the controls and made a steep, climbing turn. By the time he could see the field, the little trainer was stopped in the center of it. Dust was drifting away. It was a beautiful sight: The blue and yellow Stearman sat all alone—and it was in one piece. Ross released his pent-up breath. A figure emerged from the rear cockpit as fire trucks and an ambulance raced to the scene.

A haggard, gray-faced Major Wilson forced a grin. Seated in the patients' sunroom, he regarded Ross through tired eyes. "They tell me that I'll be good as new in a month or so. They're shitting me, of course. I'll be lucky as hell just to stay on active duty. Nobody's even mentioned flight status. One heart attack at the controls is the max allowable. Who knows? I may get a chance to use that law degree that's gathering dust in a storage bin in Akron."

He sighed, then continued. "I could go on all day about what a great job you did, how grateful I am, et cetera, et cetera. But you're a pro, Ross. You kept your head and did what had to be done—and you did it right. So, instead of laying a lot of bullshit on you, I've done something I think is in the best interest of the Air Corps. I called General Smithers this morning and did some fast talking. Your orders for B-24 school are in the mail."

"Major, I don't know what to say—"

Wilson cut off Ross's response in midsentence with a weary wave of his hand. "You have the stuff it takes to go all the way to the top, Ross. But I'm going to take advantage of my rank and tell you something about yourself that can hold you back. You can be a cold bastard; you don't make close friends. The other instructor pilots are an example. They respect your flying ability and leadership, but they don't particularly like you. Not to say that's a bad trait for a troop commander to have, but it can make for a lonesome existence. Sooner or later everybody needs a friend.

"Now go out there and let Doris blubber all over you, get drunk, get laid, and pack your bags—not necessarily in that order."

21 July 1942
Honolulu, Hawaii

BT lay on the hotel bed, propped up by two pillows. He lit a cigarette and slit the flap of a heavy envelope. Janet hummed and splashed water in the tiny bathroom. She called something, but BT was engrossed in reading and didn't respond. The letter was from his father. It was written on high-quality bond paper, heavily embossed with the United States' seal and Broderick Templeton II, Senate Office Building, in heavy script across the top. He read rapidly.

Dear Son,

I'm sorry not to have written sooner, but these are hectic times— as you are no doubt well aware. Your mother and I have closed the house in Newport and have an apartment here in Washington. I spend all my time here anyway.

I read your last letter with great interest. You were quite correct in having it hand-carried from the islands. The brass wouldn't be happy with what was in it. We haven't gotten around to censoring personal mail yet, but that lunatic in the Oval Office will think of it someday. I plan to use some of your information during a committee hearing next week, in fact. The army is talking of procuring another one thousand B-17s. A thousand! Can you visualize that? At close to $200,000 per copy? From what you tell me, they are worthless in the Pacific theater. Wait until I ask for specific results of their use at Midway. Only nine of fourteen could get airborne, and you say those nine failed to score a single hit on the Jap fleet. Disgraceful! I can't wait to see that General Whittington's expression. The pompous ass is privately claiming at least two battleships and a carrier sunk or heavily damaged.

About your request. I agree with your analysis and will do what I can. But we will have to proceed carefully. I had lunch with one of my sources in the War Department only yesterday. He told me that your pilot rating creates some difficulty. Do what you suggested at your end and keep me informed.

Your mother sends her love. We both offer prayers of thanks that you survived that awful Sunday, and although we can't speak openly of it, we are proud of your action at Midway. . . .

BT laid the letter aside as Janet emerged from the bathroom.
"Aren't you dressed yet? We're due at Mother's in less than an hour."
He scowled. "We aren't going to play bridge, are we?"
Janet turned from the dressing table and laughed. "BT, you know how Mother and Father enjoy the game. Just make an effort for their

sake, okay? And remember, there will be two other couples. Really, dear, you knew we would be playing cards. I told you that last week."

"If we ever get a house of our own, we'll never so much as own a goddamn card table," BT grumbled. He detested the game of bridge. The finesse and subtlety of the game escaped him. He always felt foolish when skillful opponents executed a coup at his expense.

Losing at anything did not come easily to Broderick Templeton III. Poker was a good example. He had quickly concealed the check folded inside his father's letter. Forwarded at BT's request, it was earmarked to pay off a couple of the regular Wednesday night players at the officers' club. A hundred bucks in one pot! It had been a chance to recoup his entire evening's losses. Okay, he'd get even come payday—as long as Janet didn't catch on that he was a chronic loser.

"Speaking of 'house of our own,' are we making any progress on the housing list?" Janet's query penetrated his thoughts.

"Not a lot," BT responded. "But it may not matter. We could be shipping out before long."

Janet paused in the act of adjusting a bra strap. A look of surprise on her face, she regarded her husband's reflection in the dressing-table mirror. "Shipping out? When did this come about? Where?"

BT silently berated himself for the slip. Reassignment had been uppermost in his mind ever since the ill-fated Midway incident. Progress was being made, but nothing he was prepared to discuss, not even with Janet.

"It's classified for now," he said lamely. "I probably shouldn't even mention it."

"BT!" Janet turned from the mirror, her face flushed with anger. "Are you trying to say that you can't even tell your wife that we may be moving?"

"I'm sorry, dear, but it has to be that way. Don't mention it to anyone—even your parents. It's very hush-hush."

"Not to Father? BT, what is all this? I demand to know what's going on."

BT squirmed in discomfort. Damnit—how could he have let that remark pop out. "I'll let you know as soon as I can," he muttered.

Janet was coolly furious during the drive to Colonel Richards's quarters. BT concentrated on rehearsing his remarks to Col. Elliott Sprague, assistant deputy for Bomber Operations, who would be one of the other players present that evening. Much depended upon the impression he created. Janet needn't worry that he would be surly or ungracious. Colonel Sprague was on the soon-to-be-released brigadier general promotion list. Even Sprague wasn't certain of that, but BT's father knew—thus BT knew.

Furthermore, if promoted, Colonel Sprague was promised the command of a new bomber wing, to be activated at Mountain Home Airfield in Idaho in September. Ida, the curvaceous, blond secretary to the deputy for personnel, knew that. Thus BT also knew. A few clandestine rendezvous and a diamond-studded wristwatch had been more than enough to extract that closely guarded secret—plus a bonus sampling of Ida's uninhibited passion.

These two separate facts, when combined, gave birth to BT's plan for his immediate future. General officers were authorized a junior officer as an aide-de-camp. An aide who could also be the general's personal pilot was considered ideal. BT would be just the right selection. True, an aspiring officer would need a combat tour on his record, but BT had seen enough of the Pacific war for the time being.

"Yes, Sir," BT deftly swirled exact proportions of gin and vermouth over ice, "I'm a bomber man through and through. The heavy bomber will win this war."

Colonel Sprague accepted his chilled martini and nodded in agreement. Peering from under beetling black eyebrows, shrewd eyes observed the smooth-talking young officer with interest. The two had strolled to the corner bar while the players at table one completed their rubber.

"My father probably talks more than he should," BT laughed self-consciously. "But he told me in a letter last week that the Big Three have agreed that emphasis will be given to winning the war in Europe first and that strategic bombing will be a key factor." BT shook his head with a rueful grin. "*That's* where I would like to be. The '17s are out of place here in the Pacific. That was made pretty plain at Midway; I was there. The heavies were made for fixed targets. A moving target, like a battleship—well, we didn't lay a glove on them. Quite frankly, Sir, I plan to make a career of the army. I don't see that flying combat in heavies out here is going to do much for advancement."

Janet's father triumphantly announced the conclusion of the evening's play with a successful three no trump contract. BT and Colonel Sprague drifted over to join the conversation. The latter wore a thoughtful expression on his rough-hewn face. He was fully aware that the darkly good-looking young lieutenant was the son of a senator. Sprague was well versed in War Department politics. He was also in agreement that the war in Europe offered vastly greater opportunity for promotion than did the Pacific air forces. Say he made that BG list—say he was given a wing. . . . To have the son of a senator on his staff—well. . . .

Chapter Seven

11 September 1942
Mountain Home Army Airfield, Idaho

"I'm Loo-tenant Smedley, gentlemen. Me and this beauty here," he patted the parked B-24's slab side, "we're gonna be taking up just about all your waking hours for the next few weeks. If you got girlfriends in town—well, you can just tell 'em that you got yourself a new sweetheart." Facing Ross and three other student pilots, the laconic instructor pilot leaned against the bomber's shoulder-high main landing gear and continued his time-worn welcoming speech.

Lucas Smedley was an avid movie-goer—his attire patterned after Hollywood's best. Green-tinted aviator glasses concealed close-set eyes. A saucer-shaped dark green Class A uniform cap drooped over his ears in soft wrinkles as if the veteran of long, harried hours beneath a headset. Actually, one could speed up a "fifty-mission crush" by wetting the cap in the shower, sprinkling it with dust, then cramming it into the angles of a wire coat hanger to dry. Where the others wore khaki flight suits, Smedley wore smartly pressed gabardine altered by the base tailor. Bony facial planes were the only thing detracting from his portrayal of Mister Army Air Corps.

Ross Colyer was ready to start flying; he had been for two weeks. Getting settled in, records updated, and a new physical exam, and sweating out a training slot in the B-24 program—he was anxious to get on with it. The entire base resembled the unfinished state that Thunderbird had been in when he reported there.

The 361st Bombardment Group was housed for the time being in one end of a maintenance hangar. Buildings of raw Oregon pine were springing up like yellow warts. All new pilots assigned to the 866th Bomb Squadron were housed in a building completed only a week before. The sign in front read "Bachelor Officers' Quarters"—the euphemism for a standard two-story barracks building with cubicles formed by thin plywood to create an illusion of privacy.

Two major differences existed between Thunderbird and Ross's new station. First, Mountain Home was larger and had paved runways—and obviously was to grow even larger. Second, the fall air at this altitude was like inhaling a whiff of pure oxygen. The view was one of un-limited space; a mountain range, already snowcapped, dominated the distant horizon.

The atmosphere here was totally different than at Thunderbird. War—combat, urgency, and grim, impersonal efficiency motivated every action. There was no place for military pomp and circumstance. Sundays and holidays passed unobserved, except for a one-hour church pass. There was a sobering, if unspoken, realization that the next move would be to a combat zone. Verifying that wills and emergency addresses for next-of-kin were current implied that the time for fun and games was past. A ground school course in emergency medical treatment was entitled "What to do when the doctor *isn't* going to come." The prevailing attitude plainly indicated that this was a fighting outfit.

Aircrew training reflected the same grim motive. The drab-painted B-24s were designed for one purpose: to inflict maximum damage on the enemy while incurring minimal damage in return. They were nei-ther graceful nor beautiful. Squatting in symmetrical rows, they re-flected lumpy, brutish strength. Battle damage was anticipated. Learning by rote the emergency procedures for coping with fires, explosions, and the loss of essential systems was imperative.

Lieutenant Smedley reveled in his status as an instructor pilot. The title alone conveyed knowing more about a given subject than your contemporaries. The fact that Smedley had completed B-24 training himself less than six months ago became insignificant. No one ever challenged the casual "And when you guys get to combat you're gonna find that . . ." that he was prone to weave into his instruction. Ross gave the posturing lieutenant his undivided attention.

"The four of you will be assigned to me until you solo. After that, you'll fly 'buddy' with each other until you have eighty hours. You'll be assigned to a crew then and enter the Combat Crew Training syllabus. There'll be one four-hour training period in the morning and one in the afternoon. You'll stand down every third day for ground school. Night flying will be worked in when the time comes. I'll take two of you at a time—one will fly left seat for two hours, then you'll switch over. This morning I'll give the four of you a walk-through. Colyer, you and Agee will fly together. I'll take the two of you this afternoon. Wilkes, you and Noonan will be buddies and start tomorrow morning. Okay?"

After a grinning nod of agreement from his four charges, Smedley continued, "You're looking at the D model of the B-24 Liberator, gentlemen. It's a big hunk of airplane to strap on your ass. She has a wingspan of a hundred and ten feet, is sixty feet long, and will weigh sixty thousand pounds fully loaded at takeoff. Now, I understand that some of you have flown the B-17, so it won't be as big a change for you as it will for those who've come straight from twin-engine advanced. But she's still a lot of bird; for example, you sit almost twelve feet off the ground when you're in the pilot's seat."

Smedley's voice droned on as he led the foursome around the aircraft, looking like a tour guide as he pointed out items that needed to be inspected carefully during the preflight check. After they had thoroughly scrutinized the B-24's exterior, Smedley stopped under the right wing root and pointed at the bomb bay doors.

"You got three ways to get inside," he said. "The best way is here, on the right-hand side—through this little door, see? Inside is this handle marked 'Auxiliary Bomb Door Valve.' You pull it and the doors are opened by hydraulic pressure. You got another hatch up inside the nose-wheel well and another one in the underside of the tail section.

"You climb up on this catwalk that divides the bomb bay lengthwise." Smedley paused, standing on the twelve-inch-wide metal beam until the others had clambered inside. "You got a forward and rear bomb bay with shackles for twelve thousand-pound bombs or twenty-four five-hundred-pounders. These little cranks here on the center support will let you open or close the doors by hand. . . ."

Ross drank in the array of cables, metal tubing, wires, mysterious-looking switches, and handles. Soon, this would all be his to oversee. He glanced downward at the concrete ramp and tried to visualize traversing the sixteen-foot cavern in flight—clad in a bulky sheepskin flying suit and wearing an oxygen mask plugged into a walk-around bottle, a parachute harness, and carrying the chest pack—with twenty thousand feet of nothing below. True, a safety line was rigged the entire length, but the two vertical center supports were little more than a foot apart, so it was impossible to squeeze between them while wearing a chest-pack parachute. The '24 was no different than a B-17 in that respect, but scary in any event. He followed as Smedley led the way up a short flight of steps to the flight deck.

"Later on, you all are gonna be seeing plenty of the 'office' here, so we'll mosey on and take a quick peek at the nose compartment," Smedley said as he snaked through a passageway on the right side of the nose-wheel well. Smedley stepped past an array of radio gear and the radio operator's console, then disappeared into a narrow tunnel between the nose-wheel well and fuselage.

It was scarcely three feet wide and four feet high. Ross dropped to his hands and knees and followed. This is no place for a fat man, he observed to himself as he brushed past two silver-painted bottles labeled "ENGINE FIRE EXTINGUISHERS." "You all'll have to come two at a time," Smedley called back.

Lieutenant Smedley settled himself in the right seat and draped a headset over one ear. "Okay, Colyer, you take the left seat. That's were the head honcho sits—you may as well start out there. Agee, you lean over Sergeant Castillo's shoulder and pay attention. Preflight complete, Sergeant?"

"Yessir. We have the standard local fuel load. Only Form-1 write-up is an overdue compass swing. Wheel chocks in place, fire guard standing by, external power on line."

Ross adjusted his seat, rudder pedals, and control yoke as he scanned the cockpit. Not a lot different from a '17, he thought. A bit wider, perhaps—he would have to stretch to reach the copilot's seat. This was his first plane with a nose wheel instead of a tail wheel. The forward perspective was strange—level, instead of tail down.

Smedley unsnapped a strap holding the ground control lock in place and stowed it overhead. "Okay, you two. The first thing you should always do is run the controls through while you have a ground controller to observe. It's surprising how many times control cables get reversed during maintenance. Just be damn sure that when you pull back on the yoke, those elevators both go in the same direction. Next, the battery switch. We have external power, so we leave it off. Generator switches?"

"Off," the flight engineer responded.

"We leave 'em off until all engines are on speed—keeps the points from arcing at low RPM," Smedley explained. "Master switch and all four ignition switches, over here on the extreme right, are on. Now, we got power to all systems, so we turn the electric auxiliary hydraulic pump on. That gives us hydraulic pressure until we get an engine going. Check your brake system pressure; the gauges are on your lower left panel, pilot. You should have between 850 and 1,125 psi. Now you can set the parking brakes.

"Inverters on—that gives you AC power for your instruments. Autopilot off. Intercoolers open. You may be used to using a carburetor heat control. The engine intercoolers do the same thing—they heat intake air to prevent carburetor-throat ice. Engine cowl flaps— the controls are on my side—are open for starting. Props—high RPM. See those four toggle switches on the throttle pedestal? Hold 'em forward with this gang bar until all four lights flash."

Smedley looked sharply at Ross, then glanced back at Agee before continuing. "I'm going through this pretty fast, but I'll tell you now: There's exactly eighty-one controls, gauges, and switches in this cockpit. Every one of 'em must be checked and double-checked before take-off. Before you graduate you'll get a 'blindfold check.' You'll have to run an entire checklist from memory and touch. Someday the ability to do that will save your airplane.

"Okay. We're ready to start engines. Superchargers off. A gate valve in the exhaust tail pipe diverts exhaust gas to the supercharger turbine wheel. If that gate is closed, and the engine so much as farts on startup, well—you're gonna blow the whole damn exhaust system off. Engine starting sequence is three, four, two, one. Three first because it has the hydraulic pump. After that, inboard to outboard, to keep the ground fire guard from walking close to turning props. All the switches are on my side."

Smedley paused, then began to hurriedly explain his actions as he flipped toggle switches and punched buttons. "Engine fire extinguisher armed. Fuel booster pumps on, to give us pressure for priming. Prime number three—four or five shots on a nice warm day like this. Energize number three starter for about a half minute, then press the crank switch. There, she fired right up. Move the mixture control from idle cutoff to auto-lean." He glanced at Ross. "Adjust the throttle for 1,000 RPM and I'll crank number four."

Ross's nervousness left him as they moved easily through the engine start and taxi-out. This big bitch is a pussycat! He allowed himself an inward grin. The first indication of what was in store for him came as he turned the big craft into the wind at the runway run-up area. He tapped the left brake to tighten the turn.

Smedley erupted like a miniature volcano. "Goddamnit!" he shouted. "Do I have to tell you every fucking detail? Didn't you even look at the pilot's handbook? Never, never, never use brakes in a turn. You wipe rubber off the main gear and put side pressure on the nose gear. From now on, I want to see both feet flat on the floor when you taxi. You use the brakes only when stopping on a straight line."

Ross bit back an angry retort. He recognized the browbeating technique—had seen examples of it demonstrated by the civilian instructors at Thunderbird. Roger Gibbs had been a prime example. Under the guise of being tough with students, they reinforced their egos by browbeating. Ross forced a smile—for some reason that always pissed off Smedley's type.

"Ready for the pretakeoff check, copilot," he announced as if nothing had happened.

The surprised instructor glared back. "Okay. See if you can manage to stabilize the engines at 2,000 RPM and check the mags—max allowable drop is seventy-five." Smedley's voice dripped with sarcasm. "Now, if it's agreeable with you, *Sir,* we'll set flaps for 10 percent and close cowl flaps to one-third open. Takeoff power is forty-nine inches of manifold pressure and 2,700 RPM. If I'm not doing things to suit you, *Sir,* just let me know."

Ross returned the sarcasm with a steady look. Smedley pressed his mike switch. "Mountain Home Tower, Army Six-Two-Six is ready for takeoff." He continued in a more normal tone as the tower cleared them into position on the runway. "I'll follow you through on the throttles and set the friction lock. Start easing in some back pressure at about eighty. Lift-off, at this weight, will be at about a hundred and ten. Establish your climb and get the gear up. At one-thirty-five, reduce power to forty-five inches and 2,550 RPM."

Ross negotiated the takeoff and climb-out smoothly and without difficulty. He spent the remaining time in the air listening to Smedley's version of flight instruction. Caustic comments, arms-flung-outward expressions of despair, screams of disbelief at Ross's and Agee's ineptness. "Jesus Christ, where did they find you? My ten-year-old sister can hold a heading and altitude better than that. You find those wings in a Crackerjacks box?"

Four long hours later, Agee set the parking brake and moved the mixture controls to idle cutoff. Exhausted, tempers frayed, the trio of pilots dropped through the open bomb bay to the parking ramp. After a muttered thanks to Sergeant Castillo and brief instructions to the ground crew, they swung aboard a passing shuttle.

Smedley did a Jekyll and Hyde act. All conviviality, he lit a cigar and asked, "Well, how do you like her, huh? A real dream to fly in weather, by the way. Tomorrow we'll get down to business. Do a stall series, shut down an engine, put you under the hood, and do some instrument work—you hit the books in between, hear?" Then, as they were leaving the personal-equipment shack where they turned in parachutes and oxygen masks, he tapped Ross on the shoulder. "Oh yeah, Colyer. A word with you, over here, before you go."

In a remote corner he faced Ross with a friendly smile, a smile that didn't reach to his cold gray-green eyes. "You're a smart-ass, Colyer. I don't like smart-asses. You thought you were pretty cute this afternoon with that, 'I'm ready for the checklist, copilot' shit. You think you're a big man. B-17 time. Shitpot load of medals from Pearl Harbor. Instructor pilot. You think you're going to show us how it's done. Well, I've got news for you, hotshot. Don't unpack your bags. I'm gonna make it my personal business to run your ass off this reservation." With a broad smile for the benefit of onlookers, the dapper pilot turned on his heel and strolled out the door.

Ross watched him go. He knew it was going to be a long winter. He would make the grade—no way was he going to let that supercilious little bastard wash him out—but it would all be uphill.

Chapter Eight

22 October 1942
Advanced Airstrip *Blau*
The Caucasus, USSR

Leutnant Kurt Heintze peered though a tiny side window of the Junkers
Ju 52 trimotor transport. An anticipatory smile creased his blond good
looks, and the laugh lines it formed softened his deep-set steel blue
eyes. A prominent jawline stopped just short of giving him a pugnacious appearance.

He clambered over a rope-secured jumble of oil drums and cartons
containing an assortment of food and clothing, hoping for a better look
at their destination—an oblong grassy area lined with weather-beaten
tents. Surrounded by fields of bright sunflowers and green gardens,
its grim purpose was revealed by two rows of sleek, camouflaged
Messerschmitt Bf 109F fighter aircraft parked to one side. *Flugplatz
Blau,* temporary home to *Jagdstaffeln* 7 and 8 of III *Gruppe, Jagdgeschwader* 89.

The heavy transport settled to earth with a protesting rumble and
waddled toward a cluster of a dozen waiting men. Kurt straightened
his already impeccable uniform, squared his cap, and, following the
transport's two other passengers, stepped into the warm Georgian sunlight.
If one is to fight a war, far better to fight it in the sunny clime of a
Black Sea province, he thought. Not that he objected to fighting a war.
The fledgling fighter pilot had worked toward nothing else for the past

year. Casting covetous eyes on the slim, deadly fighters parked nearby, he wondered, How soon? How soon can I make my first sortie against the enemy?

A chunky officer wearing captain's insignia stepped forward. "Welcome to JG-89, gentlemen. I am *Hauptmann* Gerhardt Korts; I'm the adjutant here." He gave the three assembled airmen a shy smile and continued, "We still have time to meet *Gruppenkommandeur* Eckert before lunch. If you'll follow me, I will see that your baggage is placed in your tents."

The tent they entered served only to protect a flight of crude wooden steps leading to an underground bunker. A pair of naked overhead bulbs cast dim light against raw earthen walls. Two bomb cases served as desks, and heavy planks across empty fuel drums formed a map table. A trace of benzine fumes from the drums lingered, mixed with the dank mustiness of the underground command post. A worn bag of battered golf clubs, propped in one corner, lent an incongruous note to the stark surroundings.

"Ah, my new babies," a smiling, lantern-jawed man said as he stood to greet them. Unfolding his six-foot-two-inch frame from behind the larger of the two bomb cases, he reached forward to shake their outstretched hands. "I am Maj. Carl-Otto Eckert, your commanding officer. You are most welcome additions. But come, before we talk business, tell me the latest news from home." A wry grimace crossed his lumpy, misshapen features. "What we hear on the shortwave R/T is not always, shall we say, totally accurate."

He retrieved a battered garrison cap from the map table and placed it carelessly atop his thinning black hair. "We will be at the mess tent, Franz," he called over his shoulder to a slightly built figure hunched over the other desk.

Settled at a trestle table, a bottle of wine open before them, the foursome devoured an exceptionally good lunch: stew with more meat than Kurt had seen for almost a year. He looked closely at their commander. Carl-Otto Eckert needed no introduction. He had become an ace in Spain flying with the Condor Legion, and his name became a household word during the Battle of Britain. He looked the part, Kurt decided. A man more dedicated to flying than to the niceties of military bearing, his uniform was baggy, soiled, and wrinkled. Oil spots on the tunic appeared to have been there since the garment was new. His boots, muddy and wrinkled around the ankles, had obviously not seen a brush in recent weeks. In fact, Kurt had noticed that the other pilots, lounging in the background to observe their arrival, were similarly attired. His drill sergeant at the flying school near Regensburg would have had apoplexy. Kurt was uncomfortably aware of being a conspicuous newcomer in his smartly tailored and recently cleaned uniform. He vowed to alter that situation without delay.

With plates cleared and news from home digested, Eckert grew serious. "Heintze, you are assigned to *Jagdstaffel* 7." Addressing Kurt's two companions, he added, "Bachneck and Hoth, you will report to *Jagdstaffel* 8. Heintze, you will be wingman to *Oberstabsfeldwebel* Lipfert. Now, one thing you will learn immediately is that rank has no place in JG-89. Those with the most kills fly lead. You observe, you remember what you see and hear, and you will survive. In time you will become *rottenführer* and get your share of victories. Above all, you follow orders in the air. Military discipline on the ground is one thing. Air discipline is strict. For example, there is no place for a display such as you put on after graduation at Zerbst, *Leutnant* Heintze."

Kurt flushed. How the hell had the man learned of that episode? He listened closely. "That you can fly across the airfield at ten meters altitude upside down demonstrates admirable skill. But here, the ability to do that is taken for granted. You will never again so foolishly risk a precious airframe and pilot.

"You will learn new techniques for destroying enemy aircraft. We are outnumbered by the Russians. It is only by using your head instead of your muscles that you will score victories. Dogfighting is out. To engage twenty of their fighters in a free-for-all resulting in their losing two and our losing two is a loss for us. Until now your training has been aimed at making hands and feet obey your will—to control your aircraft. That competence must be instinctive. You will add the traits of cunning and judgment, and develop the ability to anticipate what the enemy is going to do. Pick your time and place—seek out the unwary and unsuspecting. Do the unexpected. Now," the weary-faced major glanced at his watch, "you will get settled in and meet your element leaders. Tomorrow you meet the enemy."

Kurt wrote swiftly by the light of his flashlight. Electricity did not extend to individual tents. The laboring generator, dimly audible in the distance, could supply essential power only to the command bunker and its all-important radios. First, a letter to his parents in Munich. It would be couched in guarded language. *Herr* Heintze, senior, was a most avid Nazi party member. Kurt's enrollment in the Hitler Youth and later in the officers' academy had been arranged by him. It never occurred to Rudolf Heintze that his son did not share his devotion to the party. Kurt's decision to become a flyer had come as a surprise. Everyone knew that the SS was the elite corps; the man Goering, head of the flying service, was secretly laughed at by party higher-ups.

It had been the same way with the plumbing business founded by Kurt's grandfather. It was assumed that the son would follow in *his* father's footsteps. Kurt had no such intention of following his father in *his* father's business, but was wise enough to avoid a confrontation. He used the strict censorship of military information as an excuse to deal in the most general of terms when corresponding with his parents.

Corresponding with Gretta was something else. He frowned with concentration as he sought to convey the depth of his feelings:

My dearest Gretta,

I can only tell you that I am now at an advanced base on the eastern front. My time has come! After more than a year of training, I am at last about to do my part in this war. The airplane! It is the fastest machine built—anywhere. We simply cannot lose. More than half the pilots in my squadron are already aces! I will have to fly wing for a time, but I hope to have my ten victories by Christmas!

My only regret is that we must remain apart. My first act was to unpack your picture and set it on the crate alongside my cot. It brightens up what would otherwise be a most dreary place. There are few comforts here on the front. I share the tent with another pilot I have yet to meet, but I'm sure I will like him. All the men I've met so far are friendly. What a great group to have at our wedding when this is all finished! Do you still plan to wait until your eighteenth birthday to tell your parents? . . .

Kurt concentrated on *Feldwebel* Lipfert's words as they leaned on the wing of the airplane Kurt would fly. The man who would be Kurt's crew chief, *Feldwebel* Erich Merschatt, stood nearby. "This is an improved version of the plane you flew in training," Lipfert explained. "She has a more powerful engine, a Daimler-Benz 1150, and can do almost 360 mph. She's a bit heavier on the controls, but landing speed is still about 75. You have a 20mm cannon firing through the prop, a pair of 7.9mm machine guns, and the same type of reflective gunsight.

"So far, we don't carry bombs. Our task is to support our ground forces by disrupting the Russian air attacks. The greatest threat to our tanks is their Il-2 Stormovik. It's a very tough airplane; we call it the 'concrete bomber.' It's difficult to shoot down—you've got to get in close and shoot for the oil cooler underneath or directly upward through the wing roots. It has armor plate all around the cockpit and engine."

Kurt was surprised to hear in Lipfert's voice the note of respect for the Russian planes and pilots. They had been told at fighter school that the Russians were inferior in all respects. His instructor continued. "They mostly use La-5s and La-7s for top cover. Don't underestimate them. They don't have our firepower, but they're fast and maneuverable—and *they* also have pilots who flew in combat in Spain. Today we'll just do a sweep in the southeast sector to get you acquainted. Not much is happening down there. The rest of the group is going north to support a push toward Stalingrad. But we have to keep an eye on the south flank as well. Just stay close to me and I'll keep you informed as to what we're doing."

Kurt, excited, watched Merschatt wind the hand-cranked inertial starter to max RPM. Please, please, let us see some action, Kurt begged silently. The sleek fighter quivered to life as the engine caught and settled into a comforting rumble. He concentrated on *Feldwebel* Lipfert's lead ship as they completed the uneventful taxi-out and takeoff. Kurt knew he was a good pilot. Holding formation was elementary, and he was proud of the way he maintained precise position on his leader's right wing.

The R/T crackled to life. "*Achtung,* Blue Flight. Seven Il-2s are strafing roads near Yerevan. They have fighter cover. Intercept and attack."

Kurt grinned from ear to ear. What luck! His first mission and he would have an opportunity to demonstrate his marksmanship. He was embarrassed when Lipfert's emotionless voice advised him to stay in tight and check that his guns were armed—he had overlooked that essential item.

After ten minutes' flight, Lipfert called, "Bandits—ten o'clock low. Prepare to attack."

Kurt searched the area below; he could see nothing. Where were they? By now he and his squadron had reached five thousand feet and were howling at near red-line speed. Then he saw them. The enemy. Dark green shapes slightly above and directly ahead. They were going so slow! This would be like shooting skeet. He shifted his gaze from Lipfert's plane and moved into firing position.

The rearmost plane filled his gunsight. Kurt depressed the firing button and held it. Amazed, he watched as red tracers fell far short and to the right. How could he have missed at point-blank range? Then he was among them, surrounded by shifting shadows. A peripheral glance showed them turning to attack from his tail—my God! Where was his lead? Desperately, Kurt hauled back on the stick and hurtled upward into a thin layer of cloud. Bursting out on top, he scanned the clear air for pursuit—he had lost them!

Feldwebel Lipfert's reassuring voice advised, "Okay, just stay calm. I was on your tail but lost you in the clouds. Come back underneath and join up."

Kurt shoved the stick forward and tore through the obscuring clouds. He gasped in alarm—an enemy plane was coming head-on! It was scarcely a thousand meters away. He wrenched the stick to the right and dove for the treetops. His alert opponent executed a split-S and was once more on his tail. Kurt slammed the throttle to the firewall and streaked for home. Lipfert's voice followed him, but was broken and indistinct.

Major Eckert spoke from behind feet crossed at the ankles atop his bomb-crate desk. A bemused *Feldwebel* Lipfert stood to Kurt's left rear. "Now, *Leutnant* Heintze, if I understand correctly, you have managed to violate all the rules of aerial warfare on your first mission."

The group commander held up his left hand with index finger raised and, staring into Kurt's eyes, said, "First, you lost your leader. It is your job to protect his tail during an engagement." He extended his middle finger. "Second, you flew into his field of fire, thus preventing him from attacking." Then the ring finger. "Third, you mistook your leader for the enemy. It was Lipfert you saw after you descended through the clouds." The little finger joined the first three. "Fourth, you failed to follow orders from your leader. And," the major said, extending his thumb, "fifth, most serious of all, your actions prevented accomplishing your assigned mission. Those Russian fighter-bombers slaughtered one of our truck convoys this morning."

Eckert balled his hand into a fist and slammed it against his thigh. He assigned Kurt three days of duty with the armament and maintenance section as punishment. The major's parting words had burned his ears: "There is no place in a fighting squadron for a pilot who cannot follow orders. Perhaps you are better suited to duties not involving flying. We shall see."

Kurt remained in his tent when not actually performing duties on the flight line those first two days. The other pilots would be certain to make fun of him. It had happened before. The memory of being forced to wear his sister's pink hair ribbon to a meeting of his Hitler Youth group still rankled. His father's summary punishment had been imposed because he had gone to the rescue of a boy being savagely beaten by a street gang. The boy was a Jew.

On the third day, he drew the lowliest of duty, that of winding up the inertial starters of planes standing immediate alert. A pilot he vaguely recalled meeting on the first day joined him to do a preflight check. The pilot laughed and slapped Kurt on the shoulder. "You set a new squadron record, Heintze. In the major's doghouse after only two days. Most of us were here a week or more before we were banished to flight-line duty. Don't take it too badly. You'll be flying again soon, and you have one of the best for a *rottenführer*. *Feldwebel* Lipfert has eighty victories and has never lost a wingman."

Thus heartened, Kurt was a veritable sponge as he prepared for his second combat mission. "Do not take long shots, especially at the Stormovik. Think, think, think before you attack. Break away and try from another angle if conditions are not in your favor." Lipfert made no reference to their first, disastrous sortie.

A grim-faced Heintze allowed *Feldwebel* Merschatt to help him settle his parachute pack in the seat, then adjust its straps and plug the R/T into his helmet. Leaving the folding canopy top open, he ran through the before-starting-engine drill: Fuel selector open . . . throttle one-third open . . . prime—three, four, five strokes . . . water cooling closed . . . propeller to automatic . . . master ignition switch on both . . . All while two mechanics wound the inertial starter to max RPM.

"Free!" a ground crewman shouted, indicating the prop was clear.

Kurt tugged the internal clutch control and the prop started turning. The perfectly tuned Daimler-Benz caught immediately, filling the surrounding area with a comforting thunder. After verifying that the oil pressure, fuel pressure, generator, and coolant instruments had satisfactory readings, he checked both magnetos at 1,700 RPM and released the parking brake. A broadly smiling *Feldwebel* Merschatt gave him a thumbs-up sign.

Lipfert, with Kurt on his right wing, led one element of a four-ship *schwarm* dispatched to deal with a reported strafing attack on German positions a scant fifteen minutes north. They leveled off at eight thousand feet. This time Kurt spotted the enemy at the same time *Leutnant* Gratzman, the *schwarm* leader, indicated contact. He saw Lipfert make an upward motion with his hand and arm. Kurt looked up. Sure enough, just above and to their right, a dozen speedy La-5 fighters loafed in a lazy snake maneuver flying top cover. Gratzman broke left with his element as Kurt followed Lipfert in a spiraling climb to the right, keeping the sun between them and the still-unsuspecting Russian fighters.

Gratzman broke radio silence with a shouted, "Now!" Kurt followed Lipfert in a sharp nose-over. They raced through the astonished Russian fighter formation, scattering them with a few random bursts of cannon fire. Engine screaming at peak revs, Lipfert pulled out of their dive a scant five hundred feet above the terrain. Sagging in his seat from g forces, Kurt glimpsed the familiar dark green shapes of the foraging Il-2s. He bitterly recalled his previous mistake and dropped back slightly, scanning the sky to the rear and above.

Closer, closer—Christ, they were within less than a hundred yards! Lipfert's first burst was dead on target. The Stormovik's oil cooler erupted like a blowtorch. They had caught the rear gunner asleep and flashed underneath without a shot being fired at them. It required all of Kurt's skill to stay with Lipfert as the canny element leader zoomed upward, then bored into a screaming split-S to challenge four La-5s streaking belatedly to the rescue of their charges.

Again Lipfert disregarded an opportunity to engage the fighters, even though he had the decided advantage. Their target was the flight of marauding Stormoviks. A desultory burst to disrupt the fighter formation and once more the now fleeing Il-2s were in their sights. Lipfert resorted to his secondary strategy. The enemy had dropped to a scant one hundred feet—too low to slide underneath and go for the vulnerable oil cooler. Executing a perfectly timed pursuit curve on the lead plane, Lipfert held his fire until Kurt was certain a collision was unavoidable. Then a long burst at the wing root, just behind the armored cockpit. The sturdy Russian plane visibly shuddered at the impact. The tail section separated from the forward fuselage. Kurt, trailing the action, glimpsed a blossom of fire as the stricken ship tumbled toward the ground.

Then Kurt had his opportunity. Racked in a turn that drew vapor trails from the wingtips, Lipfert attempted to regain a firing position. As Kurt slid to the outside, the profile of another plane eased into view through the windscreen, an unmistakable red star on its side. A lightning survey behind and above—all clear. Kurt tightened his turn ever so slightly so as to cut across his target's turning radius. He was in a perfect position—so close that the reflective gunsight was filled with clear plastic canopy and spinning prop blades.

He savagely depressed the firing button. A stream of reddish orange balls erupted from the nose cannon. He watched them terminate along the engine cowling of the fleeing Stormovik. A kill! Nothing could survive that deadly fusillade. The Russian flipped away in the opposite direction as Kurt, open-mouthed with dismay, watched his tracers ricochet harmlessly off the armor-plated engine compartment. Dazed and dejected, he rejoined his lead. Following Lipfert as they jinked their way clear of the now swarming Russian fighters, Kurt was consumed by fury. Two opportunities with the enemy helpless before him and he had failed to down a slower, less maneuverable aircraft than his own. Kurt Heintze, a silver medal winner in gunnery school, was still without a victory.

5 March 1943
Advanced Airstrip *Silber*
Ukraine, USSR

Kurt gulped soggy bread, cheese, and cold coffee while huddled beneath the wing of his dripping aircraft. Weary ground crews, braced against the chilly March drizzle, pumped fuel and fed new ammo belts into machine-gun receivers. There was enough daylight for one more sortie, his fourth of the day, then he could collapse in his tent.

The Russian bear was stalking westward. There seemed to be no stopping the daily pounding of German positions by Russian guns. Take off, grope through the low clouds and mist, and hope to stumble onto an enemy convoy or a tank column. Empty the ammo cans, return, splash down on the sodden turf, refuel, rearm, and do it again. Five times yesterday, four the day before that. Still the massive Russian counterattack moved forward, elbowing aside the smoking skeletons of trucks and tanks and the remains of hundreds upon hundreds of inert bodies. Entire villages lay in smoldering ruin—no sign of life remaining. Kurt, at first sickened by the carnage, had grown calloused to the bloody aftermath of ground warfare.

He was still without an officially credited kill. He considered protesting to Major Eckert. He had flown as *Feldwebel* Lipfert's *rottenflieger* for more than four months. The tall, serious Lipfert commended the skill that Kurt displayed in holding position and in anticipating attack opportunities. A number of times Kurt had given the coup de grace to an enemy that his leader had failed to shoot down cleanly. In fact, his long-range gunnery was superior to Lipfert's. Still, no mention was made of removing him from the sergeant's tutelage and making him a flight commander. The opportunity to become a fighter ace continued to elude him.

Feldwebel Merschatt crouched beside him, a worried frown marring his usually cheerful expression. "We very much need to stand this plane down," he grumbled. "The oil-scavenge line has a dangerous leak, the right magneto shows an almost 200-RPM drop, the elevator control requires complete rerigging, and I will be the entire night just replacing the damaged coolant doors."

Kurt swallowed the last of the cold, rancid coffee and grinned. "I couldn't agree more, Chief. But with Red artillery only thirty miles distant, we fly until the wings drop off. I see *Feldwebel* Lipfert is strapping in, so give me a leg up and I'll try to bring your precious airplane back in one piece. You will have the entire dark, cold night to nurse it to health. And see what you can do about clearing out some of this damnable rain in the meantime."

The weather did improve as the *schwarm* drifted south toward the scene of its last engagement. It was Kurt who first spotted a string of five Il-2s racing on the deck toward dark clouds of smoke. "Bandits, low, two o'clock," he called over the R/T.

His heart leaped as Lipfert replied, "I don't see them, Two. Take the lead."

Twisting down with patches of mist whipping past the canopy, Kurt led the streaking 109s in pursuit. He watched the range close, two hundred . . . one hundred yards; he double-checked that the guns were armed, then, when the sighting pip centered on the Stormovik's left wing root, he opened fire. Large pieces flew from the Russian plane as it entered an uncontrollable rolling dive. Slight back pressure and he turned toward a second target.

Jarring explosions threw the Messerschmitt into a violent turn. Kurt saw an engine door rip off and disappear—acrid blue smoke enveloped the cockpit. What the hell was that? Debris from the exploding Il-2? Ground fire? No matter—he was going in.

An open field lay ahead. Switches off, fuel control off, canopy open . . . now hold off from touchdown, hold it off—now! The careening fighter touched down in a burst of flying mud and rending sheet metal. Executing a sluing turn, the once-proud aircraft grated to an ignominious halt.

A quick examination of vital body parts revealed no injury—everything seemed to work. A good landing. But, which side of the lines was he on? No ground troops were in view. He reached forward and calmly unscrewed the clock from the instrument panel. Clocks were in short supply; instructions had been given to salvage them after a crash if at all possible. Stepping onto the crumpled wing, he breathed a sigh of relief as he saw a field-gray truck jouncing toward him. It bore German markings.

Alarm replaced complacency as three bulky figures tumbled from the truck's canvas-covered rear. They wore mustard-colored uniforms and carried stubby automatic rifles. The faces were distinctly Asiatic. Jesus Christ! Russian soldiers, driving a captured German truck. Not many pilots crash-landing behind Russian lines were ever heard from again. He searched overhead. It was standard procedure to provide cover for a downed pilot. Where was Lipfert and the other element? If ever he needed top cover, it was now. The sullen cloud layer remained empty—and silent. Only a not-so-distant series of reverberating explosions disturbed the peaceful meadow. He heard a string of guttural orders, shouted over the muzzles of three rifles.

Stall for time. A buried sixth sense for survival induced his instinctive reaction. Kurt crumpled into a moaning heap on the muddy, weed-covered ground. One of the soldiers approached cautiously, prodding

Kurt's inert form with his rifle barrel. There was a rapid-fire exchange of dialogue between his captors, then an arm slipped beneath his shoulders and rolled him face up. The sour smell of garlic overlaid with last night's vodka sent a wave of nausea through Kurt's innards.

He recalled a trick he'd learned as a teenager at boarding school. After much coaching by more accomplished companions, he learned to roll his eyes backward into his head until only the whites were visible. Accompanied by a sepulchral groan, the act invariably struck terror into the hearts of onlookers.

The stunt served its purpose. His startled captor dropped him and stepped back. A few minutes of discussion and Kurt was dragged, more or less gently, into the rear of the truck. A surreptitious peek through eyelids opened to slits revealed that two of his captors remained alert and on guard. His mind sorted through escape schemes. He recalled someone saying that the odds for escaping were greatest during the first thirty minutes following capture.

The sound of aircraft engines approaching at low altitude and high speed brought him out of his reverie. Good God—they were driving a truck with German markings! If the aircraft were Stormoviks—and they were almost certain to be just that . . . His captors were of the same mind. The truck skidded to a halt in a side ditch. The driver emerged, yelled something, and his two guards disappeared with a scrambling leap. The sound of pounding feet faded.

Kurt became aware of a faint vibration in the metal truck bed. The driver had failed to shut off the engine in his rush to escape what could be a sudden deathtrap.

The low-flying aircraft passed overhead with a snarling roar. Either they had another, more tempting, target in view or they had expended their armament elsewhere. Kurt raced to the cab, engaged the transmission, and floorboarded the accelerator. He looked around. The Russians were probably headed toward their own rear. He spun the wheel, jumped the ditch, and headed toward what he hoped was the west. After passing the crests of two rolling hills he decided he'd gone far enough—there was bound to be a roadblock on that major roadway. Kurt steered left off the road and drove as far as he could into a clump of trees. He dismounted and proceeded on foot after first jerking a handful of wires from beneath the dash.

Kurt stopped walking before darkness fell. He was totally disoriented.

The sound of small-arms fire punctuated by the popping thud of mortars marked the direction he must travel to reach German lines. Prudence told him to wait for the cover of darkness. Exhausted, he curled into a ball within the scant concealment offered by three trees growing close together. He watched mist from a nearby stream intensify the rapidly deepening dusk. Barely visible movement on the opposite slope caught his attention. A dozen or so shadowy figures were moving toward the skyline. A patrol? It seemed likely. If so, they offered cover. He rose from his hiding place and waded the icy, knee-deep stream to follow them.

Cresting the low hill, Kurt lay prone and searched for movement. The patrol finally revealed its location in a most dramatic fashion: White star shells illuminated the slope and a hail of machine-gun fire sent the Russian troops scrambling toward him in pell-mell flight. He burrowed into the cover of low shrubs and waited, breathlessly, for them to pass to his rear. After ten minutes of silence, he raised his head and surveyed the next hundred yards he must negotiate—without being shot by his own side.

A shot and the order to halt overlapped. Kurt heard what sounded like an angry bee buzz just inches from his left ear. He dropped flat. "Don't shoot, you idiot! I'm German!"

Silence. Then, "Stand up—arms high above your head." Kurt complied. "Advance—one step at a time." Moments later he felt a rifle muzzle thrust into his kidneys; rough hands patted him down.

"I'm a German pilot. I was shot down . . ."

"Shut up!" came the harsh rejoinder. "Lie flat, face down."

Kurt sank to the muddy ground, so weary he didn't believe he would ever stand again. A new voice entered the conversation. "You say that you are a German pilot. Where is your identification?"

"We don't carry identification on missions," Kurt said through lips half-blocked by cold mud. "If you will let me up, I'll give you my name and number. You can call my squadron and verify it."

"You may stand." The new voice reflected strain and fatigue. Kurt struggled to his feet and faced the speaker. "I am *Leutnant* Woerner, commander of what's left of the 114th Battalion. I'm inclined to believe you, but there is no telephone to headquarters. I have a radio that is for essential operational traffic only. We've been withdrawing for the past four days. Now that they have located these positions, we will have to withdraw further, probably yet tonight. We'll be getting incoming artillery as soon as that patrol reports back to its unit. Come with me. I have captured brandy in the command post. There's nothing hot to eat or drink. I'm sorry."

Kurt flopped to the dirt floor, exhausted. "Can you arrange a ride for me back to my squadron?"

The pink-faced lieutenant, his eyes looking like dark smudges in the candlelight, spoke with a cynical grin. "Are you sure you know where your base is tonight? Everything is moving west—even your advanced fighter bases. As for a ride, we have an ammo and supply delivery scheduled for daylight only two kilometers from here—if the Russians haven't strafed it today."

"I'll take it." Kurt didn't hesitate. "Just to get someplace where I can report to my unit—wherever it may be. Just now, all I ask is a place to curl up and get some sleep."

"Very well. Right here is probably—" The jaded young officer's reply was interrupted by a mind-numbing shriek. As Kurt watched, the lieutenant flattened himself on the floor. A deafening explosion rocked the underground bunker; dirt trickled from bare earthen walls. Speechless with shock, Kurt barely heard the lieutenant say, "So much for anyone getting any sleep tonight. That one was close for a first effort. Hope you have your walking boots on. We'll be on our way as soon as I can coordinate with our flanks." He reached for the portable radio pack.

Kurt's eyes refused to stay open, even as a second shell passed overhead. Its bone-rattling detonation shattered the night only meters away. *Leutnant* Woerner was forced to shout into the radio. "Withdrawing to coordinates BW15-HH12. Estimate in position at oh-three-hundred. What? Say again?" A pause, then, "*Jawohl*. It is understood."

Switching off, the officer stared thoughtfully into space, then broke into bitter laughter. "It is beyond understanding. It is insanity." Youthful features, already aged beyond his twenty-two years, sagged further as he turned to Kurt. "If you are to return to your unit tonight, *Herr Leutnant*, you will travel alone."

"Alone?"

"Yes, alone. *Führer*'s orders. Further withdrawal is forbidden. *Leutnant* Gerhardt Woerner is ordered to halt an entire Russian armored division along a two-kilometer front—with sixty survivors of the 114th

Battalion. Unless you are prepared to stay and share our fate, I suggest you depart immediately. Here, I will show you the best route to safety. On second thought, take the damned map with you. God knows I have no further use for it.

"I have only one request of you. Here," Woerner removed a fine metal chain from around his neck. It supported an elaborately engraved silver medal. "If you reach Germany, return this to my mother." He tore a page from a small notebook and scribbled an address. "It was her gift to me the day I reported for duty. A good-luck talisman. Tell her luck plays no part in the war on the eastern front."

Chapter Nine

2013 Hours, 22 March 1943
Over Salt Lake City, Utah

Ross watched the ADF needle revolve erratically, then point to the rear. Station passage; he set the time into his E6B computer and read ground speed and time en route to Mountain Home. Thumbing the throat mike button, he drawled, "Salt Lake Radio, this is Army Six-Two-Six, over."

"Army Six-Two-Six, Salt Lake Radio, go ahead."

"Salt Lake, Six-Two-Six over your station at two-zero-one-four. Altitude, twenty thousand; IFR, on top. Estimating Mountain Home at five-six. Requesting Mountain Home forecast for our arrival, over."

"Roger, Six-Two-Six. Stand by for your weather, over."

Ross released a weary sigh and sat back to wait. It had been a big day. Their final practice mission. Combat Crew Training would end as soon as they cut the engines. He corrected himself. If pictures of their bomb results and gun camera film got past Captain Ellis's critical eye, they would be finished. Eight hours, most of it at high altitude on oxygen. A simulated bomb run on Omaha, then two hours of mock fighter attacks by P-40s training at Topeka. The intercom, filled with excited chatter earlier, was silent as the tired and hungry crew huddled for warmth. Even set to full hot, the heaters fought a losing battle with the frigid night.

He glanced to his right where copilot Rex Compton was correcting their heading toward home. Ross toyed with the idea of letting the cocky little flyer set up the autopilot and take a break. No, damnit, Compton needed the discipline. His headset crackled.

"Army Six-Two-Six, Salt Lake Radio with Mountain Home weather, over."

"Go ahead, Salt Lake. Ready to copy, over."

"Mountain Home forecast as of twenty-hundred hours calls for ceiling to be one thousand feet, visibility two miles, and light snow for your arrival, over."

"Roger, Salt Lake. Thank you. Six-Two-Six, out." Ross slid his oxygen mask to one side and rubbed his red-rimmed eyes and stiff, cold face. Shit! Mountain Home's weather was dropping like a shot. He had suspected a busted forecast when they had to climb from fourteen thousand back up to twenty thousand feet at Denver to stay on top of the clouds. He had used Boise as an alternate when he filed his flight plan that morning, but if they lost Mountain Home, Boise would also go below minimums. He thumbed the intercom. "Pilot to navigator."

The delayed response told Ross that navigator Art Tyson had not been following their progress. He was probably reading one of those paperback thrillers he was never without. "Nav to pilot, go ahead."

"We got a problem, Art. Mountain Home weather looks shaky for our arrival. Do we have enough fuel for Reno if things close down on us?"

"Uh, it'll be tight, Ross. Why don't we just make a go for it from here?"

"No," Ross's voice was firm, "if the weather forecast holds, we'll make at least one pass."

The bombardier, 2d Lt. Stanislaw "Stan" Cryhowski, came on, his voice breezy. "Hey, Ross, ol' boy, don't even talk about a missed approach. I got a date with that waitress at the Purple Onion later, and we got us a celebration laid on for finishing CCT, remember?"

Faintly disgusted, Ross didn't bother to reply. Christ, he would be glad to finish training and get the hell out of this place. What with his ongoing feud with Lieutenant Smedley and trying to whip a crew into shape, the past three months had him about ready to throw in the damn towel. Getting sent stateside for instructor duty had been galling enough. He'd thought that once he had a crew and an airplane like the B-24, everything would be great; he could start getting even for the humiliation that was Pearl Harbor.

It hadn't been great. The crew he had drawn was a collection of misfits. The officers were playboys; Ross had lost his temper and come down hard on Stan for referring to the silver wings, of which Ross was so proud, as "leg spreaders." The enlisted men made mistakes that had yet to be invented—all except TSgt. Hamilton "Ham" Phillips. The taciturn flight engineer was tops. His slow Tennessee drawl concealed a sharp mind, and he was deadly with those twin .50s in the upper turret.

Ross checked the instrument panel clock and again thumbed the intercom switch. "Okay, crew. We're going to make just one pass at the base. I'll make a standard range approach on the low-frequency command set with ADF backup. Rex, Art, Stan: I want you to follow me on your approach charts. I'll call every change in heading and altitude; double-check me. And stay awake. I don't have to remind you that the clouds north of the base have eight-thousand-foot rocks in them.

"If we miss, we climb back out and head south." He switched to channel A, the air traffic control frequency. "Mountain Home Approach, this is Army Six-Two-Six. Fifty miles south at twenty thousand, estimating your station at one-eight. Request approach and landing at Mountain Home Army Airfield, over."

"Roger, Six-Two-Six. You are cleared for a range approach to runway three-two. Weather is ceiling one thousand, indefinite, visibility one mile with blowing snow. Wind from three-five-zero; twenty, with gusts to thirty. Altimeter two-niner-zero-six; be advised that runway is snow covered. You are cleared from your present position to the Mountain Home range; cross high cone at ten thousand. Report leaving twenty and leveling ten. Call outbound from high cone, over."

Ross acknowledged his clearance. Observing Rex setting the new pressure reading into the altimeter, he eased the throttles back to a descent setting of twenty inches of manifold pressure. The dull roar of the four Pratt & Whitneys died to a whisper. The airspeed edged back to 160; he took one last, wistful look at the star-studded sky and allowed the nose to drop into the cloud cover. Their navigation lights reflected halos of red and green around each wingtip. "Better turn on the windshield defroster, Rex. There's gonna be rime ice in this stuff."

With a five-hundred-feet-per-minute rate of descent stabilized, Ross turned his attention to the coded radio signals emanating from earphones enclosed in his helmet. The letter "A"—dit-dah—with a slight background tone. A glance at the approach chart, clipped to the control column, told him he was approaching the southeast beam leg from the south quadrant. The ADF needle, pointing slightly to the left, confirmed that he was on a good intercept course. The altimeter wound through sixteen thousand feet.

The intercom crackled. "Windshield's icing over." It was Compton, his voice sounding strained. "Defroster won't handle it."

"Okay," Ross responded calmly. "Ham, throw a flashlight on the leading edges; see if we're picking up any ice." Wing deicing boots and alcohol tanks for prop deicing were considered hazardous during combat and were not installed at the factory. Now, a rattle resembling thrown gravel told Ross that the spinning props were shedding ice. Why the hell couldn't they wait until we were in a combat zone to remove the deicing boots and alcohol tanks? he asked himself.

The background hum in his headset was building, blending with the fading "A" of the south quadrant. Things were looking good. All he had to do was hold this heading until the solid on-course signal changed to an "N"—indicating he had crossed the southeast range leg—then make a left correction, bracket the solid on-course hum, level off at ten thousand, and wait for the "cone of silence" that indicated he was directly over the station.

Ross settled his lean, athletic frame into his seat and concentrated on the approach. It was proceeding right by the book. Another fifteen minutes and they would be rolling into their parking slot. "Pilot to crew," he announced via the intercom. "We're at ten thousand. Rex—you, Ham, and I will stay on oxygen right down to the ground; it'll improve our night vision. The rest of you can take your masks off now. How do those leading edges look, Ham?"

"Lieutenant, we're picking up ice like crazy," the engineer replied. "Looks like we're getting some clear ice mixed in with the rime."

"Oh, great," Ross muttered disgustedly. "Rex, watch the carburetor air temp—use the intercoolers to keep it above thirty-two. Carb ice is the last thing we need." He was having trouble hearing the on-course signal through building static. He glanced at the ADF needle. It was rotating aimlessly. Station passage? Impossible—he had at least ten minutes to go. What the hell? Now the blurred "dah-dit" had disappeared completely—replaced by a sound like frying eggs. Antenna ice! The goddamn low-frequency antennas were iced over. As he considered his next move he detected a sudden yaw to the right. As he applied corrective rudder pressure, he heard Rex yelp, "Number three! We just lost number three."

"Okay, crew, I'm breaking off the approach. We've lost our navigational radios. Art, give me a heading for Reno. Rex, feather number three. Then call Mountain Home—we should still have VHF voice radio. Tell them we're aborting and climbing to sixteen thousand on a heading of two-zero-zero. Ham, what the hell happened to that fucking engine?"

Sergeant Phillips's voice was calm. "Haven't got a clue, Lieutenant. Fuel and oil pressure are okay, carburetor temp's in the green. I'll check everything I can. Almost has to be a blockage in a fuel line."

Ross became aware that Compton was sitting motionless, a dazed, blank look on his face. "Get with it, Compton!" he snapped. "Get that damn engine shut down—check for fire—run your checklist, damnit! Mixture, idle cutoff—fuel boost pump off—ignition off—cowl flaps closed."

Ross noticed that it was Ham Phillips who had punched the big, red feathering button and was carrying out his orders. Christ! he thought. And I'm supposed to go into combat with this guy for copilot? Ross shook his head. He'd have to handle the radio himself. He thumbed the mike button.

"Mountain Home Approach, Army Six-Two-Six. We're declaring an emergency. We've lost our low-frequency radios and have shut down number three engine. I'm climbing to sixteen thousand on a heading of two-zero-zero. Destination, Reno. Will keep you advised, over."

"Negative! Negative, Army Six-Two-Six! Unable to approve. There is conflicting commercial traffic on Green Six. Return to Mountain Home range and hold southeast for further clearance, over."

Ross felt his temples throb with sudden ire. "Mountain Home, I'm not sure you get the picture. I'm not requesting clearance, I'm *telling* you what I'm doing. I can't even *find* your damn station, much less set up a holding pattern. This is an emergency, do you understand? Now get that airway cleared until I report south of it."

A shocked silence followed, then, "Army Six-Two-Six, Mountain Home Approach. Be advised that you are proceeding at your own risk. I will issue an advisory as to your approximate flight path. Contact Mountain Home Radio for a revised clearance, over."

Ross gave a laconic "Roger," then turned his attention to the instrument panel. He realized that the struggling, ice-laden bomber was not going to climb on three engines. Setting max continuous rated power did little more than cause the cylinder head temperatures to edge toward the red line. They could never clear the ten- to twelve-thousand-foot mountains immediately to the south. Ross entered a shallow turn, reduced power, and let the plane settle slowly downward; he should be able to hold it at nine or ten thousand. But what to do then?

He recalled his B-17 checkride of so many months before. He had been required to demonstrate a last-ditch emergency approach—one he had never dreamed of using, one he had never heard of anyone else using.

Ignoring the panicked Rex, Ross switched to intercom. "Art, get on the ADF set. Switch to the 'loop' position. The loop is in a shielded housing and should work. Use the rotate control and see if you can hear Mountain Home. When you turn the loop directly toward the station, the signals cancel out and you get what is called an 'aural null.' You get the strongest signal when the loop is sideways to the station. Got that?"

Art responded in less than a minute. "It works, Ross. Switch over and listen—clear as a bell!"

"Okay!" Ross shouted. "We're headed home, guys! Now, here's what we do. Rex, get with it and set the ADF needle to a wingtip position—that's ninety or two-seventy degrees. I'll take up a heading of due north. We have to be east of the station now. When we get the null, we're abeam the station. I'll turn left to due west and hold it until we get another null. Then we do it again, holding each heading for one minute and letting down. It's called 'boxing' the station. When we get to minimums, I'll intercept the inbound range leg and complete the landing approach. Here we go."

Ross switched back to channel A. "Mountain Home Approach, this is Army Six-Two-Six, over," he announced in crisp tones.

"Army Six-Two-Six, Mountain Home Approach. Go ahead." The controller's voice was chilly.

"Mountain Home, we have another problem. We're unable to climb to minimum en route altitude. I'm returning to your station and will make an aural null approach. I'll call you leaving each thousand feet and on landing approach."

"Uh, roger, Six-Two-Six." The controller sounded confused. "Is this a published approach?"

"Negative, Mountain Home. It's an emergency."

"You are cleared for nonstandard approach at pilot's discretion, Army Six-Two-Six. Contact Mountain Home Tower now, VHF channel B, for landing clearance."

Ross punched the VHF channel selector. "Mountain Home Tower, Army Six-Two-Six, over."

"Mountain Home Tower, Six-Two-Six. Read you loud and clear. I understand you are experiencing difficulty."

"That's a roger, Tower. We've lost low-frequency radios, and have number three shut down. I've declared an emergency and am proceeding with an aural null letdown."

"Roger, Six-Two-Six. Your operations officer is here and would like to discuss your situation, over."

"Colyer? This is Captain Ellis, do you read me?"

"Roger, Sir. Go ahead."

"What seems to be the problem?" Ross quickly explained the situation for him.

"I see," Ellis replied. After a long pause, he asked, "Have you ever made an aural null approach before, Colyer?"

"Just on a checkride, Sir. A demonstration actually, but I don't see any other way to go, over."

"You can always leave it, Lieutenant. Right now, I figure you're over reasonably flat terrain."

"Bail out the entire crew, Sir?"

"You're in a tight spot, Colyer."

Ross frowned. "Stand by one, Captain. I'll have to let the crew vote on this one."

"Negative, Lieutenant!" Ellis snapped. "You are in command; *you* will make the decision. If you feel confident that you can land the airplane under these conditions, then do so. If not, consider all the alternatives; bailing out is one of them."

Ross didn't hesitate. "Roger, Mountain Home Tower. Be advised that I am continuing my approach. Now leaving five thousand, will call leaving four, over."

Ross glanced at Compton and Phillips, but it was impossible to observe their reaction behind oxygen masks. He switched to intercom. "Pilot to crew. We're making an emergency approach to Mountain Home. Check your parachutes and assume crash-landing positions. If we don't break out of the clouds at a thousand feet, I'll take up a southerly heading and ring the crash alarm bell three times. Everyone will leave the plane as rapidly as possible. The surface temperature is twenty-eight degrees with snow. Try to retain a flashlight and secure your footgear. You don't want to lose your boots on the way down. Acknowledge, over."

After a series of shaken "Rogers," it was time to start the final approach. The stubborn ADF needle still refused to give him a reading in the auto position. He was getting the feel of the aural null, however, and turned to the runway heading. He should be less than five miles out: Set up a three-hundred-feet-per-minute descent—altimeter coming through fifteen hundred feet.

"Set twenty degrees flap—props, high RPM—booster pumps on— aux hydraulic pump on—pressure is up—supercharger controls off— landing gear down."

Compton had recovered a degree of composure and was carrying out his duties with increased confidence. "Airspeed, one-forty-five, descending through twelve hundred. Gear down, locked. Three green lights. Standing by landing lights. Airspeed one-forty; altitude coming up on minimums."

Ross sneaked a quick glance outside and saw nothing but the red glow of the port navigation light in the swirling snow. He looked back at the instruments and noticed that the airspeed was dropping. He nudged the number one and four throttles forward gently. Decision time coming up, he thought. A flashing amber light on the instrument panel told him they'd passed the outer "Z" marker. Ross let out a sigh of relief; he was on course and only a mile from the end of the runway. The large hand on the altimeter sagged through seven hundred feet—minimum approach altitude!

C'mon, c'mon, hold for thirty seconds, then break off, he muttered to himself. Then he heard Rex's terse, "Runway lights in sight! One o'clock. Standing by for full flaps and lights."

2133 Hours, 22 March 1943
Mountain Home Army Airfield

Ross dropped to the snow-covered parking ramp and reached back for his chute pack and flight bag. He was last to join the others, standing around in the headlights of two vehicles while they unwound with wisecracks about the hard landing, the cold—everything to avoid admitting that they had been scared shitless just minutes before. He saw Phillips regarding the posturing group with an amused, tolerant smile. Ross punched the lanky engineer on the shoulder and said, "I don't know about you, Sergeant, but I don't care if it *ever* gets any hairier than that."

Phillips nodded, a look of happy relief on his face. "If it wasn't for all this goddamned snow on the ground, I'd kiss it, Lieutenant."

As Ross ducked a worried crew chief who wanted clues about what had happened to *his* engine, a voice called out from the second vehicle.

It was Captain Ellis. "Colyer! Throw your stuff in here. I want a word with you before you check through ops. You had some worried folks down here, you know. That was a good show," he said, grinning and shaking his head. As Ross slammed the door closed, Ellis added, "One helluva good show, in fact. C'mon, close your flight plan and I'll buy a drink while you tell me about this goddamn 'aural null' approach. Where in the hell did you ever pick up that one?"

After a fast shower and change of clothing, Ross sat facing Ellis across a red checked cloth–covered table in the officers' club dining room. Ellis raised his bourbon and water in a mock toast. "So your last mission got sort of hairy?"

Ross laughed. "You might say that. We'd be sitting in Reno right now if that damned number three engine hadn't crapped out on us. Phillips thinks we had some kind of obstruction in the fuel line. I don't know what it was, but we were picking up a good load of ice."

"Well," Ellis shrugged, "we'll know tomorrow. What I wanted to talk about was next week. Movement orders are being typed up right now. Tucson, first, to pick up new airplanes, then overseas."

Ross grinned. "It's about time. Which direction?"

"Can't say. I don't know—and couldn't tell you if I did. Does it make a difference to you?"

"Damn right." Ross's jaw set. "I want to have a crack at the little yellow bastards who put that slug in my hip."

"I see." Ellis made circles with his swizzle stick. "My guess is we'll go east, but we won't know until we open those orders."

"We?" Ross gave the captain a quizzical look.

"Uh, yeah," Ellis said, regarding him with a self-conscious grin. "They cut orders today reassigning me from the school to the 866th as squadron ops officer. I'm going along."

"Hey, that's great." Ross raised his glass in salute. "Congratulations."

Ellis grew serious. "Colyer, you're a good pilot. I know Smedley rode your ass the entire time and I like the way you handled it. I'd like to have you as one of the three lead crews the squadron is authorized, but I've been instructed to ask you to stay on here at the school and take my job as chief of ops and training. Before you decide," he held up his hand as he saw Ross about to speak, "it won't mean staying here for the duration. After two classes you get to pick the outfit you want to go overseas with. The job calls for the grade of captain, too, by the way."

Ross closed his mouth in the act of uttering a firm refusal. Lead crew? Pilot of the plane responsible for leading the squadron to targets deep in enemy territory and providing pinpoint bombing. True, a senior officer always rode in the lead ship to make necessary decisions, still. . . . Art's navigation, Stan's bombing, Rex's flying— were they that good? He frowned. "What would happen to my crew if I stay?"

"No problem there. We have a dozen IPs waiting for a chance to pick up a crew. I guarantee that he'll be a good one."

"Let me think about it; this is all pretty sudden. I want to talk to my crew first. Can I let you know in the morning?"

"Of course. I—" Ellis stopped when he noticed that Ross's attention was elsewhere, his gaze riveted on two officers leaning at the bar. At Ross's muttered, "I don't believe it," Ellis inquired, "Someone you know?"

"Yeah, to my regret. That dark-haired lieutenant—good God, he's a captain! Do you have any idea what *he's* doing here?"

Ellis swiveled in his seat. "Oh, that's General Sprague's aide; Templeton, I think his name is. Sprague's going to be our wing commander. He and his aide have been going through the '24 school at Hobbs, New Mexico. Guess the general is up here to take charge of the overseas move. Where do you know the guy from?"

Ross drained his drink and signaled for a refill. "From way back, Captain Ellis, from way, way back. But please, just please, keep me away from that son of a bitch. I've got just one word of advice: Don't ever turn your back on him."

He paid for the drinks while in deep thought. Without tasting his, Ross continued, "I don't guess I need time to think about staying here, Captain, even if it means serving in the same outfit as Templeton. I had my fill of instructor duty at Thunderbird. I have a score to settle if we go west, but even if we go to Europe—well, I wouldn't feel right about dropping out now. If it's all the same to you, I'm going with the squadron."

Ellis grinned. "I was hoping you would, but I was told to ask. And don't worry about the general's aide. They'll be based someplace else; you'll probably never see them. Well, I gotta run. See you in the morning."

Ross finished his drink and left minutes later; he had no wish to talk with BT at the moment. He had some thinking to do.

Captain Broderick Templeton III was very much aware of Ross's presence in the O-club bar. He saw his old rival enter in the company of the officer he knew to be in charge of ops and training. BT's scotch and water quickly developed a flat taste and he stubbed out a cigarette that was suddenly too harsh. How to handle their first encounter since that confrontation at Hickam? Breeding and background told him to stroll over and initiate some witty, sophisticated needling: Well, I do believe that we are honored with the presence of the hero of Pearl Harbor. Earned a Purple Heart, I believe. Oh, and a Silver Star, too, I see. Tell me, Ross, what was the nature of that wound? The details escape me.

He shrugged off the impulse. Maybe after a few drinks, but not just then. Colyer's very presence stirred his anger. Besides, BT knew he would end up looking like an ordinary boor. He hadn't handled the whole affair with Janet very well either, in fact. Her admiration for Ross's effort to save at least one of the B-17s had touched off a snarled response from him. Janet snapped back and their first real argument ensued. No, unless the bastard saw him and came over to talk, he would ignore him.

BT turned instead to the fuzzy-cheeked lieutenant beside him, the base public information officer, and drawled, "Okay, so her name is Nancy and she's your secretary. But you are strangely silent with regard to vital facts. Is she married? Where does she live? What's her telephone number? Can it be that you are, perhaps, helping yourself to a portion of the lovely young thing's favors?"

"Down, boy," the lieutenant said, affecting a man-of-the-world chuckle. "As a matter of fact, she *is* married—to an army sergeant who is right now stationed somewhere in the CBI theater. She's a nice kid and strictly off-limits, BT."

"Says who?" BT hooted. "Why, the poor thing. I do declare that she is missing that which old BT provides best. We shall see if that deplorable situation can be remedied. But, back to business. The general wants pictures of every 866th crewman sent to his hometown paper. Tomorrow morning I'll give you General Sprague's bio and arrange for his press conference. Do you have any contacts with a major magazine, such as *Life,* Cox?"

"Not really," came the reluctant response. Lieutenant Cox, loathe to admit that his commission was less than six months old, changed the subject. "But if you want a good lead profile, we can start with that pilot who just walked past. He's over there at that corner table. The 866th already has a genuine hero. His name is Colyer and he won the Purple Heart and Silver Star during the attack on Pearl Harbor. I know him well," he boasted. "Hey, come on, I'll introduce you."

BT, with admirable restraint, said offhandedly, "Don't bother, I already know him. Frankly, I don't care for him a bit. You see, I was at Pearl when Colyer got that so-called wound."

"The hell you say?" Cox's eyes widened.

"Yeah, that incident was the joke of Hickam—still is. How he got that Silver Star is a mystery I haven't solved. Here's what really happened. . . ."

0918 Hours, 26 March 1943
100 Miles East of Saint John's, Newfoundland

Rex idly examined the plate covering his control wheel hub as he listened to the conversation. The Consolidated logo was upside down and the screws were loose. Sloppy damn people. With nothing better to do, he would fix some factory worker's goof. Removing three screws, Rex rotated the cover plate, but stopped short of replacing it. A folded piece of paper rested inside the wheel hub.

Scanning its contents, he announced on intercom, "Hey, listen to this. I just found a message from the gals who put this bird together. Listen: 'To the sharp-eyed flyboy who discovered this note. This is our first night on the job after finishing training. We'll do most of the finish work in the cockpit. This will be the best bird to come off the line 'cause we're sending all our love with it. Be good to her and if, after the war, you're ever in Seattle, call . . .' " Rex paused and added, "They give their telephone numbers and sign it, 'Bonnie, Trish, and Flo.' And get this, they call themselves 'The Three Happy Hookers.' "

The intercom erupted in a babble of wisecracks. Stan broke through to ask, "Okay, what are those phone numbers, Rex? Give."

"Never happen, lover boy. Those numbers are gonna be the best-guarded secret of the war." The grinning copilot stood firm in the face of good-natured abuse, tucking the wrinkled slip of paper inside a secret compartment in his billfold.

Ross was struck by the irony of going into combat with the blessing of three frivolous girls. It seemed sort of like a knight of old riding off to battle with his lady's scarf streaming from his helmet. Stifling an urge to tell Rex to return the talisman to its hiding place, he made an unnecessary adjustment to the autopilot. Was it his imagination or had the plane responded with a new eagerness?

Chapter Ten

5 April 1943
Karinhall Estate, Germany

Reichsmarschall Hermann Goering, his corpulent rouged cheeks flushed with anger, turned toward his two grim-faced visitors. General Adolf Galland, commander of the *Luftwaffe*'s fighter forces, and Gen. Alfred Gerstenberg, commander of the Romanian defense forces, sat determined and unyielding. Neither man was comfortable in the opulent setting of Goering's office. Either one of them could have housed his entire staff inside its paneled, lavishly decorated walls. Priceless paintings, courtesy of the Nazi-occupied territories, covered more than half their surface; rare vases and statuary adorned a profusion of antique end tables. A huge white wolfhound lounged in front of an ornately constructed fireplace. Both generals knew full well that to defy the volatile *reichsmarschall* could mean banishment from his inner circle. But too much was at stake, including Germany's very survival, for them to defer to Goering's political maneuvering.

The slender, sandy-haired Gerstenberg reiterated his demands. "*Herr Reichsmarschall,* you tell me that Ploesti's oil production is crucial to the *Führer*'s plans. You honor me with the post of overall commander. Yet you allocate me resources that amount to little more than a home guard."

Goering screwed his porcine features into a dark scowl. "Ploesti is too deep for American bombers to reach. Our air defense forces battle for their lives to stop the incursions from England. Our eastern front

106

is receiving unbelievable pressure. Rommel begs for additional forces to prevent him from being driven into the Mediterranean. Until our secret weapons are operational, we must contain these attacks. I cannot strip my first line of defense."

"The *Führer*'s 'secret weapons' exist only on paper, *Herr Reichsmarschall,*" the obdurate Gerstenberg replied bluntly. "If and when they do enter the arena, they will require oil. Until then, our tanks and planes drink enormous amounts of it.

"I require four wings of first-line fighter craft, forty batteries of antiaircraft guns, and seventy-five thousand troops to man them. The day is not far away when the Americans will be within striking distance of Ploesti. From Italy. You know yourself, *Herr Reichsmarschall,* that Mussolini cannot repel an invasion. The big bombers will come by the hundreds when they come. Nothing short of an iron ring of planes and guns can deter them."

"Alfred, old friend, you ask for the impossible!"

"It is just as well that you allocate them to me now," the little Prussian officer said, stern lines furrowing his features. "Otherwise, you will see at least an equal number sitting idle, starved for *benzin,* after Ploesti lays in smoking ruin."

The beleaguered Goering, commander of all German air forces, did not take such blunt opposition kindly. No one, not even an old friend who had flown on his wing during World War I, could defy him in this manner. But the canny field marshal cum politician restrained a thundering rebuke. He gnawed an immaculately manicured thumbnail as he pondered Gerstenberg's assessment. The man could be right. The damnable Yankees seemed to replace every bomber shot down with two more. He hadn't reached his exalted post by failing to hedge his bets.

"Place your requirements on paper, Alfred," he finally grumbled. "I will present them to the *Führer.*"

Gerstenberg extracted a slim folder, bound in blue buckram, from his briefcase. "I have taken the liberty of preparing my defense plan in advance, *Herr Reichsmarschall.* Will you require my presence when you present it?"

Goering dismissed him with an impatient wave of sausagelike fingers and glared at the impassive General Galland. "Your comments, Adolf?"

"The *Führer* must be told the truth, *Herr Reichsmarschall,*" Galland replied carefully. "A most difficult decision must be reached. Alfred is quite correct in one respect: The threat posed by Allied heavy bombers is only beginning. I do not have sufficient machines, or enough experienced pilots, both to repel counterattacks on all fronts and defend the homeland. Territory, although won at great sacrifice in terms of men and equipment, must be relinquished more quickly and our perimeter tightened if we are to save Germany itself."

Goering leaped to his feet. "You speak defeatism!" Spittle spewed in a fine spray from his effeminate red lips as he pounded his rosewood desk with a fat fist. "What you say amounts to treason. I will never tell the *Führer* such a monstrous lie. The *Luftwaffe* will die to the last man before more territory is surrendered!"

Relatively young for his rank, handsome, and with the treasured diamonds to the Knight's Cross displayed at his throat, Adolf Galland stood his ground. "The English night raids do not seriously threaten production facilities themselves; they saturate a general area in hopes of finding a key target. What they do, however, is to terrorize the sleeping workers. Speer tells me that production at factories producing our fighter aircraft slumps dramatically following a night raid.

"The Americans have developed the ability to bomb during daylight hours. The few times they have crossed into Germany proper have not resulted in heavy bomb damage, but our fighters are suffering heavy losses attacking their formations. Just now, they are able to send only small formations of their 'Flying Fortresses.' As they acquire more airplanes they will present a truly formidable force."

"You worry like an old woman, Adolf," Goering scoffed. "I have talked with our brave fighter pilots; their name for the 'Flying Fortress' is the 'Flying Coffin.' We will knock them from the skies like so many clay pigeons before they can penetrate our defenses and reach our important targets."

"I don't know which of my pilots you talked with," Galland replied soberly, "but they were either very foolish or, as the young are prone to do, they told you what they believed you wanted to hear."

"Impossible!" Goering snapped. "They would not dare lie to their *Führer*. It was only days ago when a dozen were presented the Knight's Cross at Rastenburg. They assured both the *Führer* and myself that they would destroy the American threat."

Galland's groan of despair was inaudible. He made a mental reminder to identify the group responsible for such rash talk and provide some polite counsel. "They would not mislead you intentionally, *Herr Reichsmarschall*. They are understandably confident. Please accept my more sober assessment of the situation. We will see huge formations of enemy bombers over Frankfurt, Dresden, and Berlin by fall. I propose to augment our fighter defense in the north with two additional wings in central Germany. Between them they will harass the invaders every step of the way to and from their targets."

"I forbid you to carry out this plan!" Goering's eyes bulged and his voice bordered on hysteria. "The *Führer* himself has instructed me to stop the daylight bombers before they can reach our industrial heartland. It will be done! Do you understand? It will be done if it means that every man and machine is sacrificed. It is the *Führer*'s order!"

The two dispirited generals strolled toward their parked staff cars, where drivers stood at rigid attention. Gerstenberg stopped short and laid a gloved hand on Galland's arm. "The war goes badly for you, I gather."

The fighter commander paused and turned with a wry grimace. "The eastern front—it devours men and equipment; the Russian bear is aptly named."

"I know." Gerstenberg regarded the haggard features of the younger man with shrewd appraisal. "Do I have your support for my fighter defense?"

Galland's response was a bitter laugh. "My support? I will gladly provide you with reams of it. Airplanes with pilots? That is another matter. Ploesti oil? Of what use is oil with nothing to put it in? More than 50 percent of our aircraft production is vulnerable—and most of that is engaged in producing bombers that will be lost on their first missions."

Gerstenberg hesitated. The substance of a fleeting conversation with a fellow officer of Prussian background, Col. Count Von Stauffenberg, rested on the tip of his tongue. There had been no mistaking the implication of the intense young count's words. He had asked Gerstenberg to join a conspiracy to overthrow the *Führer*. Gerstenberg had pretended noncomprehension. But the feeling persisted that the group might succeed. The objective: Destroy Hitler, who was showing signs of mental disorder, and negotiate an honorable peace. Galland's strategy was squarely on target.

The sandy-haired general resisted an urge to confide in one who was, after all, an unknown quantity. Instead he looked Galland straight in the eye and told him in matter-of-fact tones: "General, as an independent command, I have the ear of others close to the *Führer*. I intend to press my case for the defense of Ploesti. Shall I include your argument for a Central Air Defense Force?"

Galland returned Gerstenberg's piercing look with a smile of wry amusement. His companion's abrasive methods were well known: a combination of Prussian arrogance and shrewd persuasion. A renegade, brilliant, Gerstenberg had steadfastly refused to align himself with the Nazi party's hierarchy. He had been relegated to a backwater command in order to rid the General Staff of a major irritant. Did he really have Hitler's confidence? No matter; Galland was making no progress alone. He extended his hand. "I would be happy if you would," he answered, staring sharply into Gerstenberg's eyes. They exchanged salutes and parted company.

6 April 1943
100 Miles Southwest of Reykjavik, Iceland

"Okay, stir your ass, Dutch. Lieutenant says we're letting down for landing." The tail gunner, Pfc. Mickey Reed, prodded the recumbent, blanket-shrouded figure with the toe of his flying boot. "Swear to Christ! This guy can go to sleep *anywhere*. I haven't been warm since we left Goose Bay. I'm hungry enough to eat the ass out of a skunk. Eight fucking hours in this aluminum igloo—and this turd-head sleeps the whole time."

Reed directed his remarks to the right waist gunner, Pfc. Milt Dirkson, the third member of the miserable little group huddled in the uninsulated waist compartment. The men were almost identical in appearance. Each wore a parachute harness and yellow Mae West life preserver over bulky, sheepskin-lined chocolate brown flying suits and boots. The only difference was that Reed towered over the others by almost a full head.

Dirkson stretched and hugged the GI blanket draped around his shoulders. "You oughta put on long johns, Mickey. No wonder you're cold. What you got against long johns, anyway? Hey, if you're hungry, I didn't eat the fruitcake in my ration; you can have it if you like."

"Long johns are for old men and kids," the muscular tail gunner snorted. "You keep in shape, you don't need 'em. Hell, we used to go ice skating with just pants and a sweatshirt. I played football when it was below freezing and snowing like hell and didn't even wear a long-sleeved jersey. As for that fruitcake, shove it. It tastes like the tin can it comes in." He pressed one hand to his intercom headset as the mind-numbing note of the B-24's four engines softened.

"C'mon, Dutch, you lazy bastard. They say up front that we're about twenty minutes from touchdown. Hot chow and a warm place to take a piss."

Private First Class Helmut "Dutch" Guenther, the left waist gunner, rubbed sleep from his eyes and removed the leather helmet covering his close-cropped blond hair. A wide yawn distorted his doughy features. Dutch was everything Mickey Reed disliked in a man: overweight, slow witted, and lazy. He was always last to arrive at formation, and his continual requests for help with cleaning his .50-caliber waist gun, adjusting his parachute harness, or properly hooking up his electric flying suit were a source of constant irritation to Reed. What irked him most, however, was Guenther's appetite for chocolate bars. "I'll bet the greedy son of a bitch eats one even while he's taking a crap," Mickey had been heard to grumble.

"Where are we?" Dutch asked plaintively.

"Iceland," Dirkson volunteered as Reed ignored the question. "Wonder if we're gonna stay overnight or just refuel and keep going?"

"Lieutenant Colyer's been talking to Ham about number three engine," Reed grunted. "It's been running rough; they think maybe it needs a plug change—a magneto even. That'll take about four hours. Make us too late to get into England before dark. Can't fly over England after sundown for some reason or other."

"Well, I hope we get a chance to sleep in a bed." Guenther stretched and grunted. "I'm plumb wore out."

"Jesus Christ!" The irate Reed threw up his hands. "I swear, Dutch, you gotta be part bear. You were asleep before we got the gear up. Wonder what the women look like here?" He switched the subject abruptly.

"They'd be Eskimos, wouldn't they?" Dirkson conjectured. "Would you screw an Eskimo, Mickey? I don't think I'd want to. Bet you anything that she'd be fat and smell like fish. That's all they eat, you know."

Dirkson's question went unanswered as they heard the props surge to high RPM, signifying final approach. Dark clouds dripping cold drizzle into sullen gray waves became visible out the waist window.

Dutch Guenther watched Mickey doing push-ups in the narrow space between their iron cots. He swallowed the last of a Hershey bar and asked mildly, "Why do you do that all the time, Mickey? Damn, when you ain't out running you're doing sit-ups or chin-ups—you figure on killing Germans with your bare hands?"

Reed favored his critic with a scornful glare. Most people avoided
meeting Mickey's eyes when he glared at them. The basically brown
irises contained tawny golden flecks. When angry they resembled the
orbs of a stalking lioness. Perspiration beaded on his acne-scarred
features as he responded between effortless movements, "Guenther,
you dumb asshole. Just because we ride around in the back of an airplane, there's no reason not to keep in shape."

He sat up and toweled his bare torso. "This war isn't going to last
forever. We get our twenty-five missions in and we go home, right?
We'll probably be eligible for discharge by then. First thing I'm gonna
do is look up that major league scout I talked to after our last game;
I hit two triples and a double that day. He wanted me for spring try-
outs with the St. Louis Browns. If I go out there huffing and puffing
like an old woman, they'll tell me to come back next year."

"Well, I don't know," Guenther said as he examined a toenail
that showed signs of becoming ingrown. "Seems to me they'd give
you a chance to get back into condition. Ain't like you'd been goof-
ing off or something. Besides, Pop's union steward told me that any
vet coming home from the war would have a job waiting at the mill.
Seems to me that the pro baseball and football teams will have the
same rule."

"That's all you know about it, fat boy. Pro sports is a tough racket.
But that's where the money is. No sweating your balls off for nickels
and dimes in some stinking Chicago steel mill for me. Not that you
couldn't stand to sweat off some of that flab." He poked a derisive
finger into Guenther's plump abdomen. "Well, I'm off to a long, hot
shower." The lithe, brown-haired athlete slipped on wooden shower
clogs and clomped off toward the latrine.

Guenther gazed after the arrogant figure, his features pinched in a
puzzled frown. "Milt, why doesn't Mickey like me? Hell, I haven't
ever said or done anything to piss him off. He's always bugging me
about being a dumb krauthead and being fat. He makes fun of Judy's
picture—says she looks like a potato dumpling. Damnit, Judy's a pretty
girl. She's promised to marry me when I get home. If he wasn't so
damn big, I'd have decked him when he said that."

"Aw, Dutch, don't let Mickey get under your skin," Dirkson said.
He rolled on his stomach and added, "Mickey's just mad about the
war screwing up his chance to play big league ball. He takes it out
on everyone. He and his old man didn't get along. He told me that

his dad used to beat up on his mother, that he drank too much. Mickey had to work his way through high school. He's not a bad guy."

"Well, I just wish he'd find someone else to make fun of," Guenther pouted. He looked down the aisle as a half-dozen flight suit–clad figures burst into the low, overheated barracks room.

"Hey, there you are, you lazy bastards," a chunky, dark-haired airman called out. "How come you're still on the ground? Everybody else is pressing on. You decide you wasn't going with us, huh?"

"Hey, Mancuso, you wop asshole." A grinning Mickey Reed, towel wrapped around his waist, joined the noisy group. "We decided to wait for you. Didn't think you screw-offs would ever find this dinky little island. We was gonna go out and look for you tomorrow."

"Well," said Mancuso, "you might just get the chance." The group, suddenly sobered, took seats on adjacent cots. "Lieutenant Litton's plane is overdue. They ain't sent a position report since about an hour out of Goose Bay."

"The hell you say. What do you suppose happened?" asked Guenther.

"Dunno. Litton drew eight thousand for an altitude. Jiggs McCarthy was in the airplane just ahead. Said *they* picked up a bunch of ice climbing to ten."

"Jeez!" Guenther's eyes reflected alarm and concern. "I just saw Rosie Wilcox at breakfast. He's one of Lieutenant Litton's waist gunners. What are they going to do about them?"

"Ain't gonna do shit," snorted Mancuso. "I heard some talk in ops. Search and Rescue'll look for 'em. We go on—we're in a combat zone now. No time to screw around looking for stragglers, they said."

"Don't hardly look right, does it?" Dirkson asked with a worried scowl.

"Well," Reed observed, "just be glad it wasn't us."

The group stood in silence, eyes averted, but no voice was raised in indignation at the big tail gunner's seemingly callous remark. Dirkson opened his mouth to speak, then closed it. The sobering aspects of passing from a peacetime to a war footing registered for the first time.

"Where's your RO, Leckie?" Mancuso asked. "I tried to raise him on thirty-five-sixty all the way over. Maybe he talked to them. He and Litton's radioman, Henchly, are asshole buddies."

"Wiseass Leckie?" Reed asked. "He's out sucking up to the officers. Where else? Lieutenant Colyer and Sergeant Phillips are out helping change plugs on our number three engine—that's why we're stuck here. Leckie knows as much about working on a Pratt and Whitney as he does about brain surgery. But he's out there, you can bet your ass on that. If Colyer wants to fart, he'll have to ask Leckie to move his nose."

Corporal Robert Leckie was indeed "out there," the wind-whipped drizzle trickling down the back of his neck. His numb hands could scarcely hold the extension lamp steady as TSgt. Ham Phillips wrestled with the set of rear plugs. The sheet-metal floor of the maintenance stand, slick with oil and water, made just standing up difficult. Lieutenant Colyer and the single NCO from transient maintenance huddled on the other side of the engine nacelle, communicating in monosyllables as they checked magneto leads.

It was hardly the arrangement Leckie had in mind when he volunteered to help. When he had strolled over to where the officers were attempting to consume a revolting fish stew and mentioned casually to Lieutenant Colyer, "Sir, if I can be of help out there. . . ." he was thinking of something like rigging an intercom between cockpit and work site. To serve exactly what purpose, he wasn't certain. But it was bound to extract a measure of praise for his ingenuity. The plan placed him in the cockpit, warmed by a Herman-Nelson heater, monitoring progress and relaying urgent communications to the tower—acting as a sort of facilitator.

Afterward, he fantasized, tired and cold but happy with success, they would casually adjourn to the officers' hut to share a drink. Conversation would be relaxed and witty, and that irksome caste system between officers and enlisted men would drop away. His opinion would be sought on the impending air war.

Shit! Would that clumsy Phillips ever finish? he wondered.

Lieutenant Colyer helped secure the last fastening on number three's engine cowling and trudged over to Leckie, his face drawn with fatigue. "Okay, if you'll stand fire guard, Ham and I will run 'er up and see what we have."

Crouched to one side, Leckie stomped stiff, numb feet as the cold engine reluctantly coughed to life and settled into an uneven rumble. After the oil and cylinder head temperatures moved into their operating range, the rumble surged to an ear-shattering thunder. Was there a roughness? Leckie was too miserable to care. His spirits hit bottom when a grinning pilot and engineer dropped to the rain-wet ramp.

"Purrs like a contented cat," the lieutenant announced. "Okay, everyone, let's hit the sack. Takeoff time is oh-eight-hundred."

Fucking inconsiderate officers, thought Leckie. This was going to be the last time he would volunteer for anything.

Leckie briefly considered a hot shower but instead shucked cold, wet clothing and flopped onto his bunk. Sleep wouldn't come. He ached with fatigue, but the blessed wave of darkness avoided him. Time was running out. He had to face the fact that he was going to have to fly some combat missions. That goddamn recruiting sergeant. "Even if you can't pass the aviation cadet physical," the son of a bitch had said, "with your test scores you're a cinch for Officer Candidate School." Bullshit. After he was inducted no one had paid the slightest attention to his great test scores. Dull-faced personnel clerks had glanced at his repeated applications for OCS and said, "Yeah, I know that's what the regs say, but you can't apply while you're already in a school. Apply again when you get to your next station."

Well, by God, he'd run out of "next stations." Now it was, "Apply after your combat tour." Home in the Bronx on a stingy three-day pass after radio school, he had told the gang at the pool hall, "I should have waited to be drafted. Old Lady McGonigle, hell I didn't know she was on the draft board. She told me after I enlisted that I probably would have qualified for a deferment." He never mentioned the private conversation he'd had with a stony-faced municipal judge. The mysterious disappearance of two fur jackets from the department store where he'd worked went uninvestigated in exchange for his enlistment.

I'm not afraid of flying combat, he told himself. Street fighting was probably a bigger threat to life and limb. Didn't he have a six-inch knife scar to prove it? It's just so stupid. I'm smart. If I could get to OCS, maybe I'd become a supply officer or a finance officer; damn, I'd be a great finance officer. I'd be in line for a good job after the war. But a radio operator? Who the fuck would want a radio operator? He'd buck for communications officer school, but stay on Colyer's good side. Endorsement by his aircraft commander would be essential.

Gentle snores filled the darkness. Corporal Robert Leckie drifted into dreamless sleep.

7 April 1943
Reykjavik

Second Lieutenant Arthur Tyson stiffened in his seat as the briefing officer droned, "After checking Nutt's Corner, Ireland, you will be in the combat zone." The balding captain's bored tone lent an ominous note to the casually worded statement. So offhand, so matter-of-fact.

In four hours or less you may be dead. Art wouldn't have been surprised to hear him add: "Be sure your next-of-kin's address is up-to-date." Today was the day. Until now, keeping on course, hitting reporting points, and making good estimated times of arrival had been his sole concern. A new hazard to navigation now existed—they flew in hostile airspace.

Art realized how subtly the evolution from training to combat had transpired. The carefree days at Mountain Home, alternating between classroom, airplane, and the nightclubs in town. Knowing that civilians associated the wings and uniform with danger and courage made a slight swagger inevitable. A casual, "Oh, there's some risk involved, of course. But, hell, someone has to do it" invariably caused the current cute number to go wide-eyed with adoration. Live for the moment. Tomorrow may not come. The insidious passage of time betrayed them, however. Despite preparation for the final plunge, this morning's casual discussion of their possible fate was a shock.

Four of the twelve B-24s departing from Goose Bay the day before had remained overnight at Reykjavik. Seven had refueled and continued the previous afternoon. One, Lieutenant Litton's, was still carried as "overdue." It was more comfortable to think of nine missing men in such abstract terms. Conversation excluded any conjecture about where those men might be.

Art observed the change in attitude with some concern. At Mountain Home the brass would move heaven and earth to locate an overdue airplane—fly search patterns over the desolate mountainous terrain for weeks, if necessary. None of that concern was now evident, only a brittle, "They didn't make it. Too bad, but you have to expect losses in combat."

The four crews, scheduled to depart at twenty-minute intervals, huddled close together on wooden benches in the high-ceilinged, drafty briefing room. The odor of stale tobacco smoke, sweat, and wet wool wafted through the dank chill. Art bit into an apple carried from the mess hall and examined the packet of papers issued to each navigator.

"The Jerries have a habit of running in single Ju 88 and Me 110 intruders during mission takeoff and landings," the captain continued. "They look for singles, then hit and run. After passing ten degrees west you will arm and test-fire your guns. Gunners, man your positions and remain alert—and I mean right down to entering the traffic pattern. Your destination, identification codes, radio frequencies, call signs, and IFF codes will be given to you in a sealed envelope to be opened after takeoff. The IFF codes are crucial. The Limeys live by these Identification Friend or Foe signals. They change every day, and anything not transmitting the proper code gets shot at. The bastards are very good at shooting down stray aircraft—very, very good. They aren't choosy about the make and model they shoot at, either." He paused and looked around the room before continuing.

"The frequency given for your destination is a nondirectional radio beacon located one mile off the approach end of the main runway. It is low output, so you have to be almost on top of it to pick up its transmission on your ADF. Pilots and navigators can pick up flight plans at the ops counter. You can get transportation for coffee and in-flight lunches at the same time. Oh, yes. One of the flimsies, the pink one, gives you procedures for reporting surface sightings while over water. *Don't* let down from your cruise altitude for a closer look. Surface ships have itchy trigger fingers where airplanes are concerned. Are there any questions?"

Art was panting slightly after he squeezed through the narrow nose-wheel hatch. The nose compartment was damp and chilly in the gray overcast morning light. He arranged himself into a halfway-comfortable position on the undersized seat and spread a Mercator Projection on the map table. The pocket watch–sized chronometer, carefully checked for split-second accuracy by shortwave radio signal, was clipped into its special rack.

Preflight checks of radio and navigation aids completed, Art stowed his oxygen mask, sextant, and chart case, then crawled aft to the flight deck for takeoff. His predeparture procedures out of the way, he was free to contemplate the immediate future. He didn't like to dwell on the subject. The others could wisecrack and joke about being afraid, but to Art it was a most serious matter. That devil-may-care attitude he'd presented to the world at Mountain Home had been a facade.

His decision to enlist in the aviation cadet program, for example, was no spur-of-the-moment thing. He had talked at length with his father about this unwarranted intrusion in his life—a life that had been proceeding according to his well-thought-out plan. After premed, veterinary school. After graduation, marry his high school sweetheart, Vera Baxter. An option to acquire a forty-acre horse farm adjoining the Baxter holdings was in his safe-deposit box. A lucrative practice, on the fringe of the famed Kentucky thoroughbred country, was almost guaranteed. His father, proprietor of Tyson Brothers' Fine Clothing for Men and Boys, had warmly endorsed the plan. His mother was overjoyed with his selection of a fiancée. The possibility of his relocating away from Bartlesville was never entertained.

Obviously, the outbreak of war dictated alteration of his plan. To await the draft was the least viable option, since it removed any choice in the matter of how and where he served his country. Discovery at an early age that large bodies of water created more than normal apprehension ruled out a naval career. The Army Air Corps, his father agreed, offered the best opportunity to serve with dignity in commissioned officer ranks, with civilized living conditions, and without the prospect of engaging in hand-to-hand combat with a savage, godless enemy. Tyson senior's concept evolved from his own experiences during World War I.

An hour after takeoff, Art cross-checked his dead-reckoning position with the ADF bearing off Reykjavik range and made a neat, penciled cross on the navigational chart's pristine surface. Lieutenant Cryhowski's head and shoulders appeared in the crawlway leading from the flight deck. Stan wasn't wearing his helmet, exposing close-cropped reddish brown curls. Beneath them, his ruddy complexion and laugh lines around his eyes reminded Art of a slightly debauched pixy.

"Hey," the cheerful bombardier shouted, "how about a hot cup of coffee? Christ, it's cold down here." He shoved a thermos in Art's direction. "Kinda crowded up there though; thought I'd come down and keep you company. How we coming?"

"Well," said Tyson as he gratefully accepted the flask and poured a steaming cup, "considering that we've been airborne less than an hour and the coastline is barely out of sight, I feel confident that we're on course."

Stan, somewhat surprised at the usually stoic navigator's attempt at humor, laughed and slapped Art's sheepskin-clad shoulder. "Way to go, Arthur. Don't sweat the small stuff." He arranged a chute pack for a backrest and seated himself on the floor before continuing. "Ross just opened the envelope. We're headed for a place that just has a number: Station 78. It's close to two little towns northeast of London named Biggleston and Walden Abbey. Rex and Ross are trying to locate them on a map. Ross said to tell you he'd brief you as soon as they have it doped out. It ain't gonna be a bike ride into London, though."

He changed the subject. "Wonder how soon we get to fly on a mission? And how about this 'lead crew' shit, anyway? It doesn't bother me, having twelve ships dropping on my aiming point. But it's gonna be different, being shot at while I'm on a bomb run."

"I'll bet I get replaced," Tyson announced.

Stan arched his eyebrows. "Replaced? What the hell makes you think that?"

"I'm not all that good a navigator—hell, you know that, Stan. I almost blew our last checkride. If Ross hadn't been on the stick, we'd have missed the IP by twenty miles. I'm not sure I want to be responsible for an entire squadron. What if I fuck up and get a lot of guys killed?"

Stan scowled. "Art, don't even think that, much less say it. Look, this is a chance for us to show everybody that we're the best damn B-24 crew in the ETO. It'll mean promotions; lead crews get promoted almost automatically. Ross says it will take longer for us to get our twenty-five missions in; lead crews rotate—we won't be flying every mission. But, for the first time in my life, I'm in a position to show people what I can do on my own. My mother didn't let me do a single damn thing without her approval. She picked out the schools I would attend, my clothes, where and when we would go on vacations. The final straw was when she sent her interior decorator to do my room in the frat house at Princeton. That's the day I went down and enlisted.

"You know what she did? She wrote the fucking secretary of war! Told him I 'wouldn't be able to cope with the rigors of military training.' Wanted him to invalidate my enlistment! Well, by God, I won the silver medal for excellence at bombardier school. The first, the absolute *first* thing I ever received that she didn't somehow manage to buy for me— and that includes a place on the Little League baseball team." Stan fished a cigarette from a crumpled pack. Neither man spoke as he straightened one and lit it with cold hands.

"There were three parents at our graduation; naturally Mother had to be there. Why? To give me a red Jaguar convertible for a graduation gift. The other guests sat on some bleacher seats; Mother sat on the reviewing stand with the commanding general. She means well, I know that, but she just can't keep from meddling in other people's lives. I don't know where my dad is. Her story is that he ran away with a chorus girl when I was about eight. I barely remember him; he didn't spend much time at home. I'd like to find him and hear his story. I'll bet I know why he ran. Anyway, I'm going to be the best goddamn bombardier in the Eighth Air Force. And you're gonna be the best fucking navigator."

Stan stood and stamped his chilled feet. "I'll buy the first drink tonight. By the way, I saw you in the class-six store at Goose Bay. What did you bring along to celebrate our last mission with?"

"Well . . ." Art shrugged and grinned. "I don't know one kind of liquor from another. Someone told me that Johnnie Walker was good stuff, so I got a bottle of the Black Label."

Stan stared at the pudgy navigator, eyes wide with shock. "Art, you brought *scotch?* To *England?*" He rolled his eyes heavenward. "Man, England is where the fucking stuff is made! Oh, well, first trip to London, I'm going to take you in hand." He grinned wickedly. "I'll bet you didn't even bring silk stockings. You're gonna learn more than just navigating during the next few months—I'm gonna see to that." Clapping Art on the shoulder once more, Stan disappeared through the crawlway.

"Copilot to crew. Unless our navigator has us hopelessly lost, again, that's the Irish coastline coming up. Time to arm your guns. Stand by for test firing. We're in the war zone, troops. Keep your eyes peeled."

Second Lieutenant Rex Compton couldn't conceal the excitement in his voice. He squirmed on the cushion he used to elevate his five-foot-eight-inch frame to windshield height. It embarrassed the hell out of him to use it, but Ross insisted. "Visibility is everything, Rex. Plus, someday it's going to take both of us on the controls; a cushion will give you more leverage." It irked Rex that he didn't have something essential to do, like manning a .50 caliber. Copilot on a goddamn flying elephant. Fat, plump targets when the German fighters came up. Ross didn't trust him. Did everything himself. "Monitor the instruments, Rex," he would say—shit, Ham Phillips did that. It was always the sad-faced engineer who came up with, "Number one's oil pressure is fluctuating, Sir; looks like number four's fuel pressure gauge is inop, Sir; I'll write it up. I'm also going to write up the heaters again, Lieutenant. They should be putting out more than they are. Number four's prop is surging, Sir. Maybe we should run it up—oil is probably wanting to congeal in the dome at this temperature."

Ross wasn't satisfied with the way Rex held formation, either. You'd think it was a matter of life or death: "Stick that wing right in lead's goddamn window, Rex. *Anticipate* those turns. You get on the outside of a turn and you have to pull max rated power to catch up. Make *small* changes to the power with just the outboards to hold your position. Don't ride the rudders—makes you skid into the lead ship. Watch that fucking prop wash! Stack *above* your lead. Shit, Rex, you're all over the place. Settle down, goddamnit!"

Ross had pissed and moaned for a week about the way Rex had gotten confused that night they'd lost the engine. He'd hinted that Rex had let the carburetor ice up.

And, since they had been selected to be a lead crew, Rex wouldn't get to fly every mission. Whenever they flew squadron lead, one of the brass would fly right seat and Rex would either cool his heels on the ground or, if he was lucky, take one of the gunner's positions. The rest of the crew paid no attention to him. It was his size; he had to look up to talk to all the others—especially that smart-ass Reed. The big tail gunner had come close to insubordination a couple of times.

How the hell had he ended up in this job? Single-engine advanced training had been heaven. The AT-6 was a hotter airplane than some of the first-line fighters, and he had been good—dogfights were his meat. He set his sights on P-47 school, then damn near bawled when the orders were posted. No reason was given; only about half the class got fighter assignments. The rest ended up as twin- and four-engine copilots. It was gunnery phase, he decided. His scores had been close to the bottom. But, goddamnit, he had gotten the touch there close to the end. His instructor had been a real bastard, though. Probably had his mind made up after the first week: Compton is a loser; send him to bombers.

Rex could hear Phillips in the upper turret, an arm's length behind, keeping his guns in motion. He listened to the *whirr—whine—klunk* as the turret hit the stops and reversed. He tried to imagine that they were over Germany, drilling deep into enemy territory. Nothing happened. Personally, he felt foolish going to action stations over neutral territory. Someone's idea to get them fired up, he guessed. From the chatter and wisecracks on the intercom, the rest of the crew wasn't taking it all that seriously either. Then the atmosphere of laissez-faire terminated—abruptly.

"Bandits—we got bandits at, uh, seven o'clock high!" Nine sets of muscles froze.

"This is the pilot. Who called bandits?"

"This is Dirkson, Sir. It's one bandit really. Seven o'clock, but he's closing fast."

"Bombardier to pilot. I see him, I think. Let me try to pick him up with binos." Stan's head appeared in the astrodome as he peered aft. "Can't identify him, but he's a twin engine. Looks like he's crossing behind us about three or four thousand feet above. Probably a Limey on antisub patrol."

Nine sets of lungs emptied in relief. "Hey, Milt. Can't you tell a Limey bomber from a German fighter? Huh? Back to aircraft-recognition school for you."

"Yeah, you nervous in the service, Milt? Why didn't you cut down on him?"

"All right, you guys, knock it off. At least Dirkson was on the ball. How come no one else saw that plane?" Ross was using his no-nonsense voice. "Later on, that kind of alertness can save our ass. Good work, Milt."

The incident jarred Rex from his self-pity trip. He scanned the instrument panel, wishing desperately for something to call to Ross's, and Phillips's, attention. He finally settled for "Copilot to engineer. Don't forget to do a compass swing soon as we get settled in, Ham. It's way overdue."

Sergeant Phillips, manning the upper turret, permitted himself a slight smile. "Roger, Sir, it's written up in the Form-1."

Lieutenant Compton was a nice enough guy, but he sure had a lot to learn about engines and airframes. Ham had wondered how the cocky copilot would behave if, for instance, Lieutenant Colyer got hit bad during combat. He winced at the prospect of battle damage to their factory-fresh Liberator. God, she was a beauty. He had seen pictures of the damage that flak and fighters could inflict. The thought of a perfectly working machine turned into so much junk was depressing. He wondered if it was wrong to be more concerned about damage to *his* airplane than about physical injury to its human cargo.

Maybe Ham's feeling for perfect performance resulted from the fact that things mechanical had never seemed to work at home. Pop was always too tired after driving his rural mail route to repair and tinker. Besides, the old man seemed to be all thumbs whenever he *did* make an attempt. By the time he was ten, Ham discovered that if he studied a toaster until he figured out how it worked, it was easy to fix when the toast didn't pop up. Without it ever being discussed, he became the one who kept household appliances and their old Model A Ford operational during the lean years.

Sun, streaming through breaks in the overcast, painted the jade green hills of Ireland with a soft glow. They resembled the rolling Tennessee landscape back home. Would he ever see it again? Ham drove the thought from his mind. Losses of aircraft and crews were high, he'd been told. The papers made much about the devastation the American bombers were creating inside Germany. A neighbor, given a medical discharge after losing a leg when his B-17 was shot up, had given him a different viewpoint. But he had confidence in his ability to keep the big bomber flying, and he was a crack shot with those twin .50s. Lieutenant Colyer was one of the best pilots in the squadron. Between them they'd bring the crew back home in one piece.

Conscious that he had been daydreaming, he resumed his visual sweep of the sky ahead and above them.

After another hour, the jagged eastern coast of Ireland behind them, the crew's diligence lapsed into boredom. The matter of a name for their plane came up.

"We just gotta have a name for her before we fly a mission," Stan announced firmly. "C'mon, you guys, what's wrong with *Dangerous Dolly?* We can paint a sexy babe on the nose with boobs that look like five-hundred-pounders."

"Yeah," Milt Dirkson chimed in. "We can get Digger O'Dell, he's on Lieutenant Eubanks's crew, to do the tits. He did three pictures at Mountain Home. He's the best tit man in the whole outfit. I can do the legs; everyone wants me to do their legs. We'll get at it first thing."

"Sounds dumb to me," Rex objected. Then, remembering the note he'd found in the control wheel, he added, "How about calling her the *Happy Hooker?* That has more class."

"Look, Ross, you decide," Stan responded. "We have to come up with something; hell, we might be sent out in just a day or so. We don't want to be the only plane in the squadron with a slick nose."

Ross grinned and made a course correction with the autopilot turn knob. "Art, get out a coin. Flip it and let Rex call it. If he's right, he gets to decide."

By the time Rex called, "Wolfpack Tower, this is Wishbone Seven, over your splasher beacon at four thousand. Request landing, over," the issue was decided. The B-24 with serial number 402117 was named the *Happy Hooker*. With USAAF crew 1227 aboard, she touched down on the rain-slicked macadam runway at Walden Abbey, England—prepared to challenge Adolf Hitler's *Festung Europa*.

Chapter Eleven

"Navigator to pilot, over."

Lieutenant Ross Colyer pressed the intercom switch. "Go ahead, Art."

"I think I know what happened, Ross—the reason we didn't find the bombing range, you know."

Ross's voice was frosty. "You don't have to tell me what happened. I know what happened. You, Stan, and Rex—all with maps in front of you—got lost before we were fifty miles from home."

Tyson seemed oblivious to the biting sarcasm. "It's this damned country, Ross. Everything is so close together. It all looks alike from twenty thousand feet. Now, there were two towns, both with railroads and highways crossing. The only difference is they're ten miles apart. Without—"

"We'll talk about it on the ground, Art," Ross snapped, cutting him off. "In great detail, believe me. Captain Ellis is going to be real curious as to why we're bringing our practice bombs home with us."

The other crew members, sensing the displeasure in Ross's voice, remained mute. As they descended through irregular breaks in the clouds, Ross concentrated on avoiding patches of fog and mist hugging the swampy shoreline. Damnit! He cursed under his breath. They had wasted the entire afternoon. First, they couldn't find the bombing range. After circling aimlessly, they had proceeded to the gunnery range, marked

124

by huge buoys in the "Wash"—the notch in the English coastline carved by the North Sea. Even with the gunnery instructors borrowed from experienced crews, there hadn't been enough hits in the towed target sleeve to knock down a Piper Cub.

It was their attitude. With the exception of Ham Phillips, none of the crew—officers included—seemed aware of what they faced. The remnants of the B-17 group they found on arrival at Walden Abbey should have been a sobering portent. Only five airplanes and crews remained out of what had been an eighteen-plane group. Six had been lost on one mission to the German submarine pens at Bordeaux, France. Two more had crashed on takeoff in near zero visibility. There were no replacements, even now. The remaining five planes and crews were used, as needed, to fill in a composite group.

Ross had talked at length with the veteran pilots. They told him in bitter tones that the German fighters didn't employ the same tactics the P-40s had used against them in training. And the flak! Nothing could prepare new crews for those deadly little black puffs. Their own tactics changed as a result. They had been taught to fly a flat spread of three-ship elements. The German fighters ripped these formations to ribbons. Then Eighth Air Force countered with a "box" formation in which elements were stacked both vertically *and* horizontally. They flew close together—wingtips almost overlapping—in order to take better advantage of their own defensive firepower. Ross couldn't visualize holding position for eight to ten hours at a time under those conditions.

Finally they were underneath the cloud base, a comfortable two thousand feet above the terrain. The mosaic of newly constructed airfields flitted by below. Locating "home" among that profusion could prove embarrassing. It was as if some playful giant had passed along and flung a handful of identical black triangles onto a green and beige checkerboard. Ross saw Rex attempting to tune in the low-frequency radio beacon. As the needle steadied, Ross selected the tower's frequency and tapped Compton on his shoulder. "All right, you have it—your turn for a landing, I believe."

"Okay!" Rex's darkly handsome features formed a pleased smile as he assumed a more attentive position.

Ross lifted the hand-held mike and, using the bored drawl cultivated by flyers the world over, advised: "Wolfpack Tower, this is Red Dog Seven. Five miles north for landing, over."

"Roger, Red Dog Seven, Wolfpack Tower. Landing runway one-eight. Reported weather is three thousand broken, visibility seven miles with haze. Wind south, fifteen knots. Altimeter two-niner point eight-one. Call downwind, over."

"Roger, roger, Wolfpack. Understand altimeter two-niner point eight-one. Will call downwind, out."

As Ross leaned forward to set the field's barometric pressure into the altimeter, Rex asked, "How about a practice number one peel-off? Captain Ellis was chewing ass about planes getting strung all over hell-and-gone, landing out of element formation. Number one has to keep her in real tight."

Ross shrugged and nodded agreement as he retrieved the mike. "Wolfpack Tower, Red Dog Seven here. How about a practice three-sixty overhead, traffic permitting? We'll simulate number one position for a formation landing, over."

"Roger, Red Dog Seven. Request approved. No reported traffic. Call one mile out on initial, over."

Ross acknowledged and switched to intercom. "Pilot to crew, prepare for landing in about five minutes." He heard muttered acknowledgments and watched Rex swing the *Happy Hooker* onto a heading lining them up with the active runway.

"Any mechanical write-ups?" he asked Ham Phillips, now in position between the pilot and copilot seats.

"Naw," the rangy flight engineer responded. "Nothing I can't take care of myself. That number two supercharger still wants to surge on takeoff. I'll flush the system and check the filter. I'd rather do it myself than have that bunch of shade-tree mechanics screw around with it."

Ross knew he would be out there at midnight if necessary. Phillips regarded the *Happy Hooker* as his personal airplane. It was a love affair that started the day they picked up their factory-new Liberator in Tucson.

Observing that Rex was entering initial approach, Ross double-checked his seat belt and reached for the before-landing checklist.

"Wolfpack, Red Dog Seven. One mile out on initial, over."

"Roger, Red Dog Seven. I have you in sight. Call on your break."

Ross shifted his attention to Rex's approach. He noted with a slight frown that his copilot was descending through the standard pattern altitude of one thousand feet, still carrying cruise power. Airspeed was building toward the 220-mph mark. Just as he was about to comment, the approach end of the runway passed beneath the nose. Rex simultaneously threw the big Liberator into a forty-five-degree bank and hauled back on the wheel. "Half flaps at one-fifty, then gear down," Rex directed.

Ross repressed a slight smile as he realized what Rex was up to. The frustrated fighter pilot was attempting a fighter-style landing with a boxcar. Okay, let him learn the hard way. Ross called the tower: "Red Dog Seven on the break, Wolfpack."

When the compass indicated the runway's reciprocal heading and their airspeed had fallen to 150, Ross announced casually, "Roger. You have flaps fifty, gear coming down. The tower's cleared us to land."

Without leveling the Liberator's wings, Rex dropped the nose and chopped power; the B-24 sank like a wounded goose. Neck muscles straining visibly, he struggled to horse the ungainly bird's nose through a tight turn and onto the runway heading. They sank below three hundred feet, still turning. Ross made a mental note to remind Hotrod about the hazards of low turns with fifty-some feet of wing hanging toward the ground. He double-checked for three green gear lights, placed the props in high RPM, and settled back to watch.

Passing over a dry ditch that marked the field's boundary, even Rex realized he was high and hot; belatedly, he called for full flaps.

"Naw, let's take it around and try again," Ross ordered disgustedly. He reached for the mike to advise the tower of their intentions when he realized that Rex was continuing his approach. "Go around—go around!" he yelled.

Rex threw him a startled look but made no move toward the throttles. With runway disappearing beneath him at an alarming rate, the flustered copilot attempted to force twenty tons of metal, still at flying speed, onto the uneven black-topped surface. Too late, Ross grabbed the controls with a terse, "I got it."

Rex resisted briefly and the main landing gear touched down. In his eagerness, the hapless copilot applied brakes. The *Happy Hooker* skipped once and settled back to the runway, left wheel first. Then the right gear touched down, its brake fully locked.

The act of passing a stationary rubber tire across macadam-covered gravel produces a result something akin to scraping a slice of ripe Cheddar cheese across a grater. Rubber tread disappeared with a smoking screech. Nylon carcass threads flew off next. Within seconds the right tire ruptured. The sound, resembling a pistol shot, caused mechanics working on parked airplanes to raise their heads in interest.

"Get off the fucking brakes!" Ross screamed. As the confused copilot complied, the aircraft commander undertook the not inconsiderable task of averting disaster. His thoughts raced while the entire episode assumed eerie, slow-motion aspects. Ross knew a go-around now was out of the question. He nudged the number four throttle. There—that stopped that sickening swerve to the right. Left brake—don't lock it, for Christ's sake! Okay, airspeed's dropping, but not fast enough. We're going off—which way? Let her go to the right and ground-loop inside the airfield? Or keep straight ahead and roll off the end? Keep the goddamn nose wheel off! Let that candy-ass nose gear touch down at over a hundred and you buy the farm.

He glanced toward Rex. Shit! He's practically catatonic, useless. He saw Phillips still standing between the seats, face tense but under control. Good, he'll be the one to give orders to. End of the runway coming up—damn! Isn't this bitch ever going to slow down?

Okay, down to eighty—suck the wheel into your gut. Keep that nose wheel off as long as possible, but it should hold at this speed. Is Art out of the nose? He'll be trapped if we belly in. Fire. The ruined right gear is causing the whole airplane to vibrate. That tire will catch fire— or maybe it blew so bad it came off the rim. Pray that it did. Dad, I tried. I really did. I hope you have a chance to know.

Good, we're still on the runway. I'll keep her straight ahead and start shutting down. Cut the master switch? No, number three has the main hydraulic pump. Still need brakes.

As if from a distance, Ross heard his voice calmly order: "Feather one, feather two, feather four."

Compton didn't budge, so it was Phillips who reached forward and pressed the big red feathering buttons, almost mashing them through the instrument panel in the process. The engineer then proceeded to toggle off the fuel booster pumps feeding the three dead engines. Good, Ross thought, that will reduce the danger of a fire.

"We're going off the end, troops. Hit the crash bell, Ham." Ross searched the ground ahead. It didn't look too bad. He figured they would stop before they reached the stone-and-wood rail fence marking the airfield perimeter. Airspeed dropped below seventy as they lurched off a slight drop marking the runway's end. It felt as if he could step out and walk that fast. Then he recalled what Pinky Woods's car had looked like after it hit a tree while doing sixty. Jesus Christ! He'd forgotten they still had three bombs and some unexpended .50-caliber ammo aboard!

*   *   *

Perched in his glass-enclosed cubicle atop the 365th Bomb Group's operations building, the tower operator was quick to recognize the signs of an accident in progress. He hit the crash klaxon with one hand while reaching for the field phone with his other.

Captain Claude Ellis, the 866th Squadron's operations officer, left his seat in one fluid motion as the raucous, though not unfamiliar, *Ooooo-Aaaah, Ooooo-Aaaah* signaled trouble. Vaulting into a parked jeep, he watched the *Happy Hooker* rumble across the last of the runway and come to a halt some fifty yards into the soggy English meadow. Ellis held his breath, prematurely aged features set, waiting for the telltale flicker of orange flame. He exhaled with relief as black figures poured from the crippled bird and raced for safety.

Ross was the last to drop from the open bomb bay. A quick head count showed seven crew members bunched about a hundred feet away. The eighth, Ham Phillips, was crouched over the mangled, smoking remains of the *Happy Hooker*'s right main gear. He straightened as Ross approached.

"The sumbitch didn't collapse," Phillips announced proudly. "New tire and wheel and she'll be ready to fly tomorrow morning." Then he averted his eyes. "Lieutenant," the normally sanguine flight engineer mumbled with an embarrassed effort to appear casual, "that was some piece of work you just pulled off. Thanks."

The sound of screaming sirens racing toward the scene prevented further talk. In seconds the base fire truck, a weapons carrier elevated to the status of emergency vehicle by the addition of a huge chemical tank, drew alongside the smoking wheel and tire. An ambulance, the flight surgeon still wearing hospital whites and stethoscope, moaned to a halt nearby. With the danger of fire removed, the other crew members surrounded Ross and Ham. Tension eased as everyone began talking excitedly and laughing with nervous release. Dutch Guenther was catching the brunt of their crude humor. The dark stain that had spread across the crotch of his flight coveralls would take some time to live down.

By the time Captain Ellis skidded his jeep to a stop in front of the damaged bomber, his sick apprehension had evolved into a foaming rage. As he swung his lanky legs over the jeep's side, he shouted, "What the fuck did you think you were doing? Can't you clowns even go on a goddamn *training* mission, f'Christ's sake, without wiping out an airplane?" Reaching the huddle of suddenly quieted airmen, he thrust his face inches from Ross's. "Well?"

Already dejected, Ross could only respond with a resigned, "Goddamn tire blew on touchdown. Engineer doesn't think we have any more than minor damage, though."

"Well, when Major Deckard finishes with you, *you're* sure as hell going to have more than 'minor damage.' He got to me on the radio on the way out. He wants to see you in his office. Right now! He's breathing fire. Even the goddamn radio was smoking. I'm to take you straight to headquarters. A truck's on the way out to pick up your crew and gear. C'mon—let's hustle."

As Ellis clashed through the gears, Ross turned to take a last look. The once proud *Happy Hooker* had acquired a dispirited list to starboard. Forlorn and lonely, she slumped there in a foreign environment. Even the curvaceous, scantily clad female painted on the nose, her saucy, seductive face peering over one shoulder, looked a bit dowdy. He noticed Rex, cigarette in hand, chatting casually with Stan and Art. He was shrugging his shoulders.

The squadron commander's office was situated inside one of the corrugated sheet-metal Nissen huts that had sprung up around the operations building. Resembling a huge tin can sliced lengthwise, the Nissen hut was the U.S. Army version of home away from home. A hastily applied coat of olive drab paint and boarded-up ends hardly qualified the structure for display in a home-decorating magazine, however. After a perfunctory knock on the wood-plank door, Captain Ellis led Ross inside.

Major Deckard's supply sergeant had done his best to lend dignity to the crude interior. An American flag drooped from its stand behind the CO's desk. A fair reproduction of the Eighth Air Force shoulder patch hung alongside two wall charts reflecting the current status of crews and planes. Overshadowing all, however, was the sergeant's prize find. A luxurious Persian rug, its rich red, blue, and beige tones carefully kept free of dirt and dust, covered most of the rough-finished concrete floor.

Ross saluted and stood at rigid attention. Major Deckard was comfortably seated in the reflected heat of an electric space heater, seemingly engrossed in polishing a gleaming brass trombone with a Blitz cloth. The major's trombone solos, his favorite means of alleviating stress, were the joke of the squadron.

A deceptively benign expression gracing his round pink features, Major Deckard regarded Ross from behind a battered desk, resurrected from a Royal Army warehouse. He occupied the one upholstered swivel chair carried on the supply officer's inventory.

Placing the trombone aside, he leaned back and laced plump fingers across his ample girth. His outwardly relaxed manner was betrayed by the incessant tapping of both thumbs against each other. Ross had never before noticed that Major Deckard's pink fingers were covered with a profusion of white hairs. An odd contrast. Then Deckard's bland words penetrated his thoughts.

"Lieutenant Colyer. Allow me to tell you of a funny thing that happened to me on the way to deliver Lieutenant Colonel Brookside to his airplane just now. Colonel Brookside is assigned to Eighth Air Force Ops, I might add. We had been in this office for, oh, about two hours, when the colonel wearied of chewing on my ass regarding the sorry state of our training. I was only too happy to learn of his plans for immediate departure and was in the act of delivering him to his plane when I heard aircraft engines overhead. I looked up. Colonel Brookside looked up.

"Guess what we saw, Lieutenant? An airplane on an overhead approach. But wait—it was executing a fighter-type pattern. 'Gadzooks,' I said, 'that has to be the biggest fighter I have ever seen!'

"'No, no, Eric,' Colonel Brookside replied. 'That is a B-24. Could it be one of yours?'

"'Oh, no, Colonel,' I told him. 'Our pilots fly bomber-type approaches for landing.' Then that B-24, with this group's markings plainly visible, proceeded to land long and hot, blow a tire, then run off the end of the runway. For the present, Colonel Brookside languishes in our sumptuous officers' club waiting for us to clear that wreck off the end of the runway, chuckling good-naturedly to himself all the while, no doubt, over his delayed departure."

"Sir . . ." Ross's voice trailed off as Major Deckard raised a hand, palm outward.

"No, Lieutenant, this is not an interview. I will talk and *you* will listen." The squadron commander paused, his eyes burning hotly into Ross's before he continued. "So, I return to this office and tell myself that there is, of course, a perfectly logical explanation for this bizarre event. I will question the pilot and relay this logical explanation to Colonel Brookside. Now, Lieutenant, I'm listening. You may speak."

Ross swallowed and blinked, then focused his eyes on a point twenty inches above and to the right of the irate major's shoulder, just as he'd been taught by his cadet tactical instructor. He could only respond with a miserable, "It was a fuckup, Sir."

Deckard feigned a judicious pursing of his lips. "Yes. Yes, one could say that. That was my very thought, in fact. But, somehow, I don't believe that your revelation will come as much of a surprise to Colonel Brookside. Continue."

"Well, Sir, the last formation landing was screwed up because the number one made wide, sloppy turns. We were practicing a tighter pattern, Sir."

The major averted his face and rubbed a sandy stubble of hair with both hands. Facing Ellis, he asked, "And, Captain Ellis, do you have anything to add?"

"At zero-eight-hundred hours tomorrow, Major, I will give Lieutenant Colyer two hours of practice landings."

"Splendid. A much more humane solution than the one that keeps crossing my mind. But yes, by all means, more practice is certainly indicated. I only hope Colonel Brookside agrees that your measures are adequate. Now, Lieutenant, how did other aspects of your training mission go?"

Ross groaned inwardly. "We brought our ordnance home, Sir. We couldn't drop. You see, Sir, we didn't find the target area."

He heard Ellis, standing behind him, utter a strangled sound. Deckard's feigned air of joviality slipped, badly. "What did you say?" he asked in a hoarse whisper.

Major Deckard watched the door close behind Ross, then leaned back in his chair and stripped the cellophane from a fresh cigar. "Well, what do you think, Claude?"

Captain Ellis chose his words carefully. "He'll come along, Major. None of the crews are all that sharp yet. Colyer is one helluva good pilot. It's just—well—that crew of his seems to have trouble doing anything right. Take that business about missing the bomb range. All the crews are having trouble doing pilotage in this little country. But thirty miles? That has to be a new world record. All the same, I'm having serious second thoughts about putting that crew in a lead airplane."

Deckard, seemingly ignoring his ops officer's words, examined his cigar as he spoke. "Claude, you keep an eye on that boy. He's a comer."

"Oh?" Ellis raised his eyebrows.

"Bet on it. Anyone who'll stand there and take the ass chewing he did without putting the blame on his copilot has balls. He'll handle lead crew, all right."

"His copilot? You mean it was Compton who made that half-assed fighter approach?"

"I'm sure of it. The tower operator said he recognized Colyer's voice on the radio. Stands to reason he wasn't doing the flying."

"Well, I'll be goddamned." The ops officer chuckled wryly.

"Yeah, but that's not the only reason I say the boy's a comer. Oh, he's a good pilot—salvaging that landing was a work of art. I was watching; he did everything perfectly. But, in addition, he's smart and he's cagey."

"How's that?"

"Well, you see—" Deckard paused to retrieve the trombone from beside his desk and blew a few bars of "When the Saints Go Marching In." Ignoring Ellis's expression of pretended pain, he continued, "Compton's a frustrated fighter pilot. He's already applied for a transfer. I have a hunch that Colyer would be glad to see him go, so I figure he's busting his butt to get the little shit left-seat qualified.

"That's one reason he kept his mouth shut just now," Deckard said, then paused to put down his trombone and relight his cigar. "He isn't about to throw sand in the gears. Oh, I'm not saying he wouldn't have covered up for the kid if that wasn't the case, but I had trouble trying to keep from laughing.

"But we'll cross that bridge when we get there. In the meantime, Brookside's visit wasn't altogether to chew my ass—although he did do a bit of that. Something big is in the air, and it's not too far away. I'd guess it has to do with that big powwow at Division today. The brass is getting antsy because the Eighth isn't living up to its advance press. Yeah, I'd guess that we're going to see some foreign real estate—real soon."

The beefy major closed his eyes and blew softly into the trombone, easing into a soft blues melody.

1430 Hours, 29 April 1943
Headquarters, 2d Air Division
Buxton Hall, England

Captain Broderick Templeton III occupied one of the two dozen chairs arranged against a richly paneled wall of the parquet-floored meeting room. In gentler days the room had served as the dining hall for residents of the Whittington Academy for Girls. The sixty-odd young ladies in residence were summarily returned to the custody of their wealthy families to make room for a forty-man contingent of the Eighth Air Force's 2d Air Division—not until after overcoming determined opposition voiced by influential members of Parliament, however. Advance elements of Maj. Gen. Ira Eaker's Eighth Bomber Command were finding that their British cousins did not, in all cases, view their arrival as divine intervention.

Seated directly behind his boss, Brig. Gen. Elliott Sprague, BT dutifully took notes. His actions were duplicated by the aides and assistants of the ten other generals and colonels convened around the highly varnished dining table. Relegated by protocol to the perimeter, the junior officers were limited in their input to an occasional whispered statistic in the ear of their principal. Later, each would be expected to relate the substance of all matters presented.

BT hoped that he could read the cramped scribbles; his hands were chilled and stiff. Wartime fuel rationing extended even to meetings of tribal chieftains.

An intense, pink-faced colonel was expounding on the need for expanded public relations. "We are, after all, guests here . . ."

Bored, BT's thoughts drifted. The damn building must be a hundred years old, he conjectured. Lighter rectangles on the floor-to-ceiling oak paneling revealed that Dame Whittington's curators had, perhaps wisely, elected not to entrust priceless paintings to the care of their unwelcome guests. Somber blackout curtains hung at mullioned, lead-glass windows—no doubt replacing heavy brocade draperies. Outside, clouds almost low enough to touch oozed endless quantities of fine rain. Low ceilings and visibility had effectively emasculated the vaunted aerial might of Allied forces for the past ten days.

Barely visible through a pall of cigar smoke, pink and lavender cherubs cast their benign gaze on the gathering below from a pastel-frescoed ceiling. The irony of their pastoral oversight did not escape BT; the topic under discussion by this grim-faced assembly of wing and group commanders was how most efficiently to destroy large numbers of the human race.

The inanely babbling colonel was replaced by a Colonel McNaughton, from General Eaker's Eighth Air Force headquarters. BT ceased regarding the brilliantly polished toes of his uniform shoes, handmade by a London bootery, and listened with increased interest.

"Gentlemen, Eighth Bomber Command is facing stiff opposition on a number of fronts." The colonel's beetling salt-and-pepper eyebrows drew together, emphasizing his resemblance to a chronically disgruntled mastiff.

"It looks as if the goddamn Germans may be the least formidable opponent we face." He paused at a polite chuckle from the select audience, then continued. "General Arnold and the Air Staff in Washington sent General Eaker over here to develop a capability of bombing strategic targets deep inside Germany during daylight. Our Forts and Liberators were designed to defend themselves in combat, and our Norden bombsight allows extremely precise target selection. The British, including Prime Minister Churchill and Air Marshal Harris, assumed from the beginning that we would follow their lead in flying our missions at night.

"Therein lies our major problem. The RAF remains convinced that even our heavily armed bombers can never stand up to German fighters. Theirs couldn't and the Germans were defeated in their attempts to destroy England with daylight bombing. Their attitude is, 'Come now, chaps, we've been doing this for the past three years. We know best, so be reasonable and do it our way, what?' Churchill came close to convincing President Roosevelt at Casablanca to redesign the B-17 as a night bomber. General Eaker talked him out of it. Now it's up to us to prove once and for all that the Eighth Air Force can operate independently and surpass the RAF by placing bombs on the target with pinpoint precision."

McNaughton stopped and looked slowly around the table before continuing. "One clue to their thinking: Air Marshal Harris is supposed to have told a visiting dignitary from Washington, 'We're shutting down the factories we miss at night by taking out the workers asleep in their beds, don't you know.' Well, they're not doing a very good job of it. German fighter production continues to increase, as does their output of tanks, subs—damn near everything."

"Mac, I don't want to be a wet blanket, but we're taking a helluva beating from the Jerries," growled flinty-eyed Brig. Gen. Clinton Goss, commander of the 1st Air Division. "If this run of abominable weather hadn't given us a chance to patch up our battle damage, I couldn't even put up a decent practice formation."

BT eyed his boss, General Sprague, to see his reaction. BT liked what he was hearing less and less. To hell with all this talk about numbers of airplanes; they were losing crews faster than replacements could be provided. Machines could be replaced, but for every bomber shot out of the sky, nine or ten men either died, were horribly maimed, or were captured. The statistics ignored rank and position—an unsettling fact.

"And we'll continue to take a pounding until we can mount a force large enough to protect itself," McNaughton barked. "A bomber's defense against fighter attack rests with having a high concentration of fire-power—enough to discourage attack.

"The combat box formation developed by Colonel LeMay can do that, but such a formation would require three hundred planes to be effective. Our best all-out effort so far is a hundred and twenty-five."

Goss stripped a cigar and took several minutes to light it. "We've got to get fighter escort all the way to the target, Mac. We all know that. What's being done to get it for us?"

McNaughton's face darkened. "It's going to take time, damnit, Sir. Word is the P-51 Mustang won't be operational until the end of the year. Even with the new seventy-five-gallon drop tanks, the P-47s barely reach the German border—less than that if they run into enemy fighters and have to drop them early. We're getting some longer range P-38s but not many. Most of them are being diverted to the Pacific. For now, we can really only count on having Spits and Thunderbolts as far as the French coast, maybe a little farther."

"Okay, so when are we going to be able to launch three hundred bombers, Mac?" This from a lean, nervous colonel whom BT recognized as the 354th Bomb Group's commander.

Colonel McNaughton regarded the tabletop in front of him, his lower lip thrust out like a belligerent bulldog's. "Enter the second and third fronts, Wiley. Admiral King is raising hell in Washington. He wants to scrap heavy-bomber production and build fighters for his carriers. As if that isn't enough, General Arnold has been told that the next three groups of heavies will be diverted to North Africa—for Operation Torch. No, we're going to have to launch a deep penetration of Germany without escort. And soon. The British are claiming that so far we've accomplished little more than the destruction of occupied France. Targets deep in the German homeland will be another bucket of eels. To prove our point we *must* take out a big target inside Germany without fighter escort. And keep our losses below 20 percent."

A shocked silence filled the room with electricity.

"Twenty percent?" an astonished Colonel Wiley asked. "Jesus Christ, Mac—you're saying that 20 percent is *acceptable?*"

"If we can show at least 90 percent destruction of the target—yes. The RAF is running below 20 percent of their bombs on target. If we can demonstrate that deadly accuracy is possible with relatively green crews while under heavy attack, we'll have saved the daylight concept. And that, gentlemen, is paramount. The Eighth sinks or swims with our first major effort."

BT crawled into the rear of the staff car. A homely, red-haired WREN held the door for him.

"It's back to High Wycombe, General?" she asked with a rolling Scot's burr.

Sprague roused himself from a gloomy silence. The meeting had broken up on a somber note. "No, Miss." He gazed thoughtfully at the estate grounds. They were already showing signs of neglect. "Take us to Walden Abbey."

"Aye, Sorr—Walden Abbey 'tis then. A bare thirty minutes' run, Sorr; quick as a wink we'll be now." BT regarded Sprague with a puzzled frown.

"BT, my lad, we are about to get this war off the ground." The general flashed a wolfish grin and relit his cigar. "While that bunch of old women are tiptoeing around wringing their hands, the 7th Wing is going to lead a strike right square at Jerry's jugular vein. The formation will be built around the 365th Group. I'll make Walden Abbey my command post. The 866th Squadron will lead; that Major Deckard did a damn fine job back at Mountain Home. Tomorrow morning every airplane in the wing that can get off the ground is going to start training missions. They're going to learn how to shoot. Did you know that average gunnery scores are less than 25 percent of all rounds in the target? They're going to sharpen up on bombing, and most of all, by God, they're also going to learn how to fly this new box formation."

"General," BT responded with a dazed look, "some of the planes arrived from the States only yesterday. Not all the ground crews have reported in. The crews haven't had theater orientation. This stupid English weather —we aren't forecast to have decent weather for another week—"

"Minor details," Sprague said, waving an impatient hand. "The crews need to know how to load bombs and ammo and pull routine maintenance, anyway. Our pilots are just going to have to learn to fly in this weather. The goddamn British do. What better time to start? The 7th Wing, by God, is going to set the pace. We'll have the rest of those bastards asking, 'How the hell do you do it, Elliott?'—and that includes those blue-nosed Limey sons a bitches. And I'll tell 'em, 'You got to kick ass, boys.' That's been the problem over here. Everybody's afraid to rock the boat. There's too many meetings like that one back there—too many cocktail parties, and no one doing anything.

"Well, I'm not going to sit around with my thumb up my butt. The Seventh is going to hit the German heartland within the next two weeks. Eaker won't dare turn me down when I show him what we can do. And you and I, my boy, we're going to be right up there in the lead ship!"

BT sat in a state of total bewilderment. The goddamn man was crazy! he thought. The general was putting together what was bound to be a suicide mission. A queasy feeling of panic assailed BT's senses. He had known when he used Sprague to get out of the Pacific theater that the man was ambitious—had counted on that. His misgivings mounted as he realized the depth and enormity of those ambitions. Well, in the unlikely event that Eighth Air Force approved the mission, the dumb bastard could be in that lead airplane if he wanted to; but BT planned to be elsewhere. He needed an escape route, and right now wasn't too soon to start laying the groundwork. His handsome, composed features concealed a feverish search for a solution as he watched, without seeing, the sodden countryside passing by in a gray-green blur.

A trip to London was essential, he decided. BT turned and waited for Sprague to finish an impassioned account of his plans for the upcoming two weeks. "General," he interjected smoothly, "we need a target on Eighth's priority list if a mission is going to be approved. A guy I went to school with is on General Overbrook's staff up at headquarters. He'll have access to the list. What if I run into London, buy him a few double scotches, and see what I can pry out of him?"

Sprague grunted, his eyes acquiring a cunning squint. "You're right. I can't very well go to Division and tell them in advance what we're planning. Good thinking. As soon as we check in at Walden Abbey, you catch the next train for London."

1605 Hours, 29 April 1943
Walden Abbey

An hour after leaving Major Deckard's office, Capt. Claude Ellis propped his feet on the rickety worktable that served as his desk. His office, a niche formed by chipped green file cabinets in one corner of the ops/briefing hut, was strictly functional. A large-scale regional map of Germany covered one wall, flanked by twins of the status charts in Major Deckard's office. The only contrast in the stark, utilitarian surroundings was a picture. Situated among a litter of reports and manuals atop the long table, a striking brunette, wearing a sardonic smile, surveyed her strange surroundings from within a heavy, sterling-silver frame.

Ellis lit a cigarette and regarded his silent companion through a wreath of smoke. Well, old girl, he said to himself, maybe I'll get my chance before too much longer. He used to talk aloud to his dead wife, but ceased that practice after a roommate asked if he felt okay. Dragging smoke deep into his lungs, he savored Major Deckard's parting words about a "big" mission in the offing. It could represent his opportunity to start that long climb back to the top.

It had been a hard struggle. The booze—he had damned near drowned himself in it after that nightmare accident. It had already cost him one promotion when he had been bumped two hundred files on the seniority list. "A brilliant, energetic officer . . . capable of handling increased responsibility . . ." had been replaced on his efficiency ratings with "Requires close supervision. . . ."

He'd had it all in the palm of his hand—the potential to go all the way, to general officer, perhaps. A superlative instructor pilot, strong command presence, and, as a bonus, a well-known admiral for a father-in-law.

Then there had been the promotion party. Captain at the age of twenty-two. The ride home from the club in his powerful Lincoln convertible. Beautiful Lisa feeding him champagne at eighty miles an hour as the warm Texas night whipped past. That glimpse of a rusty pickup truck without headlights. The hospital room. A somber chaplain telling him that Lisa, his wife, hadn't survived. The occupants of the pickup—a Mexican migrant worker, his wife, and three children—all dead.

He'd borne the pain of the funeral alone. His stony-faced in-laws never spoke to him again. An equally glacial colonel suggested that he request immediate assignment to a combat outfit. He'd been sent to Mountain Home. The next several weeks passed in an alcoholic haze. Rumors of a new B-24 wing being formed. Restless weeks spent in an office job in base headquarters. Then he'd met Deckard, imported to command one of the newly formed squadrons.

The gruff, rotund major had seen something in Ellis that others didn't. After reading the dissipated young captain the riot act, Deckard had offered him the job of operations officer with the 866th. "If you can keep your nose out of the goddamn sauce and whip this rabble into combat readiness, you might make a comeback, Claude," the major had told him bluntly.

Now, an imperial quart, a "forty-pounder," of Red Label Scotch gathered dust in Ellis's footlocker—proof, to himself, that he could still cut it. He would never have another chance, he knew. Captain Claude Ellis would kill for Eric Deckard.

He saluted the beautiful object of his thoughts and turned to his current problem: 1st Lt. Ross Colyer and crew. He liked Colyer. The man was probably the best pilot in the squadron. But damnit, he just seemed to be unable to get a handle on that bunch of misfits he called a crew.

Ross wandered aimlessly along the flight line before finally dropping off his parachute, oxygen mask, and Mae West at the personal-equipment hut. Now, retrieving the single bicycle issued each crew, he stumbled toward the Nissen hut shared with Art, Stan, Rex, and the officers of Lieutenant Eubanks's crew. He pushed the bike; it didn't seem worth trying to ride the thing on what little hard surface existed. Mud. The entire base seemed to sit on nothing else. He plodded down a narrow lane leading toward a copse of trees sheltering the drab cluster of huts assigned to 866th officers. Spring was doing its best to make an appearance, but other than bursting pink and purple blooms on unidentified fruit trees, the season still resembled winter.

What a pisser of a day, Ross thought. Goddamn it! He knew he was a good pilot, and he worked hard at being a good crew commander. He had looked forward to flying combat. As he'd told Rhoda, that last night, he was going for a flying career instead of engineering. Entering Aviation Cadets was the reason he'd dropped out of Michigan University during his third year. But things just kept going wrong. His crew was a goddamn laughingstock. One or more of them seemed to find something new to fuck up every day.

Take that session back there just now: Any other aircraft commander in the group would have gotten nothing more than a sharp warning. Deckard and Ellis made it clear that they expected perfection from his crew; after all, they were a lead crew.

His stride quickened; he was going to get this bunch of misfits whipped into shape or know the reason why. And he was going to start with one each Compton, Rex, Smart-Ass.

Ross was greeted by wary looks as he entered the dreary metal shell they called home. Stan and Art sat on one of the four cots at their end. Rex stretched full length, hands locked beneath his head, on the remaining one. Other than splintered wooden footlockers and a polished steel shaving mirror hung from a center post, the interior was spartan. A personal touch had been added by each occupant in the form of a Betty Grable pinup above Rex's cot, an ornately engraved Arabian sword above Art's, and a nightstand adapted from a 105 howitzer shell by Ross's. Stan used the DD-sized cups of a forty-two-inch black lace brassiere suspended overhead to store his watch, billfold, cigarette lighter, and assorted coins.

Art and Stan took one look at Ross's expression and babbled, "Gonna try and be first in line for a hot shower." They fled as Ross sank to his cot and gave Rex a long, unwavering look.

"Well, I guess my ass is jolly well in the old sling," said Rex, opening the conversation with a flippant air. "That goddamn Phillips needs a good ass chewing for letting us take off with a bad tire. From now on, *I'm* going to check those things."

"Oh, for Christ's sake, Rex, cut the bullshit," Ross snapped. "You screwed up a landing. You froze when I needed you. You damn near got us all killed. Now, face facts and let's talk about what we're going to do about it."

"Okay, just what did the almighty Major Deckard tell you to do about me? Am I restricted to base?" the little copilot asked.

"Major Deckard didn't say a damn thing about *you*. He doesn't know that you were at the controls. But first thing tomorrow morning, *I* get two hours of touch-and-go landings with a highly pissed-off Captain Ellis. I'll be lucky if he even lets me have all four engines for the first takeoff."

Rex lit a cigarette and made an abortive effort to produce a smoke ring. "You telling me that you took the fall all by yourself?" His voice was skeptical.

"Rex," Ross's voice was hoarse with strain and fatigue, "goddamnit, you went to the same preflight school I attended. Didn't they teach you anything about accepting responsibility? You keep telling me about how you want your own plane. Well, I'm telling you now, friend, when you strap that left seat onto your butt, you, and no one else, are responsible for everything that goes on. You don't lay blame on your crew. Now, you either forget about the lousy deal you think you got and shape up, or so help me God, I'll see to it that you're still in that right seat when you retire. Got it?"

Rex, his spirits buoyed by the news that Ross had shouldered the blame, reassured his aircraft commander. "I'm sorry if I made trouble for you, Ross. I'll try harder, really I will. Now, let's hit the shower while there's still some hot water." He grabbed a towel and flashed his most winning smile.

Ross gazed at Rex's disappearing back and slowly shook his head in dismay. He shivered in the dank cold of the unheated hut. The daily ration of one bucket of coke sat undisturbed beside the tiny cast-iron stove, dubbed a "turtle" by the English. The lazy bastards hadn't even bothered to start a fire. After several minutes spent staring at the floor and thinking, Ross plodded across the wooden duckboards, half buried in the mud, toward the shower hut, soap and towel in hand.

First Lieutenant Charlie York and his copilot were returning, looking disgusted. "Goddamn hot water's all gone," they muttered in passing. Ross stopped dead in his tracks. It figures, he told himself. It figures. And if that goddamn Rex was the last one to have hot water, I'll kill him.

Chapter Twelve

30 April 1943
Walden Abbey

Zero-eight-hundred hours came and went. Ross and Sergeant Phillips, preflight complete, huddled in the damp, chill cockpit of *Weary Willie*. The *Happy Hooker* was still out of commission, having her right wheel replaced. Watching shapes emerge as an early morning mist dissipated like windblown cobwebs, Ross tried to imagine what a formation takeoff would be like in this weather. Just shooting practice landings was going to be a hair raiser. Where the hell was Captain Ellis? Phillips poured another cup of coffee from the thermos and broke the gloomy silence. "You listen to the radio last night, Lieutenant?"

Ross turned up the collar of his leather A-2 jacket and slouched lower in his seat. Eyes closed, he responded, "Nope. I wrote letters last night."

"Well, I was at the NCO club. They were listening to this German station, the one that plays all the Hit Parade songs. You ever listen to it?"

"Once in a while."

"This guy, this Lord Haw-Haw, the one who talks like a Limey?"

"Yeah."

"Would you believe it, he knows all about our group. He said, 'Welcome to England, Colonel Bolt and all the men of the Circle H 365th. Do you like your new home at Walden Abbey? Enjoy it while you can, boys. Our brave pilots at Abbeyville are anxious to give you a warm welcome when you venture across the Channel. Oh yes, I almost forgot. How many fellows back home do you think your wives and girlfriends have dated since you left?' It was spooky, I'll tell you, Sir."

"Stan and Rex told me about it when they came back from the club." Ross rolled his head and addressed Phillips with only one eye open. "He does that to all the new arrivals. It's a trick, supposed to lower our morale and make us not want to fight, you know."

Phillips considered his words with a wrinkled brow. "How the hell does he know all this stuff? Christ, do we have German spies on the base?"

"Probably not. But look at the place. I understand all the bases are like this one—wide open. You see the old geezer and his family out there farming? Well, he isn't farming on our airfield; we put our airfield on his farm. The English need every scrap of food they can raise. So they don't let a square foot of land go to waste. Hell, the only decent paved street we have is the main highway to Ipswich. There's another reason we have our airplanes and living quarters dispersed all over the place: The Jerries are only about thirty minutes' flying time away. Believe me," Ross's tone turned grim, "I saw close up what happens when you line airplanes up in nice, neat rows.

"So the civilians come and go as they please. Kids beg for chewing gum outside the PX and they import truckloads of girls for dances once a month. It stands to reason that the Nazis know everything that goes on."

While Ham was still digesting Ross's words, a jeep sped down the perimeter taxiway in their direction. Splashing through puddles from the previous night's rain, it drew to a stop alongside. A fatigue-clad corporal jumped to the pierced-steel planking that formed *Weary Willie*'s parking hardstand and stuck his head inside the open bomb bay. "Anybody up there?"

"Yo."

"Ops says your flight is scrubbed. Officers' Call in the briefing room at ten-hundred, okay?"

Ross and Ham exchanged disgusted looks. With a muttered, "Well, shit," Ross started securing the cockpit. "Ham, would you hang around and tell the crew chief what happened? I'll catch a ride and see what's so all-fired important. I'll let you know if anything is up, but you'll probably hear all about it in the mess hall before I do anyway."

"Okay, Sir." Phillips wore a perplexed scowl. "Lieutenant?" he called to Ross's departing back.

"Yes?"

"What this Haw-Haw said, you know, about girlfriends dating? Do you think they do—right away, anyway?"

Ross laughed. "I'm sure some do, but a lot don't."

"Dutch got all worked up about it. He's really crazy about that girl back in Chicago."

"Well . . ." Ross let his voice trail off. What the hell could he say? Secretly he wondered about Janet. Then he grinned—he didn't have to wonder about Rhoda.

What was so "all-fired important" turned out to be the 365th Bomb Group's first look at its wing commander. A few minutes before ten, Ross, Eubanks, and their officer crew members slid onto backless benches crowded into the ops/briefing room. The building was one of the few on the base constructed of rough red bricks and stuccoed with a material the English called "Maycrete." Painted the ubiquitous olive drab, it stood out as yet another scab on the pastoral landscape.

Desultory chatter filled the air. A dense cloud of cigar and cigarette smoke swirled lazily under naked overhead bulbs. Two cherry red coke-fired heaters helped dispel the early-spring chill. The map of Eastern Europe covering one wall drew the immediate attention of every new entrant. It remained uncovered and no string of red yarn marked a route into enemy territory. This was not to be a mission briefing; the mood relaxed.

"So when I came out after breakfast, it was gone," said Lieutenant Eubanks, complaining bitterly. "Some bastard stole my bicycle! I gave the number to the provost marshal, but he says it will be near impossible to locate it. All the bikes are identical, even the ones you can buy off base. Anyone can paint a new number on it. Goddamnit! I'd like to get my hands on whoever is riding it."

"Well, why didn't you just take the one next to where you parked it?" Stan asked in a mischievous voice. "That's what everyone else does."

Eubanks's indignant response was cut short by a ringing, "Ten-hut!" A hundred-odd pairs of boots hit the floor as the assembly sprang to rigid attention. From the corner of one eye, Ross watched a half-dozen uniformed shapes stride across the rough-finished concrete floor. He recognized Deckard and Ellis bringing up the rear. A tall—well over six-foot—figure stepped onto the low rostrum and turned to face his audience. A single silver star glittered from each shoulder of his natty forest green tunic. He didn't remove the soft, floppy cap; beneath it,

Ross could see that his close-cut hair was dark—chestnut brown. Dark eyes, set well apart, regarded the world from either side of a straight, slightly oversized nose. It was not a handsome face, but rather one that projected power and confidence. Ross decided, for some indefinable reason, that he didn't like the man.

The brigadier general's first words did little to alter his first impression. "Take seats. Gentlemen, I am Gen. Elliott Sprague, your wing commander. And I am pissed off—highly pissed off. Why? Because we aren't out there flying a combat mission this morning. But this will be the last morning we spend on the ground, I guarantee it. Until crews of the 7th Wing can shoot, bomb, and fly formation better than any wing in Europe, we practice. Around the clock if necessary. . . ."

Ross's attention strayed. Oh, shit, we've drawn an eager-beaver type, he thought. He studied the officers who followed the general in and took up seats in the front row. One looked familiar, but he couldn't see the man's face. Ross's gaze slid over Deckard and Ellis, then stopped. He did a double take. The oak leaves on Deckard's shoulders were silver, and Ellis sported gold ones. Promotions! He was in the act of nudging Eubanks, seated beside him, when the officer with the familiar-looking back turned to present his full profile. Ross dropped his head and regarded the floor. It was BT!

Eric Deckard could hear the mousey whispers behind him grow as more of his officers discovered the change in insignia. It was hard to keep a shit-eating grin off his face. As for the general's words, he'd heard them the night before.

The tall, arrogant bastard knew how to get results, Deckard thought. After an hour spent berating Eric and everyone else in a position of responsibility, he'd become chummy. "But, first things first," Sprague had said as he settled himself opposite Eric's battered desk. "As of zero-zero-zero-one hours tomorrow, the 365th will fly wing lead with the 866th as its lead squadron." He waved an impatient hand. "I want you to stay on as squadron commander. I read your file. B-17 ops with the 14th Bomb Group when you got wiped out at Manila. Shuffled off as an instructor pilot in the States. Latched on with "Hurry-up" Halverson to get the hell out of instructing. Stuck at Ninth Air Force headquarters in North Africa when his crazy attempt to bomb Japan from a base in China fizzled. Then back to the Training Command. You made yourself such a nuisance there that they gave you this job to get rid of you."

While Eric was recovering from his surprise at the man's extensive knowledge, Sprague continued. "Your wife divorced you while you were overseas and married a navy commander. Your daughter is living with your parents in Dallas while your lawyers and ex-wife squabble for custody. You're a cynic, Deckard, but you have a knack for getting people to work for you—that's why I'm going to establish my command post here at Walden Abbey. I gave my word to General Eaker that the 7th Wing would be combat ready ten days from now. You and your squadron, Major, are going to help see to that." A wintry smile on his face, he regarded Eric's dazed countenance. "You're wondering how come I know all this? I was on General Short's staff at Honolulu. I make it my business to know these things.

"Now, I don't want a major and a slick-winged captain helping to run my training program." He fished in a side pocket and extracted two small boxes. He tossed them onto the desk in front of Deckard. "As of today, you're promoted to light colonel. Your ops officer is a major. I'll get out of your hair now. There'll be a group Officers' Call at ten-hundred hours tomorrow. An eighteen-ship practice formation at daylight the following morning. The two of you have work to do. I'll ride as tail gunner in your lead ship. I want to see what goes on."

Deckard's reverie was interrupted by subdued coughing and the shuffling of feet behind him. He knew his men—Sprague was right—but the crews had heard this kind of stuff before. Their restless reaction said "bullshit." It would be up to him and Claude to hone their combat skills. Suddenly those new silver oak leaves seemed to weigh a ton.

Chapter Thirteen

1 May 1943
London, England

BT refilled his dinner companion's glass from the bottle of old port sitting at his left elbow. Service at London's Allied officers' club seemed immune to the ration controls imposed upon the English population at large.

"He's a damned idiot, Deke," BT said, shaking his head. "Remember that wild man we had for a quarterback our last year at Princeton? Convinced he could carry the ball better than any back we had? Well, that's Sprague. He's a headline hunter and has aspirations of acquiring four stars before this war is over. He may do it, too, but he's going to get a bunch of people killed in the process. Ol' BT isn't keen on being in that group."

Deke Brownell shifted his immaculately tailored figure in the leather-upholstered dining chair and favored BT with a lazy smile. "BT, knowing you, you have some devious, probably unethical, possibly illegal, scheme in mind. I recognize the symptoms. Please, do me the favor of enlightening me. I refuse to touch it, by the way. I may learn slowly but I have a long, long memory."

"Deke, boy. Spare me your wholesome, true-blue act," BT chided. "I recall more than a few unsavory projects bearing the unmistakable prints of your shifty hands. Now," his voice lost its bantering tone, "quite simply, all that is needed is for your boss, General Overbrook, to nix this moronic plan of Sprague's to lead a strike deep inside

Germany at this point. I'll take a priority target back to Walden Abbey to keep him happy, but when he springs it on 2d Air Div, it gets stomped. Okay?"

"You certainly have a high opinion of my influence," Deke drawled in mocking tones. "I am a lowly captain, strictly peon grade in this outfit. I'll do what I can, but don't make book on my success. I'll level with you—the big brass is desperate for something to wave under 'Bomber' Harris's nose. If your guy makes a good enough presentation—well, it just might get Eaker's approval."

BT scowled into his empty wineglass. "Unbelievable," he mumbled. "Oh, well, just do your best. But, this leads to something else: Do you know a light colonel named Weatherby in B-17 ops?"

Behind a frown of pretended concentration, Deke masked his knowledge of the man. He had learned never to be open and forthright with his old classmate; doing so invariably resulted in burned fingers and sore toes. "Vaguely, maybe. Black hair, hawk nosed—looks like a football halfback?"

"Sounds like him. I got his name from Janet's dad when he found out I was coming to England. Weatherby is an old 14th Bomb Group man; he was with Brereton in the Philippines. You know I took B-24s just to get here, but my heart is still with the old Fortress. I'm going to see Weatherby tomorrow—see if he might have room on his staff for another veteran of that December Seventh business."

"My, but you've been busy in the short time you've been here, BT," Deke responded with a chuckle. "Next thing you know, you'll be asking for someone like my boss to give you a recommendation."

"Well," BT said, his expression all innocence, "it would be one way he could show a little gratitude for learning of Sprague's suicide mission in advance."

Deke laughed outright and shook his head in admiration. "I wish we had you to deal with the Limeys for us, BT. Your mind runs on devious lines exactly parallel to theirs. Good luck with your pitch, but I see one great obstacle: It takes an act of God to get a combat-ready pilot assigned to this headquarters in a staff job. And how is Sprague going to react? Never in hell is he going to release you."

BT pursed his lips. Reaching for the check, he gave Deke a veiled look. "If you think I'm just trying to duck combat, Deke, you're dead wrong. Hell, rated staff officers fly missions too, you know. As for the transfer, let's say I have 'special qualifications.' As for Sprague's reaction," he shrugged, "there's always the same motivation that induced him to request that I be assigned to him as aide-de-camp."

Deke grinned and nodded. "Your old man. Yeah, you might say that you do have 'special qualifications.' "

"And . . ." BT paused. He still had trouble figuring change to an English pound. After counting it out, he continued. "I can offer Sprague a replacement who's better qualified than I am. He's even right there in place at Walden Abbey."

"Yeah?"

"Yeah. A real hotshot pilot. Already lead qualified. He even has a Silver Star, for Christ's sake. Name's Ross Colyer; I knew him slightly at Hickam." A flinty smile surfaced briefly. "He's just the right guy to fly Sprague's airplane." They strolled to the cloakroom and retrieved raincoats and caps. "Father sends his regards. I'm sure he'll appreciate any favors you can provide," he added pointedly. "I'll drop by tomorrow, after I see this Weatherby, and let you know how things look. Maybe by then you could have the name of a target for me to give Sprague?"

BT, stripped to shorts and propped by two pillows wedged against the headboard of his bed, wrote swiftly. A friendly Air Transport Service pilot had readily agreed to take BT's letter with him when he took off for a return trip to the States the next morning. BT's story about the urgent need to cheer up his despondent wife, plus a five-pound note, did the trick.

The letter to Janet was concise and said all the things that wives left behind like to hear. The instruction to draw two hundred dollars from their joint savings and send the money to him had been tucked in as an apparent afterthought. "An opportunity to pick up an antique silver service," he told her. Sprague's cronies played a mean brand of poker. The letter to Janet was already stuffed inside the envelope. The second letter, the one Janet was to deliver to his father immediately upon receipt, would be enclosed with the first.

Dear Father,

Only six weeks and it seems as though I've been here forever. I believe I've seen the sun exactly twice. We have yet to fly a mission; weather either prevents takeoff or hides our targets in Europe. Which leads me to the reason for this letter. Father, I am very concerned that General Eaker, and possibly General Arnold, are being misled about our daylight bombing capability. Frankly, it's a failure. The few missions going more than a hundred miles or so inside enemy territory suffer horrendous losses to German fighters. Our own fighters cannot provide escort much beyond the English Channel. Most alarming is the fact that we are ignoring advice offered by the RAF. They tried daylight bombing and were forced to stop. Now they bomb by night, when the fighters can't find them. Their losses run less than half of our rate and they are having excellent results. I understand that a number of our senior officers, Admiral King among them, are violently opposed to the daylight bombing concept. I must say I agree with their arguments. Perhaps you . . .

He laid his pen aside and consumed a healthy belt from the half-tumbler of scotch at his elbow. Okay, you're doing it again, he told himself—going to papa on your knees for help. When was it going to stop? Janet had seen it. The night she'd told him that he lived in his father's shadow had set off a real quarrel. Okay, he'd go it alone. He was smart, he was a good pilot. He would tell the old man to fuck off. He reached to crumple the unfinished letter, then paused. It was just so goddamned *easy.* He set his drink aside and retrieved the pen.

10 May 1943
Office of the Commander, U.S. Army Air Forces
Washington, D.C.

General "Hap" Arnold leaned on propped elbows and listened intently. The briefing officer, a beefy colonel from Intelligence, tapped the last chart with his pointer and summarized: "The timing is right for this mission, the capability exists, the target is essential to Hitler's war effort, and resistance will be light. General Spaatz's assessment is positive; you have it in the briefing folder. Even General Eaker and 'Bomber' Harris of the RAF concede that it should take priority."

General Arnold's eyebrows arched. His drawn gray face reflected surprise. "Ira agrees? He's willing to provide three groups of his B-24s?"

"Yes, Sir. General Eaker is most aware that a crippling strike, deep in the heart of Europe, is essential if his theory of daylight bombing is to be vindicated. With the P-47 drop-tank problem unresolved and

P-51s with the improved Merlin engine not due before late fall, he feels that a major effort launched from England, without fighter escort to the target, is impractical with the force he presently has combat ready. A deep strike from North Africa will catch the enemy completely by surprise."

"What number is Ira reporting combat ready?" The harassed general's voice had a hard edge.

"Not more than three hundred, Sir. General Eaker considers twice that number necessary to defend themselves against a rapidly growing enemy fighter force."

"Three hundred?" Arnold thundered. "Goddamnit, by my figures, he has almost seven hundred!"

"Well, Sir—" The perspiring colonel was out of his depth and searched the faces of the half-dozen Air Staff representatives, hoping for someone else to come to his rescue. He confronted six blank, unhelpful stares. "General Eaker's combat readiness report carries almost two hundred and fifty planes down with combat damage. A temporary shortage of spark plugs and starters has another sixty out of commission. The remaining shortage is a matter of combat-ready crews."

The assembled members of Arnold's staff watched with concern as their commander's rage grew. That the overworked Arnold had a heart condition was common knowledge. One of the braver members cleared his throat and volunteered, "A plan for the Eighth to fly two crucial missions in late July will be on your desk tomorrow morning, General. In line with striking 'bottleneck' industries, the Me 109 plant at Regensburg and the ball-bearing factories at Schweinfurt will be coordinated with a mission in force from the Twelfth in North Africa. They will hit the Fw 190 plant at Wiener-Neustadt. Orders go out tomorrow for a strike on Dortmund, weather permitting, on the twelfth. While not the "heartland" of Germany, it will help provide an idea of how strong their defenses are."

Arnold grunted, only slightly mollified. The portly briefing officer continued. "With oil resources being a critical factor to the *Luftwaffe,* this mission should sharply curtail the number of sorties they can mount against our bombers."

"How soon and by how much?"

"Within thirty days, their oil reserves will be depleted. We estimate that Tidal Wave will destroy 30 percent of their production."

The still-irate general drummed his fingers on the polished mahogany tabletop. "Very well. Go ahead with your ops order. I'll brief the Joint Chiefs and the president." He stood and turned toward the exit. "Ploesti, Romania," he mumbled. "Good Christ, nobody's even heard of the place."

10 May 1943
Aboard the *Happy Hooker*
Over East Anglia, England

Lieutenant Matt Dillon, face invisible behind oxygen mask and sunglasses, lounged between Ross and Rex on the flight deck. "Half you guys aren't gonna come back from your first mission, you keep flying like this," he drawled. Dillon's voice didn't reflect a great deal of interest one way or another.

Ross, who was concentrating on holding the *Happy Hooker* precisely beneath and behind the lead airplane, shot a quick glance at the laconic Dillon. The altimeter showed that they were at exactly twenty thousand feet. Lieutenant Eubanks, in *Weary Willie,* was barely visible off their left wing; Milt Dirkson had advised that Lieutenant Millikin in *Forever Yours* was perched on his right.

Christ, it was cold, thought Ross. Forced to keep his right hand on the throttles, he flexed stiff fingers inside his leather flying gauntlets. It was a trade-off: Heavy, lined gloves destroyed his feel, but thin leather wasn't all that much protection against the twenty-below-zero temperature.

"How come we won't be back?" asked Ross.

Dillon shrugged. He was a most unwilling volunteer to fly with the raw B-24 crews as coach. It had been Deckard's idea—to impress the idle B-17 pilots into the role of advisers. Veterans of at least five combat missions, they had "seen the elephant"—an apt analogy coined by the old sergeant in a classic novel about the Civil War. That battle-weary veteran had compared a regiment of fresh green recruits, marching to their initial engagement with the enemy, to his first circus. He had excitedly walked five miles just to see a real live elephant. To his dismay the animal was old and dirty, with tusks barely a foot long, and had deposited an enormous pile of feces in the dusty street as it walked past.

In the four days following General Sprague's pep rally, Dillon had stood and watched, mostly noncommittal, as planes of the 7th Wing floundered above the ever-present overcast. As if begrudging every word, he responded, "You're all over the fucking sky. Shit, you need a spyglass to see each other. Jerry is going to have trouble deciding which straggler to knock off first."

"I thought things were coming along pretty good," Ross responded curtly.

"Well, you just go on thinking that way, if it makes you feel better. But think about it. A tight diamond formation of four boxes of six ships each can throw out maybe thirty tons of .50-caliber slugs a minute. Ain't no fighter pilot in his right mind who's going to try and get within four hundred yards of a formation like that. No, Sir. He's gonna sit out there at about a thousand yards and sort of lob his shots—or go look for an easier target. Now, you spread out fifty or sixty yards and you reduce the number of guns bearing on him by the square of some damn figure or other.

"And them Germans don't fly passes like those '47s that made that mock attack yesterday. They see a loose, sloppy formation like this one and the fuckers come barrel-rolling right down your goddamn throat. They like to attack, in line, head-on. We got fewer guns up front, don't you see? They get you scattered all over the place, then swoop around to the rear and pick you off one by one."

The slender pilot fell silent, as if exhausted by the longest speech Ross could recall hearing him make.

Ross considered Dillon's words; they made sense. "How come no one has bothered to tell us that? We're flying the formation exactly as briefed. Oh, the join-up could be better, but everyone is holding a steady position."

Dillon grunted. "Probably because that wiseass general of yours hasn't bothered to ask anybody. You want my opinion—he don't know shit about combat flying."

"What the hell, why haven't you stood up in debriefing and told him this?"

"She-e-e-it. And get read off as a know-it-all? Besides, if I open my mouth I'll probably get tabbed to fly along on your first mission. And that, my friend, I have no intention of doing. You're gonna get clobbered—just like we did on our first trip to Paris. I sat there and watched nine—nine, mind you—of our planes auger in in about fifteen minutes. Shit, there were three spinning down, all on fire, at the same time. Nope, word is we're moving out our '17s to join the 93d Group at Rackenheath. I'm not about to screw up a chance to get back with an experienced outfit."

Ross flew in silence for several minutes, then asked, "Okay. Where should I be to fly what you call a 'tight' formation?"

After a pause and a sigh, Dillon replied, "Call in your wingmen. Tell 'em to tuck it in until they can feel the prop wash from your outboard engines, then slide off just a tad. Move forward until their wingtips are just about even with your tail."

"Goddamn, you're going to have midair collisions all over the place."

"Maybe. At least you'll be bailing out over friendly territory. After you get your wingmen tucked in, put your nose right up that lead ship's ass—about twenty feet below and even with his tail turret."

Ross grinned to himself: General Sprague, his head dimly visible, was in the lead aircraft's tail turret. Ross followed the B-17 pilot's advice and was rewarded when Sprague responded on the radio with a blistering, "Red Dog Baker, what the hell do you think you're doing? Get back in position. Do you hear me?"

For the second time in a month, Ross stood at attention facing Colonel Deckard across the commander's desk.

"Colyer, goddamnit, what is it with you? You got some kind of death wish or something? General Sprague tells me that you almost rammed us from the rear today," the weary Deckard spluttered.

Ross braced himself. "Sir, I had complete control of my airplane. There was no danger of a collision. I was following Lieutenant Dillon's suggestion to tighten up the formation."

"Dillon? Oh, the B-17 pilot. Well, I don't know what he had in mind, but *I'm* telling you not to pull a stunt like that again. The general was foaming at the mouth when we landed. Chewed my ass for having you lead the second element. Wants you relegated permanently to the 'Tail-end Charlie' position."

"Sir . . ." Ross drew a long breath and related Lieutenant Dillon's comments regarding the formation. Deckard listened closely without interruption. Picking up the trombone, he blew the opening bars of "When the Saints Go Marching In," a sure sign he was disturbed.

Removing the mouthpiece, he wiped it carefully with a somewhat dingy handkerchief and asked softly, "Colyer, what are your intentions after the war? You have any idea of staying on for thirty?"

"Yes, Sir. I left engineering school because I wanted to fly."

"Well, you just set your career back about ten years today."

Ross slipped from his position of rigid attention. "What? My God, just for coming closer to your airplane than he thought I should?"

"There's more to it than that, Lieutenant." Deckard checked his watch. "Look, the club bar is open. Let me buy you a drink. I'll fill you in."

The officers' club was full of weary but noisy aircrews. They had been through four days of intensive formation practice and more was sure to come. They jokingly longed to draw a combat mission and get some rest. The sizable semicircular bar was lined elbow to elbow with loudly demanding patrons. Two sweating enlisted bartenders trotted back and forth in an effort to fill the steady flow of orders.

The club, still incomplete, was housed in yet another of the jumble of Nissen huts. Fiberboard panels to insulate the curved, bare metal skin were only partially installed; the noise level was deafening. Unit emblems were grouped around the bar mirror: the Eighth Air Force's winged eight, the 775th Bomb Group's—the previous tenants—prowling tomcat, and the 7th Wing's just-adopted symbol, a fiercely scowling Indian. Those preferring to drink while seated grouped around a half-dozen trestle tables. These were stained with spilled drinks and marred with cigarette burns. The membership's pride and joy, however, was a fieldstone fireplace in which a pair of blazing logs rested on lengths of railroad iron.

A reminder that the place was not your ordinary, everyday corner saloon was mounted above the bar mirror. Two unshielded bulbs—one green, one red. A green light, now burning, announced an open bar. The red bulb, when illuminated, announced that a mission was scheduled the next day and that the bar would close at 1800 hours.

Ross and Colonel Deckard collected beers and found seats at a relatively deserted table. Raising his mug in a casual toast, Deckard leaned forward and spoke softly enough not to be overheard. "You know the general's aide, Templeton?"

"I know him."

"The captain is being reassigned—to Eighth Air Force headquarters in London." Ignoring Ross's raised eyebrows, Deckard went on. "Somebody told General Sprague that you would make an ideal replacement for Templeton. The general asked me, just this morning, what I thought about the move."

Ross felt a chill tickle the back of his neck. Deckard drank deeply from his mug and continued. "I told him you were one of the best pilots in the squadron and a good officer. I also told him it couldn't be a worse time for me to lose a lead crew. He didn't appear overly sympathetic—was all set to call you in after today's mission to break the news. Well," he gave Ross a level stare, lips pursed, "guess what? The deal is off, like in 'forget it.' "

Ross forced a grin. "Me? A general's aide? Who in the hell could have given the old man such an idea? I'm happy where I am, Colonel. I'm sorry I got him so pissed off today, but what Dillon says makes sense—and remember, he's been there."

Deckard drained his beer and stood. "I hear you, Colyer. I gotta go now." He slapped Ross on the back. "Get a good night's sleep. Same time, same place tomorrow." He paused. "By the way, Colyer. You happen to know which hut this Dillon beds down in?"

Ross captured a refill from the bar and sat nursing it, a wry smile on his sweat-grimed face. He had no doubt about the identity of that "anonymous person" who had recommended him as Sprague's aide. The question was, why? He sensed a presence behind him and turned to see BT sliding into the chair Deckard had vacated.

"BT. Have a seat," he invited unnecessarily. "I knew you were on the base but hadn't run across you."

BT placed his drink on the table and propped his chin in his hands. "And I'll just bet you ran all over the place looking for me." His handsome features wore a mocking smile.

"Not really." Ross's voice was cool. "I think we both pretty much said it all that day back there in the Fort Shafter gymnasium. You dragged me off that beach, and I thanked you. You rejected my gratitude; I think your words were something like, I'm going to hang you out to dry."

"Now, Ross," BT assumed an injured air, "we'd both had a bad day. I was pissed, sure, that you felt you had to give me an order at gunpoint. But I've gotten over it; I just wish you could forget the whole incident as well."

Ross sipped his beer and regarded his old adversary with narrowed eyes. "Okay, truce," he responded warily. "Can I buy you a drink on it?"

"Yeah, sure," BT said, his voice brightening. "Janet will be glad to know we're speaking again. She thinks a lot of you, you know."

"How is she?" Ross asked as he returned with fresh drinks. "I never did get around to congratulating the two of you."

"That's understandable, Ross. Janet's fine; I just heard from her yesterday. Our mail finally caught up with us. She's staying with her parents; Colonel Richards was reassigned to Wright-Patterson. I'll write her tonight and tell her we had this visit. Now, what on earth went on this afternoon? I understand you almost rammed the general's airplane."

Ross responded with a short laugh. "Not at all; I was just trying to tighten up the formation. But," he shrugged, "it sure put me at the top of his shit list."

"Oh, I don't really think so, Ross." BT adopted a worried frown. "The old man has kind of a short fuse, but he gets over it. I told him that the B-17 pilot you had along put you up to it. I think if you explained things to him in person, everything would smooth over."

Ross nodded thoughtfully. "I appreciate your taking up for me, BT, I really do. By the way, I heard you're getting a new job—in headquarters yet."

BT's voice sharpened. "Who told you that?"

"Oh, probably the same person who told you about what the B-17 pilot told me," Ross replied with a lazy grin.

BT scowled into his drink. "Goddamn. I can never understand how word gets around so fast. It isn't definite yet. I wish some people could keep their mouths shut. But it leads up to what I was going to suggest to you. You see, the general has already requisitioned a replacement for me. He had about settled on you."

Watching Ross's feigned surprise, he continued. "I think I can convince him that you're still the best person for the job. You agreeable?"

Ross assumed a thoughtful expression. "Damn, BT, you've caught me by surprise. I just don't know what to say right now. Let me think about it. I'm really grateful for the offer, and for your making the first move to patch up our—er—misunderstanding. But, hell, give up my crew? I'm not sure I'm 'drawing-room qualified.' I'd probably do something stupid the first time I was around a party with all the brass. But I'll give it a lot of thought. I'll let you know, oh, say after tomorrow's mission."

He thought he detected a flash of anger in BT's eyes, but the response was smooth. "It's your decision, my friend. But—" BT tossed back the last of his drink and stood. "Don't screw around too long. He could make up his mind tomorrow, tonight even."

"Well, I'll just have to take that chance, BT. I'll be in touch, just as soon as I can sit down and consider all the pros and cons. And thanks again for thinking of me. . . ." The last words scattered and died in the empty wake of BT's departure.

A wide grin replaced the serious look Ross had shown BT. That bastard, he thought. BT was about as apt to change personalities as a pig was apt to sprout wings and feathers. Now what in the hell had brought all this on? BT was up to something, and helping out his old enemy wasn't likely to be his objective. Ross shook his head. He was a combat pilot. He would talk to Colonel Deckard—resist becoming what amounted to being little more than a servant to that pompous ass, Sprague, to the bitter end.

11 May 1943
Walden Abbey

Ross was to be spared the ordeal of yet another training mission. The word was passed at breakfast. It spread faster than news that the small-town minister's wife had run off with the piano player in a whorehouse. They were assigned a combat mission.

Colonel Deckard and Major Ellis missed the standard breakfast of powdered eggs, canned bacon, and—today only—a side dish of canned peaches. The pair had been in the ops/briefing hut since 0400 hours. Two harassed communications clerks were still decoding the ops order, bits of which were continuing to arrive via Teletype.

Deckard, with Ellis reading over his shoulder, regarded the first two pages with greedy anticipation:

Operations Order No. 64:
11 May 1943

S E C R E T

Headquarters 7th Bomb Wing (Heavy)
APO 83

1.

a. (See intelligence annex)

b. 4 squadrons, destroy railroad marshalling yards and related structures at Dortmund, Germany, at 1100B: Key Point time 0740B. Alternate target: PFF on airfield runway intersection (5230N-0710E). . . .

*   *   *

Eyes racing across the crudely typewritten pages, Deckard muttered significant bits aloud: "Drop from twenty-one thousand . . . that's good. The 199th Group to fly lead . . . oh, shit—we're ass-end Charlie! Full fuel and bomb load. Twenty five-hundred-pound GPs. Wish to hell we had another thousand feet of runway—have Nate double-check flight plans. This is a deep penetration for us; we'll be sucking fumes coming home. We're to put up nine mission birds and two spares—wow! We got that many combat ready, Claude? Where the hell is the intel annex? There's bound to be flak; I keep hearing that the Jerries are moving more Me 109s north. We gonna have any fighter cover?"

By midmorning the little base resembled a turpentined anthill. Nature had seen fit to bestow an unaccustomed measure of sunshine on the little island; temperatures soared to a balmy seventy degrees. Adrenaline kept voices pitched a bit higher than usual; feet moved at parade-ground cadence instead of the customarily lethargic shuffle. A steady stream of officers and men moved past stern-faced MPs posted to secure entrances to the ops/briefing building. Inside, Nate Buckner, the squadron navigator, worked with Gus Gustoferson, the lead bombardier, cursing the dripping sweat that marred charts and mission drafts. Deckard and Ellis fled to the quiet, relatively cooler confines of the colonel's office, the business of assigning crews to formation positions uppermost in their minds.

Around perimeter hardstands, canvas covers for engines and nose compartments were, for the most part, converted to sunshades as ground crews labored to fine-tune engines and aircraft systems. Periodically, the twelve hundred horses captive inside a Pratt & Whitney engine would cough to life and shatter the morning tranquility as they were brought to full power. Mechanics made subtle adjustments, indifferent to the miniature hurricanes generated by their prop blasts. Nearby civilian residents looked at each other knowingly. It had been weeks since the now-decimated B-17 group had disrupted their peace and quiet.

Morning evaporated. The mess hall buzzed with conversation as sweat-grimed troops gulped a lunch of Spam sandwiches and GI lemonade.

"Hear it's Paris; goddamn *Luftwaffe* will be like bees."

"Kiel, I'd guess. Bounce some more thousand-pounders off those concrete sub pens."

"*Dutch Treat* won't ever make it. Needs a double engine change just to get out of the traffic pattern."

"They think I'm gonna take off with just a thousand rounds per gun, they're nuts. I already got another thousand stashed."

It was midafternoon when Ross and Ham Phillips were satisfied that the *Happy Hooker* was airworthy. "We got time to replace number two supercharger control? It's been surging," Ross told the weary maintenance chief.

"Lieutenant," said the balding master sergeant, rolling an unlit cigar to the corner of his caked lips, "we ain't got a spare. I think it'll get you there and back. If you don't think so, well, that's for you and the major to work out."

"Fair enough." Ross grinned and slapped the crusty crew chief on a sweat-soaked shoulder. "You've done a helluva job just keeping her in the air during this ball-busting training schedule. I'll try and bring her back in one piece for you."

A pleased grunt, feigning indifference, constituted the crew chief's response. Ross and Ham flagged a passing six-by-six and headed for the living area.

Rex was the hut's sole occupant. Sitting cross-legged on his cot and stripped to his shorts in the unaccustomed warmth, the copilot was using a towel to keep sweat from staining the letter he was composing. Ross discovered, to his dismay, that a huge stack of unsealed letters lay in a mound on his cot. Pens had been active during the morning hours. Everyone was apparently seized by a compulsion to write what might be a last letter to family and loved ones. Now, an officer had to read each one to see that nothing revealing location, mission, morale, or any one of a half-dozen other taboo subjects left the base.

"Well, shit." Ross regarded the stack of outgoing mail with weary disgust. "Am I the only son of a bitch on the base who can censor mail? Hell, I have a couple letters of my own to write."

Rex laid his pen aside and leaned back, favoring Ross with a lopsided grin. "The curse of high office, gallant leader. All the other a/c's huts got some as well. How's the bird?"

"She'll fly," Ross grunted. "I'd like to replace that number two supercharger, but it'll have to wait. Be sure to keep an eye on the damn thing. Where are Art and Stan?"

"They went over to the club. Decided to see if they can pick up any straight poop from the group on tomorrow's mission. Also, the red light over the bar gets turned on at eighteen-hundred. Stan wanted to scarf up a few beers before it closed."

"Those bastards. Well, I'm just going to bundle up this mail, go over there, and dump it in their laps. Let *them* pry into the private lives of our enlisted types. I hate that job. Why the hell can't someone who doesn't know these guys read their mail. Do you know there's a corporal on Polk's crew writing steaming letters to the wife of a sergeant on Wilkinson's crew? I ask you, what the hell business of mine is that?"

Rex chuckled wickedly. "Just be glad that us morally upright officers don't have our mail censored. I'd hate to have you read what I write to your dearly beloved Rhoda in Justin godforsaken Falls, Michigan."

"All right, Rex, knock off that shit." Ross flushed angrily, then changed the subject. "Speaking of mail, did anybody go to mail call?"

"I ran across Dirkson. He showed up; his dad was in a bad way before we left and he's antsy. He says the mail clerk told him that the ship carrying a lot of mail for us took a torpedo." Rex shrugged. "May be another month before we get anything besides Red Cross emergency messages."

"Damn!"

"Ross . . ." Rex paused and lit a cigarette with pretended indifference. "About tomorrow. Are you scared?"

Ross reached for Rex's open pack and extracted a cigarette for himself. While lighting it, he considered the question. "I don't really know, Rex. I've been too damn busy this morning to think about it, I guess. Are you scared?"

"Not really. Maybe I just don't know what to be scared of. But they say that anyone who isn't scared before a mission has something wrong with him. I was just wondering."

"Yeah, well maybe we'll feel different after our first one. How do Art and Stan feel about it?"

"Huh!" Rex snorted. "That stupid Stan has fire in his eye; he can't wait. In fact, that's why he went to the club. Everyone has figured out that if we put up nine mission planes and two airborne spares, it leaves one crew on the ground. He's convinced that the stand-down crew will be us. Is that general still pissed off at us?"

Ross frowned. It had never occurred to him that his crew might get left behind. "That's horseshit, Rex. But I guess Stan is right about one thing: Someone won't go. If it's us—" he shrugged. "Well, that's just how it is. Now I'd better get busy on this stack of letters. Like I say, I want to write a couple myself."

Rex stood and, in a rare demonstration of camaraderie, said, "Here, give me the damn things. I'll take 'em to the club and the three of us will play censor. You write your letters."

Ross fished writing materials from his footlocker and settled down to compose letters to Rhoda and his parents. Rhoda first—not that he harbored any illusions that they had a future. But it was nice to get her letters, pretending that she was madly in love with him. What the hell to say? Anything of interest was classified. "I love you and miss you," he wrote, then looked at the trite words disgustedly. If only he could tell her about his running conflict with Rex; the way his crew was constantly screwing up; the need to have a confidante; how being aircraft commander was a lonesome job. One didn't dare confide doubt or indecision. The chances of being stood down tomorrow—how did he feel about it? Had he experienced a fleeting feeling of relief when Rex mentioned the possibility?

Justin Falls, a foreign place he had departed scant months ago, took on aspects of a lifetime in the past. It seemed he had been here in this cold, damp place forever. Ross sighed, and bent to his task. "I've lost some weight. The crew is a really super bunch of guys," he lied. "Guess you're all set to return to school this fall. God, it seems like ten years since we went to classes together. I have no idea how long I may be over here. Maybe we could get married at the same time you get your degree. You do still want to get married, don't you? After that last night with you, I sure want to! And you'd better, if you know what I mean! Ha-ha."

By the time the men came to evening meal, hyper attitudes noticeable during the day were becoming more subdued. But men still laughed too loudly over remarks that really weren't that witty; they walked with forced casual swaggers, acting the way they thought old, seasoned combat veterans would act on the night before a raid. The handful of B-17 crews who had experienced combat were easily identified. Sober-faced troops surrounded them, hanging onto each word.

The cooks had done their best—the lamb stew was actually edible. And, from someplace, fresh melons had materialized. Pineapple up-side-down cake, with seconds, won grudging words of praise.

Ross, Rex, Art, and Stan returned directly to their hut. A stroll past the officers' club showed that the red light above the bar was indeed burning. None seemed inclined to mention feelings prompted by that somber reminder.

Inside their suddenly homey domicile, personal effects were stowed in footlockers without comment. They would fly with only their dog tags for identification. Unspoken attention was given to removing potentially embarrassing items, such as condoms, clandestine love letters, and "black books" with the telephone numbers and addresses of former girlfriends. There was no point in upsetting the folks back home if they didn't return.

Rex produced his Dop kit and mumbled that he was going to shave so he could catch a few more winks after wake-up. The others, at a loss for constructive activity, announced that they would do the same.

Chapter Fourteen

0315 Hours, 12 May 1943
Walden Abbey

"Lieutenant Colyer, Lieutenant Eubanks, Sirs—wake-up call. Chow in thirty minutes; briefing at oh-four-thirty." A flashlight beam brushed briefly across sleeping faces. Boots crunched with unnatural loudness in the morning quiet, as the enlisted charge-of-quarters proceeded to the next hut with his unwelcome message.

Ross, flashlight spraying the darkness, fumbled for his flight suit, which he had left folded atop his footlocker the night before. Drawing the garment over his long johns, he stumbled to the light switch and filled the hut with sickly saffron light from the overhead bulbs. From the way Art and Stan bounced into action, Ross suspected that they had been awake for some time. He slipped bare feet into flying boots, collected a towel and shaving kit, then headed down the muddy duckboards toward what the English architects had labeled the "ablutions building." He scanned the still murky horizon and savored the stillness.

It was hard to believe, he mused, that a day commencing with such tranquility could soon become a hell of heat, blood, and mayhem.

Ross and his companions trudged down an uneven cart path toward the blacked-out mess hall, each preoccupied with private thoughts. Across the field the voices of weary bomb-loading crews, the long night nearly behind them, provided grim verification that the moment of truth was at hand. Spirits lifted somewhat as the stimulating fragrance of freshly brewed coffee reached them. They joined a queue of identically

clad airmen crowding the entrance, and passed into a room filled with
a chattering cacophony of voices.

Ross choked down modest portions of powdered eggs and salty
canned bacon. He refrained from slaking a consuming thirst with
excessive amounts of juice and coffee. A full bladder aboard a combat-
configured Liberator, flying formation, presented logistical problems,
especially while at altitude and wearing oxygen equipment.

The distance between the mess and briefing huts seemed unusually
short that morning. En route, Sergeant Phillips accosted the foursome
to announce, "The rest of the crew's all accounted for and ready to
go, Lieutenant. We'll draw the guns and meet you at the bird, okay?"

"Good enough, Ham," Ross responded. "Be sure everyone double-
checks his chute pack. They've been finding some bent pins lately."

"Yes, Sir. Hey, Lieutenant, any hint about where we're going?"

"Not a clue, Ham. But we'll know in just a few minutes. We'll brief
you all before takeoff."

When they reached the briefing hall a helmeted MP wearing a
holstered side arm gravely checked their names against his clipboard
and passed them inside. Taking adjoining seats on the crude plank
benches, Ross and his retinue of officers settled down to await the
mission briefing team. Seats filled rapidly. The level of conversation
approached that of a rowdy beer hall on a Saturday night. Eyes never
strayed for long, however, from the muslin-shrouded briefing map
dominating the front wall.

"Ten-hut!" The background of voices ceased in midsentences as
General Sprague led his staff to the front of the room.

"At ease, at ease," said Sprague.

Colonel Deckard, following his officious executive officer toward
the front, was a smiling figure of joviality. His attitude prompted one
brave soul to yell, "You gonna drop that god-awful trombone on the
Jerries today, Colonel?"

The quip was rewarded with a hearty belly laugh from Deckard and
a piercing scowl from Sprague. The half-dozen officers trailing in his
wake wore, by contrast, expressions of grim efficiency. They took seats
in front, as did General Sprague, without speaking, while Deckard and
the other squadron commanders joked with crew members in aisle
seats. The group commander, Col. Arny Bolt, stepped onto the raised
platform. His face sagged, showing the effects of a long night with
little sleep.

Eubanks muttered to Ross, "I heard that the old man is pissed off at not being in the starting lineup. As group CO he insisted on flying lead, but the general elbowed him out of the way."

"Well, I for one wish he was," Ross responded. "At least he flew combat before he got the 365th."

The group commander became the focus of every eye in the house as he stuffed a stubby pipe in his pocket and said, "Gentlemen, today we're hitting railroad marshalling yards at Dortmund. That's in Germany, you know." The sally prompted nervous laughter.

As he spoke, a pair of clerks from operations removed the expanse of white muslin from the wall map. Dead silence ensued as the crews absorbed its appearance. A length of red yarn originating in East Anglia snaked northwest across the North Sea, then cut sharply back and crossed the German coastline. After a short distance, a length of green string, marking the return route, took over and followed a path through the Netherlands, across the English Channel, then home. Interest in the route ran a poor second, however, to that devoted to a series of red circles framing the junction of red and green yarn—their target. The circles indicated known antiaircraft concentrations.

"It should be an easy target," Colonel Bolt said. He turned to the group intelligence officer and waved him to the stand. "Isn't that right, Ted?"

Major Ted Rafferty rubbed a hand over his reddish blond crewcut and faced his tense audience with a wry grin. "It appears to be, Sir," he said cautiously. "At last report, Dortmund was lightly defended with only two flak batteries. But that was more than a month ago. There's been a big increase in traffic north along this rail line toward the ports, however, and Dortmund is a bottleneck. Jerry has a habit of reinforcing places like this with eighty-eights mounted on railroad cars.

"Fighters. The *Luftwaffe* is adding to its Home Defense Force daily. Estimate now is about three hundred 109s—and they can call on their night-fighter Me 110s. We'll start out on a heading toward Kiel to draw the squadrons located in central Germany to the northeast. When we cut back toward Dortmund, they won't have the endurance to engage us for more than a few minutes. Spits and P-47s will rendezvous with us as we cross the coastline and again over Belgium on the way home. Other than that, we're on our own. Ops?"

Major Dale Weathers, the group operations officer, stepped onto the raised briefing rostrum. His short-cropped black hair sprinkled with gray, he was older than the young air crewmen he faced. "We'll be providing a fourth squadron for the boys at Siddley," he said. "Our airborne spares will fill in, as needed, anyplace in the group. Since we're the new kids on the block, guess what? We'll be the last group in the wing, Tail-end Charlie."

He grinned at the unified groan that arose in response. "Now that 'Purple Heart Corner' stuff is mostly a myth. Fly tight formation, keep those guns moving, and your chances are no worse than anybody else's. And I do mean keep those guns moving around! From the time we turn south, fighters are a possibility. A plane screwing around, way out of formation, guns dangling every which way—that's a fighter pilot's dream."

While the ops officer talked, a sheaf of papers was distributed to each aircraft commander. On top was the group formation diagram: twenty-seven hand-drawn T's, in groups of three, nine to a squadron. Across the top of each T was an aircraft commander's name. Ross scanned his flimsy with lightning swiftness; his heart sank. His name wasn't on it. Then, in the lower left corner, he spotted six more names under "Airborne Spares." Colyer and Wilkinson were slotted from the 866th. Disappointed but not dismayed, he showed it to the others.

Airborne spare. It meant that his crew and Wilkinson's would board combat-configured airplanes, do the takeoff, and follow the group to the bomb line; then, if no one dropped out with mechanical trouble, they would return home. It was a cruel hoax. Get all fired up psychologically to do a mission, go through a hazardous takeoff, and get sent home as nonessential.

"We're not out of it yet," he muttered, in an effort to retain his composure. "I'm betting that somebody's gonna blow an engine before we get two hours out."

That goddamn general. They had been dropped from the starting lineup because of that stupid practice formation. An air of gloom remained with the four through the remainder of the briefing, including the weather officer's attempts at levity as he told them to expect good weather for the entire mission. It was a rare day when both England and the Continent enjoyed clear skies. They were not to worry about the fact that, just now, they couldn't see across the runway; the skies would clear by start-engines time. The officer trotted off the platform in mock terror amid a chorus of boos and catcalls.

Then General Sprague took the rostrum. He was dressed in a tailored forest green gabardine flight suit. BT, seated in front, wore an identical getup, Ross observed with a sardonic grin. BT didn't appear to share his boss's vim and vigor.

"This is our first opportunity to draw blood, men," Sprague stated in cryptic tones. "We'll be flying with experienced crews in the other groups, and they'll be looking for us to screw up. Let's disappoint them. The 7th Wing, I'm here to tell you, is going to be the outfit others try to keep up with: more kills, more tonnage delivered, and the lowest circular error in the entire goddamn Eighth Air Force!"

The briefing over, Stan split off to attend a special target briefing, and a casual-looking Rex strode away in the other direction to draw escape and evasion kits. Art and Ross piled onto a canvas-shrouded six-by-six headed for the flight line. The gray half-light of dawn gave no indication that the dense, heavy mist would obey the optimistic weatherman.

Sergeant Phillips met Ross's crew truck, a worried frown creasing his forehead. "We got problems, Lieutenant."

"How so?" Ross queried as he leaped to the ground and retrieved his gear.

"Well, for one thing the goddamn VHF radio is out. Supply doesn't have a spare, so they got a man on the way to *Weary Willie* to cannibalize a set. It's down for parts anyway. He promised, but you know how that goes. Worst thing is our oxygen. We have only about two hours in the system aft of the bomb bay."

A harassed crew chief joined them. "Goddamn practice missions, Lieutenant. The systems just bled off since they weren't being used. We get only one oh-two truck and he's topping up the rest of the mission birds fast as he can. Since you'll be spare, *Happy Hooker* is last on his list. It'll be close."

Ross bit back an angry retort. How the hell could something like that be overlooked? Simmer down, he told himself. The radio. Strict radio silence was observed anyway. He would have the low-frequency command set. It had a ten-mile restricter on the transmitter to prevent plane-to-tower conversations from being intercepted by enemy listening posts. It wasn't good. He could miss such things as a recall or important formation changes. Those orders would come by VHF. Still, they could go without it. Wait and see.

The oxygen supply was something else. "Art, how much time are we scheduled to spend at altitude?"

The navigator squatted alongside a main gear and fished out his log. Using his flashlight he ran down the entries. "We climb to bombing altitude at oh-nine-fifty-three. We get back over water and start our letdown at twelve-forty-seven. That's more than three hours at altitude, Ross."

Seething at the morning's helping of obstacles, Ross's mind raced, seeking a solution. "Where's Mickey?" he snapped.

"Right here, Sir," said the towering, athletic tail gunner as he materialized beside Sergeant Phillips.

"Mickey, catch the first thing on wheels that goes past here. Get the hell to the parachute shack. Tell them I want a dozen bailout bottles—right *now!* That'll give you guys in the back enough oxygen to get by on if that truck doesn't show up. Get cracking. You have," he peered at his watch, "twenty minutes before start engines. Okay, Ham, let's do a walk-around."

Stan rolled off a passing six-by, lugging his bulging briefcase and the all-important Norden bombsight. This miracle of precision was the single most crucial instrument Ross would have on board. Its proud manufacturers boasted that the sight could place a five-hundred-pound bomb in a pickle barrel from twenty thousand feet. They weren't too far wrong, either. It was also the most closely guarded component on the entire base. Bombardiers drew the sights immediately prior to takeoff. Regulations required them to wear side arms while in possession of the hush-hush system, and they were escorted to the airplane by an armed MP. Mickey was turned away when he attempted to board the delivery truck for his own top-priority errand.

Stan gently placed the sinister-looking black box aboard and clambered up to mount its contents in the Plexiglas nose. Then, while Ross and Ham performed their meticulous inspection of the exterior, Stan entered the bomb bay. Using his flashlight to augment the weak yellowish light cast by the airplane's lighting system, he checked that the nose fuses in the cargo of twenty deadly instruments of destruction had safety pins installed and that their shackles were securely locked. He dropped to the ground through the open bomb bay doors and looked up at the innocent-appearing cargo. A wide grin split his freckled features.

Cryhowski, you dumb shit, you're actually enjoying this, he thought. Mother, you would faint dead away if you could see me now. Your baby boy, living in a disgusting steel building, sweating, and getting filthy dirty.

Even Princeton hadn't provided a refuge from her smothering oversight. And in addition to the War Department, she had actually called their goddamn senator.

"The boy just got carried away, Edward. Could you tell those people at the army that my Stan could *never* cope with living in a barracks and eating that awful food?"

Well, he was having a ball. He was as good as most of his contemporaries— better even. His most prized possession was the small silver plaque attesting to his excellence, awarded upon graduation from bombardier school. No way would he trade it for the red Jaguar that Mother had given him at his graduation. He would stay in the army as long as they would keep him.

At twelve minutes prior to start-engines time, the *Happy Hooker* was still minus a VHF radio and a full charge of life-sustaining oxygen. Ross assembled the crew for a hasty briefing and final checkoff. "Okay," he snapped. "So we're assigned as a spare. Don't let that change a thing you do. I'm betting that we go—call it a hunch. Any more bitches before we load up?"

Art joined the group with more news. "We only have five flares for the Very pistol. Two green-green, a yellow-red, and two reds."

"Oh, shit! What's the recognition code of the day?"

"A green-green followed by a red," Art advised.

"Well, we'll have to make do. The goddamn Limey gunners shot down three gooneybirds full of troops off Dover last week because they didn't have the right code. Coffee jugs and water get here, Ham?"

"They're pulling up right now, Sir."

"Okay, everyone check your buddy's chute harness and let's strap in. Where the hell is Rex, Mickey, that radio, and the friggin' oxygen truck?" he added to no one in particular.

Major Ellis, bitter at being left behind on their first mission, chose that moment to bring his jeep to a sliding halt alongside. "Okay, Colyer, why isn't your crew on board? You fuckups miss start-engines time and I'll have you all on detail for a month, so help me."

Ross would have bitten his tongue off before asking for help. They would make takeoff if he, by God, had to put Rex on a wing and order him to flap his arms. "Nothing we can't handle, Major. We'll start on time."

"Okay, you'd damn well better." The harassed ops officer roared off into the gloom, surface water spurting from beneath the wheels. Ross continued his predeparture briefing through clenched teeth.

Pretakeoff events culminated in swift succession. As the ground crew cleared the area of extraneous gear, preparatory to starting engines, a green flare arced from the tower platform. "It's a go," Stan cried elatedly.

Ross frowned. He could see across the field, but the skies were far from clear. Rex and Mickey arrived in the same jeep. Mickey headed for the waist entrance, a stack of slim dark green cylinders clutched to his chest like firewood. Rex hastily passed around plastic cases containing items deemed helpful to airmen who parachuted over enemy territory: a map of the region surrounding the target printed on waterproof silk; a button that was really a compass; forty dollars in gold coins; a length of hacksaw blade; and assorted items such as matches, concentrated rations, and, to the hilarity of all, a single condom. "To waterproof matches and other items" had been the official explanation offered by an indignant classroom instructor.

Ross and Rex were poised over the engine-starting controls, concentrating on their hack watches, when a weapons carrier slid to a halt in front. A disheveled ground crewman stood in the illumination of the vehicle's headlights, holding an oblong black metal box, a beseeching look on his face.

"Leckie, can you install a VHF set in flight?" Ross called over the intercom.

"Sure thing, Lieutenant," the eager voice of their radio operator responded.

"Okay, have this guy outside pass it through the waist window. As soon as we get settled down, have a go at it. Turning three," he added as the sweep hand of his watch crossed the twelve.

Thirty-three fingers pressed thirty-three toggle switches as the sweep hands of thirty-three watches, synchronized at the mission briefing, crossed twelve. The number three engines of thirty-three warplanes stuttered, coughed blue smoke from mixture-rich cylinders, and settled into an uneven cadence. Ross experienced a visceral tingle of pride as he observed the precision start. Professionalism in combat flying began at this point; the 365th Bomb Group had just passed its first test.

One by one the *Happy Hooker*'s remaining three power plants rumbled to life. The heavy black umbilical cord supplying electrical life until engine start was jerked free and the clattering little auxiliary generator shut down.

"Checking number one," Ross announced. Advancing the throttle until the number one tachometer steadied at 2,300 RPM, he reached for the dual magneto switch. "Checking right mag."

"No drop," Rex responded as the needle barely quivered.

"Left."

"No drop."

"Set the supercharger." Ross advanced the throttle to full open.

Rex nudged a stubby lever forward until the needle registering manifold pressure covered a tiny red line at the forty-seven-inch mark. Producing its full twelve-hundred horsepower, the big Pratt & Whitney bellowed in protest at remaining tethered. Rex, Ross, and Ham studied instruments reflecting engine performance while the entire ship rocked and shuddered. Ross glanced at Ham, who nodded. The aircraft commander retarded the number one throttle and the engine settled down to a contented burble.

Ross repeated a power check on *Happy Hooker*'s remaining engines and gave the ground controller a thumbs-out hand signal to pull the restraining wheel chocks. Allowing the aircraft to roll forward slightly for a brake check, Ross turned his attention to takeoff procedures. Nine lives and thirty tons of machinery were committed to take their places in the deadly air battle consuming the European continent.

Backlighted by a dimly visible sun emerging from the fog and haze, Eric Deckard's *Hard Times Ahead* lurched across the uneven perimeter track toward the number one takeoff position. A sullen BT, his reassignment a casualty of Sprague's grandiose plan, rode as his copilot. General Sprague perched on a stool in one corner of the flight deck.

With subdued throttle burps, Sprague's little flock eased from their hardstands in slow pursuit. Ross assumed the squadron's last position in line, buffeted by the combined blasts of forty props preceding him. Rex braced himself against the wheel to prevent the swirling air currents from damaging fragile control surfaces.

Major Ellis was seated in a solitary jeep at the takeoff point. He aimed a steady green light from an Aldis lamp toward the cockpit of

Hard Times Ahead. The squadron commander directed his lumbering, bellowing craft along a newly painted runway centerline as the noisy conga line behind him shuffled one step forward.

The *Happy Hooker,* at long last, took her place astride the runway's white centerline. Rex, showing his first sign of tension, had prepared the crew for takeoff at least three times. Ross flashed his copilot a tight grin and—with a confident, "Here we go!"—set the brakes and ran all four engines to full takeoff power.

Ham Phillips uttered a terse, "All instruments in the green, Lieutenant." Catching the green "cleared for takeoff" light from the corner of his eye, Ross let the heavily laden bomber slip her leash. He experienced a fleeting pang of sympathy for Chaplain Smythe, standing alongside the control jeep. The sturdy figure had remained there, enveloped in a choking hurricane of gritty prop blasts, throughout the mission's departure. He held an oversized wooden cross clasped between both hands.

Ross's throat tightened with emotion, then he was forced to return his attention to the business of getting this death-defying act airborne.

Acceleration was agonizingly slow. A stolen glance at the airspeed indicator showed the needle quivering at sixty-five. Rex would start calling airspeed at eighty. Slightly less than half the runway remained. Rex spoke, but it was not to call out airspeed. "I've got number two! Son of a bitch's surging," the copilot advised in clipped tones.

Too late to abort. Ross stole another glance—this time at number two's manifold pressure gauge. Jesus Christ! Sixty inches! A few seconds of that and she'll blow a jug for sure, Ross thought. Messrs. Pratt & Whitney had never intended for their cylinders to withstand that kind of punishment. Gratefully he observed Rex ease the supercharger control downward. Then the plane's nose wheel lifted and the pounding runway dropped away beneath them. The *Happy Hooker* swept across the end of the field and buried her nose in the blinding mist. A wide grin split Ross's face—the old girl was climbing like a champion! "Gear up; flaps up," he called cheerfully.

Ross could feel his crew members shed tension as they emerged into clear, sparkling air. Through hastily donned sunglasses he picked up the squadron formation, circling lazily as the last to take off joined up. He aimed for his position, a thousand feet up and one mile behind the main formation. He would hold that position, poised to replace any ship having to return to base with mechanical problems. If there were no aborts by the time they reached the bomb line, the German coast today, Ross and Wilkinson would jettison their bomb loads and return to base. Speaking of which, where the hell *was* the other spare?

As if reading his thoughts, Mickey spoke from his rear turret. "Tail to pilot. *Winsome Winnie*'s taking up position on our left wing." Ross craned his neck in time to see Wilkinson slide his Liberator into the number three slot. He grinned at the copilot's thumbs-up signal.

This was it! he told himself, silently exultant. This was what it was all about. The frustrating months of pilot training, practice combat, separation from home and sweetheart, the ass chewings. It was all in the past. Now he was doing something worthwhile. The boy who had worried about term papers, pop quizzes, and Saturday night dates now worried about winning a contest where the rules were harsh. It was a man's world—a world only the courageous dared enter—a world in which only professionals survived.

You have what it takes, Colyer, he told himself with savage satisfaction. You've stood up to the best of them and won your point. All you have to do in this business is to know that you're right and stick to your guns—and earn a reputation. People didn't argue with a person who was regarded as tops in his field.

Corporal Leckie squatted at the radio console, its array of electronic gear representing the *Happy Hooker*'s voice to the outside world. Don't make it look too easy, he told himself. Grumble, curse the inept radio maintenance technicians; then, at the last minute, solve the problem by applying superior knowledge and technique. That would impress them, by God. He, Corporal Leckie, would save the entire crew. A modest shrug would be his only acknowledgment of their praise.

He removed a small screwdriver from his breast pocket and glanced toward Ham Phillips; the flight engineer's back was turned. A half-dozen turns to tighten a recessed screw head located on the rear of the crackle-finished black casing. A screw loosened only two hours earlier—his first act upon arriving at the airplane. The balky set came to life with a humming vibration.

A veteran at radio school had suggested the trick as a means to ground his plane to gain a night on the town. Leckie had used the trick for a more lofty purpose. He didn't even know what backing off the screw did to the circuitry, but he was assured that ground crews couldn't find the problem. He thumbed his press-to-talk switch. "Radio to pilot. I found the trouble, Lieutenant. We won't need the new set. Those idiots on the ground didn't run a resistance check. She's up and running anytime you want to use it."

Ahead and below the *Happy Hooker,* 1st Lt. Adrian Polk, flying *Iron Maiden,* applied conscientious effort to hold his ship in precise, standard formation. Proud of his selection to fly three-on-one off his wing commander's left wing, he took care that his right wingtip remained abeam of his leader's tail and even with the slender wingtip ahead. Concentrating on holding textbook formation, alas, caused him to ignore some alarming indications of disaster.

Iron Maiden's number four engine contained an insidious malignancy. Undetected, its oil filter had become clogged with gritty dirt. A bypass continued to permit unfiltered oil to enter moving parts, however. The slotted oil ring fitted into the number eight piston to supply lubricant to the cylinder wall slowly built up an accumulation of sludge. The first clue that all was not right came when the flight engineer shouted, "Number four is trying to run hot, Lieutenant. How about cracking the cowl flaps a notch?"

As the cylinder-head temperature stubbornly crept past 215 degrees, the waist gunner called a worried, "Waist to copilot. Number four is smoking quite a bit."

Disgustedly the copilot moved number four's fuel mixture control to auto-rich, muttering to a concerned flight engineer, "There, that oughtta cool her down." His words coincided with an immediate drop in indicated oil pressure. A hasty cross-check revealed the afflicted engine's oil temperature edging higher. The flight engineer never completed his transmission to the pilot: "We got a problem with—"

The laboring engine, its pounding components denied their life blood, disintegrated.

The copilot reacted immediately to Polk's command to "Feather number four!" But the order came seconds too late. Without oil pressure to hold the prop blades in a controlled position, centrifugal force drove them into a fully flat pitch. The resulting wind resistance could be compared with placing a barn door across the outer engine.

Lieutenant Polk countered the sickening lurch toward his lead ship reflexively. Applying full left aileron and rudder, he sought to avoid colliding with Colonel Deckard's *Hard Times Ahead* by dropping his nose and passing underneath. The young pilot failed to reckon with the prop blast from Deckard's number one and number two engines. The *Berlin Express,* directly beneath and leading the second element, never had a chance. Temporarily out of control, *Iron Maiden* slammed atop her sister ship's nose and cockpit. Locked together, the two heavily laden craft entered a deadly flat spin, attached to each other like two obscenely copulating insects.

Ross observed the disaster from his position one mile to the rear of and a thousand feet above the formation. Stunned, he realized a full two minutes later that the *Happy Hooker* and the *Winsome Winnie* were expected to move into the vacant slots.

Chapter Fifteen

Sergeant Ham Phillips relaxed slightly as the sun-dappled English Channel appeared in the distance, waves dancing with flashes of light. The crew was in good spirits as they descended from altitude, homeward bound. Really, Ham thought, it was more of a giddy reaction, the crushing tension of the mission draining from their tired muscles. They had acquitted themselves well. Their's had been the only squadron to hit the primary. Mickey had reported from the tail position that shit was flying in all directions down there. Even railcars and engines. Lieutenant Colyer's solution for their oxygen shortage had worked perfectly. They excitedly counted flak holes: twenty-seven.

In the nose, Leckie, Lieutenant Cryhowski, and Lieutenant Tyson argued loudly over possession of a two-inch fragment of the stuff. Lieutenant Cryhowski finally suggested a solution. The first one who could light a cigarette during descent got to keep the souvenir. They were passing through nineteen thousand feet at the time. After a protracted silence while the trio attempted to make a lighter operate in the rarified air, shouts of indignation filled the intercom.

"Foul! You can't do that! That's cheating!"

"Like hell it is," the bombardier responded gleefully.

Rex could stand it no longer. "What the hell's going on down there?"

"I just lit a cigarette at exactly eighteen thousand six hundred and forty feet," Stan explained.

"Yeah," Art added bitterly. "You know what this prick did? He loosens one side of his oxygen mask, cracks the emergency flow valve, and uses the trickle of oxygen to light a cigarette!"

"Learned that trick in bombardier school," Stan explained. "Takes a fine touch, though. Just a tad too much oh-two and you only get about two drags before she burns up."

Ham saw Lieutenant Colyer smile as he cut the banter short.

"Okay, that's enough bullshit! We're still in fighter country. We dodged the bullet on the way in, but you saw what they did to the groups ahead of us. Let's look lively and keep those guns moving."

The crew once more became all business. The pack of German fighters had circled warily at a distance on the outbound trip but apparently decided to concentrate on the leading formations. Now Ham focused his attention on the lowering sun, the place from which fighters preferred to launch an attack.

There! A dozen or so specks—just to one side of the blinding solar glare. He pressed his intercom switch. "Turret to copilot. Were we expecting a fighter escort for the return trip, Sir?"

Rex glanced at Ross, who nodded his head. "Over the Channel, turret. You got something?"

"Bandits at two o'clock, real high—in the sun, in fact. If they ain't Spits, they sure as hell look like Me 109s are supposed to look."

A hushed silence descended as all eyes strained to pick up what Ham's keen vision had observed. Stan's voice, shrill with excitement, called, "The bastards are peeling off. Here they come!"

Someone in the lead crew had been equally alert. Ross recognized Deckard's voice.

"Red Dog Formation. Bandits, two o'clock high. Let's bring the formation in—tight now. Look alive."

Frozen temporarily, Ham watched with fascination as a whirling prop disk grew in size. The premature shuddering clatter of the nose and waist guns jarred him from his paralytic state.

"Hold your fire," he snapped. "Those two are damn near a thousand yards." He licked dry lips and forced himself to follow his own advice.

The experienced enemy pilots decided to assess the mettle of their quarry. Breaking off, well out of .50-caliber range, they set up a swirling circuit around and over the now tightly knit formation. Ugly, mottled gray-green camouflage, marred only by ominous black crosses, left no doubt as to their identity—and their intentions. Raw, untested, the 866th Squadron's B-24 crews faced the deadly Me 109s.

The formation of Liberators droned straight ahead as the speedy fighters prowled around its flanks. They would launch their attacks from all directions, Ham recalled a gunnery instructor telling his class seemingly eons ago. "They'll distract the gunners and try to break up the formation."

The *Happy Hooker* was especially vulnerable. Lieutenant Colyer had drawn the last slot in the last element. And, damnit, the sons a bitches were ignoring the advance squadrons! The Red Dogs, flying tail end, had been singled out. Eyeball to eyeball with the enemy, Ham clenched his jaw muscles and waited, tracking the sharklike shapes with unwavering concentration. He discovered that he was holding his breath. He relaxed slightly, forcing himself to inhale and exhale slowly. He was surprised to hear the copilot angrily order, "Cut the chatter; keep the intercom open." The crew fell quiet; Ham realized that he hadn't heard a word.

The attack materialized with dazzling speed. Simultaneously, it seemed, the dozen attackers rolled their wingtips into vertical turns and came barreling in like a swarm of bats. A fusillade of arcing red tracers reached out to meet them. Ham felt himself flinch involuntarily as little orange sparks signaled incoming fire from the 109s' cannon.

Almost as soon as it started, the firing ceased. Ham took time to scan the formation. Not quite as precise as before, but all nine ships appeared unscathed. Ahead and to the left he spotted the fighters climbing in graceful curves to a new vantage point: They too appeared to have escaped without serious damage. Is it possible, Ham thought, that so much firepower could be unleashed with no visible result? The smell of hot metal and gun oil caused him to examine his twin Brownings. He didn't remember ever firing them. What made the thing so unreal was the relative quiet. More than a hundred guns must have been firing at once. Other than a subdued clattering from the *Happy Hooker*'s own armament, the engagement could have taken place in a vacuum.

Their respite was brief—only enough time for the a/c to ask, "Everybody all right? We take any hits?"

"Tail okay. Looks like some minor damage to the left rudder."

"Radio okay."

A silence.

"Waist, you okay?" Lieutenant Colyer barked.

"Uh, Sir, this is Dirkson. Dutch doesn't have his headset on just now."

"Well, why not? Is he all right?"

"Sir, I think he's pretty shook up. He wants to bail out."

"Good God. Stop him, Dirkson. Do whatever you have to, but get him back on that gun, hear? We'll straighten this out on the ground."

Guenther's plight was forgotten with the sound of someone shouting over the intercom. "Here they come again! Eleven o'clock, nine o'clock—hell, from everywhere!"

As if from outside himself, Ham watched the attack develop. Apparently the strategy this time was for the German fighters to concentrate their firepower toward the lightly armed nose positions of their prey. Ham selected one of the oncoming enemy and followed its path as the pilot broke from his firing pass to disappear underneath. The grim-faced engineer wheeled his turret and waited for the target to reappear behind. Sure enough, the snarling fighter streaked by in a steep climb from below, the pilot already searching the sky above.

The German was out of accurate range, but Ham recalled his dad teaching him how to snap-shoot quail. Ignoring his computing gunsight, Ham squeezed off three quick, instinctively aimed bursts above and ahead of his quarry. The lazily arcing tracers were placed precisely where he wanted them. The ghost of his first gunnery instructor had arrived to perch on his shoulder. "Given an option, fighter pilots tend to break left when in trouble. You see, torque created by that big prop makes a turn to the left easier to control. Plus, most landing patterns are to the left, so they just get into the habit."

While the enemy pilot was still deciding on a course of evasive action, Ham moved his aim slightly left and down from the path taken by his previous bursts. He clamped his thumbs to the firing trips and held them there. The startled pilot broke hard left—directly into the path of a solid hail of .50-caliber fire. Ham's continuous stream of armor-piercing projectiles arrived just in time to rake the speeding fighter from nose to tail.

The pilot died with the stick clutched full back. The agile 109's nose rose to a vertical position, then, as the aircraft lost flying speed, it dropped into a rolling spin.

Lieutenant Russell Duckworth of Chicago, Illinois, had no place to escape: The tumbling fighter struck just aft of his left wing root. The explosion—and fireball that followed—consumed both craft as if they were caught in the maw of a blast furnace.

No one saw any parachutes as bomber crews watched the planes fall apart like scorched glass in a hideous kaleidoscope.

Major Claude Ellis leaned against the iron-pipe guardrail surrounding the tower platform, his lips pressed into a thin line. Another long, hard look to the north and he lowered the binoculars to resume pacing.

"Shouldn't be long now, Major."

The tower operator, face inscrutable behind dark sunglasses, slouched before his radio console. Lighting a cigarette, he added, "We usually get a radio call before we can see anything. Dunno, though, not as much haze as usual just now."

Ellis seemed not to hear. "Where in the hell did you find those cigarettes? They smell like wet rope."

The impassive sergeant ignored the rebuke. "Turkish, Sir," he replied. "Sort of acquired a taste for 'em."

"Well . . ." The impatient ops officer's voice trailed off as he lost interest in the conversation. Raising the binoculars, he scanned the horizon once more. His anxiety had started with the failure of the airborne spares—or any aborted birds they would have replaced—to return. Oh, well. Maybe they had filled in for someone dropping out of one of the other squadrons. The cryptic strike message, relayed by HF radio, had consisted of the code "MA" for mission accomplished. That was good. It meant that the bombing results were at least satisfactory. But his uneasiness persisted.

Below his vantage point, every ear was cocked for the sound of engines; eyes turned to the north with increasing frequency as the empty roost waited for its birds to return.

At last, long-awaited words squawked from the tower's tinny loudspeaker. "Wolfpack Tower, this is Red Dog Leader. Ten miles east. Request landing for formation."

Those close to the open doorway heard the squadron leader's cryptic message and the word spread. Even as the tower operator provided landing instructions, ground crews were piling into trucks and racing for their parking hardstands. Inside the briefing hut, intelligence officers prepared to meet and debrief the returning crews. The mess hall bustled with activity. On a more somber note, the flight surgeon hoisted himself aboard a waiting ambulance; firefighters donned their bulky asbestos suits.

There they were! Ellis glued his glasses to the dark specks that gradually turned into tiny crosses. One, two—four, five: The first two elements were minus one, but holding tight formation, he noted with pride. Then he spotted the rear element, lagging behind: One, two . . . Stragglers, not even attempting to fly formation. Each had a propeller in the feathered position. He was still searching for four missing airplanes as the lead element swept overhead. The rear wingman racked his plane into a tight turn onto an abbreviated downwind. As the remaining ships peeled behind him at twenty-second intervals, Ellis descended from the tower and started his jeep. A worried frown puckered his brow as he observed a red flare emerge from two of the landing aircraft. Wounded aboard. And four ships missing?

Lieutenant Colonel Eric Deckard dropped to the ground and reached back inside for his gear. General Sprague had preceded him, striding wordlessly to his waiting staff car. Ellis noticed that Deckard's usually vibrant, cherubic features sagged with fatigue and—was there something else? Ellis stepped forward and relieved his weary commander of flight kit, oxygen mask, and chute harness. Deckard still had not spoken. Tossing the recovered items into the rear of his jeep, Ellis could contain himself no longer. "Good to see you on the ground, Colonel. How did it go?"

Deckard swung into the right seat and stripped a cigar. As Ellis supplied a light from his Zippo, the colonel confirmed his worst fears. "Bad. We lost three. Maybe four. We think Eubanks may have made it to a base on the coast."

Ellis stopped short of starting the jeep. "Three? Good Christ, how? This was supposed to be a milk run."

"A midair got two. Polk and Askew. Then on the way home, we got jumped by 109s."

"And they got two more?" Ellis asked in astonishment.

"Bet your ass. There were about a dozen of them, and it wasn't a bunch of green kids flying them. Had to be some of Goering's best. We got one; they got a couple—Duckworth and Eubanks. One Kraut son of a bitch came barrel-rolling, out of control, right through our formation after he got hit. Took Duckworth head on; he blew up. The last I saw of Eubanks, he was over the Channel with two feathered. He should have made the coast."

Ellis recovered sufficiently to start the jeep. Nothing more was said until they parked in front of the briefing room. "How was the flak? I saw a couple land with engines shut down."

"There was flak, all right. Light, but deadly accurate. Of course, we were the only ones they had for a target. Dumb-ass lead squadrons flew into broken clouds. They couldn't see the fucking target, so they didn't drop. Can you believe it? Nate caught the goof, flew around the stuff, and we bombed the primary all by our lonesome. The others hit the secondary. I think we creamed the marshalling yards, though. We'll have strike photos developed by the time debriefing is over."

Conversation lapsed as Deckard withdrew his trombone mouthpiece from a zippered pocket and softly blew a few notes of New Orleans jazz.

The pair joined the end of a line straggling into the briefing room, Deckard pausing to take his postmission shot of liquor. A smiling flight surgeon dispensed a choice of scotch or bourbon while attempting to joke with the dispirited fliers. Most just accepted the offering and tossed it back without comment.

Deckard faced an audience vastly different from the cocky, self-confident group that had gathered at 0430. Still stunned by their losses, most sat without expression as, without preamble, he stated, "Well, we won't be going back to Dortmund anytime soon. We don't have strike pictures developed yet, but we had a good pattern right on the main point of impact. In general, we gave a good accounting of ourselves. There's sure as hell no reason to apologize to that bunch up there at Division. Should be the other way around, if anything."

The first hint of a chuckle rippled among the assembled crew members. "And you got a chance to see your first German fighters. I hope you were impressed, because we'll be seeing more of them. That I can guarantee. Anyway, that rumor intelligence passed on about Goering moving in more crack fighter outfits is no longer a rumor. We won't know who gets credit for the kill until it's confirmed, but it was some damn good shooting." Deckard's last comment prompted a faint, ragged "Yeah."

"We paid a price, a high price—a third of our mission force. It's a tragic part of fighting a war, however. Midairs need not happen, but they do. Formation flying is terribly unforgiving of error. You pilots just have to remain aware of what's going on around you, from takeoff to touchdown. And, while we're on the subject, we drew those fighters because we let our formation loosen up. One of the old heads from the B-17s tried to tell us. We had to learn the hard way. Okay, get your individual crew debriefing, chow down, and hit the sack. Close-formation practice starts again tomorrow afternoon. General, do you have anything to add?"

"You're goddamn right, I have something to add." Sprague's face was a furious mask. "The 7th Wing looked like a bunch of bear cubs trying to jack off out there today. Tomorrow I get to go to Division headquarters and explain how the 866th managed to lose more than a third of its number. I was just handed a message, by the way. The fourth airplane crash-landed on the coast and burned. Two men died in the fire."

Ross's face tightened at the news. He barely heard the angry wing commander's next words. "We were able to hit one, I repeat, only one of those damned fighters. I'll have more to say to squadron commanders later." He stalked from the room without a backward glance.

The *Happy Hooker*'s crew was next to last to sit down with Major Ellis, who was helping out with the crew debriefers. Ellis fit a clean form on his clipboard and grinned. "Well, if it isn't the killer crew. Two other crews have already confirmed your kill, Sergeant Phillips. Congratulations. Have to have you give the others some lessons. Now, Sergeant, what can you tell me about the kill? What kind of attack pattern did the enemy fly? What were the markings? How many fighters did you count, altogether? . . .

Ham Phillips faced his interrogator with a stony lack of expression. What could he tell the major about it? Was the major interested in knowing how it felt, in effect, to kill nine of your friends? That scene would be burned into his mind forever. The sick "No—no—for Christ's sake, no!" as he'd realized that Lieutenant Duckworth could not possibly evade the stricken German fighter.

Ellis waited for Ham's response.

So what is it you want me to tell you about "how it was" Major of the Air Force Ellis? Ham thought. That I was thrilled and elated with my demonstration of superior marksmanship? How excited I was to see one of the enemy spin, crash, and burn—taking nine of our own with him? How proud that I didn't lose my nerve, like Guenther did? Well, it wasn't that way, not that way at all. Maybe you would rather I told you how I puked up my guts on the hardstand after we landed.

Phillips spoke at last. A brief, unemotional account of the incident. Ross was perhaps the only one among the current hero's elated fellow crew members to observe his inner turmoil. He wasn't sure, but he thought he understood.

Ross, stumbling with fatigue, proceeded to the hut he shared with Eubanks and his officer crew. Two hadn't survived the fire. Who? He observed Chaplain Smythe standing beside a six-by-six in front of the Nissen hut shared by Duckworth and his officers. The sober-faced chaplain was supervising a half-dozen enlisted men engaged in removing footlockers and duffel bags from inside. Ross paused and watched. The big truck was already half filled. My God, did you ever get used to this? The Eighth Air Force tour of duty was twenty-five missions. He had one. Entering their quarters, he found Rex, Stan, and Art sitting on their bunks. Still in flight suits, they were staring at the empty beds belonging to Eubanks's still-absent crew.

Reed, Guenther, and Dirkson were already sprawled on their bunks when a dispirited Sergeant Phillips entered the dank, gloom-filled enlisted men's hut. Reed was engaged in his favorite pasttime—baiting Private Guenther.

"What th' fuck did you think you were doing, you Kraut asshole? Bail out over Germany, f'Chrissake? What the hell, you expecting maybe to find a goddamn relative down there?"

Guenther, his face pinched and with white lines framing his mouth, didn't respond. Reaching into the musette bag beneath his bunk, he extracted a Hershey bar and consumed it in three bites.

Ham collapsed on his own bunk with a disgusted, "Oh, knock it off, Mickey. Stay off Dutch's back for once. Everybody gets the clanks now and then. Your time will come—bet on it."

"Hmmph," Reed snorted disdainfully. "Maybe. But I'm not stupid, f'Chrissake. I don't care how bad it gets inside the airplane—it's bound to be a helluva lot worse outside. How come they was in such a big hurry to get Eubanks's guys' stuff out of here? Goddamn. They don't know for sure that they're not coming back. Besides, Gus told me if anything ever happened to him, I was to get that silver cigarette case he won in the crap game last payday. Well," he pulled on a pair of sneakers, "I'm gonna run around the perimeter. Eight hours cramped into that little bitty turret gets to the old leg muscles." Reed departed, whistling and with a spring to his step.

Guenther's venom-filled gaze followed the arrogant tail gunner. "Someday I'm gonna kill that big son of a bitch," he muttered without conviction. When there was no response, he continued, "Wonder what Lieutenant Colyer's gonna say to me?"

There were no celebrations in the officers' and NCO clubs that night—only a forced show of bravado by some, and angry resentment at General Sprague's caustic words. The missing crews were barely mentioned. There were no maudlin toasts. The 866th had seen the elephant.

12 May 1943
Munich, Germany

Kurt stared earnestly into the violet depths of his fiancée's eyes. "Go, Gretta, my dearest. Tomorrow, if possible. Switzerland is the only possible sanctuary. My second cousin and his wife in Bern will provide a place for you to stay. I will give you a letter."

"But Kurt, I don't understand," the lissome, dark-haired girl replied. "The news film at the cinema tonight. Your father and others at the party for you last night. We are winning the war, my darling. You heard."

"I heard nothing but lies, Gretta. We are *not* winning this war, we are losing it. On all fronts. Father's hero, *Herr* Goebbels, is feeding the German people nothing but tripe." Kurt's voice was grim as he took both of Gretta's hands in his. His mind still reeled from the enormity of the deception being perpetrated by his nation's leaders.

The welcome home party. His father's boastful introduction presenting him as a hero of the eastern front—a fighter ace (which he wasn't); his sister Elise's new husband—a smirking, corpulent major in the SS—confiding "secret" tidbits designed to titillate his unsuspecting audience. Westphalian ham, caviar from Romania, champagne "liberated"

from France—all served by the Nazi party faithful while the general
public fought for scraps of fresh meat, butter, and ersatz coffee.

Kurt ignored their waiter's throat-clearing hints and poured more
wine. Closing time had passed, but one didn't eject a *Luftwaffe* pilot
with the Knight's Cross dangling from a multicolored ribbon. "I finally
rejoined JG-89 after I was shot down," he said softly, staring into space.
"We had withdrawn a hundred kilometers to the northwest. We were
reduced to two squadrons of a dozen planes each. I barely recognized
my unit. *Feldwebel* Merschatt, my crew chief, was there. Major Eckert,
Leutnant Gratzman—most of the old "Tigers"—were still around,
except Feldwebel Lipfert, the man who taught me all I know about
fighter tactics. He crashed and burned only a week after I went down.
He was flying a plane with a faulty prop control. There was no
replacement part on the field and no time to install it if one had existed."
Kurt's voice carried a bitter edge.

"Youngsters, mere boys, were replacing our losses. Some had as
little as sixty hours' total flying time. I was made leader of a *schwarm*
and promoted to *oberleutnant*. But hunting was no longer on our terms.
The Russians grew more powerful by the day. New airplanes—from
the Americans—faster and better armed than the Stormoviks and Lavochkins
we were used to. Hit and run—evade engagement when the odds were
one-sided, as they usually were. Flying airplanes that would have been
scrapped only months before. I managed nine victories, one short of
becoming an ace, before I was reassigned."

"Kurt, this is terrible," Gretta whispered with shocked disbelief. "I—
we had no idea. . . ."

"*Ach, nein,* of course you didn't. And still don't. Furthermore, if
I were to try to convince my father, and others, of the truth, the Gestapo
would come calling. That is why you must go, my darling. Bombs will
fall on Munich before the year is out. Yes," he continued as Gretta
uttered a cry of dismay, "all too soon. That is why I was reassigned.
Major Eckert called six of us into the command-post bunker that
afternoon. 'Goering and Hitler have shifted our major effort to defending the Fatherland,' he told us. He was angrier than I had ever seen
him. 'The defense force requires skilled pilots, expert gunners, leaders.'

"The Americans have based heavy bombers—Flying Fortresses and
Liberators—in England, *liebchen*. They are already penetrating the
German homeland—Kiel, Bremen, Cologne—one raid as deep as Frankfurt.
They are escorted partway by a new American fighter, the Lightning.

While not equal to our newest 109s or the Focke-Wulf 190, they nevertheless disrupt our patterns. The Americans bomb by day, the British by night. These are not obsolete Russian airplanes flown by inept Russian pilots. Their numbers will continue to increase, unless we can make their losses so high that they must change tactics.

"That is the reason for my new assignment, dear Gretta." Kurt drained his wine and signaled for the check. "I leave for my new base day after tomorrow. Our degree of success remains to be seen. That is why I will rest easy only after I know you are safe in a neutral country. Speak of this to no one, but go, I beg of you. Our life together doesn't appear to have a bright outlook, I fear. I promise to do my best, but for Germany I see nothing but tragedy."

Chapter Sixteen

9 June 1943
Aschaffenburg, Germany

"Achtung, achtung! Indianers!" Heads raised in the pilots' ready room of 4 *Staffel, Jagdgeschwader* 21, as the ornate Grundig radio set blared its strident message. Kurt Heintze turned to his wingman, *Oberstabsfeldwebel* Anton Stepinac, with a weary smile. "Three times this week. How do they do it? Do they never rest? Two days ago, twenty of those devils were shot down over Kiel—and they return for more punishment."

"That is because they are fools," the dark, energetic Stepinac replied with a savage scowl. An expatriate Slav, the spirited, impulsive Stepinac was always spoiling for a fight. Lantern-jawed, with a chronic shadow of black beard, he hurled his fighter into the fray with the abandon of a hungry wolf.

"I'm giving you that wild Slav for taming, Kurt," his *staffelkapitän, Hauptmann* Fritz Bümen, had told him. "He's a good enough pilot but he lacks air discipline. Take him under your wing and make a fighter pilot of him." Kurt, recalling his early mistakes, took pride in his record of having yet to lose a wingman. That he would continue his string with Stepinac was questionable, however.

"Use patience, Toni," he implored. "You are not driving a tank. You say you learned guerrilla tactics under General Mihailovich. Use them. Avoid those tightly bunched formations. Look for single stragglers, ships out of position."

His instructions fell on deaf ears. Tactics against the big bomber formations differed from engaging Russian fighter-bombers. Wingmen broke off to attack singly, in trail. Stepinac was unable to ignore the tempting, fat target offered by box formations. Already he had lost three airplanes. Two shot to pieces as he dove, head-on, into the bristling guns of massed Flying Fortresses. The third had simply shed its wings after the ferocious Chetnik pressed his 109 beyond its structural limits. Today a strip of gauze adorned his battered forehead—badge of his last parachute exit.

The buzz of idle conversation ceased as *Hauptmann* Bümen strode into the ready room and crossed to the big wall map. "Very well," he announced without preamble, "a 'Fat Dog' just crossed the coastline at Emden. First estimate places the size at two hundred bombers. *Jagdgeschwader* 4 has scrambled and will attack shortly. We are in luck today." His eyes glittered with anticipation. "Eastern Germany is under solid cloud cover. They are committed to targets west of Hanover. My guess is the Frankfurt area."

The bouncy, energetic captain faced his pilots with unconcealed glee. Selected by *Reichsmarschall* Goering himself to lead one of his personal squadrons, Bümen, with his red-nosed craft, was locked in a deadly struggle with *Hauptmann* Rostock, leader of the yellow-nosed ships in 2 *Staffel,* for the title of Best *Luftwaffe* Fighter Unit. His men were the best. His priority for aircraft and parts, unchallenged. Even the accommodations were superior to the tent-surrounded grass strips endured by those with less status.

This morning his pilots lounged on leather-upholstered sofas, their booted feet propped on low, Italian-made antique tables. Sun streamed through tall windows forming one wall of the abandoned castle appropriated for the use of 4 *Staffel*. An urn dispensing scarce, genuine coffee rested on a heavy Bavarian sideboard—flanked by bottles of cognac and schnapps. An original oil painting of Adolf Hitler, hung above the sideboard, grimly exhorted those of faint heart to give their all for the Fatherland.

"I suggest you eat an early lunch and be prepared for takeoff in one hour. The force will be within our reach by then and their escort will have turned back. We should have time for two sorties. Hunting will be excellent."

Kurt wished he could share his leader's optimism. The big, four-engine bombers were not, in Bümen's words, "excellent hunting." They bristled with heavy machine guns and they were devilishly hard to shoot down. Seldom did one firing pass result in a kill. Kurt had seen ships with two engines feathered, gaping holes in wings and fuselage, and trailing black oil and smoke struggle to the target and dump their deadly loads. The professional pilot in Kurt had to admire the courage of the American airmen.

A dozen of the assembled pilots stood, then strolled away as Bümen finished speaking—some to tidy up personal effects before they faced an increasingly tenacious enemy, some to commune with a protective God whom a dedicated Fascist could not publicly admit to knowing, some to make last-minute checks of plane and equipment. A few hoped to do no more than evacuate their bowels in the solitary comfort of a heated latrine.

Kurt approached the departing squadron leader. "Sir, may I speak with you a moment?"

"Of course, *Leutnant* Heintze." Bümen smiled. "Are you going to add a half-dozen Forts to your record today?"

"You flatter me, *Herr Hauptmann*," Kurt replied with a shy grin. "The American bombers are more difficult to destroy than the Russian Il-2. Different techniques are called for, and this is what I wish to discuss. If you would step over here, Sir?" He waved Stepinac and *Feldwebels* Moeller and Weiss, the other two pilots assigned to his *schwarm,* to join him and Bümen in a far corner of the room. Pointing to two oversized models suspended from the ceiling—one a B-17, the other a B-24—Kurt waited until he had their undivided attention. "Observe the fields of fire, please." He tapped white cones attached to each gun position. The others nodded; these models had been the object of repeated study by the pilots charged with destruction of the full-sized versions.

"Our basic tactic has been to fly the standard pursuit curve against gaps between the tail and fuselage guns, approaching from beneath at a thirty-degree deflection." Kurt paused as the others nodded in agreement. "This works quite well for a solitary plane, but when we attack a massed formation, observe what happens." He used a flattened hand to simulate an attacking fighter. "As the attack is broken off, our ships are exposed to as many as ten of their machine guns, providing our underbelly as a target. We move in the same direction as the bombers, so our relative speed is greatly reduced. This is the point at which we suffer our greatest number of losses."

"That is why we shifted to a head-on pass," Moeller observed.

"True," Kurt said. "And what happened? The Americans are adding guns to their nose positions. We are once again exposing ourselves to heavy fire after we break off.

"Consider," Kurt continued, his features curling into a wolfish grin, "our 20mm cannon has twice the effective range of their .50 calibers. If we stay with the head-on attack, we must complete our firing pass and escape before entering their cones of fire."

"Then *we* shoot at distances too great for accuracy," *Feldwebel* Weiss objected. "By the time we close to a thousand meters, fire, roll, and split-S, we are among them."

"Not if we fire from an inverted position!" Kurt's eyes glittered with excitement as he watched the three pilots' shocked reaction. "We roll, open fire at a thousand meters, hold for exactly three seconds, then break straight down. The American gunners will have less than a second to aim and fire within their effective range—and it will be a difficult deflection shot at that.

"We, on the other hand, will be firing straight ahead. This improves accuracy. Also, by attacking their lead ships, we will disrupt their formations—loosen them up—create stragglers."

"*Gott im Himmel,* Kurt! You would have us flying upside down, straight at a dozen bombers, and firing at the same time? We will disrupt their formation all right—when we crash head-on," said *Feldwebel* Weiss, shaking his head in dismay.

"It will require split-second timing," Kurt conceded, "but it reduces your chances of being shot down while limping away from a conventional attack. Your closing will be in the vicinity of two hundred meters per second. Open fire with your cannon at maximum range, fire a controlled burst, and break. I will be the first to attempt it. Who will follow me?"

Stepinac's face lit up with anticipation. His "I will be right behind you" came as no surprise to Kurt. It was his obstreperous wingman's favorite tactic: Press the attack right down the enemy's throat. Moeller and Weiss exchanged nervous glances, then gave *Hauptmann* Bümen a questioning look.

"I will permit it," the stocky commander said at last. "Don't attempt the maneuver unless you are fully confident that you can execute it perfectly. We have not had an opportunity to practice it, but the theory is sound."

The pair of dubious pilots flushed. The *hauptmann*'s tone implied they lacked nerve. "We will follow your lead, *Herr Leutnant*," *Feldwebel* Weiss responded stiffly.

Kurt slapped each on the shoulder and smiled encouragement. *"Hals und beinbruch!"* he admonished them cheerfully. The pair responded to Kurt's traditional good-luck wish to "break an arm and a leg" with wry good humor.

Bümen laid a restraining hand on Kurt's forearm as the others trooped off. "Kurt," the grizzled veteran wore a worried look, "I must speak to you."

"Jawohl, Herr Hauptmann," Kurt replied. He had the utmost respect for their commanding officer. Like his *gruppenkommandeur* in Russia, Major Eckert, Bümen had been blooded in Spain. He lagged behind Eckert in kills, his action having occurred in North Africa and now Europe. But there was no doubting his ability as a killer. Bümen's greatest concern was that age and his ever-increasing bulk were making it difficult to squeeze into the confines of the 109's cramped cockpit.

"I applaud your aggressiveness, but . . ." He hesitated. "I must tell you that your fame as a hunter has spread to the English and American fliers. The rapidity with which you have been racking up kills since your arrival last month from the east is becoming legendary. Your picture, receiving the Oak Leaves to your Knight's Cross from the *Führer* himself last week, is being circulated in their ready rooms. It is not enough that they recognize the *reichsmarschall*'s squadrons as being a formidable force—they refer to us as the 'Abbeville Kids' —but *you* are identified by name. It is known that you fly a ship with black and silver spirals on the prop hub. More than that, you are associated with that distinctive blue falcon painted on the nose. You will receive their undivided attention so long as you display those markings."

Kurt returned Bümen's look with a quiet, "Are you ordering me to remove them, *Herr Hauptmann?*"

Bümen hesitated. Wise in the ways of fighter pilots, he knew the importance placed on talismans. "I would not so order, Kurt. I can only remind you that the already considerable risk you run is increased so long as you flaunt your superior airmanship. One more thing—this propensity you have of attacking without the backup of your comrades. Wingmen can provide only so much cover."

Kurt frowned. "I learned on the eastern front that scattered, surprise attacks are more productive than the massed frontal attacks advocated by General Galland. I will follow your orders, *Herr Hauptmann,* but I prefer to hunt alone, not in a pack."

"Very well," Bümen said with a sigh. "I can hardly argue with your record, but I worry. Don't disappoint me." There was no effort to mask his concerned affection for the blond young man. He liked to think he saw glimpses of his former self in *Leutnant* Kurt Heintze.

Kurt, "on the perch" at thirty thousand feet, led his four-ship *schwarm* in a lazy orbit. He fixed his position by the city of Dortmund, a hazy sprawl of dun-colored buildings and factory smokestacks. The fighter was near its upper limit of performance, responding mushily to the controls. Kurt wished for one of the newer Me 109s with methanol injection. They were reported to fly as well at thirty thousand as at twenty. No matter, the bombers were reported to be at twenty-four. His altitude would give him time to build up maximum speed in their dive to attack.

Where were they? Dortmund represented the extreme limit of his radius of action. They would have no more than twenty minutes before they would have to break for home and more fuel.

He switched to the radio frequency used by *Jagdgeschwader* 4, which should presently be engaged with the invading air armada. He wasn't in time to hear more than interplane conversation as the spent fighters raced for their base at Antwerp. His attention sharpened. The next voice was that of Gold Eleven, the Ju 88 surveillance plane. Stripped of all excess weight, the speedy ship was launched early in an attack to pace the enemy bomber stream and report its altitude, location, and direction.

What Kurt heard caused him to frown. The lead group was at twenty-two thousand. That was good, but the formation had changed direction and was heading for Dortmund. It appeared that the target was not going to be Frankfurt. The remainder of the squadron loafed to the south, ready to harass the bomber formation on its anticipated route to Frankfurt. They would see no action today. The change in targets further reduced his time for engagement. Oh, well. He would land and refuel at the *Jagdgeschwader* 4 base. He allowed his *schwarm* to drift north-ward, straining to pick up the American formations.

Kurt saw flak bursts before he saw the bombers. The lead group emerged from an indistinct background of green and brown terrain, its camouflage blending perfectly. The formation appeared to be in a turn, skirting the closely bunched bursts of antiaircraft fire. The maneuver told Kurt that they would shortly make another turn to line up for the bomb run. Perfect. Turns invariably caused neophyte crews to slide out of position. He would pounce before they could regroup. He formed a mental picture of his position in relationship to the sun. Again, perfect. The four lurking fighters would be seen as mere specks against its brassy glare. He pumped a clenched fist above his head, signaling the others to arm their guns.

The ponderous formation of bombers swung into a turn toward the west. Kurt could see that they were Flying Fortresses. He counted thirty and frowned. Apparently *Jagdgeschwader* 4 had not scored significantly. His frown deepened. The ships remained tightly bunched as they swung onto what had to be their bomb run. The Amis were learning!

Kurt nodded in respect at the display of skilled airmanship. All right. He would wait. He had learned patience on the eastern front. According to the first sighting, more than a hundred of the raiders had yet to make their appearance. He led the *schwarm* into another orbit.

A second group appeared farther east. Its leader apparently had no intention of running the gauntlet of flak greeting the first group. This formation was obviously missing some ships, but it still maintained a tight, formidable box of heavily armed B-17s. Then Kurt's pulse quickened. Yet another target swam into view—widely spaced and well off course. His face became a frozen mask. With the stick in its furthermost position forward and to the left, Kurt's 109 streaked toward its prey.

A backward glance confirmed that his wingmen were following in trail. Concentrating on the lead element, he sensed the controls shudder with protest at the screaming, full-throttle dive. He glanced at the airspeed indicator; it was well into the red zone. Kurt eased off power and commenced a sweeping turn toward the oncoming bomber for-mation. Crunching g forces drove him deeper into the bucket seat. His conviction that the enemy gunners would be sweeping the skies above and behind gave him renewed confidence.

Kurt leveled off at twenty-two thousand. He had judged his turn precisely. Black crosses with translucent disks representing whirling propellers filled the center of his windscreen. Christ, they were closing fast! Left pressure on the stick. The speeding fighter spun to an inverted position with lightning quickness. Forward pressure on the stick to hold the nose level. His reflective gunsight was filled with the nose of the leading bomber. It was time. He thumbed the red firing button and caught a glimpse of golf ball–sized red tracers. Some impacted squarely on target. He hauled the stick into his gut and prayed. "God, let me miss a collision," he murmured.

The checkered landscape of Dortmund's suburban sprawl blurred past as Kurt recovered from his vertical descent. Then he was hurtling straight up, the altimeter winding toward twenty-six thousand. He pressed forward on the stick, rolling to observe what was happening. His heart leaped. A brown and green shape was twisting earthward. A second one, outboard engine on fire and faltering, slid from the right side of the formation. Stepinac had scored as well! He throttled back and let the others join up. They had enough fuel left for at least one more pass.

Stepinac joined his right wing, waving his arms wildly. Where were Weiss and Moeller? Kurt caught sight of a spiraling, smoking shape out of the corner of his eye. Small. It was a 109. Shock almost made him miss the sight of red tracers, like hot coals, arcing past his right wing. Kurt swiveled his head and saw Stepinac's familiar ship enveloped in red and yellow flame. Good Christ, they had been bounced! But by whom? The American Thunderbolt escort was limited to a range that ended just inside the coastline. Instinctively he slammed the stick down and to the left in a negative g break.

Twisting and turning, Kurt headed for the checkered landscape below. Frantic glimpses to his right and left revealed his pursuit to be four twin-engined, twin-tailed craft. American P-38s! They were easily recognizable. He searched his memory for words and images from aircraft-recognition classes. He recalled that the big ships had far greater range than the Spits and Thunderbolts. They were heavily armed and difficult to knock down, but, he also recalled, they were less maneuverable and had a slower rate of climb than the 109.

Kurt's confidence returned as he hurtled earthward. He should be able to evade them easily. Faith in his ability to escape unscathed was shaken, however, by his next glance at the overhead mirror: The fork-tailed devils were gaining; they were outdiving him! Very well, he would turn south and head for home—lead them deeper into lethal skies. Their endurance couldn't be unlimited. A stream of red tracers past his left wing caused him to abruptly discontinue his turn.

Kurt waited until individual details of the terrain were discernible before hauling back sharply on the control stick. The 109's slender wings groaned and the gray beginnings of blackout blurred his vision. Could the heavier Lightnings pull up in time? Streaking west, throttle to the firewall, on the deck, barely above treetop level, Kurt stole another glance at his mirror. The Lightnings' pilots had anticipated the pullout. These were not inexperienced aviators.

Their leader had divided them into pairs. One flight roosted above and slightly behind on his right wing, another on his left. He was boxed.

The Lightnings had taken away his favorite escape maneuver—the sudden, rolling pitch straight down. Lessons he'd learned in Russia flashed before him. Do the unexpected. A sharp turn right and squeeze off a short burst. There was no chance of a hit, but the sight of tracers often unnerved the foe—caused him to make a mistake.

An immediate stream of fire from the hotly pursuing craft proved the folly of that attempt. Nevertheless, Kurt repeated the move, turning left this time. The response was the same. Kurt recalled Bümen's words, ". . . you can expect to receive their undivided attention. . . ."

His mind racing with possible options, Kurt saw the Rhine River flash beneath him. He was in France. A crash landing could very possibly place him in the hands of French Resistance fighters—a fate to be avoided at all costs. Then his decision was made for him: A winking red light on the lower right corner of his instrument panel told him he was nearly out of fuel. Evasion with honor—returning home with his aircraft intact and unscathed—was out of the question. Now he was fighting just to stay alive. Kurt drew a deep breath and hauled the stick to its rearmost limits.

The agile fighter's nose lurched straight up, rate-of-climb indicator on the peg. He held his breath. If one of his four adversaries had reacted in the necessary split-second interval, Kurt could expect to be raked by the four .50-caliber machine guns and one 20mm cannon that he knew the Lightning carried in its nose. The opportunity passed. Kurt waited until he was approaching stall speed, then flipped to inverted flight and released the canopy. Snapping his seat belt open, he watched his feet float from the deck of the upside-down cockpit. Framed briefly against blue sky, he entered a tumbling, spiraling fall. He counted to ten and pulled the D-ring on his parachute.

The sharp pressure he felt as leg straps bit into his groin told him that the canopy had deployed. Swinging wildly, he searched the suddenly silent skies for his attackers. Two of them were in a tight turn, returning to the scene. He could hear the deep snarl of their Allison in-line engines. He faced the deadly oncoming threat with no small amount of trepidation. Shooting down parachuting airmen was an unspoken violation of civilized warfare. He laughed in spite of himself. Did the Americans, newly involved in the war, observe this contradiction in terms—"civilized warfare"? Then the pair of avenging fighters was upon him.

Involuntarily, he closed his eyes and spoke aloud into the rushing wind, "Gretta, my darling, if you grieve, do so for a lost cause, not for a lost lover—"

Chapter Seventeen

9 June 1943
Walden Abbey

Ross stood apart from the team of crash-rescue and medical technicians as they removed what remained of 2d Lt. Arthur Tyson from the *Happy Hooker*'s shattered nose compartment.

"Okay, we gotta have more room. Take that crash ax and cut away the rest of this Plexiglas panel," a voice from inside called.

A slicker-clad man standing alongside the jagged opening, which revealed a tangle of wires and tubing, accomplished the task with noisy precision. Gloved hands reached inside to extract the laden stretcher.

"Wait a minute," a second voice inside mumbled, "there's so many of these goddamn shell casings on the floor, I can't hardly stand up."

Someone had mercifully covered the remains with a rubberized black tarp. A limp hand, with leather flying gauntlet still in place, dangled beneath the protective sheath. "Easy, now," said one of the men. "Hank, get the fuck over here and give us a hand."

Stan, unmindful of the steady, soaking drizzle, sat at the edge of the PSP hardstand, head resting on forearms crossed on his knees. The remainder of the crew mingled under the wing with the huddled ground crew, scuffing the rain-slicked surface with their flying boots and mumbling meaningless phrases. Rex had been the first to depart in the boxy OD ambulance—his face white with shock, his lower leg fixed in a hastily devised splint.

So this is what it's like to die in combat, Ross mumbled to himself. Why don't I feel grief? Remorse? He watched woodenly as the second ambulance drove slowly away. There was no need for haste; its destination was the morgue.

A blank-faced team of maintenance specialists descended on the crippled bomber. "No big deal," Ross overheard one say. "No structural damage. I'll need a sheet-metal crew first thing. Get this inside cleaned out before we start on the hydraulic and electrical systems. Tell the lieutenant it'll be two days at the outside."

Captain Hurd, the intelligence officer assigned to debrief the *Happy Hooker*'s crew, scanned the drawn, strained faces assembled around him. Their expressions were all too familiar. It wasn't the first time he'd had to face men who had just seen a buddy reduced to a limp, bloody, inanimate object. There was little to be gained just now. He would check off the mandatory boxes and release the slack-faced crewmen to cope with the situation as best they might.

"Unless you have something new or different about fighter markings or tactics, I won't take up any more time," he said. "Questions? Comments?"

Stan raised his head. "It was a new kind of Me 109," he replied softly. "There were only four of them. Their noses were painted red. They just kept coming—straight at us, but flying inverted. My goddamn gun jammed. I don't know, maybe I could have made him break off if I'd been firing at him. It's funny, you know. If I hadn't been squatting down trying to get that jammed round out of the track—that 20mm shell had my name on it, for Christ's sake.

"I'll know that son of a bitch if I ever see him again. I should recognize him—we were practically eyeball to eyeball when he pulled a split-S and dove straight down! His airplane was different, too. He had the prop spinner painted with black and silver stripes. I had a glimpse of the nose—it had a light blue bird painted on it. A hawk maybe, or an eagle. Its wings were spread just like they are when they start to dive on a rabbit."

The captain had been doodling interlocking triangles on the margin of his debriefing form, but he stopped and stared at Stan as the bombardier described the attack. "Those new 109s—they're G models by the way—were the 'Abbeville Kids.' There's two squadrons of 'em—one with yellow noses and one with red noses. They're Goering's personal favorites and very bad news. That inverted head-on attack is a new twist, though. The plane you described is also known. The markings are Lt. Kurt Heintze's. He's racked up quite a score since arriving from Russia. He was personally decorated by Hitler last week. It's interesting to know that Goering is moving his top guns to defend the homeland. We're hurting them and they're worried, by God! Well, why don't you all take off now. You did well just to get back home. You tangled with the best they can throw at you, if that's any consolation."

Ross roused from his dejected slump to take a long pull from the clear glass bottle and hand it back to Eubanks. "Christ, what is this stuff? Tastes like av-gas," he spluttered.

"Orange gin," the grinning pilot responded. "Only stuff you can get that isn't rationed. The orange flavor is better than the rest. Stan?"

The bombardier formed his mouth into a lopsided grin. "Why the hell not? Alcohol is alcohol."

Ross stared across the stark, chilly room at the deserted space formerly claimed by Art Tyson. The mattress was rolled at the head of the iron cot, revealing faintly sagging steel springs. Any evidence that the navigator ever existed had been removed: his footlocker, pictures—everything. "The goddamn ghouls didn't waste any time getting rid of his stuff," Stan muttered.

"I know how you feel," Eubanks responded. "I don't know why, but I expected to see Roy's things still here when we got back that night. We had talked about it, you know. I told Roy to take anything of mine he wanted; he insisted that I have his tailored dress jacket— it fit me better than it did him. Well . . . You say Rex is okay?"

Ross stirred. "Yeah. I just talked with him for a minute. The medics told me that a fragment from the shell that got Art broke some small bones in his foot. Four weeks in a cast and crutches. Rex, that dumb shit, is already planning to use this as a way to get transferred to fighters." He reached for the gin bottle. "Anyone interested in changing and going to the club? I think I'm going to get blind drunk."

Further conversation halted when Major Ellis, after a perfunctory knock, strode into the hut. He eyed the half-empty gin bottle and grimaced. "God, how can you stand that stuff?"

When there was no answer, he continued. "Listen, Colyer, I thought I'd stop by and tell you that you're on the board for tomorrow. You'll take one of the new replacement birds. Since Wilkinson is stood down, you'll have his copilot and navigator."

Ross gaped in astonishment. "Tomorrow? Jesus Christ, Major, my crew isn't in any shape to fly another mission without some rest. Art Tyson got killed today—or didn't you know?"

"I know," Ellis responded, his tone cold and impersonal. "I also know that if you don't get back in the air, your crew is going to sit around brooding and getting cold feet." He turned to leave. "Oh-four-hundred briefing. Mission is coming in on the Teletype right now." The shocked trio watched the door close behind him.

"That cold-blooded son of a bitch," Ross raged. "I won't go! Damnit, Art isn't even cold yet."

"Go, Ross," Eubanks said quietly, staring at the floor. "He's right, believe me. I had to stand down for a week after we got back. I had the shakes so bad I could hardly get the engines started. But it goes away as soon as you get the gear up. We can't quit. It's been only five missions since Roy and my radioman bought the farm. And you know what? I have trouble remembering what they looked like."

Ross stared blankly at his suddenly aged friend. I can't do it, he thought. To hell with the rest of the crew. Let them find another aircraft commander. I have to come to grips with what's happened.

The others didn't know—would maybe never know—but Ross needed time to think. It was that last conversation with Art. The worried navigator had suggested that they take their bikes and visit the Blue Ox, a little pub just outside the base. Over mugs of weak wartime beer Art had told him, "Ross, I'm going to request that I be taken off flying status. I can't hack it. Look, I've done some figuring. The average crew lasts fifteen missions. The odds against finishing twenty-five are astronomical. I have too much to go home to, damnit. I'm not going to be a sacrificial lamb for that overbearing, egotistical bastard, Sprague. He can walk across somebody else's corpse to get his second fucking star."

Ross made a pattern of interlocking wet rings on the bar with his mug as he tried to think of what he should say. Finally, he said, "Don't do it, Art. Sure, Sprague is obsessed with making the Seventh the hottest wing in England. But this thing is bigger than that. If we don't stop Hitler in his tracks—well, you won't have much to go home to anyway. And the odds are improving. As we get more planes and crews, the formations get bigger and better able to defend themselves. We have

two new P-38 groups for escort now, and better long-range tanks for
the '47s are coming. Pretty soon they'll be covering us all the way
to the target and back.

"C'mon, Art, you won't be able to live with yourself. What will
you tell your kids? 'I went to the war, but I got scared and turned tail'?
The rest of us get puckered up on every mission, too. Don't think you're
the only one who's figured out the odds. Look, we're past that magic
five-mission figure. That's when most new crews get clobbered. We're
going to make it, I can feel it."

The argument went on until Art finally shrugged and said, "Okay,
Ross, okay. I'll do it your way. You're the best damned pilot in the
outfit. If anyone is going to keep bringing that big, ugly bitch back,
it'll be you."

That had been two nights before. Ross reached for the nearly empty
bottle. Okay, Art, don't sit up there and sneer at my high-sounding
words, he thought. I'm going, damn you.

26 June 1943
Walden Abbey

Ross slumped against the boundary fence, breathing heavily after
his dash from third base. Rex, his right leg encased in a dirty cast,
slouched beside him. "Good hitting, Skipper." The grinning copilot
slapped Ross's shoulder. "If you'd kneed Mickey Reed in the nuts as
you went into second base, you could've probably stretched that hit
to a triple."

The lanky pilot mopped his sweating forehead and chuckled. "Get
someone else to do that, guy. I'm the catcher, remember? That big
bastard would like nothing better than a chance to come charging home
and flatten an officer in the process. All in the name of good, clean
sport, of course. You really have a hard-on for that boy, don't you?"

Rex's jaw muscles bunched. "He's an arrogant son of a bitch. I'd
like to see *someone* deck him." They watched their tail gunner throw
his glove in the dirt and hurl cursing criticism at the outfielder who
had just made a wild throw.

Reed treated the officer-enlisted softball games as a serious challenge. Now, with the game in its last inning, the score seven to six
in the officers' favor, Mickey's temper was growing short.

Ross stretched lazily in the warm, late-June sunlight. "I can't understand it," he mused aloud. "Three days of weather like this without a mission. You picking up any rumors at ops?"

"Nothing else but," Rex replied. Carried as "limited duty," the copilot was spending his days as an assistant ops officer at group. "There's a big one shaping up. Division is busting its balls to get every bird it can operational. The big buzz just now is the next shipment of new planes. We're getting another squadron, and both the 866th and the 771st, the new one joining the group, are being increased to nine ships each. Hey, you going to the bash tonight?"

"Wouldn't miss it," Ross replied cheerfully. "Payday *and* a party— with *two* busloads of girls from Ipswich? C'mon now. I heard Colonel Deckard giving a real tongue-in-cheek order to the adjutant: 'All girls off the base by Tuesday.'"

Lieutenant Eubanks struck out with a lusty swing, ending the inning. Ross stood as the officers took to the field for the last time to defend their one-run lead. "You making any progress on your reassignment?" he asked Rex casually.

Rex shrugged. "Can't tell. Fighter Command is willing—soon as I'm returned to flying status, of course. The thing is sitting at wing in somebody's hold basket. Colonel Deckard will have to release me, if and when. And he ain't talking."

"I'll see what I can do," Ross reassured him. "If that's what you want."

"I'd appreciate it." Rex gave him a level look. "You don't seem to miss me."

Ross used the clamor to get behind the plate to evade an answer. I don't play God anymore, he told himself as he crouched behind the first batter. Let Deckard, Sprague, Division—whoever—do that. Rex wanted to fly fighters, so okay.

Then there was Guenther. Guenther of all people. Wanting permission to marry an English girl he'd met in the Red Cross canteen in Ipswich. What about the fiancée he'd left behind in Chicago? She was out of reach; the girl in Ipswich had round heels and put out. The broad was just looking for a ticket to the U.S. of A. Piss on it. He would recommend approval.

Stan. Ross had awakened early the morning of their last mission —before the wake-up call. He'd seen Stan sneaking a jolt from a bottle of orange gin concealed beneath his bed. He realized then that

Stan had been hitting the booze hard since the day he'd flown the bomb run with Art's body rolling loose under his feet in the nose compartment.

Leckie. The obsequious radio operator had stopped talking to everyone—unless it was to answer a direct question. Ross had asked Phillips about the man. Leckie had withdrawn from life. He ate, slept, and flew missions. Supposedly, Ham had figured, he took a crap now and then, but no one ever saw him. Otherwise he just sprawled on his bunk and stared at the ceiling.

Dirkson was throwing up on every mission. Ross first learned about it when Milt vomited into his oxygen mask and almost choked to death before Reed could come to his rescue.

Ross recovered from his introspection just in time to catch the batter's foul tip for a third strikeout. He joined the noisy throng around a tub of cold beer for the victory celebration. He scarcely recognized some of the men who had made that long over-water flight from Mountain Home scant weeks before. Nervous, shrill laughter. Vulgar profanity punctuating every verbal expression. Swaggering braggadocio. Blank, shifty eyes. Few had made it to ten missions yet, but the strain was taking its toll. The flight surgeon had issued a stern admonition during their last briefing: "Hereafter, frostbite cases will be treated as being 'in line of duty' only after convincing proof that they are not self-inflicted." Too many stories had circulated in the clubs about men removing a glove and sticking a hand into the subzero slipstream. Anything to gain a brief respite from the gut-chilling prospect of cheating death one more time.

Chapter Eighteen

0400 Hours, 1 July 1943
Walden Abbey

Since only officers attended mission briefings, the enlisted crewmen developed their own intelligence system to obtain a clue about the target's identity. One member stood just outside the closed door to the briefing room. The officers' reaction when the wall map with its skein of colored yarn was revealed spoke volumes. If the enlisted crewman heard a loud groan, he would race to his plane to advise his buddies that they faced a rough one. If the reaction was mild—muttered jokes or laughter—the crew could relax.

On this damp, dark morning marking their tenth mission, it was Ham Phillips's lot to play spy. He listened closely, then looked at the other crew representatives similarly engaged. The reaction was different today. Subdued murmurs, then silence.

Ham caught a ride to the armament shack. "Mike," he told the slender, worried master sergeant in charge, "I want another two thousand rounds of .50 caliber on board."

"Hey, Ham—you got your full load. I saw to it myself."

"Gimme another two thousand, Mike."

"Now, damnit, Ham. You're over max gross weight already. I could get my ass in a sling. Your pilot know about this?"

"What my pilot knows, or doesn't know, is my worry, Mike. Just get that truck on its way and I won't tell anyone about your stash of extra ammo—the one your captain doesn't know about." He flashed a vicious grin at the discomfited NCO and strode toward the *Happy Hooker*'s hardstand.

Inside the briefing room, Ross and Stan, seated alongside their recently acquired navigator and copilot, stared at the big wall map as if hypnotized. The piece of red yarn seemed to have no end. It zigged north, zagged east, then finally plunged due south. "Frankfurt, by God," Hanson, the navigator, his face drained of blood, breathed in awe.

Ross glanced at the worried man's pale, acne-scarred face. They had acquired 2d Lt. Kevin Hanson from the "casual" pool of crew members without crews. At first it appeared that Ross had been lucky. Hanson had completed fifteen missions in another group before he became the sole survivor of a midair collision. But, Ross soon discovered, the man was "flak happy." His nervous apprehension rubbed off on the others. It was something that Ross needed like a rubber crutch. This would be their fourth mission with him since Art's loss, and Hanson's tangible fear only increased as he approached the end of his twenty-five-mission tour.

Ross scanned the flimsy showing formation positions. *Happy Hooker* was to fly group lead. Hot damn! He showed the assignment to Stan. The bombardier grinned broadly, seemingly unconcerned that the responsibility for laying the cargoes of thirty-odd airplanes on the main point of impact sat squarely on his shoulders. Ross searched Stan's relaxed features for clues: Was he sober?

Colonel Deckard slid in beside them as Major Weathers ran down the briefing. "I'll be riding right seat for you," Deckard told Ross. "You want your copilot to stand down or fly a gun position?"

Ross glanced at 2d Lt. Bob Whitaker's morose features. He was on loan from one of the new crews that wouldn't be flying the mission. It was to be his first exposure to combat. "I think I'll leave him, Colonel. This promises to be a hairy one. My gunners may not be the best in the ETO, but I know what to expect from them."

"I agree," Deckard muttered softly. "I doubt that Whitaker will put up a fuss." He grinned at Ross. "Seventh Wing is leading today. We're the second group. General Sprague is leading with the 199th. And you're right—this is apt to be a pisser."

They all stood as the briefing came to an end and the group commander returned to the platform. Deckard leaned over, his mouth close to Ross's ear. "Wait til you hear this," he whispered conspiratorially.

"If it's any consolation to you, gentlemen," said Colonal Bolt, "history will be made today. This is the largest and deepest daylight penetration into the enemy's industrial heartland to date. It could be something else, I might add. It could be the *last* daylight mission of any size. The RAF has been pressuring us to switch to night operations. It's reached all the way to Washington. We have a senator here right now, a member of the Military Affairs Committee, raising hell about our daytime losses. He agrees with the Brits.

"Some of *you* may agree with him. But consider this, gentlemen. The Jerries are getting better and better with their night fighters. The RAF is losing damn near as many planes as we are, but we're putting ten bombs on the MPI for every one of theirs that finds a strategic target. We'll be over here forever using their tactics. You won't be flying twenty-five missions—you'll be doing more like fifty. Anyway, Senator Templeton is going to be watching this raid today. If we blow it, he's going to go running back home screaming for blood."

Ross stood with raised eyebrows. Templeton. Was BT going to be in that lead airplane with Sprague? His old adversary must not have pulled off his scheme to be reassigned. Imagine that pair leading the entire Eighth Air Force. The idea was downright scary. Ross listened to the group commander's summation.

"Everything that will get off the ground is going to be up there today—two hundred and fifty Forts and B-24s. Let's make it look good." Bolt strode to the rear door, leaving the sobered crew members to digest his words.

Ross dressed carefully. First he drew on woolen long johns. Next, he eyed the electrically heated blue suit issued by personal equipment. It would allow him to dispense with the bulky sheepskin jacket and pants, but the damn thing had a habit of shorting out—leaving a hand or foot unheated. The outside air temperature at twenty-four thousand feet would be in the neighborhood of twenty below. Plus, a major hit in the electrical system would render the thing useless. He opted to leave the questionable item behind and donned a green gabardine flight suit before struggling into the two-piece leather outer garments. Checking to ensure that both CO_2 inflation cartridges were unpunctured, he added the yellow Mae West life preserver and, lastly, the all-important parachute harness.

The shoulder-holstered Colt .45 automatic made an uncomfortable bulk under his left armpit, and he briefly considered leaving it behind. The pistol was a subject of innumerable arguments. Escape and evasion briefers said, "Leave it at home. You aren't about to shoot your way out of enemy territory. Just the act of drawing it can get you shot by some civilian." A counterargument was that there may be only one guy between you and freedom. It had taken the tight-mouthed Lieutenant Dillon to put the matter in perspective for Ross: "Throw the son of a bitch away if you bail out, but take it. Someday you may have to use it to control one of your own crew." Only Ross and Mickey Reed wore side arms.

After examining the rubber oxygen mask, a new type supposedly less prone to ice up, Ross waddled toward the door, resembling an arthritic chocolate penguin.

There were no cheers as a green flare, arcing through the gloom and mist, signaled a "go" for the mission. This was one trip that nobody was looking forward to, even though it counted toward that magic "get-the-fuck-home" number.

Ross waved his crew aboard the repaired *Happy Hooker* and clambered into the open bomb bay, giving the shadowy array of thousand-pounders only a cursory look. Other than some extra riveted seams distorting the painted derriere of their mascot, there was no reminder of that grim last flight home with Art Tyson's remains.

As Ross entered the flight deck and slid into the left seat, Colonel Deckard arrived, the stub of a dead cigar clamped between bulldoglike jaws. In the act of helping Ross hook up to the oxygen and communications systems, Ham Phillips advised offhandedly, "She may feel sort of heavy on takeoff, Lieutenant."

Ross turned and gave the bland-faced engineer a questioning look. He received only a nod in return. "Check," said Ross softly. He gave Ham a weary thumbs-up. Dispensation to exceed mission directives that specified allowable ammo was thereby bestowed.

"Fuck 'em," Ham whispered as he left the flight deck.

0652 Hours, 1 July 1943
199th Bomb Group (Heavy)
Siddley, England

Captain Broderick Templeton III arranged half-pages of notes and clipped them to the copilot's control column. Leading a bomber stream was a complicated business. Call signs, signal codes, times—the goddamn timing. Failure of one group lead to be in the right place at the right time could blow the entire mission formation.

BT watched his pilot, Maj. Eddie Masters, the 199th's ops officer, adjust his seat and rudder pedals. Masters was one of the best and this would not be his first mission lead. BT felt reassured. His boss, General Sprague, would be on the flight deck, but when it came to the intricacies of assembling 250 airplanes in an area smaller than the state of Rhode Island, Sprague was worthless.

The old man was talking a blue streak as BT and Masters ran the before-starting-engines checklist. The general's words were a distraction. BT wished he would shut up. But this was his big day. BT had been with him when Sprague had presented his plan to hit the Daimler-Benz factory at Frankfurt.

"More than half of the engines for the Me 109 are made there. Not to mention the five hundred engines per month for tanks and trucks." The general's words were falling on fertile ground, BT observed. Eighth Air Force staffers needed a convincing display of daylight bombing deep inside Germany in the worst way.

Major General Eaker had joined the meeting for the summation. The subject of a mission commander was broached. Colonel Montague—BT recognized him from the meeting at Buxton Hall—turned to Eaker. "I'm sure that Colonel Timberlake will want this one."

Sprague interrupted with a smooth, "Please, gentlemen. This strike is my baby. I did the spadework, I know all the details. I believe I should have the opportunity to lead it."

A stony-faced Eaker appeared to ignore the array of dissenting frowns turned in his direction. After a moment's silence while he drummed the tabletop with stubby fingers, he answered. "I agree with the plan. We need a demonstration now, while Senator Templeton is, er—" He stopped short of saying "in our hair," after a quick glance at BT. The general's private intelligence net was thorough. "And Ted Timberlake is out. I don't want to risk anyone briefed on Tidal Wave falling into German hands."

Faces froze at the mention of an obviously highly classified project. Except Elliott Sprague's. BT could almost see his boss's ears twitch. Was something big cooking that he was unaware of? BT sighed. He could anticipate his next task: Find out what the hell gives with this Tidal Wave operation.

"Elliott will fly lead," Eaker concluded.

Sprague seemed oblivious to the fact that they were scant minutes away from start-engines time. "We make our mark today," he was telling Masters. "Night Train"—he had selected the code name himself—"is going to make history. Seventh Wing will prove to even the most doubting Thomases that daylight precision bombing is the answer." He seemed to forget that he was repeating, verbatim, the inspirational message he had delivered during the briefing. You could almost see him mentally buffing that second star.

BT's irritation with the pompous bastard almost made him forget the butterflies in his gut. Night Train was apt to make history, he agreed. But not in the context Sprague had in mind. If not for Colyer and this publicity-seeking general, Broderick Templeton III would be sitting behind a desk in ops plans right now. That damn Colyer would be the one looking down the gun barrel.

It was ironic. If Night Train got wiped out, BT's dad would raise so much hell that the Eighth would switch to night bombing—too late to save the ass of the guy who had planted the seed.

His father. How to broach the subject of a five-hundred-dollar "loan"? It just had to be forthcoming—and soon. Sprague's warning had been casual but firm: "BT, Colonel Yates mentioned that you still owed him from that game of, oh, what was it—two weeks ago? You can't let a thing like that run on, you know. A lot of good officers have gotten cashiered for bad gambling debts. Better see to it."

Major Masters's next words brought BT back to the immediate task at hand. "Stand by to start number three."

The soft-spoken major had not confided in BT, who was, after all, the general's aide. BT had caught enough of an unguarded conversation, however, to know that the big, rawboned pilot was far from happy with his lot. Anyone who had faced a determined *Luftwaffe* and that ring of 88mm antiaircraft guns around a target knew the odds on this one. Without fighter escort beyond the coast, losses would be heavy. To be under the command of an egotistical, promotion-hungry mission commander for the single most important strike to date was not a reassuring prospect.

BT read from his crib notes as they waited for the green takeoff light from the tower. "Climb out on a heading of zero-six-five to three thousand. Set up a left-hand orbit off the Sugar-Fox beacon. Depart Sugar-Fox at two-niner on heading one-eight-zero climbing to eighteen. Engineer, after we enter orbit, commence firing green-yellow flares at two-minute intervals. Everybody copy?"

"Copy, pilot."

"Copy, engineer."

"Navigator, copy."

General Sprague watched Masters set up the autopilot and, as the ADF needle indicated passage of the Sugar-Fox beacon, enter a shallow bank to the left. "I'm going to the tail position," Sprague announced crisply. "I'll control the assembly from back there where I can see."

Major Masters leaned toward BT as Sprague minced his way along the narrow bomb bay catwalk. "Stand by for rough weather," he advised with a wry grin. Scanning the relatively clear morning air, BT raised his eyebrows in an unspoken question.

"The comm junction in the tail wasn't wired into the VHF set," explained Masters. "The general didn't tell anyone he was going to ride tail gunner. He can see what's going on, but he sure as hell can't talk to anybody—except you, that is." Masters gave BT a sadistic leer and returned his attention to maintaining a constant altitude and airspeed.

The explosion wasn't long in coming. "Masters, there's no VHF position back here!" Sprague roared into the intercom.

BT took a deep breath and responded. "This is Captain Templeton, Sir. Major Masters is on the command radio. I'll tell him to switch over." He favored Masters with a sardonic smile and indicated that the lead pilot should switch to intercom.

"Evidently an oversight by the ground crew, Sir," the major responded smoothly. "I assume they were aware that you planned to fly in the tail turret, General?"

"Assume nothing," came the snarled reply. "That engineering officer is going to get a rocket up his ass when we land. He should know enough to prepare a lead plane for any eventuality. I'm coming forward. Already I can see that things are screwed up. Airplanes are all over the sky behind us."

Their lead ship had completed half of its first circle. BT could see what indeed appeared to be a confused gaggle of B-24s and B-17s milling aimlessly. But even as he watched, he could see order emerging. The lead planes of the other groups, each loosing different-colored flares as they circled, were picking up strings of ships easing into position. BT thumbed the intercom switch. "How's our join-up coming, waist?"

"Lead squadron is formed, Sir. Low squadron is moving in; high squadron is pretty well back. I'd guess it'll take one more circle for them to catch up."

BT leaned over to advise Masters that their ships were almost in place. Observing a grim expression on the pilot's face, BT hesitated.

"Goddamn those weather forecasters. Look at that." BT followed the major's furious stare. To the southeast, their intended course, puffy white cloud tops were visible well above their altitude.

General Sprague chose that moment to burst onto the flight deck. Before he could vent his wrath, however, Masters pointed ahead and yelled above the engine roar, "We got problems. That stuff is right at our rendezvous point and altitude."

Sprague, his anger diverted, grunted. "Why wasn't that stuff in the forecast?" Masters, at a loss for an answer to the rhetorical question, remained silent. "Okay," the scowling general snapped, "we'll climb above it. Announce a change in assembly altitude to twenty thousand."

"Sir," Masters replied carefully, "that'll throw our times off. Plus, the '17s were to assemble at twenty. Because they're slower, they were to hold and let us pass beneath, then fall into the rear of the stream."

Sprague was unconcerned. "Then, goddamnit, they'll just have to go to twenty-two. Increase your climb speed by five miles an hour and make up lost time on the way to the buncher beacon. Here, give me the mike. I'll issue the order." Masters's protest was cut off.

"Navigator to pilot. We're coming up on oh-seven-two-niner. Time to depart Sugar-Fox on heading one-eight-zero."

Trapped by events, Masters uttered a disgusted, "Okay, Nav, turning now. Engineer, fire a double green to tell the group that we're turning on course. Tail, are all of our birds in position?"

"High squadron is still about two miles behind, Sir."

BT knew what was bothering the experienced lead pilot. It required split-second timing to form up ten groups of twenty-eight squadrons, including one group vacating its assembly radio beacon as another was approaching. The tolerance over buncher beacons was plus-or-minus one minute. Now the group lead had increased airspeed. With their own high squadron out of position, the error would magnify as assembly proceeded. BT regarded the carefully thought-out flight plan clipped to his control column. They may as well tear it up. Fragments of box formations would be scattered all over Europe—and they would be facing as many as three hundred German fighters. In addition, BT overheard Sprague bellowing into the VHF set in violation of the radio silence edict. Night Train, BT decided, was getting off to a piss-poor start.

The core of General Sprague's—and Night Train's—problems was embedded in an undetected upper-level atmospheric disturbance drifting southward from the polar ice cap. Bitter cold arctic air poured over the warmer landmass of England. Not only were clouds building where none were supposed to exist, but strong upper winds were moving the climbing formations in an unpredicted southerly direction.

Masters leveled off at twenty thousand. A deft touch on autopilot and throttles allowed the eighteen ships in the lead and low squadrons to maintain good position. The high squadron still lagged behind, using gas-guzzling power settings in an attempt to catch up. The lead ship was above the cloud tops, but a copper-bright sun burning through heavy haze reduced visibility to less than the five miles required for the rest of the planes in the formation to maintain position.

"What the hell?" Masters let out a startled oath as the ADF spun aimlessly, then pointed to the rear, indicating station passage. "We're four minutes early at the buncher beacon, Nav. What gives?"

"We must have picked up a hellacious tail wind, Major."

"Well, crap. General, I suggest we do a four-minute orbit here to get our timing back on track."

Sprague frowned out a side window. "No," he responded shortly. "We're going to have to get above this haze. Reduce climb speed to let the formation catch up and keep climbing. I'll set a new assembly altitude when we break clear."

Masters bit his lip. He and BT exchanged glances. Masters shrugged and added power to the already laboring engines. The general was ignoring an ironclad rule—one established by bitter experience. Never, never lead an unformed mission into enemy territory.

0755 Hours, 1 July 1943
Aboard the *Happy Hooker*
20,000 Feet Over the North Sea

Stan Cryhowski returned the target photo to his mission folder. The pattern formed by railroad tracks, roads, and the river was etched into his memory. The impatient bombardier resented the long hours of grinding through cold, hostile skies until he had the opportunity to do his job. Glancing outside, expecting to see the wind-whipped surface of the North Sea beneath, he frowned. They were flying through a shimmering haze of ice fog. Below was an opaque gray blanket. Turning, he tugged Lieutenant Hanson's booted ankle. "We over water yet?"

At the navigator's nod Stan called into the intercom, "Bombardier to crew. Time to test-fire guns."

He heard staccato burps from the rear and worked the charging handle on his own nose-mounted .50. It sounded unnaturally loud—but reassuring—as he squeezed off a short burst. He hoped someday to get at least one kill of his own. It didn't seem likely, though. An eagle-eyed bomb aimer, yes. Deadly gunner, no. The fact that he hadn't fired at the 109 that got Art still gave him occasional cause for reflection.

"Bombardier to pilot. I'm going off intercom to pull the safety pins before we go on oxygen. Over."

"Roger, Stan," Ross said. "Don't stay away from that nose gun too long. I don't see our fighter escort yet. I can't see the lead group ahead either. We're kinda hangin' out here flapping in the breeze."

Stan eased onto the narrow bomb bay catwalk. The roar of the howling slipstream and four engines at climb power was a physical force pounding his eardrums. Starting at the rear, he extracted the heavy wire pins inserted into the nose fuses of the dozen thousand-pound bombs and four strapped clusters of slender incendiary sticks. The fat green shapes of twelve high-explosive containers seemed benign. The bomb-loading crews had scrawled graffiti—"Up yours, Adolf," "With love from Sam and Dave"—on some of the casings. Although hardly original, the slogans were their way of participating in the dangerous missions.

The incendiaries were an entirely different matter. Crews were never comfortable with them on board. Packed with magnesium shavings, they burned with a white-hot intensity that was impossible to extinguish. Water, in fact, made them burn even more fiercely. Training films showed the hellish weapons burning their way from roof to basement of a four-story building. They made a sinister addition to an already lethal cargo, and Stan wasted no time admiring them. He hustled back to the flight deck and dangled the sixteen pins, with little red warning streamers attached, in Ross's view.

"Bombs are armed, Skipper," Stan yelled over the thunder of the straining engines. Ross nodded and resumed scanning the blinding haze for the missing formations as the plane continued to claw for altitude. Both he and Deckard wore scowls of concern on their faces.

Hanson tugged at Stan's sleeve as he slithered past on his way to the front. "Where the hell is our fighter escort?" he asked, face drawn taut with nervous tension.

Stan shrugged and turned his palms up. The altimeter was edging past twelve thousand. He hooked up to his intercom cord and announced, "Bombardier to crew. Time to go on the old oh-two, troops. Check your masks, flow regulators, and check in." After mumbled acknowledgments he slouched in his kiddie-sized seat. He, like the other crewmen, scanned bleak skies that could turn hostile at any moment.

Mickey Reed's voice broke his concentration. "Tail to pilot. Sir, I just got a glimpse of what I thought was our high squadron. But Sir, so help me, they was a formation of B-17s!"

"Tail, are you certain they were '17s?" Stan recognized Colonel Deckard's rasping voice.

"Sir," an anguished Reed responded, "they only had one vertical tail and they sure as hell had four engines. I—I'm almost certain. One thing for damn sure, Sir—they wasn't B-24s."

"Oh, for Christ's sake," Deckard muttered over the intercom, unaware his mike was still hot. "The goddamn Forts are supposed to be twenty miles from here. Nav?"

"Yessir?"

"How far are we from Point Indigo?"

"I haven't had a good fix since we left the buncher beacon, Colonel. My dead-reckoning position puts our first turning point at one-four. That's in three minutes, Sir."

In the ensuing silence, Stan switched his comm selector to VHF. Not monitoring the intercom at all times was contrary to standard operating procedure, but shit—what was going on? Deckard apparently had switched to channel D, the fighter channel. He heard a bored voice say, "Big Friend Leader, this is your Little Friend Leader. Be advised we are at angels ten, in the clear and no joy."

Stan stiffened. The fighter escort was ten thousand feet above the coded base altitude of twenty thousand feet and didn't have the bomber stream in sight! He listened closely, but there was no acknowledgment from the lead bomber formation. Christ! They were lost, mixed in with a bunch of Forts who were supposed to be twenty miles behind, no fighter cover. It promised to be a long day. Would they abort the mission at the coastline?

Decision time came without warning. The shearing effect of that river of polar air cleared the cloud mass like a gargantuan broom. One minute the *Happy Hooker* was virtually blind, the next they were in brilliant sunshine, the neatly checkered terrain of the Third *Reich* clearly visible below.

"What the hell?" Deckard exploded. "We're still supposed to be over water!" Hanson scrambled down to squat beside Stan, scanning a map, trying to pick up a landmark.

"Flak, four o'clock low!" shouted a waist gunner.

"Two bomber formations, three o'clock," called out another gunner.

Stan could see tiny specks, high and distant, straight ahead. Far more visible than the planes themselves were the contrails they generated. Upper air conditions appeared perfect for the formation of those streamers of ice crystals—the result of disturbance created by wingtips and whirling props. Flak gunners and enemy fighter pilots loved them.

As Stan tried to decide if it was the lead group he saw, Hanson fixed their position. "Christ, we're right over the coastal defenses west of Bremen, Colonel. Do a hard right."

Hanson's words coincided with four simultaneous detonations that jarred the big B-24 as though it was entering a thunderstorm. Whining pings marked the passage of shell fragments through the fragile aluminum skin.

Ross commenced evasive action. Only small changes in heading and altitude were possible while leading a cumbersome formation, however.

The next bursts were less accurate but still inflicted damage. Stan watched, fascinated by the random appearance of the ugly black puffs of smoke. They looked so harmless. First an even round ball, then two little legs formed. It was said that the only danger came from ones with red flame visible when they exploded. He had been told by other crew members that if you could spot muzzle flashes on the ground, you could actually see the black shell coming up toward you. Stan wasn't inclined to test the hypothesis.

"Tail to pilot." Reed's voice was tight. "Number three in the high element just took a hit in its number one engine. No fire, but it's smoking bad. The squadron behind us is catching it now—shit, there goes one on fire. He's spinning in. No chutes."

"Top turret to pilot. Bandits. They're after that group ahead of us. You can just barely see 'em, but—my God! There must be forty or fifty."

Deckard's voice came over the VHF channel with calm assurance. "Red Dog Formation from Red Dog Leader. Close up. I repeat, close up. We're out of the bomber stream and proceeding to the target alone. Keep those guns moving and don't waste ammunition—we have a long way to go. We'll bomb from group formation. Once more, bring it in tight and keep it that way."

Reassembling Night Train into a coordinated bomber stream was physically impossible. Pilots, blinded by clouds and haze, had tacked onto any formation they could find consisting of two or more ships. The B-17s, having climbed to a higher altitude, picked up stronger tail winds than the B-24s. Very soon they were overrunning the ragged remnants of the leading Liberator groups. No one was on the briefed course, nor were they on any semblance of a time schedule. Of concern to all was the excessive fuel consumption created by the disorganized departure. Getting home was going to be squeaky. Would the forecast hold for good ceilings and visibility over their English bases?

Stan tore his gaze from the mayhem being inflicted on the group ahead. He had work to do. He switched on the Norden bombsight to allow it to warm up. He would make running entries of wind drift and ground speed at every opportunity. His rough estimate was more than an hour to the IP. He started to call on Hanson for assistance, then saw that the harassed navigator was scribbling furiously, attempting to create a revised flight plan. Stan observed the winking indicator on Hanson's oxygen flow regulator. The man was breathing rapidly. He made a mental note to watch for hyperventilation. Rapid breathing on oxygen could be as dangerous as a lack of the life-sustaining stuff.

Stan looked ahead. The swirling fighters were giving what he assumed to be the lead group a thorough going over. He gulped. Good Christ, he could see three bombers falling away from the formation; one appeared to be inverted. As he watched, its tail assembly separated, falling away like a severed limb, a mute expression of despair and defeat. The other two wounded planes were trailing smoke and flame. White shapes tumbled from one. Chutes. One—three—six. It registered with grim finality that these, for Christ's sake, were people, not inanimate objects.

Where the hell was the fighter cover? The P-38s had this much range. Shit, the bomber formation was lost. If their escort was where they were supposed to be, they'd never make an appearance. Stan mashed the press-to-talk switch.

"Bombardier to radio, over."

"Yessir."

"Leckie, come forward and stand by to man the nose gun if we get hit by fighters on the way in. I'll have my hands full before bombs away."

A short silence. Then, "Radio to pilot. Do you think I should leave my radios, Sir? We may have to get off an urgent message."

"Get your ass forward, radio," Deckard snarled.

Stan smiled to himself. He would instruct Leckie to make one exception to his targets. If he spotted that goddamn black and silver prop spinner—the one that reminded him of those little whirligigs he used to get at the county fair—then *he*, by God, would take over the gun. He wanted that bastard in the worst way.

Chapter Nineteen

1121 Hours, 1 July 1943
22,000 Feet Above Frankfurt, Germany

Well ahead of the *Happy Hooker,* BT did his best to concentrate on the instrument panel, alert for the first sign of mechanical trouble. It was no use. His gaze kept returning to that sphincter-loosening sight of a hundred 88mm flak guns spewing tons of explosive shells heavenward. No formation could survive passage through that seemingly solid wall of death-dealing metal fragments. Why the hell didn't Masters break off and come in from another direction, at another altitude? BT wondered.

The major, face concealed by flying glasses and oxygen mask, kept his gaze straight ahead. Except for occasional orders to the crew, Masters could have been a machine. He had maintained that demeanor throughout their nerve-shattering engagement with the fighters. BT had been spared the sight of most of that ordeal; the action took place mainly out of sight to the rear. Apparently this group did not have the stomach for those devastating head-on tactics.

The 199th had taken heavy losses; BT knew of six of their number blasted from the sky by 20mm cannon fire. The gunners had kept up a running account of the savage air battle. In addition to smoking ruins dotting the landscape behind them, three other planes had engines feathered. They had jettisoned their bomb loads, allowing them to stay within the protective womb of the box formation.

General Sprague, standing behind BT's seat, was out of the copilot's view. He had been most vocal, however, cursing the other group leaders for not being able to form a protective screen. The missing fighter escort came in for especially scathing criticism. Gunners who missed opportunities for a kill were threatened with dire consequences. But the awesome vista confronting them now had silenced even the vociferous task force commander.

The navigator—BT didn't know him, didn't care to know him or any other member of the crew for that matter—calmly intoned, "Coming up on the IP, Major."

His announcement was punctuated by a deafening blast. Its concussion rocked the thirty-ton airplane like a toy. BT sensed, rather than heard, a screaming chunk of metal penetrate the flight deck.

"Masters is hit!" Sprague called. "Take over the controls, BT. Engineer, get down here; see what you can do."

BT, temporarily paralyzed with shock, could only gape at the figure slumped in the pilot's seat. The front of Masters's helmet was a mass of streaming blood streaked with bits of gray brain matter. His dark glasses had been torn aside, and viscous red fluid filled sightless eyes.

The bombardier's sharp "What's going on up there? We're losing altitude" jarred BT back to awareness. The autopilot was engaged, giving directional control to the bombardier, but the pilot's slumping body rested heavily against the control wheel. The servo motors transmitting corrections to the control surfaces were designed to be overridden by forty pounds of pressure. The ship had entered a gentle glide and was losing altitude.

BT horsed back on his wheel. The plane leveled. "Pilot's hit," he announced tersely. "I have us back in level flight."

"Okay" was the unemotional reply. "Bombs away in five minutes."

BT saw the general and their flight engineer struggling to remove Masters from his seat. He heard Sprague say, "Lay him in this corner. He's alive. Grab that first-aid kit and get a compress on that gash. Hook him up to 100 percent oxygen, then get back to your position before we pass the target—there'll be more fighters waiting for us. I'm taking over the left seat."

BT, confused by the lightning speed of their disaster, clutched the wheel in a death grip.

What do I do next? he thought helplessly. The plane was flying itself once again. The array of yellow lights on the autopilot panel winked in random succession as its mechanical brain held them on course—straight into the maelstrom of flame and smoke.

He watched in awe as Sprague slid into the left seat and calmly wiped the wheel and controls free of their covering of slippery blood. The son of a bitch had veins filled with antifreeze. Did he have no compassion? Was he leaving Masters down there, unattended, to die? He barely reacted to a cry over the intercom.

"Waist to pilot. Carson's hit bad! Piece of flak went right through his throat!"

"You have two minutes to do what you can for him," Sprague barked. "Then get back on your gun! Radio, take over that empty gun position. We'll be under fighter attack again in less than five minutes."

Senses reeling, BT realized that they were in the midst of the worst of the flak barrage. He glanced to his right. Christ, less than a hundred yards away the air was clear. The urge to wrench the wheel to the right and flee their pounding nightmare was strong, but respite could come only after they crossed the target. How soon? From what he could see of the ground below, it would be some time before they were over the target area.

He scanned the instrument panel. In front of Sprague, the "BOMB BAY DOORS OPEN" light glowed. The jeweled light adjacent to it, labeled "BOMB RELEASE," remained dark. As if attracted by a magnet, BT's gaze was drawn to a red-painted T-handle situated at the base of the control console. Printed in white letters were two words, "BOMB RELEASE." It was a design feature that allowed the pilot to override the automatic system in the event of an emergency.

BT's mind raced. Bomb release equaled a hard, diving turn to the right, which in turn equaled escape from the inferno. He glanced to the left. The engineer had returned to his turret. Sprague was gazing to the left, shouting over the VHF radio. Seemingly of its own volition—BT powerless to stop it—his left hand moved the necessary inches to grasp the release handle. A surprisingly short tug and he felt the struggling ship lift as its four-ton bomb load dropped clear.

The startled bombardier called out, "Bombs away! What the hell? The release was premature—Christ, we won't even come close."

BT ignored him. He had already hit the autopilot release and entered their run for open territory.

1132 Hours, 1 July 1943
Aboard the *Happy Hooker*
Approaching Frankfurt

A sullen Corporal Leckie edged his way into the nose and hooked up to oxygen and communication. Stan turned his attention to the bombsight. Pressing the two knobs that erected its stabilizing gyros, he waited for a confirming indication. Nothing. Angrily, he mashed the erecting knobs a second time. A sluggish response, then they toppled. Damn. After ensuring all switches were in the "on" position, he removed a glove and slid his hand beneath the electrically heated blanket that enveloped the device. Stone cold. Pounding a fist on one knee in frustration, Stan reached for the press-to-talk switch.

"Bombardier to pilot, over."

"Go ahead." Stan recognized Ross's voice.

"Got a problem down here, Ross ol' boy. The goddamn bombsight heater is out. It's too cold for the gyros to stabilize."

"Oh, great," Ross said, his disgust tinged with anger. "What the hell can you do about it?"

"The bombsight is worthless without gyros, Ross. What we should do, I guess, is let the deputy lead take over."

"I'll talk to Colonel Deckard about it, but I doubt that he'll want to do that unless it's absolutely necessary. Stand by."

Deckard came on the intercom. "You have any other ideas, Cryhowski?"

"Well, Sir. I know one guy who claims he wrapped his electric underwear around the thing and got it working."

"You want to try it?"

"I'd sure like to make the drop, Sir. Only thing is, I'm not wearing my heated suit today."

"I see. Okay, any volunteers?"

"This is the engineer, Colonel. I'll give him mine. We have what little heat there is up here on the flight deck. I'll get by."

Deckard's response was broken off by a frantic shout. "Waist to pilot. Bandits! Lots of 'em. Nine o'clock low and climbing."

Ross spoke calmly, his voice devoid of emotion. "Okay, crew, get set. Ham, hold your position; the bombsight fix will have to wait. Colonel, I have an idea of how to deal with those head-on attacks. Request permission to break radio silence and advise the rest of the formation."

Deckard grunted. "The whole goddamn world knows where we are. Go ahead."

Stan switched to VHF and listened. "Red Dog Formation, this is Red Dog Leader. We have bandits at nine o'clock low. Anticipate head-on passes. When they roll, lower your noses to bring the upper turrets to bear. All planes will have to do it in unison, and *don't* let the formation loosen up. Let's give it a try."

"Top turret to crew. There they are. Eleven o'clock and circling. The bastards are looking us over—about twenty of 'em. They don't have red or yellow noses, thank God."

Stan looked up from the balky bombsight. Ugly mottled green and gray shapes moved into view.

"Damnit, I almost wish they were Goering's red-nosed bunch," he breathed. Holding a two-ship formation in trail, the wary attackers moved rapidly out of sight to the rear.

"Tail to pilot. They're after the low squadron!"

Happy Hooker's crew remained silent, listening to Mickey Reed's running commentary. It was almost like tuning in a ball game on the radio, Stan thought. He felt a trickle of sweat course down his back as he waited.

"There they go—four of 'em in trail, head-on into the lead ship! The first one broke too soon—he missed."

Stan found himself reading a placard above the manual bomb-release handle as he waited. "CAUTION!" it read. "WHEN AIRPLANE IS ON GROUND MAKE SURE ALL PERSONNEL AND OBSTRUCTIONS ARE CLEAR OF BOMB BAY DOORS BEFORE DOOR CONTROL IS OPERATED." Makes sense, he told himself. Funny, I don't recall ever reading that before. His inane diversion was broken by more combat chatter.

"The second one is rolling on his back," Reed shouted into the intercom. "He's shooting—oh, my God! Lead took hits right in the nose section."

Stan winced.

"They're hit bad; the nose is coming up. He's gonna stall! Oh, shit. He flipped over and the rest of the squadron is trying to miss him. The tail is breaking up—I see chutes. One, two—there's four."

Silence.

"I don't see any more. Now the bastards are attacking from the rear; the formation is scattered all to hell.

"We got one! It's just like you said, Lieutenant: The deputy lead lowered his nose when they came in head-on, and got one. Oh, oh. The low element is taking hits—there's an engine on fire. He's dropping back. Get out! Get out! Oh, you dumb bastards."

Reed's voice broke. "Those dumb fucks were still shooting back when they blew up."

The intercom remained silent as Reed reported in dull tones, "They're breaking off—going back into their circle. Guess we're next."

Stan waited, muscles tensed, for news of the next attack.

The formation of 109s, their black-crossed numbers reduced by two, streaked across the nose, well out of range. "The bastards are leaving!" Ham Phillips called from the upper turret. "They're headed north. How about that?"

Tension was released in a rush of chatter until Ross put an end to it. "Okay, hold it down. That was just the first bunch. We aren't even to the target yet. Stay alert. But if anyone ever doubted the wisdom of keeping a tight formation, you just saw proof that they prefer hitting the sloppy ones."

Stan returned to his attempts to coax the stubborn bombsight gyros to life. By repeated caging, he discovered they were holding for as long as five minutes. It would be risky, but they might stay up long enough for the bomb run.

He thought briefly of the two unfortunate crews in the low squadron. I'm glad it was them instead of us. It can't happen to the *Happy Hooker;* it'll always happen to someone else. Art had been different. Then Stan guiltily recalled Eubanks's words: "I have trouble even remembering what they looked like. . . ."

Stan realized that he felt as if he'd been flying with Hanson forever.

"Navigator to pilot. IP coming up in seven minutes." Tension caused Hanson's voice to emerge as an adolescent squeak. "It looks like the lead group is on their bomb run right now—Jesus, look at the flak!"

Stan raised his head long enough to observe the leading group's plight. The number of black puffs caused his jaw to drop momentarily. It was unbelievable that the smoke could be so thick—like a solid cloud. Individual bursts were impossible to detect. Barrage flak—he'd heard about it. When the enemy gunners figured out what target was to be hit and the bomber's altitude, they ceased trying to aim at individual

planes and just laid up a continuous pattern, letting the attackers fly
through it.

It appeared that the mission leader had decided to drop by squadrons
rather than in group formation. One by one the nine-ship squadrons,
now ragged and decimated by savage fighter attacks, disappeared into
that hellish six-minute alley from IP to target. Deviation from the flight
path was not possible; you just had to sit there and ride it out, knowing
all the while that the goddamn fighters hadn't gone home—they'd just
bypassed the flak and were circling, waiting like sharks at the bombers'
posttarget rally point, anxious to resume their feeding frenzy.

Stan elbowed the frightened Leckie to one side and settled himself
in place. He crouched over his magic box like one of Macbeth's witches
peering into her cauldron. He felt an icy calm descend upon him as
he waited for Ross to announce, It's all yours, bombardier. Autopilot
engaged; we're on the bomb run, crew.

When the order came, Stan went to work, his mind speaking to him
as his hands carried out their duties.

First he ran the telescopic sight forward until the target appeared
in its eyepiece. There it was. A sprawl of huge buildings with three
smokestacks. A four-lane highway passed to the north, crossing the
Main River at a thirty-degree angle. Check, check, check. It was
definitely his target. Then he put the course line on the aiming point—
a gray building just beyond the stacks—the power plant. The course
line drifted left—a minute correction. There, it's holding. Now the rate
hair. He lined it up so it crossed with the course line on the aiming
point, then adjusted the rate knob until the cross hair stopped moving.
Oops, we're drifting left again, he thought. He made another adjustment
and felt the airplane bank onto a new heading. He made another
adjustment. It was looking good. He glanced at his watch—another
three minutes.

Stan ran through his prerelease checklist: panel—all lights burning,
release switch on "auto," involometer set to salvo the GPs, incendiaries
on four-second delay.

Violent motion threw the cross hairs off. He glanced up from the
bombsight—holy shit! Smoke from bursting shells was so thick it was
beginning to obscure the target. Forget it, he thought; concentrate on
keeping those cross hairs centered. Where were the explosions from
the lead group's drop? Why couldn't he see them? He peeked out the

nose. Oh, for Christ's sake! Blossoms of smoke and dust rose a good mile in front of the target! The formation's main point of impact, a complex of assembly buildings, was barely touched. Stan guessed that only one squadron had managed to score a hit.

1527 Hours, 1 July 1943
En Route to England

BT spent the return trip in a daze of rattling machine-gun fire, slashing passes by enemy fighters—Me 109s with yellow noses this time—and a cacophony of intercom messages: "Two down in the low squadron." "*Bouncing Betty* is hit; I see six chutes!" "Watch out, tail, there's a half-dozen coming your way." "I'm about out of ammo; we got any more back here?" "Hey, good shooting turret. You got that bastard!"

BT's numbed mind could absorb no more. He discovered with slight surprise that his oxygen mask prevented him from biting the knuckle of his index finger. The swarming P-47s above the French coast looked like angels. In the lull that followed their rendezvous, Sprague screamed his displeasure at the bombardier.

"What the hell do you mean, 'the system made a premature release'? Somebody sure as hell had to toggle those things. Who, I ask, but you?"

BT smiled behind the concealment of his oxygen mask. He knew his boss. With his career riding on the success of Night Train, a determined investigation to place responsibility would never materialize. Hadn't the general ordered the radio operator to abandon his gun position long enough to send their coded strike report? They were already on record as having "bombed primary with excellent results."

BT's euphoria at being free at last of enemy threat was short-lived. Their radio operator relayed a coded weather forecast for their return. England was covered by dense cloud cover with ceilings and visibility reduced by fog and drizzle.

As BT sat digesting this glum news, the engineer advised that their fuel situation was critical. They were an hour behind flight plan and had used up critical reserves with high-power settings. Again, BT cursed the day Colyer and Sprague had thwarted his opportunity to evade this madness. Never again. If the senator couldn't wrangle a reassignment for him. . . . In the meantime he had to get this wreck on the ground—and walk away from it.

The practice runs of Bomber Command's version of a formation landing in bad weather were chilling enough when flown in clear air. The margin for error was virtually zero. Somehow BT had never really believed he would ever be called upon to actually make one. But there was no alternative. Roughly two hundred bombers, all low on fuel, were descending on bases no more than five miles apart. Recovery time for the entire swarm was limited to about twenty minutes. Midair collisions could equal combat losses.

When Sprague gave no indication that he would attempt the approach and landing from the left seat, BT checked his seat belt and started his descent toward the Siddley marker beacon. He turned as the flight engineer tugged his sleeve.

"Sir, the left mains don't even register on the gauge. It's gonna be close."

BT could only nod. What the hell did the man expect him to do about it? Invent some fucking gasoline?

With only five of the original nine-ship squadron formed on him, BT skimmed the cloud tops at four thousand feet. When the ADF needle indicated they were nearing the station, he mentally reviewed the procedure as he called for gear and flaps down. He recalled that the lead ship was to cross the beacon on the main runway heading. The lower left-hand ship would peel on station passage and set up a standard rate, one-needle-width turn. Descent would be adjusted to place the plane over the beacon on runway heading at an altitude of one thousand feet at the completion of its 360-degree turn. Succeeding ships would follow at thirty-second intervals.

BT, as formation lead, was the fifth ship to peel off. He noted station passage and punched the instrument panel clock to start his timed turn. One minute passed. At a minute and forty seconds the waist advised that his left wingman was turning. BT took a deep breath. Timing was crucial. He waited exactly thirty seconds, then wrenched the wheel to the left.

Bright, late-afternoon sunlight turned to gray murk as the nose plunged into the cloud cover. Keep a standard-rate turn, he said to himself; that's essential. His pattern was larger, so a five-hundred-feet-per-minute rate of descent would be adequate. He saw the airspeed building and eased the throttles back to hold at 150 mph. Sprague started calling airspeed and altitude. At one thousand feet, with the ADF needle pointing over the left wing, BT leveled off and rolled out on the reciprocal of the runway heading. He heard Sprague call, "Station passage."

BT homed in on the ADF beacon and started slowing to 140 mph. He breathed easier after station passage but winced as prop wash rocked the wings. Damn! he thought; that means we're awfully close to the plane ahead. BT dropped the nose and called for full flaps, his voice hoarse with strain. He sneaked a peek ahead. It was like staring into a pail of gray dishwater. He turned back to the instruments. Hang on engines, he thought, we almost have it made. The altimeter sagged through three hundred feet. BT almost sobbed with relief when he heard Sprague call out, "Runway at one o'clock."

BT looked up in time to see two yellow flares cross in an arc. He pointed the nose between them, silently blessing the two men standing on either side of the approach end marking the touchdown point.

The runway! A black ribbon of glistening, wet macadam stretched before him. Summoning the last vestige of his sagging energy, BT hauled back on the throttles and sucked the wheel into his gut. The bomber touched down hard, bounced once, then hugged the ground. He added power to clear the runway—knowing that the next aircraft was only thirty seconds behind.

BT entered the circular hardstand, wheeled the big bomber in a tight circle and called for engine shutdown. He couldn't suppress a giggle as number one coughed and died of fuel starvation. Men poured from a waiting ambulance and clambered into the open bomb bay entrance. With hands shaking too badly to write, BT wordlessly tossed the Form-1 flight log onto the instrument console. Piss on it, he thought wearily. Let someone else do the paperwork. He was finished.

☆ ☆ ☆

THE HEARING

DAY TWO

29 November 1945
Hearing Room B, Building 1048, War Department

Colonel Blankenship, standing before his file-laden table, spoke into the hush following General Woods's call to order. He faced the witness attired in a fashionably tailored civilian suit seated in what the army inventory listed as a "side-chair, wooden, w/arms."

"Would you state your name and address for the record, Sir?"

"Walter Smithers. I live at 3485 Holly Circle, Alexandria, Virginia."

"Thank you. I believe you were employed as a civilian consultant to the Targeting Subcommittee at Headquarters, U.S. Army Air Corps during the period 5 January 1942 to 10 July 1944. Is that correct?"

"It is."

"And would you describe the nature of your duties there?"

"TarSubCom, headed by Maj. Gen. Edwin Jones, was charged with selecting and prioritizing targets within the European landmass for destruction by our strategic bomber forces."

Janet regarded the witness as she sought to restore circulation to her still-numb toes. An overnight arctic chill had descended on the nation's capital, and her parking slot left her with a two-block walk. She wished for her sketch pad. The previous day's proceedings had been nothing short of boring. If she had paper and charcoal, she could at least record some of her impressions. Writing material of any kind was forbidden in the hearing room, of course. The only written record of the hearing would be the official report.

She would caricaturize Smithers as a fox, she decided. A receding chin and forehead emphasized his long, pointed nose. Jet black hair— a dye job, she wagered—worn with an old-fashioned part down the center, terminated above elongated ears plastered flat against his head. His dainty, well-shod feet were crossed at the ankles in a slightly feminine manner. Equally dainty hands lay in his lap. He exuded a poised, confident air; he was obviously at home when providing testimony and proud of his store of important facts. Janet decided she didn't like the man. Perhaps instead of a fox, she would sketch him as an ass.

Caught up in her game, Janet turned her attention to the five members of the investigative board. Her father had given her a thumbnail sketch of them. All had served in the Pacific, so theoretically they had no bias regarding events that had taken place in Europe. It was a good theory, her father had snorted, but not realistic. Army politics among its relatively small family of general officers transcended geography. Everyone knew everyone else, had been at West Point at the same time, or had served with or under each other at some point. Personal likes and dislikes were formed early and extended over entire careers.

They had in common, however, identical uniforms: forest green tunics and the gray-beige "pink" trousers. Only one affected the popular "Ike" jacket favored by the Allied supreme commander in Europe. Each wore silver command pilot's wings, with a star surrounded by a wreath, atop rows of multicolored ribbons denoting awards for valor and service— "fruit salad" in the military vernacular. General Woods's array extended from his breast pocket upward almost far enough to conceal his wings beneath his lapel.

Janet decided she would superimpose the board president's features on a bear—there was no other way to describe the man. General Woods's caustic, hard-driving demeanor was legendary. He would go far, her father had predicted, maybe even become chief of staff.

To Woods's extreme left sat Brig. Gen. Orville Kinzer, the chief of Fighter Operations in Pacific Command's headquarters. He had brush-cut reddish blond hair and a florid, chronically sunburned complexion. Heavyset, he viewed the world through pale blue eyes with a squint of sardonic amusement. He looked like an overgrown Saint Bernard puppy, Janet decided. Were there such things as reddish blond Saint Bernards?

The brigadier general seated between Kinzer and Woods should have been an undertaker. Lean to the point of emaciation, the pale-complected

Jack J. Black projected cold austerity. A military intelligence specialist, the man thrived on unraveling the enemy's secrets. Janet shivered as she made brief eye contact with his opaque black eyes; he gave her the creeps. She would adorn his portrait with a skull and crossbones.

Her interest was diverted by a sharp exchange between the witness and General Woods.

"Mister Smithers, the board is generally aware of agreements reached during the Casablanca Conference. We were told yesterday of the internal friction that existed within the Combined Bomber Offensive staff. I had hoped that, today, we could get down to the specifics of what went into the planning of the Ploesti raid. Could you oblige us, please?"

Smithers compressed his lips. "I will endeavor to present my testimony as succinctly as possible, General. It was just that those policies formed our planning framework. The destruction of Germany's oil resources was not, in the beginning, a high priority. I thought you should be made aware of that."

"We know. Get on with it." Woods waved a ham-sized hand impatiently.

Blankenship attempted to soothe the ruffled witness. "Sir, what led you to move Ploesti ahead of other, higher priority targets?"

"Politics" was the waspish reply. "The British were exerting pressure on President Roosevelt to abandon daylight bombing. General Eaker told General Arnold that a convincing demonstration deep in enemy territory was essential."

"Then the destruction of the Ploesti oil refineries themselves was not deemed essential to the Allied war effort?" Blankenship's eyebrows raised fractionally.

"I didn't say that. The refineries and cracking plants at Ploesti provided at least 35 percent of Hitler's petroleum products. The twelve refineries there had the capacity to produce almost two hundred thousand barrels per day. Certainly it was an important target. But oil was fourth on the priority list emerging from Casablanca—behind submarine and aircraft production and surface transportation systems."

"And when was this decision made, that Ploesti would be a priority target?"

"In late 1942. But Ploesti was not selected for its strategic significance. As I understood it, the target represented one of the few major installations that could be safely attacked without a fighter escort for the bombers."

Blankenship chewed his lower lip. "You say, 'As you understood it.' You did not, I take it, have a hand in that decision?"

"No, Sir. TarSubCom was cut out of the pattern completely. General Jones protested vigorously to General Arnold, but he was ignored."

"I see." Blankenship turned to General Woods. "Does any board member have a question for Mister Smithers?" After negative head shakes, he continued. "I suggest we take a short break, gentlemen, before our next witness."

"Yes, Colonel, I was present at the March 1943 meeting during which General Arnold was briefed on Tidal Wave."

Blankenship paced the uncarpeted floor in front of an alert but relaxed brigadier general. "Who submitted the plan, General Laxalt?"

"A General Brereton. He had been selected by the Air Staff to do the detailed mission planning." The wary officer, young for flag rank, gave no indication that he would volunteer information.

"What was the essence of his plan, Sir? Just a general overview, if you can."

"He proposed to strike the oil refinery complex with at least a hundred and fifty B-24s from bases in North Africa. The mission would be flown at extremely low level to gain the advantage of surprise."

"Why such a large force for such a seemingly vulnerable target?"

"The distance represented the B-24's extreme range. A redundancy factor was included to provide for planes aborting because of mechanical difficulty, navigation errors, weather, and fuel exhaustion."

"The use of a heavy bomber at low altitude must have created some question," said Blankenship. "What was the rationale for departing from the customary B-24 mission profile?"

"Pinpoint accuracy; the key main points of impact were sometimes no more than a powerhouse or cracking plant. There was also the surprise factor. Brereton believed it was essential."

"Did you agree?"

"It was not up to me to agree or disagree. It was my impression that the decision had already been made. The briefing was to provide information, not to solicit approval."

"Would you care to express an opinion as to the plan's overall feasibility?"

"I would not."

Blankenship stroked pursed lips. "Thank you for your cooperation, General." He made no attempt to conceal the sarcasm in his voice.

Chapter Twenty

5 July 1943
Headquarters, 2d Air Division
Buxton Hall

Seven pairs of eyes regarded the tabletop display with much the same fascination reserved for a piece of lewd sculpture. The eyes belonging to the pink and lavender cherubs staring down from the frescoed ceiling didn't count. Already those eyes were filmed with the residue from countless cigars and cigarettes consumed in the echoing dining hall since its conversion.

Major General Lewis H. Brereton, slender pointer in hand, carefully recorded his uniformed, bemedaled audience's reactions. His product was definitely in the hard sell category. "The boys in RAF Intelligence spent a lot of long hours creating this little display," he told his audience in a clipped, faintly foreign accent. His naturally olive-toned complexion was further darkened by recent exposure to desert sun and wind. Clearly he was not a regular member of the group standing before him, their features bleached a pasty white by the dreary English climate.

"This display reveals far better than aerial photos the difficulty of taking out this particular target. Note," he touched a number of miniaturized structures comprising the three-dimensional exhibit, "the wide dispersal of key installations."

Brigadier General Goss, arms across chest, was moved to remark, "My boy would give an arm and a leg to have that layout for his electric train. God, what beautiful work. An entire city done in microscopic detail. It must have taken months."

Brereton bristled with a sudden flash of irritation. "I doubt that you could afford it, General," he snapped. "To continue: Ploesti, as a city, has no strategic value. It merely provides bedrooms for the workers who operate this series of refineries. They completely encircle its perimeter. Furthermore, not all of the area they occupy is crucial to production. These tank farms, for example: They contain refined products, quickly replaceable. The essential structures are these cracking towers, powerhouses, and distillation plants." Brereton briskly tapped a dozen relatively small complexes. "We have it on good authority that these are further protected by blast walls."

Brigadier General LeRoy Zimmer, acting commander of the 2d Air Division, whistled soundlessly. "A real bitch," he muttered. "Those eggs are going to have to be laid in there by someone like Dizzy Dean. But before we get into that, let's talk about how we're going to get from here to there. Hell, that's more than three thousand miles round trip—right through the heart of Germany's defense forces."

Brereton, visibly annoyed at having the sequence of his presentation disrupted, dismissed the request with typical curtness. "That's been worked out, General. The task force will stage out of North Africa. Your planes will be equipped with long-range tanks. That places the target well within the range of a B-24. The crucial aspect of the entire operation is precise delivery."

"The Norden is good, General," Goss, the 1st Air Division commander, observed, "but that's asking a lot. You're talking about two or three dozen aiming points with an allowable CE of maybe fifty yards."

"Exactly. A factor that gave us considerable difficulty."

"And the solution?"

"You will drop from an altitude at which you can hardly miss— fifty feet or thereabouts."

Following a shocked silence, Zimmer expressed the reaction of all. "In a goddamn *Liberator?*"

Brereton almost lost them then. The group broke into derisive laughter and began conversing with jocularity.

Flushed with anger, the balding, stocky two-star general rapped the display table with his pointer. "All right, gentlemen. Enough of that. You were not called here to vote; you are here to receive orders. Is that clear?"

The gathering of senior officers sobered, somewhat embarrassed at the stern rebuke.

"Months have gone into planning this operation. This target is carried on the books as number one in priority. Hitler obtains more than a third of his oil from Ploesti. Its destruction will shorten the war by six months to a year.

"Unqualified success depends upon two elements: total surprise and unerring accuracy—both in bomb delivery and navigation. The complex is lightly defended at this time, for the very reason you just expressed. The Germans consider it out of our reach, especially from the west. What defense capability they possess is oriented against attack from Russian-based aircraft. Needless to say, total surprise depends upon total secrecy. No one, I repeat, no one, is to be briefed on this mission without my express approval. You will submit a list of names to me of those whose knowledge you consider absolutely essential. More than a thousand lives could depend on how the matter of security is handled."

"*How* many?" someone asked.

"Closer to fifteen hundred," Brereton replied, matter-of-factly. "The ops order calls for simultaneous strikes by five groups, roughly a hundred and seventy-five ships, over a twenty-minute period."

A thoughtful Zimmer observed, "Every one of our crews will need to undergo retraining, General. Is there a date set for this party?"

"There is. We are draining resources that General Eaker and General Eisenhower require for major operations both here and—er—in other locations. The mission must launch not later than August 1. Participating units have already been selected; you will be provided movement orders as you leave. The units will depart for Benghazi, Libya, as soon as the necessary aircraft retrofitting is complete. Low-level formation training may be commenced immediately, but for reasons of security the final phase will be carried out there.

"That about wraps it up, gentlemen. If any of you have doubts about the outcome of this operation—well, I plan to be in the lead ship. Good day."

Brigadier General Elliott Sprague left the closely guarded meeting room in deep thought. Without comment he accepted—and signed for—a bulging, double-sealed envelope. BT joined him as he descended the broad entry steps to his waiting car. Not even the generals' trusted aides had been permitted to participate in Brereton's briefing. BT was consumed with curiosity. He was to remain unenlightened. Sprague's response to his overtures was limited to noncommittal grunts.

The hawk-faced wing commander had remained silent and unobtrusive throughout the meeting. Other than a brief exchange with Brereton to establish that Sprague was in Pacific Command headquarters when the general was in command of the Philippine bomber group, he'd kept in the background. Sprague remained very much in the Eighth Air Force's doghouse, a result of the ill-fated Night Train operation. He still smarted from General Eaker's caustic criticism. The official loss figures released for general consumption listed forty-seven bombers and crews missing. After adding the aircraft disabled beyond repair, a closely guarded figure, that number increased to just under a hundred. Fortunately for Sprague, reconnaissance photos revealed extensive damage to the target. The foes of daylight bombing were successfully held at bay, and Senator Templeton returned to Washington—unconvinced, but with fangs drawn.

This did not prevent Eaker from holding a scathing, private session concerning Sprague's leadership. The fact that his lead squadron had failed to place a single bomb on the target received specific comment. The hard-faced Eaker had been blunt in his assessment of Sprague's future with the Eighth Air Force.

Now Sprague would be part of a big operation free of Eaker's oversight. It was an opportunity to recoup his status as a bold tactician. Some visits had to be made, some chits called in, some favors purchased. He eyed BT. The young captain's performance in the lead aircraft that day had left much to be desired, but . . . The little bastard *was* wired into some of the right places. Whatever, Elliott Sprague was going to play a key roll in Tidal Wave; his career might well hang in the balance.

He fished a fresh cigar from his tunic. Without looking at BT as he clipped its end, he asked, "BT, does your dad know that you're in hock to half the headquarters staff with unpaid poker losses?"

5 July 1943
Luftwaffe Command Post
Otopenii, Romania

General Alfred Gerstenberg radiated confidence and energy as he faced an attentive Maj. Bernhard Woldenga. The major, looking older than his twenty-nine years, was the last, and most welcome, staff member allocated to the hard-driving commander of Romania's defense forces. Fresh from eight months of directing the fighter defense against

Allied bombers in North Africa, the handsome but stern-faced Woldenga was a prize catch. Despite assurances by General Galland and *Reichsmarschall* Goering to send him first-line troops, too many were ill-trained, apathetic, or burned out by two years of debilitating combat.

The German troops regarded an assignment to Romania as escape from the hell of daily exposure to the firestorm sweeping Germany's ever-shrinking empire. They fell on the fleshpots of Bucharest and the unbelievable largess of unrationed meat, butter, sugar, and imported spirits like the biblical horde of locusts. Added to the feast were hundreds of nubile young women, deprived of male companionship when the Germans sent thousands of Romanian conscripts to fight on the eastern front.

The fun-seeking arrivals soon discovered that Gerstenberg was a harsh leader. Military discipline was reinstilled with stern, recruit-training measures. Skills were sharpened by never-ending practice drills. By sheer determination and driving effort, the sandy-haired general had made Ploesti's oil complex the best-defended target in all of Europe. That it had been done without divulging to the enemy the true extent of its bristling defensive firepower astonished even Gerstenberg himself.

The general, overjoyed at having an audience of professional peers, paced before the sprawling wall map as he spoke. The room, one glass wall overlooking the Situation Room, with its profusion of charts and plotting boards, reflected Gerstenberg's penchant for austerity. Plain gray linoleum covered the floor. The walls were free of decoration and the furniture was strictly utilitarian dark wood.

"The overall strategy is based on forming two rings of defense against air attack," he revealed. "Here, forming the outer ring, are fighter bases in Greece, Bulgaria, Crete, and southern Italy. A long-range Wurzburg radar is mounted atop Mount Chernin, here, on the Yugoslav-Bulgarian border. These fighter units, admittedly, are not first rate. But they will provide early warning and a measure of harassment to the invaders, both coming and going."

Major Woldenga took advantage of a pause to observe, "*Herr* General, you are basing your outer defense to deal with an attack from the southwest. That is impossible. The American heavies in North Africa have a maximum range of less than two thousand miles. Is not Russia, to the east, the real threat?"

Gerstenberg's eyes gleamed. "Today, yes. Tomorrow is an entirely different situation. Italy will fall to the Western forces; even now they prepare for a massive invasion. The Italians are weak and have no stomach for this war. In the not-too-distant future the American bombers will have bases there. Then, Major, our skies will be black with their numbers. The Russians are not a factor, yet." He waved a deprecatory hand. "Stalin has scrapped bomber production to build fighter-bombers needed for frontline troop support. The day will come when a land war must be faced—not only from the east, but from within Romania itself. Premier Antonescu is an opportunist. There are strong pro-Allied feelings among the decadent *boyer* families even now. At the first indication of support from the West, our friendly Romanian hosts will turn on us like jackals. But that is in the future. For the present we fight to preserve the supply of Romanian oil. The survival of the Fatherland is at stake."

The gesticulating Gerstenberg, warming to his task as lecturer, paused to remove his tunic. "The inner ring is devised to cope with both air *and* ground attack. *Jagdgruppe* 4, here, northeast of Ploesti at Mizil, is equipped with the Me 109F and manned by experienced German pilots. It constitutes our first line of air-to-air defense. Just east, at Zilistea, a *nachtjagdgeschwader* of twin-engine Me 110 night fighters is in the process of becoming operational.

"Two wings of Romanian pilots are based outside Bucharest, at Pepira. They are assigned to defend the capital city." A dismissive shrug. "Let them. Bucharest is of no importance as a target. Some of the Romanians are excellent pilots, but for the most part they come from rich, titled families. They play at war. On a recent drill those alerted to sit in their planes did so with champagne bottles alongside."

Major Woldenga listened intently. More and more he was impressed with his new commander's grasp of the essential elements of leadership. The middle-aged major was no stranger to the burdens of command. A master mariner with the Hamburg-Amerika steamship line at the age of twenty-five, he underwent pilot training when his employer planned its own airline. Since joining the *Luftwaffe,* his rise had been rapid through assignments to fighters in Poland, Greece, Britain, Russia, and North Africa. Woldenga's feeling that he had been relegated to a backwater of the war dissipated.

Gerstenberg went on to describe the deployment of 88mm, 37mm, and 20mm antiaircraft weapons—forty batteries in all—operated by German crews. Outside this deadly "inner ring" were machine-gun batteries manned by Austrian and Romanian gunners. The majority of these were cleverly concealed in barns and haystacks and atop factories—even in church steeples. He enthusiastically explained how they were exercised frequently with flybys of old Heinkle bombers and Ju 52 transports. The ebullient general saved his favorite device for last.

"The *Flakwagen*," he announced with pride. "A dozen railroad cars have been constructed with collapsible sides. Inside are concealed 37mm cannon and quad-mounted twenties that can quickly be dispersed anywhere. They form a deadly surprise for the unwary.

"In summary, I confess to borrowing a page from the *Führer*'s book, Major Woldenga. You see before you *Festung* Ploesti."

6 July 1943
Walden Abbey

Ross concentrated on his squadron commander's words with difficulty. The going-away party for Rex the night before had lasted until 0400. The cocky little copilot had been helped onto a six-by-six less than an hour before, headed for the P-47 base at Raydon. Despite the problems Ross had endured with Rex, he discovered that he missed the guy. The man he'd drawn as a permanent replacement was a stick— a competent pilot but devoid of humor.

Colonel Deckard's next words penetrated his pounding hangover, however. Ross jerked straight upright as he heard, "I'm taking you off operations, Colyer, effective today."

Ross frantically searched his memory. What miscreant deed, lapse of proficiency, or unwise words could have precipitated such drastic action? "Colonel! I—I don't understand. What am I supposed to have done now?"

Deckard chuckled. They were seated in his office. The Eighth was stood down that day—weather again—and the weary crews were making full use of the break.

"Relax, Lieutenant. You aren't being fired." He paused to strip a fresh cigar. Fishing for his lighter, he continued. "You've got a new job."

Ross felt the combination of brandy and orange gin churn in his stomach. But what he was hearing caused a worse sickness. That goddamn BT, he thought. The shit has pulled it off. I'm being assigned to that ass Sprague as his aide.

"Sir, I don't know what you have in mind, but I beg of you, let me stay with my crew and finish our missions. We have ten now, and—well, we're not the fuckup crew we once were. I'd like to finish my tour with them."

"Oh, you'll keep your crew—never fear—for the immediate future at least. But, to be blunt, the flight surgeon tells me that they are ready for R and R."

Ross brightened. So that was it. A week at the aircrew Rest and Rehabilitation Center. All right! Early in the war the brass realized that the constant pressure of combat would cause even the boldest to succumb. Mental aberration was something that must be dealt with; entire crews were being lost because of flawed judgment or irrational reaction by only one member. A sumptuous resort hotel was requisitioned and converted into a spa. At roughly the midpoint of their combat tour, crews were sent there for a week-long release from the pressure-cooker atmosphere of war.

"That's great, Colonel. The men were just talking last week that it was about our turn."

"Oh, I'm not talking about Southport," Deckard replied. "I won't deny that you've earned it, but it just isn't on for right now. You'll get a break from doing missions and," he chuckled again, "a change of scenery. Here's the dope.

"An important low-level operation is being planned. Where and when, I can't say. It involves a number of B-24s. The 365th is included."

"Low level? Liberators?" Ross's brow puckered as he digested Deckard's explanation. "Where? And how low is 'low'?"

"I honestly don't know where. I gather that we'll relocate to a staging base. The altitude they're talking about is a hundred feet—or less."

"A hundred feet? Good Christ, we'll get slaughtered. You can hit a '24 with a slingshot at that altitude."

"Assume total surprise and light defense—that's what they tell me, anyway," said Deckard.

Too astonished to respond, Ross considered the implications of dropping at low level with a plane the size of a B-24. He could find nothing reassuring about the prospect.

"Okay, here's what's involved," Deckard continued. "As of now, the group is stood down for training. Tomorrow we start practicing low-level formation flying in three-ship elements—at first, anyway.

It'll give the navigators fits, you can bet. How good is your navigator, by the way?"

Ross, loathe to criticize a crew member to his boss, hesitated. "I'll go with him. But, Sir, Hanson has twenty-four missions in. He's sweating his last one. He's good, damn good. It's just—well, he has the clanks right now. You know how it is—he wants to get that last one in and get home."

"I see. Well," Deckard's voice hardened, "that leads me to the next item on the agenda. You'll be the one to decide whether he goes or not. As of tomorrow morning you're the squadron operations officer. Ellis is getting his own squadron. He stays behind. You're the one who'll set up our low-level training. You'll fly this mission, whatever it turns out to be, with your old crew, but it'll be your last as an aircraft commander."

Ross's open-mouthed astonishment prompted the colonel's features to assume a broad smirk. "Oh, and by the way, congratulations, Captain. The rank goes with the territory."

6 July 1943
Aschaffenburg

Stripped to his undershorts, *Leutnant* Kurt Heintze sprawled in a wood-slatted deck chair on the west-facing patio. A dozen of his fellow pilots reclined in similar positions, allowing the summer sun to wash away the accumulated fatigue of the past three days. They'd flown double sorties, and the effects of hammering cannon, muscle-straining turns, and constant head swiveling had taken a severe toll. Pilots would collapse into bed only to awake, drenched in cold sweat, as their unconscious minds relived those brief brushes with death.

Each morning Kurt had been greeted by the raucous, nerve-jolting bray of the alert klaxon. After jog-trotting—no one ran anymore—to the parked aircraft and listening to the crew chief's briefing with numb indifference, Kurt would return to the silent world, chilled and devoid of life-sustaining oxygen. The enemy was never difficult to locate: The Americans followed a schedule that resembled that of a commuter train. Kurt would pick a target and dive, twist, and shoot—then pray that his break escaped the red curtain of tracer rounds searching for a vital spot. And still the bombers came, returning in defiance of the repeated decimation of their formations—returning in ever-increasing numbers.

Gretta's last letter had been deposited on his bed during that day's mission. Kurt hadn't waited to shower and change before ripping open the flap and devouring its contents. She was still in Munich: ". . . Papa says we are safe here. The Americans can never bomb this far inside Germany. . . . Travel to Switzerland is difficult and dangerous. . . ."

Gott im Himmel! Kurt thought. What did it take for those blind fools to accept reality? It wasn't the Americans who represented an immediate threat. Besides, their pinpoint attacks largely spared residential areas. It was the English and their nightly destruction of vast portions of targeted cities. And they were roaming deeper and deeper into the *Reich.*

Kurt turned his attention to a half-track drawing to a halt in front of the castle entrance. A dozen smartly turned out men leaped to the ground. Laughing, slapping each other's backs, forage caps adjusted at a rakish angle, they retrieved their meager luggage and strutted up the broad flight of steps. Replacements. The second shipment this month. Not a hundred hours of flying time among them. Where did they come from? Was there no end to this parade of youthful, healthy bodies? Idly Kurt tried to pick out the two or three who would still be around this time next month. *Jagdgeschwader* 21's losses had exceeded 100 percent since he had joined it. His own worried crew chief had painted his distinctive falcon and spinner stripes on a third ship.

The "old tigers," their comatose bodies arrayed around him on the sun-soaked patio, were easily recognizable. Their dull eyes focused on a point two thousand meters in space during conversation. They spoke in monosyllables. They chain-smoked cigarettes, held between fingers that frequently betrayed a tendency to tremble. And they consumed vast quantities of cognac.

Kurt's interest was drawn to the last of the new arrivals to dismount. Unlike his fellow passengers, he was hatless and wore his wrinkled tunic unbuttoned. Soiled breeches were tucked into boots that sagged around his ankles and hadn't seen a brush or polish for some time. He had ridden in the cab with the driver. The man turned his squinting gaze upward to the elevated patio. Kurt's lethargy evaporated. He sprang to his feet and raced to the low railing.

"Toni!" he called. "Toni Stepinac. You crazy Chetnik, where have you been?"

*   *   *

Stepinac, his black-bearded features split into a broad grin, held his glass, containing a full three fingers of amber cognac, under Kurt's nose. The pair perched on the patio railing's wide concrete surface.

"So, your unbelievable luck holds," said Toni. "How many more of those flying battleships have you managed to sink?"

Kurt laughed. "Not enough, but I can't wait to hear what happened to you. No one was certain that you had managed to get clear of the fire."

Stepinac sobered. It was then that Kurt detected the puckered scar tissue disfiguring the big Slav's throat and wrist. "It was a near thing. My oxygen mask, goggles, and helmet saved my face. My greatest worry was my chute. It had a hole burned in it, but I walked away from the landing. How did you manage to duck those fighters? Lightnings, weren't they? Where did they come from?"

Kurt's own smile faded. "They chased me west until my fuel ran out. I zoomed and left it. I was back here that same night. As to where they came from—I did the unpardonable. I failed to check above us before we pounced. They had me cold as I was coming down. I was certain that they would finish me off as I hung there in that chute harness. It's a terribly helpless feeling, I can tell you." His gaze strayed, unfocused, to the horizon. "I've managed to shoot down two of the fork-tailed devils since. I wondered both times if either was the man who spared me." He laughed dryly and stared into Stepinac's eyes. "Perhaps I'm getting too old for this business, Toni. I no longer have the feeling that it's all a game."

Stepinac gave his old flight leader a quizzical look. "And the big fat ones. Is your inverted head-on attack still successful?"

"Not completely. First, not many of the new pilots we're getting have the flying technique to hit and get out. Nor the inclination," he added. "And the bombers learned to counter by dropping their noses at the last minute to bring that damnable upper turret to bear." He shrugged. "I still use the maneuver, but it will never stop them. They increase like unwanted houseguests.

"The rules have changed since the bombers came, Toni. They are determined to bring us to our knees by destroying our cities, our factories—our very culture. They are workmen. They plod their way to a target, destroy it, and return home. And they give no quarter along the way. There is one in particular, a Liberator. Twice I have engaged it without scoring more than one hit. The pilot actually turns into my firing pass. I have been close enough to see that it has the picture of a naked woman painted on its nose and the name *Happy Hooker.* I barely limped home with my rudder shot away after our second encounter. The pilot looked me straight in the eye; it almost seems that he knows me. I am determined to bring that one down, Toni. That one is mine." Kurt's voice took on a strident pitch.

"Not once have we been successful in turning a formation away from its target. Not once! Their losses are often sickening, but still they come."

Stepinac's features formed into one of his ferocious scowls. "They will never break our spirit, our determination, Kurt. You will see—the swine will tire of such huge losses and seek an honorable settlement."

Kurt laughed bitterly. "There is no indication of that happening. There is a rumor that their leaders met in North Africa and announced that they will accept nothing other than Germany's unconditional surrender. No, the bombers have none of the feeling for fair play that we share with their fighters. They are bent on destruction—total and absolute destruction of Germany and all it stands for. I often wonder if the crew of that Liberator would have spared me as that Lightning pilot did."

Major Fritz Bümen interrupted the reunion, crossing the patio in bouncy strides and extending a hand of welcome. "*Feldwebel* Stepinac. What a pleasure. I just learned of your return. We could discover nothing of your fate, you know." He eyed the scars. "I see you didn't escape without damage, however."

"A scratch, *Herr* Major," Toni said, waving a dismissing hand. "But I see congratulations are in order—your promotion. By the way, is my old job still open?"

Bümen studied the eager young man at length before responding. "*Leutnant* Heintze's wingman? I fear not. No, you will be assigned an entire *schwarm, Feldwebel* Stepinac. Experience is a scarce commodity with us just now." He paused. "Here, sit at this table. I'll join you in a beer." After an orderly had replenished their glasses, Bümen continued. "I hope you learned well from your leader, Stepinac—he's leaving us."

Both men regarded the major with stares of questioning astonishment.

"It seems that Fighter Command sees things differently than we do here," Bümen continued. "I've been ordered to select one of my best pilots for reassignment to, of all places, Romania."

"Romania?" Kurt frowned. "But, *Herr* Major, we have no enemy in Romania. Or is it the Russian advance?"

Bümen responded in discouraged tones. "We have no enemy in Romania, yet, *Herr Leutnant*. What we do have in Romania is oil. Huge quantities of it. And where there is a plentiful supply of oil, my young friends, we will soon have a greedy enemy. I do not know all the details, Kurt, but a new composite *jagdgeschwader* is being formed—from units on all fronts—to defend the oil fields from heavy-bomber attack. Don't ask me where it is expected the enemy will come from, but the orders come from General Galland himself.

"You will not be disappointed, Kurt. I am authorized to tell you that you will be made a *staffelkapitän* and promoted to the rank of *hauptmann*."

As Stepinac's delighted shout died, Bümen added, "It is time to recognize your ability. Look at this as a double reward. First, you will have an opportunity to use your talent as a fighter pilot for something other than individual combat. Second, you deserve to be given a respite from your punishing schedule. You will be sorely missed, but more of that later. Heavy weather is predicted for the next two days."

"Weather?" Kurt seemed puzzled.

Bümen laughed softly. "I will elaborate on that last remark at your farewell party. Tonight."

Chapter Twenty-one

14 July 1943
Libya, North Africa

"See, there—just as I told you."

Seated atop a rare creamy white camel, as befitted a subchieftain, Abdul sighted along the line indicated by Saddam's dirt-grimed brown finger. Squinting against the searing desert sun, the white-robed Bedouin contemplated the scene below. Eyes, set deep in coffee-dark features, glittered with satisfaction. Beneath a prominent, hawklike nose he allowed thin lips to form one of his rare smiles. "Ay-i-e-e-e. What a treasure! Think of the luxury of sleeping inside those stout walls during the cursed *Khamseen*. We will remove it to the oasis and be the envy of all."

The object of their interest was a pyramid. Constructed of heavy plywood and situated in a level valley area, relatively free of sand dunes, it measured precisely eight feet in height and width. Painted a garish orange and adorned with four-inch-wide diagonal black stripes, it offered a jarring contrast to the surrounding sea of dun-colored real estate.

Saddam turned in his ornately appointed saddle and regarded his companion with wide-eyed curiosity. "What do you believe this strange object to be?"

Abdul scowled to conceal his own ignorance. "It is obviously a tent made of the finest of material," he scornfully told his subordinate.

"And why do you believe the soldiers in the truck that crawls on the sand placed it here?"

Saddam's question prompted another scowl. "They seek to hide it, of course. It is of great value."

"Might it be a place of worship for the nonbelievers? Might not they be angry if we remove it?"

"Ah, you ignorant son of a camel. The foreign soldiers do not worship. Besides, is it not written by the Prophet that 'he who destroys a place of false worship is assured a place in heaven'?"

Saddam eyed the haughty subchief with judiciously concealed skepticism. Abdul had many such quotes attributed to the Prophet. However, when Saddam had cited some of them to a visiting mullah, that worthy professed ignorance. Saddam sighed in resignation as Abdul whipped his ungainly steed into a shambling trot toward the mysterious pyramid.

"Navigator to pilot. We're over the IP. Turn now to one-eight-seven degrees. We're on our bomb run. Target should be at twelve o'clock in seven minutes."

Ross Colyer, shiny new "railroad tracks" adorning his flight suit, wrestled the lumbering B-24 onto the new heading as best he could. Low-level turbulence made precise instrument readings impossible. Thermals from the 110-degree desert surface, whipped by swirling winds, tossed the twenty-ton bomber like an errant Ping-Pong ball. Even with outside air pouring through every vent, the temperature inside the uninsulated fuselage approached that of the burning sand below.

Seemingly immune to their jolting discomfort, the sweating aircraft commander pressed his intercom button. "Okay, Stan, let me know when you have the target in sight." He let out a short laugh. "We won't be practicing evasive action on this run—it's built-in."

"Roger, Captain," Lieutenant Cryhowski responded in a doleful tone. "Christ, we'll be lucky to get within a thousand yards, bouncing around like this. Can you possibly hold this bitch just a *little* bit steady during the bomb run? Hell, you don't need a bombsight for this; just close your eyes and let her fly."

"Excuses, excuses, Stan," Ross's new copilot, 1st Lt. Norman Brewster, chimed in. "You better come up with a CE under two hundred feet. Otherwise, we get to do this every day until you do."

"Fuck you, Norm. You just concentrate on trying to learn how to put the gear up and down without having it explained to you every time. I'll worry about our circular error."

"Okay, you two, knock it off," Ross interrupted. The conversation could be considered normal crew banter, but he knew it wasn't—not altogether, anyway. Brewster just hadn't fit into the crew as yet. The victim of a last-minute shuffle back at Walden Abbey, the sharp-tongued pilot had been reassigned as one of Ross's first acts as ops officer. As the aircraft commander of a newly arrived crew, Norm couldn't handle combat formation and was bounced back to copilot. Ross decided to use him to replace the reassigned Rex Compton. Bitterly resentful, the square-jawed Brewster could be depended upon for sarcastic criticism at the slightest opportunity.

"Pilot to crew. We'll be making three bombing runs at five hundred feet," Ross announced. "After the first drop we'll enter a racetrack to the left and make two more. Then I'll drop to a hundred feet or so and we'll make two strafing runs over the same target. Now, I know it's hotter than hell in here. But don't spray your shots just to get rid of ammo and go home; make every burst count. You gunners can load now, but don't arm your guns until the copilot gives the order. How we coming down there in the greenhouse?"

"No joy, Captain," 2d Lt. Kevin Hanson announced in a worried voice. It was his job to find the target area. He would catch hell from all concerned if he didn't. "These damn sand dunes all look the same. Better come three degrees left, though—there's a bit more drift than forecast. And Stan, get set. That target is down in a little valley. We'll pop over a dune and be right on top of it. You won't have much time. I'd get the bomb bay doors open now, if I were you. Damnit!" The perspiring Kevin left dirty streaks across his face as he wiped away sweat runnels with his forearm. "You see anything that looks like a target yet, Norm?"

"Zero," Brewster told him without evident interest. "Are you sure you were over the initial point when we turned?" Before the indignant navigator could respond, Norm continued, "Wait a minute—over there at two o'clock. What the hell is that? Looks like the target—or part of it anyway. Hell, it's moving!"

"Bombardier to pilot," Stan announced crisply. "Come twenty degrees right. I think we have the target in sight." Then, as the big Liberator wallowed into a turn, his voice grew shrill with frustrated rage. "Jeesus Kee-rist! Would you look at that?" As all heads inside the racing bomber swiveled to the right, Stan continued. "Them fucking ragheads are stealing our target!"

In the ninety seconds required for their thundering B-24 to reach the scene, Ross was able to confirm the excited bombardier's observation. Two antlike black figures were frantically attempting to urge a pair of protesting camels to a faster pace. Securely roped to both sides of each animal were four triangles of plywood. The bright orange and black markings left little doubt as to their origin.

Ross advanced the prop controls slightly and, cramming the Liberator's four throttles forward, hauled the big craft into a tight climbing turn. "Well, I'll be go to hell," he muttered. "Okay, close the bomb bay doors. Secure the guns. Stan, safety the bombs. A goddamn dry run—and for all the stupid reasons. What in Christ's name do you suppose they intend to do with that thing? Colonel Deckard is flat going to have a shit fit. I just wish we had a camera. Nobody, but nobody, is gonna believe this."

"Aw, Cap'n, these A-rabs'll take anything that ain't welded down," Ham Phillips interjected in his soft Tennessee drawl. "Just last week, the perimeter guards stopped two of 'em 'bout three in the morning. Know what they were carrying? A whole goddamn propeller—still in the shipping crate. Three hundred pounds that thing weighs—at least. And just two of them scrawny little farts. MPs said they had to run to catch 'em."

"We goin' home, Skipper?" Corporal Reed asked plaintively from the tail position. "If we are, I'd like to get out of this turret. It's like one of those carnival rides back here."

"That's a roger," Ross replied with weary disgust. "No reason to stooge around here with no target."

"Let's make just one firing pass at those thieving bastards," Stan pleaded indignantly. "Not hit 'em, just kick up some sand around their fucking black feet. Put the fear of Allah or whoever it is they talk to into their miserable hides. Better yet, let's sling one of these practice bombs at 'em. You wanted a camera, right? Well, we got one, you know. It automatically takes pictures of my bomb drops. That ten pounds of black powder won't hurt anybody. Makes a helluva bang, though. And you'd get your pictures!"

"No way, no how, Stan. You want to stir up an international incident?" Ross's handsome, dirt-caked features cracked into a grin at the bombardier's suggestion, however, as he eased back power and leveled off at two thousand feet. "Give me a heading back to base, will ya', Kevin?"

Stan tried once more. "Hey, look, Ross. Why don't we just salvo these eggs, shoot up a sand dune with our ammo, and say we hit the target? Who's to know? Sure as hell nobody's gonna find that target again. We'll fill another square, and it's one less of these stupid low-level practice missions we have to fly."

"Who's to know? I'm to know, that's who. And we need all the practice at this business we can get. Our scores are close to the worst in the group. No, we do it again—and again if necessary."

A palpable sullen silence settled over the crew. Ross was known to be a perfectionist. He insisted, for instance, that all crew members wear full combat-flying gear for these practice missions. While they sweltered inside sweat-soaked flying suits and heavy boots, other crews wore shorts and tennis shoes. Ross's reason was a flat, "Wait until you see a flash burn. This bird has one weakness: You have an accident and it can torch before you know it."

It was with measured tact that Sergeant Phillips posed the next question: "Cap'n, can you tell us just exactly *why* we're practicing this low-level stuff? Look, we froze our butts off flying high-altitude formation in England. We dropped bombs from up there and shot at every fighter in the entire *Luftwaffe*. Now we start this lurching around at a couple hundred feet shooting up somebody's desert. This is one mighty fine airplane, Cap'n, but hell, it ain't made for this kind of flying. The engines. They got less than two hundred hours, but we've sucked so much sand into 'em we'll have to change every damn one if we ever get a combat mission. What gives? We being punished or something?"

Ross signaled for Brewster to take the controls while he formed a reply. "I don't rightly know, Ham. Now the rest of you, listen up. I agree that the B-24 is not a low-level bomber. Could be we're gonna provide tactical support for the guys up there in Sicily. *Stars and Stripes* says they're catching pure hell. I don't know. What I do know is that when we take off for a low-level mission, we're going to be able to toss a bomb into a two-hundred-foot circle and put 75 percent of our .50-caliber rounds in a stationary ground target. Okay?"

There was no immediate response as the Liberator bucked northward across the featureless North African desert. Crew members, weary and disgusted by the aborted training mission, went about the business of securing gear and preparing to land. Ross reached for his canteen and tried to rinse away the taste of that damned, ever-present, gritty dust. It permeated every crack and crevice of the airplane, and their clothing as well. The stuff irritated heat rash, which, the crew was fond of swearing, had its own heat rash.

Privately, Ross asked himself the same questions his crew had posed. Just what the hell *was* going on? In the wildest stretch of his imagination he couldn't picture the *Happy Hooker* flying low-level support. For one thing, Stan was lost without his Norden bombsight. And the Norden was worthless at this altitude. Kevin wasn't trained for low-level navigation and the gunners were used to shooting at high-altitude moving targets. They thought it was funny when they couldn't hit ground targets as they flew past. Well, it wasn't funny. It was obvious that someday soon they would be called on for a low-level combat mission. Their inability to hit targets could well be fatal.

As a matter of fact, aside from Ham—who was tops in his trade— the intense young pilot was not highly pleased with his crew. Was it his fault? Was he doing something wrong? None of his crew seemed to know, or care, that surviving combat depended on teamwork and professionalism. Their ten missions had seemed only to fracture relationships further, when it should have drawn them closer together. News that they had been ordered from Walden Abbey without going on R and R was greeted with near mutiny. Hanson, especially. The drawn, war-weary navigator had been livid with rage. His voice quivering, he had pleaded, "Ross, damnit, I'm within *one* of finishing my tour. Christ only knows where we're going or how long this thing may take. After twenty-four missions I'm supposed to do low-level navigation?"

Ross's promotion and the fact that this operation would mark his last as their aircraft commander added to the crew's frustration. Then there had been the shock of finding themselves in a desert camp.

Admittedly, living conditions were rotten. Rationed water, tents that did little more than slow down the constantly blowing sand and dust, mind-numbing heat, a steady diet of combat rations, and the nearest town—the only source of recreation—was off-limits. This didn't seem to affect the other crews unduly, however.

Brewster was largely responsible, Ross had decided. Brewster was just a natural-born agitator. He belittled anything and everybody that conflicted with his beliefs. And his criticism had plenty of support among the already disgruntled crew. During one of the arrogant young officer's first discussions with Ross, Norm had made it plain that he planned to move out of the copilot's seat at the first opportunity. He would appreciate Ross's support, but said that by one means or another he would have his own crew back before his combat tour was over.

Well, Ross told himself grimly, until your attitude and flying ability improve, no way in hell will you get my old crew—not as long as I'm ops officer, at least.

Ross watched "home" gradually emerge through a purple-gray haze of heat and dust. Situated outside a village bearing the proud name Djeseida, the desolate airstrip had been spawned on the site of a former British army fuel dump. Not deemed worthy of a name, the location was carried on the official list of U.S. Army Bases and Installations simply as Station 771. On the list of Precedence and Priority for Personnel and Equipment, it rated a place only two lines above the U.S. Army Band. It now hosted the grumbling ranks of the 866th Squadron.

The pony soldiers at Fort Laramie probably had better accommodations, Ross observed sourly. Troops were housed in a disorganized sprawl of drab, weathered, pyramid-shaped tents forming an irregular half-moon. They surrounded a gaggle of larger, circus-type tents housing the mess, the laughable maintenance detachment, the administrative offices, and the briefing room.

The entire depressing layout was bisected by a strip of pierced-steel planking roughly one mile in length. Barely wide enough to accommodate a Liberator's 110-foot wingspan, it was supposed to provide an aircraft landing surface superior to the packed desert soil upon which it rested. A questionable assumption, according to the aircrews.

The PSP runway separated the so-called living quarters from an aircraft parking area, where the squadron's olive drab B-24 Liberators squatted on their hardstands like so many orphaned ducklings. Canvas engine covers and nose shrouds provided scant protection to vital parts against the scouring effects of centuries-old windblown sand. Ross wished the German General Staff could see this backwater of American armed might. He chuckled to himself. Hell, he thought, we could knock them over while they were rolling around on the ground laughing.

Ross's rugged features acquired a glum expression as he regarded the scene ahead. It would be nice to get out of the hot, noisy, pounding airplane, but at least up here they were free of those goddamn flies. Where in the hell did they come from? There was no escaping them around the base. They crawled into your eyes—seeking moisture, someone had said. They crawled into your ears and around your lips. They returned as fast as you could brush them away. Ross despised the filthy things.

Station 771's PSP runway, polished by the innumerable tires of arriving and departing aircraft, winked through the hazy sunlight. Hanson's dead-reckoning navigation to a preplanned turning point west of the base had been surprisingly good. Ross complimented the sulky navigator, then turned to Norm. "Okay, you can come out from under the hood; it's your turn for a landing. Just watch those brakes in the turns. This PSP chews up tires like butter, and spares are hard to come by."

"Okay!" Brewster said, grinning. He'd show this stuck-up bastard a *real* grease job. The thought that he was the logical candidate for aircraft commander after Ross took on full-time duty as operations officer made him doubly attentive.

During the taxi-in and engine shutdown, Ross was distracted by a frenzy of activity. What the hell was going on? An army of loudly bitching troops was policing the area. Even cigarette butts were being scooped into trash sacks. Ross met Lieutenant Wilkinson's scowling navigator lugging trash from his tent toward a centrally located six-by-six. "Hey, Jiggs, has everybody gone apeshit around here?" Ross shouted.

"I dunno. Goddamn Captain Tunney is running around like a blind hog in heat screaming to 'get this rat's nest cleaned up.' He was even raving on about sending a truck for some rocks. He wants to lay out little paths with rocks on the sides and paint the fuckers white! Seems there's gonna be some kind of an inspection tomorrow."

"A what?" Ross reacted with a peal of laughter.

"You heard me, a goddamn inspection."

"Jiggs, somebody is putting you on. Who, for Christ's sake, would want to inspect this crotch area of the planet?"

"Don't ask me. If I were you, I wouldn't go to your tent, though. I just came past there. Kevin and Stan were having a fit."

It wasn't until evening chow that they learned the reason for the afternoon's cleanup party. The 365th Bomb Group had a new commanding officer and he had announced his intention to visit them the following morning. Ross relaxed. At least he wouldn't be involved. He was scheduled to give an instruction ride—an 0900 takeoff. He consumed the evening's offering of canned stew and tasteless mashed potatoes, stopped by the PX tent for a beer, and turned in early. He went to sleep chuckling.

The gooneybird bearing Col. George "Bull" Watson touched down at 0730 the next morning, precisely according to flight plan. Deckard and Ross drew their jeep into position and stood by the rear steps. Deckard had even forgone his favorite desert attire of British army shorts and short-sleeved shirt. Coming to attention and rendering snappy salutes, they eyed the stocky figure of the man descending from the battered transport.

He was an impressive-looking son of a bitch, Ross told himself. Colonel Deckard had known him from an earlier stateside post. According to him, Watson had a reputation for being an iron ass. Ross could believe it. A Class A uniform cap, looking for all the world as if it had just come from the box, sat squarely atop his lined, bulldog face. The damned cap appeared to have the grommet still in it. Ross hadn't seen a cap without a "fifty-mission crush"—the unauthorized badge of the flying fraternity—since he'd left the States.

As the stocky figure returned their salutes and strode toward them, they could see a handful of lesser lights waiting to disembark. Deckard greeted their visitor with a brisk, "Good morning, Sir. If you would ride in this jeep, I'll have this weapons carrier take your party wherever they like. The rest of my staff is waiting in the briefing tent. I thought we could start there, if the colonel agrees. Let them meet you and bring you up to date."

The colonel grunted around the stub of a dead cigar. "I don't need a briefing, Deckard. I know what the hell you have down here. I just wanted to see, firsthand, if it's as bad as I've been told." He turned a half-circle, hands on hips, and added, "I see it is. Are you responsible for the way it looks, or did you have help?"

Deckard flushed slightly. "It's a difficult place to do much with, Colonel."

"Obviously. Well, let's go to your office. We'll talk a bit, then I want to see how your men are living. After that I want to ride along on a low-level mission. We'll be gear-up and out of your hair by thirteen-hundred. Oh, yes, I'd also like to talk with your lead navigator—try to find out how his low-level navigation is coming along. The other squadrons are having problems."

The situation was totally out of control. Captain Tunney's meticulously prepared schedule of events was accurate only as far as "0730—Col. Deckard and Capt. Colyer meet Col. Watson and party."

Deckard's "headquarters" was situated inside the most magnificent edifice gracing Station 771. Constructed by Arab workmen for the British, it was laid up with a type of material resembling concrete blocks and stuccoed with mud. The low-pitched tar-paper roof and a peeling coat of whitewash hardly qualified the structure for display on recruiting posters, however. Parting strings of beads hung at the doorway to repel flies. Colonel Deckard led his new commanding officer inside.

The previous occupant, the commander of a P-38 outfit, had done his best to impart dignity to the crude interior. His efforts were largely negated, however, by a legacy bestowed by former tenants—the building had provided shelter for a nomadic goatherder's flock. No amount of effort could dispel the rancid, musky odor.

A crudely lettered wall chart provided information regarding aircrew and plane status. It hung directly below a three-by-five–foot sheet of Me 109 side paneling with the black cross still intact. Overshadowing all, however, was the fighter commander's prize find: Two elephant tusks, fully six feet in length, formed a frame for the commander's chair and desk. The yellowed ivory lent a faintly barbaric atmosphere. Deckard's trombone was discreetly tucked into one corner.

Watson accepted coffee and settled back in the only comfortable chair on the base—other than the squadron commander's.

"Before we start, Deckard, maybe you would like to alert your people that I'll want to fly with them. I assume you have some training flights scheduled."

"Yes, Sir. I'll get Captain Colyer on that immediately."

"And don't try to foist your blue-ribbon crew on me. I want to see the training schedule, then I'll pick the crew *I* want to ride with."

Deckard groaned inwardly. When the flustered ops clerk arrived, clipboard in hand, Watson took a brief look and stabbed a finger. "I'll ride copilot with this crew. The other two can fly wing."

"Fly wing, Sir?" Deckard regarded the wing commander with astonishment. "Uh, Sir, none of these crews are lead qualified. Does the colonel plan to fly a formation drop? At low level?"

"Well, *I'm* sure as hell lead qualified, Colonel. And how the hell do you think we'll do a low-level combat drop—one at a time?"

Deckard stole a look at the schedule and relaxed slightly. The colonel had chosen the crew that Colyer was scheduled to fly with as instructor pilot.

Deckard followed his new chief at a breakneck pace through the tent housing area. Other than an occasional grunt from Colonel Watson, there was no conversation. Meanwhile, Ross attempted to patch together a hasty three-ship formation briefing.

"Listen up," said Ross. "I'm going to take the left seat and the colonel is going to fly copilot for me. For God's sake, don't do something stupid. Dropping in formation is nothing new, but remember, you'll only be at five hundred feet. Don't make steep turns. Keep one eye on me and one on the ground. Don't jockey the throttles. Don't—oh, shit, just do the best you can."

They were still working on times, procedures, and the like as Deckard led the colonel into the briefing room. "Colonel Watson, this is Captain Colyer, the pilot you selected for lead, Sir."

Kirksey, the new aircraft commander originally scheduled for the flight, stood in the background, going along with Deckard's little alteration of the facts.

"Colyer, is it? Watson." The colonel enveloped Ross's hand in a ham-sized mitt. "Look, I'll step behind this partition and change. Then we'll have a mission briefing. You're in charge—I'm just along as your copilot." He bared his teeth in the only smile Deckard had seen all morning.

No one seemed ready to speak. Wilkinson and Rowley, the wingmen, stood in stunned silence. Ross was in shock. Deckard looked questioningly at Colyer. His ops officer shook his head in dismay. Deckard broke the silence with a chuckle; the others stared at him as if he had suddenly sprouted a carrot out of each ear.

The heavyset colonel strode back into the room and stopped before Ross and Lieutenant Kirksey. Clad in shorts and a khaki shirt with sleeves cut to the elbow, he didn't wait for introductions. "Hi there, I'm Watson," he greeted each in turn. "Guess we're going to be flying together." Looking at Ross he added, "Hope you boys didn't get all dressed up on my account." He eyed their regulation flight coveralls. "I like to be comfortable."

An awkward silence followed. Then Ross blurted, "Sir, I require all my crewmen to wear flight suits on every flight. Protection against flash burns, you know. Of course, that doesn't apply to the colonel," he added hastily. Deckard rolled his eyes heavenward, waiting for the thunderbolt.

Colonel Watson bent a glare in Ross's direction that would have bored holes in boilerplate. After a slight hesitation he barked, "The hell it doesn't, Captain. I said I was your copilot, didn't I? A flight suit it is. Colonel, I neglected to bring mine. Do you suppose your supply officer could meet me at the airplane with one? Forty-four short, if he has it."

"I'll go," Deckard responded. "I'll see to it, Sir. I'll bring it out to you myself." The last words were thrown over his shoulder as he fled.

Ross and his unwelcome copilot arrived alongside the preflighted Liberator a good thirty minutes before start-engines time. After meeting Watson, the other crew members found busywork, then disappeared. Kirksey, oozing suave nonchalance, issued casual orders to the bustling ground crew—instructions that were largely ignored. The lieutenant was never more than six feet from the colonel's side, however.

Their walk-around complete, Colonel Watson suggested that they wait in the area shaded by an overhanging wing. A fuming Kirksey was moving his gear to the waist compartment, where he had been relegated for the mission. Rolling the ever-present dead cigar to one side, Watson asked, "Where do you call home, Captain?"

"Justin Falls, Michigan, Sir."

"Did you go to school there?"

"Yes, Sir. I dropped out during my junior year at Ann Arbor to enlist in the Aviation Cadets. I was an engineering major."

"What did your folks think about that?"

"Well, Sir, Dad's a doctor; he's sort of pragmatic about life. He agreed that it was the thing to do. My mother is dead."

"I see. Is there a girlfriend?"

"Yes, Sir. We were sort of engaged."

"Well," the colonel said as he stood and stretched, "congratulate yourself that you stayed single. This is a rotten life for husbands and fathers. Now, I'd bet that my required uniform of the day is aboard that jeep coming this way. I'll change and it should be about time to crank up."

Ross found that, once at the controls, his nervousness dropped away. He started up and taxied carefully toward the runway. Passing *Winsome Winnie* en route, parked with engines running, he could see Wilkinson, grinning like a shit-eating ape, ready to fall in trail. Ross had an urge to thumb his nose.

Deckard and Captain Buckner, the squadron navigator, were in the tower when a gravelly voice growled, "Honeypot Tower, Red Dog One. Ten miles south with formation of three. Request landing instructions, over."

The young tower operator, well aware of the speaker's identity, snapped landing instructions with unaccustomed crispness. "Roger, Red Dog One. This is Honeypot Tower. Landing to the south. Altimeter two-niner-point-four-three. Winds light and variable. Call initial, over."

"Roger, roger, Honeypot. Understand" was the response. "Uh, we're requesting a low-altitude flyby with a circling return for landing, over."

The tower operator regarded a slack-jawed Deckard with an unspoken question in his gaze. Deckard gulped, recovered quickly, and grimly nodded. He was beginning to understand what was afoot. He mentally kicked himself for not seeing it sooner. His men needed some bizarre demonstration of leadership to jar them out of their dispirited lethargy. Their new commander had spotted that need; he was making his mark.

The passage of twelve Pratt & Whitney engines with props set in fine pitch, and the planes flying on the deck, provided an awesome experience. Even Deckard was caught by surprise—expecting "low level" to mean a hundred feet or so of altitude. His first glimpse of the three thundering Liberators was when they crossed the airfield boundary. The formation, with the wingmen tucked in tight, showed less than twenty feet of daylight beneath their olive drab bellies. The desert trembled under an ear-shattering wave of sound. In the mess tent, cooks blanched in alarm as pots and pans rattled. Those caught in the open dropped to the ground, certain that they were under attack.

Deckard and Buckner, mouths agape, watched the three blurs execute a steep pull-up and swing into their landing approach. "You know, Nate," Deckard muttered in awe, "I think we've just got ourselves one helluva commanding officer."

As Deckard's jeep with their group commander aboard pulled away from the parked aircraft, a frowning engineering officer drew Ross aside. "Well, that was a cute little show, Colyer. Feel pretty cocky, I'll bet."

Ross gave him a dazed look. "We dropped three fucking bombs from that altitude, Hank! Spare me that experience, ever again."

Back in Deckard's office, Colonel Watson, clad only in undershorts, stood on one leg as he changed into his uniform. "Well, Deckard, not a bad ride, generally speaking. We've got a ways to go, however—and we have only ten days to get there.

"But first things first." He settled himself opposite Deckard's battered desk and bit the end off a fresh cigar, but instead of lighting it, used it to jab his points home. "This job coming up—the low-level one. I've had the mission briefing and it's a bitch. You and your key staff get your asses on an airplane tomorrow morning and let the boys at Benghazi clue you in.

"This is the first move, Deckard. Back in Washington they're putting together a new numbered air force, the Fifteenth. We'll all set up in Italy after we knock the door down up there. And we're going to start kicking the shit out of that little paperhanger, only from the south."

The chunky man's lined face became even more grim as he talked. "The bastards are moving their key industries south, out of reach of the Eighth, as fast as they can. At Wiener-Neustadt, for instance, a big Me 109 factory is going up. Well, by God, we're going to be there to help them celebrate opening day."

A smug grin spread over his face. "Churchill calls the place where Germany joins onto the Balkans their 'soft underbelly.' That's gonna be our job, Colonel. We're going to slice into that soft belly until guts run all the way down to Cairo."

"You saying we're going to hit Vienna low-level?" Deckard asked in dazed astonishment.

"Nope." Watson paused to light his cigar. "That'll come later. This low-level attack—I can't tell you more now—will hit 'em where it hurts. A hundred and sixty-some B-24s, Colonel—and complete surprise. Now, I want total effort, not this Mickey Mouse stuff you've been flying. I know your training frag order set five hundred feet for drop altitude. Whoever wrote that had rocks in his head. We'll be going in so low you can reach out and pick up their fucking mail! I just showed three of your boys what we have in mind."

"I noticed that," said Deckard dryly.

"Yeah. Well, they're setting up a mockup 'bout fifty miles north of here. They're outlining the target with stripes of white lime. You'll be doing your training up there. It'll be a nine-ship formation and you'll pull a mission every day. But you'll be hearing all that tomorrow. Now," he glanced at his watch, "if I'm going to make that thirteen-hundred wheels-up, we'd better grab some lunch."

"Yes, Sir," Deckard said, leaping to his feet.

"Oh, I almost forgot," Watson said. "I understand you're drawing 'B' rations down here."

"Yes, Sir. That's because we're a detachment and not carried as combat operational."

Colonel Watson snorted. "That's bullshit. Get your supply officer up to Benghazi with a truck tomorrow. I don't want to hear that I have crews flying combat without fresh eggs for breakfast. Do you hear me?"

Watson created quite a stir in the mess hall. He brushed aside efforts to steer him to a VIP table behind a discreet screen, stating, "I said I wanted to see how your men were living, Colonel."

He stepped into line and slapped an astounded corporal on the shoulder. "I'm Colonel Watson, Corporal. Where do you call home?"

Ross and Deckard were still in shock when their group commander clambered aboard his aircraft. The amazing colonel paused as he stood in the doorway. "Oh, one more thing. You'll be getting a group SOP on it, but—starting today—I want all crew members to wear full gear for all flights. Protection against flash burns, you know."

Chapter Twenty-two

16 July 1943
Station 771
Libya, North Africa

Ross dropped from the open bomb bay behind Colonel Deckard and shielded his face from the blowing, swirling sand. He'd had a few tense moments just finding the runway; the place had to be below visibility minimums. The sand—borne on a stiff, thirty-knot wind—penetrated every orifice. Eyes grew red and bloodshot in minutes. Even short bits of conversation admitted a choking dose of teeth-grating grit. Head down, Ross scuttled for the canvas-covered six-by-six waiting for the returning squadron staff officers. He almost ran over a huddled shape with a protecting scarf wound around face and ears.

"Ross," a muffled voice called. "I have to talk with you. Can we walk back to operations?"

Ross recognized Norman Brewster's voice. "Jesus Christ, Norm," he yelled. "Get in the truck. I'm not going to walk fifty feet in this crap."

The pair scrambled over the tailgate and sank onto benches bolted to the sides of the covered truck bed. Deckard threw a quizzical glance their way as Norm unwrapped his scarf. "Now that's what I call a dedicated copilot, Ross," Deckard quipped. "The man comes out in this shit to meet his aircraft commander. Even my old bird dog at home wasn't that loyal."

Ross grinned. "Yeah, Norm. What's so all-fired important that it can't wait until I have something to cut this dust in my throat? Or maybe you're an angel and brought a beer with you?"

Norm gulped. "I'd like to wait until we can talk privately, Ross. It's sort of personal, but it's important."

Deckard raised his eyebrows. "My, my. It sounds interesting. Don't tell me that the top-secret briefing we just sat through at Benghazi is common knowledge."

Norm gave Ross an inquiring look.

"It's an eye popper, Norm," Ross responded gravely. "I'll fill in the rest of the crew first thing tomorrow. But for now, you can start thinking of a serious mission—one where we drop at the same altitude we did with Colonel Watson."

Norm didn't respond. He just sat and stared at his white-knuckled hands clenched in his lap.

"Okay," Ross said as they leaped from the truck in front of the operations tent. "You want to talk back at the tent or at chow? It's up to you."

"I'd like to do it now, Ross. Maybe we can find a corner in ops."

"Okay." Ross slumped onto a box that served as a chair and lit a cigarette. "Shoot. What's got you so lathered up?"

"I want to prefer charges against Ham, Reed, and maybe Guenther," Norm said, his jaw outthrust.

"You *what?*" Ross asked in disbelief. Sparks flew from his cigarette as it dropped to the floor.

"That's right. I want them court-martialed. Reed and Guenther were insubordinate and Phillips took a swing at me."

"I don't believe it," Ross muttered after he had recovered enough to speak. "Mother of God, what else can this crew think up to drive me crazy? Okay, what happened?"

"Well, we went to the airplane to fine-tune everything before we start this new low-level training—just like you told us to do. Guenther, the dumb asshole, somehow got a live round in his gun and shot a hole in *Weary Willie* sitting on the next hardstand."

Ross buried his head in his hands and waited without speaking.

"Naturally, I chewed his ass—threatened to make him sign a statement of charges for the damage. You'd have done the same—I hope." Norm waited for Ross to agree, but when he remained silent, Norm continued. "Then that wiseass Reed got into the act. He told me that

I wasn't the aircraft commander—that it would be up to you to settle things when you got back.

"I told him in no uncertain terms that—by God—I was an officer and I was completely within my rights to impose punishment for violations of the regs. He got uppity and made some snotty remark to the effect that I'm bucking to get the crew. Then Phillips stepped between us and told us—told me, an officer—to 'simmer down' I think is how he put it."

Brewster paused. Ross raised his head and prompted the tight-lipped copilot with a resigned, "And?"

"Well, I put the condescending bastard in a brace and read him off. Then he just stepped toward me and threw a punch. I ducked it—he didn't even get close. But that's beside the point. He assaulted an officer and—by God—he'll pay for it. I'm going to see the colonel first thing in the morning and prefer charges. I've got the entire crew as witnesses."

Ross lit a second cigarette from the butt of the first. He took a half-dozen puffs while he was deep in thought. Finally he said, "I sat in on a briefing today for what they claim will be the most important Allied strike to date. It could advance the war's end by six months. Tomorrow or the day after, we start learning how to navigate and to drop bombs from a hundred feet or less. It's never been done before. Just the damn training will be more hazardous than a lot of the missions we've flown. From what you've just told me, I doubt the *Happy Hooker*'s crew will all be on that mission—not in the same airplane, anyway."

Norm's voice rose on a shrill note. "Christ, you're talking like maybe it was *my* fault. I didn't do a damn thing wrong."

Ross's voice sagged with weariness. Norm strained to hear him. "I'm sure you didn't, Lieutenant Brewster. I'm sure you didn't. Among other things you didn't do today, you didn't keep your mouth shut. Now," he said as he stood and gathered up his gear, "I'm going to chow, then to bed. We'll talk more in the morning."

"I'm going to see Colonel Deckard in the morning," Norm called after him.

"You do that, Lieutenant Brewster. You do that. On your way, go by the *Happy Hooker* and sit in the left seat for a while. It'll be your only chance."

Ross faced Lieutenants Cryhowski and Hanson the next day before noon chow. They were both obviously unhappy. "I've talked with the rest of the crew," Ross told them. "Now, before I make up my mind what to do, I'm asking you, what the hell went on out there yesterday?"

Stan eyed his aircraft commander warily. "You gonna get pissed if I level with you, Ross?"

"Of course not."

"Okay. Yesterday, as you know, was a bitch—the damn wind blew sand all day. The crew felt that you'd sent us on a make-work detail while you were gone. The other crews were hunkered down inside. Nothing was flying. Along about noon, tempers were getting short. That's when Guenther shot a hole in *Weary Willie*.

"Norm blew his stack. Kevin and I were in the nose, but we could hear him even before we went back to see where the shot came from. It was crowded in the waist compartment, so we watched from the bomb bay entrance. We saw Norm yelling at Ham, then Ham just plain lost his head and tried to slug him."

"That's all?" Ross asked. "Could you hear what was being said?"

"Some of it," Stan replied slowly. "You're wondering if Ham was provoked. Well, Norm was being pretty abusive. He called Ham an ignorant Tennessee hillbilly—something about his mother; it wasn't like Norm, really. But, like I said, everyone was pissed about having to be out there in the heat and a sandstorm. Something had to blow, I guess."

"You *guess?*" Ross's voice was icy. "Lieutenant Cryhowski, we're in a combat theater. Everyone feels the pressure. The reason we wear these little tin badges on our shoulders is to be sure things *don't* blow, as you put it."

"Okay," Stan flared. "As long as we're preaching the gospel, an enlisted man tried to strike an officer. What do your precious Articles of War say about that? Is it *ever* justified?"

"Oh, shit," Ross said dejectedly. "It's all just so damn *dumb*. Really, I don't know why I'm bothering to do any kind of 'investigation.' Norm was going to see Deckard this morning. It'll be up to the colonel to decide if there's a court-martial."

Hanson broke his silence. "Norm changed his mind, Skipper. He didn't go. He said he'd deal with Phillips some other way."

Ross considered this surprising bit of news at length. He finally said, "I want to talk with Norm. This isn't something that he can just drop. Besides, I'd be very interested to know more about this 'some other way' business. Do you know where he is?"

"He said something about eating a snack at the canteen," Kevin offered. "He said he didn't feel like facing up to a tray of noon chow."

"Very well," Ross said as he stood. "Stan, I want the crew in formation in front of Sergeant Phillips's tent at eighteen-hundred. I have a few things to say."

"Ross," Stan called after him anxiously, "can we talk a minute before you do this?"

"Sure."

"I know you think Norm was kind of heavy-handed. But Ham was way out of line and you know it. Granted, he's tops as an engineer and a gunner. But facts are facts. If you back Ham in this, then Norm, Kevin, and I have lost any vestige of authority. That can cause trouble, especially after you change jobs."

"Who said I was going to take Ham's side?" Ross asked quietly.

"Well, you sure seem pissed at Norm."

"You'll all know at eighteen-hundred. Be there. And I wouldn't worry about Norm. He's a survivor."

Seated across a crude trestle table in the canteen, Norm eyed Ross with smoldering hostility. Washing down a bite of Hershey bar with warm Coca-Cola, Norm said, "So I changed my mind. I thought you'd be overjoyed. Your pet sergeant takes a swipe at an officer and gets off scot-free."

"Norm, what's this business about getting even?"

"Aw, I was just blowing off steam. I've already forgotten the whole silly incident."

"I don't think so, Norm. I don't in any way think so." Ross's voice crackled with anger. "Let me tell you what I think: You woke up this morning and realized you'd crapped in your own mess kit. If you prefer charges, you turn the entire enlisted crew against you, and I'd already told you to forget about ever being their aircraft commander. You want that left seat in the worst way."

Brewster shrugged and finished his Coca-Cola.

Ross, his gaze relentless, continued. "So you thought you'd kill two cats with one rock. By not going to Colonel Deckard, you ingratiate yourself with the crew. By giving me what you thought I wanted, you could maybe talk me into withdrawing my threat.

"Plus, you dump the responsibility on my back. If *I* report the fight, *I'm* the bad guy. If I don't report it, then Kevin and Stan may as well forget about the enlisted crew following their orders—and that could prove fatal."

Norm's jaw muscles bunched as Ross continued. "As for 'pretending' to forgive Ham, that's horseshit. From the time you move into that left seat, Ham Phillips's *best* day is going to be something out of an Edgar Allan Poe novel.

"It won't work, Norm. As far as the others are concerned, this conversation never happened, but I just wanted you to know the score. I've called a formation in front of Sergeant Phillips's tent for eighteen-hundred. Be there, Lieutenant—in Class A uniform." Ross stood, turned, and strode away. Norm's thoughtful gaze followed him.

Ross glared at eight set faces as the men stood at rigid attention in a precise line. Sergeant Ham Phillips wore the most abject expression of them all. Ross had a sudden impulse to back off. To rant and rave, wave his arms, issue dire threats—but *do* nothing. His inner resolve prevailed, however. He would put the welfare of the crew above his deep desire to be well liked—he owed them that. He had seen too many aircraft commanders who had made an effort to be "buddies" with their crews fail to bring them back from missions.

"Men," he let his gaze roam up and down the line, "we're obviously preparing for a big mission. Rumor has it that it'll be the biggest to date—anywhere. If we go out there with a half-assed attitude, unable to do each and every job in a professional manner, we're not going to come back—you hear me? It seems I haven't gotten that across. So, I'm going to try once more to impress on you the need for crew discipline. We've flown some tough ones. If you use what we've learned, you can go all the way.

"Now, I'm not going to overlook what happened out there yesterday just because I'm leaving the crew. There's an old saying to the effect that flying is a lot like deep-water sailing. Neither in itself is dangerous, but both are terribly unforgiving of mistakes. Mistakes were made yesterday—big mistakes. Just thank God they happened on the ground instead of over a target.

"As you know, all of you enlisted crew members are eligible for promotion. I'd intended to recommend each of you, as my last act as aircraft commander. In view of what happened, however, I intend to withhold the recommendations for Sergeant Phillips and Corporals

Reed and Guenther. Dismissed." Ross turned on his heel and left the shocked formation.

Ross and his entire crew slept through the morning's activity. Promptly at 0730 a truck convoy rumbled through the main gate. It proceeded to the aircraft hardstands and started unloading bulky shipping crates. A C-47 landed shortly thereafter, discharging a dozen military and civilian aircraft maintenance technicians.

By noon chow their work was the sole topic of conversation. They were providing supervision as squadron ground crews installed rubberized bladders into wingtips. Filled with fuel, these tanks added another seven hundred miles to the B-24's range. Another tank, a so-called "Tokyo tank," configured to fit inside a bomb bay, would extend that range by yet another three hundred. "Where the *hell* are we headed?" was the question that opened most conversations.

17 July 1943
Jagdgeschwader **99 (Provisional)**
Mizil, Romania

Newly promoted *Staffelkapitän* Kurt Heintze accepted his kit bag from the uniformed driver and turned to survey his new surroundings. Despite efforts to "age" the silver badges of rank that Gretta had so carefully added to his worn uniform tunic, he still was conscious of their newness. He was certain that the driver's exaggerated courtesy was a form of unexpressed smirk accorded to the newly promoted.

All he wanted was sleep—at least twelve hours of blissful escape from an aching head, foul-tasting mouth, and burning eyes. Two nights, largely sleepless, with Gretta in Munich followed by two days jouncing across the Carpathian Alps in an ancient railway car had taken their toll.

Kurt's first impression of the facilities at Mizil did little to lift his spirits. Drab, dirty, and hot. The driver had deposited him at the entrance to a frame building mottled with gray and green camouflage paint. "Single officers' quarters" was the driver's laconic explanation. Dare he forgo reporting to his new commander immediately? The process would require a bath and change of clothing. Those two acts loomed as monumental challenges to his flagging stamina. He pushed temptation to the background and shuffled toward the green-painted door,

its edge grimed by constant use. He wished mightily for an orderly
to appear and relieve him of the overweight bag.

If I'm lucky, the commander will be out and I can report in tomorrow,
Kurt thought wistfully. He was sweating freely as he strode purpose-
fully toward the noisy flight line. This commander, whoever he was,
had selected the busiest and noisiest location on the field for his
headquarters. I hope that means he is a fighter pilot instead of a
bureaucrat, thought Kurt.

The anemic clerk's "*Jawohl, Herr Hauptmann.* The major is in. I
will announce you" dashed his hopes for an early refuge in sleep.
He slumped onto a straight-backed bench and prepared for a protracted wait.

"*Dunder,* what manner of misfits are they sending me now?" a voice
roared from behind Kurt. Kurt turned and was greeted by the sight
of a bear of a man wearing a black eye patch. One empty sleeve was
tucked into a pocket of his tunic and he walked with a limp. Kurt opened
his mouth to form a sharp retort when recognition dawned.

"Major Eckert." He actually felt his jaw drop in astonishment as
he took in the wreck of a man that his first commander had become.
Then he noticed the new rank insignia Eckert wore. "*Herr Oberstleutnant,
mein Gott,* what happened?" Kurt blurted out involuntarily.

Eckert grinned at Kurt's immediate flush of embarrassment. "Don't
stand there like a fool, with your mouth hanging open, my boy. Come
into my office. We have much to tell each other." His weary state
forgotten, Kurt followed in a happy haze.

Slouched behind his battered desk, features wreathed in cigar smoke,
Carl-Otto Eckert beamed with pleasure. "And look who is a *staffelkapitän*
already. And with the swords to his Knight's Cross, no less. You have
been a most busy young man, Kurt Heintze. Now, tell me about the
war for the homeland. Did you destroy a hundred bombers?"

Kurt's tortured expression hadn't changed. "*Herr Oberstleutnant,*"
he stammered, "I'm sorry. I must know."

"These?" Eckert asked, waving his good arm to indicate his missing
eye and arm and shattered leg. "A gross misjudgment on landing,
I'm afraid. I believed that I could put my ship safely into a pine
forest without an engine or elevator controls. A bailout after flak had
already severed this arm didn't seem like a good idea. I didn't walk
away, I might add."

Kurt sat stunned; grief prevented him from speaking. Eckert continued. "So what am I doing commanding a fighter wing? Experienced pilots are becoming more and more scarce. I rule from this desk. My adjutant, Major Rudolph, rules from the cockpit. A far better arrangement than the old practice of relegating the cripples to filing papers.

"Not that we see any action here, mind you. Not yet, at least. Our commanding general prepares for the day when the Ploesti oil fields will become a target for the big American bombers."

He paused. When Kurt didn't respond he resumed. "Ah, you don't seem to disbelieve, as most do, that the big devils can reach our quiet little corner of the world."

"I believe it, *Herr Oberstleutnant*," Kurt replied dully. "I believe it. And they will not be long in coming. There seems to be no way to stop them. I saw their formations grow in size from a handful to hundreds—all while we were shooting down unbelievable numbers."

"But aren't the big brutes easy to shoot down? How can you miss?" Eckert had shed his capricious manner and was leaning forward, intent on Kurt's reply.

"No, they are not easy to shoot down, *Herr Oberstleutnant*. They can absorb incredible damage. Many times I have seen a ship, on fire and with two engines shut down, struggle to the target and drop its bombs. They are easy to miss because during your attack you may have as many as twenty .50-caliber machine guns firing at you. It tends to disrupt your aim.

"They fly in a formation of stacked vees—a box I understand they call it. Unless you can cripple one and separate it from the box—well, our losses attacking the massed formations are sickening. When I left, the Americans were providing long-range fighter escort as far south as Dortmund and Hamburg. It grows more difficult daily."

"Hmmm." Eckert leaned back and stroked his lantern jaw, his good eye nearly closed in thought. "This is why I was overjoyed when your orders arrived. Someone with experience, someone who can teach our young cadet sergeants how best to attack the monsters."

He gave Kurt a shrewd, penetrating look. "I detect from your appearance that you have been working hard. Rest. Go into Bucharest—you won't believe the wealth of unrationed food and drink. The women are beautiful and not unattainable. Come back in three days and assume command of your squadron."

Kurt responded with a shy grin. "Thank you, *Herr Oberstleutnant,* but, if I may, I'll settle for twelve hours' sleep, then start my duties. I have no need of the joys of Bucharest."

"As you wish," Eckert said with a shrug. "There was a young lady in Munich, I seem to recall. Do you still have an understanding with her?"

Kurt's mouth tightened. "We're in love, but an 'understanding'? Who, I ask, understands women?" As Eckert roared with laughter Kurt went on. "More than a year ago, I asked, pleaded, ordered her to flee to Switzerland and stay with my cousin. 'The bombers are coming,' I told her. 'The British by night, the Americans by day.' Her stupid parents—and mine—have convinced her that such a move is senseless, unpatriotic even. Munich will never hear a shot fired or see a bomb dropped, they boast." Kurt lapsed into bitter silence.

A sobered Eckert nodded. "A trying time, I agree. We will see worse, much worse, before we see the end. Do you grow discouraged, my young friend? Do you feel that it is useless to fight on?"

"Never!" Kurt's eyes flashed with anger. "Tired, yes. Bitter at bungling leadership, yes. But to concede defeat while I have an airplane that will fly and a gun that will shoot? If we stop telling ourselves foolish lies, the Fatherland can be saved. Until that time, I will continue. In fact, there was one bomber, a Liberator, that I consider to be my personal enemy. My deepest regret at leaving was that I would never have an opportunity to challenge that crew again. The Americans embellish their ships with lurid paintings and names. This one has on its nose the picture of a nearly naked girl and the name *Happy Hooker.* Twice I have had that plane in my sights and failed both times to bring it down. The last time, the pilot lowered his nose and attempted to attack *me!*"

Eckert nodded. "I am pleased to see that you haven't lost your fighting spirit. It would grieve me, but I would be forced to withhold your command if your feelings were otherwise. Now, tonight we celebrate. Champagne and plum brandy are plentiful. We will drink too much and talk of the old days on the Russian front, eh?"

"Ja," said Kurt, with a slight grin. If he could not fly in combat, maybe it would be good to talk about the old days.

☆ ☆ ☆

THE HEARING

DAY THREE

4 December 1945
Hearing Room B, Building 1048, War Department

Janet seated herself at the extreme right end of the polished wooden bench. Her position the previous two days had prevented close scrutiny of the fifth member of the board, Lt. Gen. Titus Blake, identified by orders appointing the board as alternate to General Woods. Blake's quiet, reserved air gave few clues to his thinking. His was the face of a man given to deliberate but resolute action, Janet thought. His visage reminded her of baseball star Lou Gehrig. He was a man at the end of his career, her father had said in an effort to sum him up.

She confided her frustrations regarding the proceedings to her parents during the lazy afternoon following Thanksgiving dinner. The three of them indulged themselves in a traditional meal, albeit limited by wartime food shortages. But the mood inside Colonel Richards's roomy quarters at Bolling Field's senior officer housing area had been festive. BT's name was mentioned during her father's longer than usual prayer at mealtime, but not afterward. She had, in fact, toyed with the idea of inviting Ross, who was in town and would testify at the hearing later. Her mother discouraged the invitation. Her reasoning was vague, but Janet didn't press her.

Titus Blake, her father explained, had committed the unwise act of submitting a minority report on General MacArthur's policy regarding use of the atomic bomb. The right or wrong of his position notwithstanding, he would retire in his present grade.

Later that evening Janet had made a brief appearance at Senator Templeton's cocktail reception. She recognized only one of the distinguished collection of largely political figures. A scattering of uniforms was present but, predictably, none of the board members were visible; the senator would avoid any hint of suborning the body he had pressed to create. Her in-laws greeted her warmly, then ignored her. She accepted the invitation of one of BT's distant cousins for a drink at the Mayfair Bar and fled the hysterical gaiety. The boy made a clumsy pass, which restored a measure of her slumping self-esteem, but nothing came of it.

The long weekend behind them, the board members bore a resolute air as they filed into their respective seats. General Woods gaveled the session to order and Colonel Blankenship rose to confront his first witness of the day. Janet's interest heightened. A stolid-faced colonel sat sullenly in front of the panel of officers. He had been responsible for preparing the intelligence annex for Tidal Wave.

Blankenship scanned an open file folder. "Colonel Ransom, your estimate of four batteries of antiaircraft guns and four squadrons of fighters defending Ploesti was in error tenfold. Why?"

"Intelligence *estimates* are far from exact, Colonel." The round-faced officer turned to address his next remarks to the board. "We had no resources of our own inside Romania. The British provided what details we had to work with. The Germans augmented their defense forces faster than anticipated and, frankly, from sources we were unaware they possessed."

The cadaverous Blake leaned forward. This was his specialty and it appeared that he would enjoy dissecting the unhappy witness. "What about reconnaissance overflights, Colonel. Were any made?" he asked with ominous nonchalance.

"No, Sir. The Combined Bomber Offensive staff, the Brits in particular, felt that the appearance of P-38 or Mosquito reconnaissance planes would alert the Germans to our interest in Ploesti."

Blake skewered the perspiring officer with a direct stare. "And the 'neutral' embassies inside Bucharest? Don't, please, tell me they were observing nothing? Hearing nothing?"

"Nothing that they reported."

"Damnit, man! Sometimes you have to *ask*. Was any effort made?"

"We were pretty well dependent on the RAF, Sir. I—I can't say whether or not they explored that possibility."

"The RAF didn't prepare that annex, Colonel. *You* wrote it. It was grossly in error and, as a result, men died unnecessarily."

Ransom, stung by Blake's caustic attack, struck back. "I followed accepted procedure, General. The need for secrecy was considered by all to be paramount. Even pictures of the refineries were obtained from British archives through a deception. Twelve other objectives were researched at the same time just to confuse the enemy. Slant-range drawings were made to make the task of target identification easier from low altitude. But even if we had been successful in penetrating German security, that mission would have gone as planned, General."

A bitter note entered the intelligence chief's voice. "Tidal Wave was not a mission launched to destroy; it was an expression—a demonstration of Allied capability to strike hard and deep. And it served that purpose. Following Tidal Wave the Germans were forced to draw on reserves. Curtailment of petroleum production resulted in a reduction of pilot training and weakened defenses in Italy."

Blake, his point made, scribbled on a notepad. When he gave no indication of responding to the flush-faced Ransom, Blankenship excused the witness.

Janet watched the officer's departure with a measure of sympathy. That he had not been promoted since his 1943 gaffe spoke volumes. How many nights had he lain awake berating his decision to "go along" with what promised to be a bold, decisive move—to withhold the fact that they had been unable to obtain a precise, accurate order of battle? *Could* he have prevented the decision to launch? Or was the disruption of Hitler's flow of oil a victory after all, in spite of the cost in terms of human life?

What yardstick did you use to judge? What would BT and Ross or, for that matter, the several hundred dead and wounded say? She sighed. Not all the tough decisions guiding the outcome of a war were made in the heat of battle, she decided.

Chapter Twenty-three

Improvements at the 866th squadron's desert home bordered on the miraculous. A truck loaded with scarce pine planking arrived, bearing a huge, scrawled "Compliments of Col. Watson." Hammers rang into the night as enthusiastic troops fashioned wood platforms for their desert-ravaged tents. Whoops of joy reverberated inside the mess tent the first morning as grinning cooks prepared *fresh* eggs, cooked to order. The word, to a limited number of insiders, was that grilled beefsteaks would be offered for Saturday night chow.

As fast as long-range tanks were added, crews took their ships to Benghazi to have new engines installed. The overnight stay, with passes into town, furnished enough material for a week of slightly exaggerated tales of debauchery. Two factory-fresh Liberators, complete with shiny new crews, touched down only two days after Colonel Watson's visit.

Ross's three-ship buzz job was soon eclipsed as the highlight of the week. Modifications complete, three-ship formations departed on practice missions from before dawn until darkness obscured the target. The new target was a puzzle. White lines, outlining what they guessed to be some type of industrial target, were laid out with lime. Fifteen-foot poles were scattered throughout the design. After lengths of red target cloth, originally used to mark them, appeared the next day in the stalls of Benghazi's noisy, crowded bazaars, bright metal cans were substituted.

Ross, Wilkinson, and Rowley were pressed into service as instructor pilots. They were considered to be veterans at Colonel Watson's version of a low-level drop. This meant that Ross flew right seat for one crew while that crew's aircraft commander flew the *Happy Hooker*. Ross, flattered by his new status, was nevertheless unhappy with the arrangement. He felt a gulf widening between him and his crew. His schedule being on a different cycle than that of his tentmates, he found himself either eating alone or in the company of other aircraft commanders.

Occasional encounters with Norm, Kevin, and Stan in the club were little more than brief exchanges of polite pleasantries. Of the enlisted crew, only Ham Phillips sought him out—in a somewhat strained encounter prompted by a need to discuss progress in modifying the *Happy Hooker*. Only Norm's sardonic cynicism appeared to remain unchanged.

As crews became accustomed to skimming the desert surface, one-upmanship quickly made its appearance. Lieutenant Anderson's crew conducted tours to display a number of deep scratches on the underbelly of *Weary Willie*.

Two incidents, however, served to return minimum altitudes to a more modest fifty feet. The first was Lieutenant Eubanks's effort to improve upon Ross's original demonstration. Colonel Deckard promptly threatened him and future imitators with an unusually cruel form of castration. The second, observed by the *Happy Hooker*'s crew, was a product of prop wash—the greatest hazard to low-level formation flying. A wingman in the three-ship element preceding Ross over the target allowed his plane to drift slightly down and in on his lead. An eyeblink later, the desert terrain was marred by a cartwheeling B-24, engulfed in orange flame as it broke up. It was a sobering, and most effective, lesson.

Colonel Deckard drove his crews to the limits of their stamina and endurance in the hellish desert heat. Either he or Ross stood in the control tower during each formation takeoff and landing.

Criticism of sloppy or nonstandard procedure was immediate and biting. "Jones," or whoever the hapless pilot might be, "if I see you landing on the wrong side of the runway one more time, I'll have you out there repainting that centerline at high noon!"

Colonel Deckard had undergone a change, as had the ops staff and lead crews who had accompanied him to Benghazi. Deckard's attitude created additional dire speculation regarding the highly secret mission that all agreed was imminent. Casual banter with those who were "in the know" became impossible. They formed their own little cliques, eating together and conversing in low, guarded voices. The muted sound of the colonel's trombone, playing New Orleans jazz, could be heard until far into the hot, windy nights.

Then, as suddenly as it had started, the low-level training ended. On Friday all foreign nationals were barred from the barbed wire–enclosed airfield. Since the foreigners' employment was for such menial tasks as KP and garbage disposal, grumbling GIs were pressed into service to carry out these essential functions. Communications off base, including personal mail, were temporarily suspended. The ominous implication of these actions was clear.

Stan, always on the prowl for news, burst into the club where Ross, Norm, Kevin, and two others were engaged in a desultory poker game.

"Okay, guys, we got orders. They've just been posted on the bulletin board. We're shipping out."

"Shipping out?" Norm asked with a frown. "Where, for Christ's sake? I thought we were going to fly a mission. You mean the whole squadron?"

"Looks like it. The a/c's get briefed at twenty-hundred hours, Ross. All combat crews assemble for departure at oh-six-hundred tomorrow."

"Now what the hell do you suppose that means?" Ross mused. "We were told at Benghazi it would be a deep penetration, but nothing was said about a staging base."

Kevin tossed a busted straight onto the discard pile and observed, "I'd say that the location of the target for this big hush-hush mission we've been beating up the desert training for is out of reach from here. We're probably gonna move closer."

"Good God, where would *that* be?" one of the other poker players chimed in. "What with those added tanks, we can go to New York and back from here. I'll vote for that, by the way."

"Well, guess we'll find out more at twenty-hundred," Ross observed. Scooping up his stack of soiled, wrinkled currency, he stood and added, "Think I'll go to the tent and start putting my gear together. What the hell are we supposed to take with us, I wonder."

"The orders say full flying gear and personal effects for two nights," Stan said.

Ross nodded. "Okay, I'll go initial the bulletin board then. See you all later."

Within a half hour, news of the impending departure had reached the far corners of the little installation. Men who had worked around the clock in support of the effort experienced a mild disappointment, the feeling of being left out.

Flight crews, meanwhile, went from the initial excitement of being exclusive members of the elite to a more sober assessment of their futures. Their dirty, disreputable, downright squalid surroundings acquired a suddenly comfortable, homey atmosphere. Orderly room clerks, supply and maintenance technicians, cooks—all who were considered sworn to make the life of a flyer less comfortable—acquired heretofore undiscovered virtues. Even those two instruments of Satan, the jerboa mouse and desert rat, were reevaluated and found to be "kinda cute"— this after it had taken a base regulation providing for severe penalties to end cases of airmen shooting at the voracious rodents with their service .45s.

Chaplain Smythe, to his disappointment, would remain behind. During the afternoon, he was confronted with a steady stream of shuffling, half-embarrassed men muttering, "Hey, Chaplain, would you hang on to this for me—until we get back, you know?" "Would you see that this gets mailed in case of—you know." "In case of—well— you know, if something goes wrong, would you call my mom when you get back to the States?" His impromptu chapel service that evening was well attended. The young chaplain's eyebrows raised fractionally at the sight of a contemplative Colonel Deckard standing at the rear.

An unusual number of crew members found themselves strolling, "taking the evening air," in the vicinity of the briefing tent shortly after 2000 hours. Their wait was not a long one, but their reward was not great. Gathering around their respective aircraft commanders, they learned only that the immediate destination was no farther than Benghazi. Colonel Watson considered their PSP runway to be inadequate for the loads they would carry on takeoff. This news caused other eyebrows to raise fractionally.

31 July 1943
Ninth Air Force Headquarters
Benghazi, Libya

Brigadier General Elliott Sprague concealed his racing thoughts behind a frozen mask of serious concern. He was shaping strategy even as Maj. Gen. Lewis Brereton dropped his bombshell. Face pale and contorted with poorly concealed rage, the architect of Tidal Wave announced, "I have been taken off the mission, gentlemen, as have Majors Reddick and Carson. The order came from General Arnold personally. I appealed to General Marshall, but the order stands. The reason given is that we three have been briefed on the plan to invade Italy. General Eisenhower insists that it would seriously jeopardize that operation if any one of us were captured and interrogated by the Germans."

The dozen officers gathered in the smoke-laden meeting room remained silent. Each was engaged in assessing the impact of Brereton's words. The lead pilot, the lead navigator, and the lead bombardier—all had been removed at the eleventh hour. Eyes strayed to the five-by-nine-foot scale model of Ploesti that dominated the room. Who would replace them? Who else possessed the wealth of technical detail that had gone into the plan of attack?

"Jesus Christ, General!" Colonel Watson exploded. "This is insanity. Three months in putting together this mission. Everyone up and down the line has known that you planned to lead it. The men have confidence in you. A change now will throw everything we've done out the window. Why did they wait until the night before to change their fucking minds?"

Sprague unobtrusively drew a long breath. It had worked! By God, that pompous ass of a senator, Templeton, had done it. Sprague upgraded his opinion of his ofttimes irritating aide. In a clandestine letter, again carried by an ATS pilot on his return run to the States, BT had alerted his father that the army was about to send three officers with sensitive information on a mission over Germany. Now, how to wangle a seat in that lead airplane?

Brereton's curt response to Watson dashed his hopes. "General Flynt will replace me as mission commander. Other changes in assignments have been worked out. I have them here." He waved a slim sheaf of papers. "You're treading dangerously close to insubordination, Colonel Watson."

Watson flushed and joined the others who cast questioning looks at the Ninth Air Force commander. Flynt had opposed the low-level idea from the beginning. The general was not a tough guy, no scratch-and-bite fighter. Could he be expected to instill the same degree of fighting spirit that Brereton had whipped up?

Sprague refrained from adding his voice to the babble of outraged protest expressed by the assemblage of group and wing commanders.

His case would be made in private. Sprague's popularity with the others was not much higher than Flynt's.

The unhappy two-star continued. "I am still very much involved in the operation, but I'll let Enoch take over the actual mission briefing. Enoch, you have the floor."

Flynt, his face more stern than usual, stood up and faced the half-circle of upset faces. "You all know that I initially opposed the low-altitude aspect of this mission. That's in the past. I gave my opinion, it was considered, and the decision was otherwise. We will sorely miss General Brereton and the others staying behind, but we're going to take out that target, gentlemen. That I guarantee.

"Target assignments haven't changed. I will lead White One, Two, and Three to Ploesti. Our targets are the Romana Americana, Concordia Vega, Unirea Sperantza, Astro Romana, and Colombia Aquila refineries. Colonel Jackson will lead Blue Group to the Creditul Minier plant south of Ploesti, and General Sprague will lead Red Group north to the Steaua Romana installation at Campina. Pay strict attention to the three initial points. They form a line and, at fifty feet altitude, navigation will be tricky. Remember, the first IP is here," he crossed to the wall map and tapped a point just north of the Danube. "The second is the town of Targoviste, and the third, Floresti, is where we turn and follow the double-track railroad right into the heart of Ploesti."

Sprague stayed behind as the meeting broke up. After the other disgruntled group leaders departed, he approached General Flynt, a forced scowl on his face. "General, I for one am happy to see you take charge."

"Oh?"

"Yes, Sir. General Brereton has done an excellent job of planning this entire mission, but I feel some of his staff may have influenced his selection of crews."

"How's that, Elliott?"

"Look at the lineup, Sir. The groups down here from England have been relegated to the least important targets. In addition, being the last ones over the target, we will receive the brunt of the antiaircraft fire."

Flynt frowned. "Elliott, this shifting of lead is creating enough disruption without your adding to it. Frankly, I find your objections somewhat childish. Believe me, there'll be enough credit for everyone."

Sprague's scowl deepened. "General Flynt, I ask you to reconsider. Morale is already sitting on rock bottom. I brought troops down here who are exhausted by the strain of facing the best the *Luftwaffe* can put up day after day. I wouldn't be surprised if the *Stars and Stripes* is bombarded by gripes if we aren't allowed to take our rightful place up front."

Flynt's jaw tightened. "Elliott, what I'm hearing sounds suspiciously like blackmail. What is it you're after?"

Sprague didn't bother to protest the accusation. "I want to lead the second wave, General."

"Out of the question," Flynt snapped. "You'll fly the mission as briefed."

Sprague did not flinch. "General Brereton and I were in the same bomb group when the Japs attacked the Philippines. General Eaker is looking to me to see that the Eighth gets a fair shake down here."

"Elliott, I don't have time for your games. Ride anyplace you damn well please. Just one thing—you won't occupy a pilot position and don't try to be a hero and screw things up."

BT took one look at his chief's tight-lipped grin and relaxed. The senator had done it again. "I take it there are some changes?" he inquired.

"Damn right! BT m'boy, we're leading the second wave—White Two."

BT couldn't contain his astonishment. "You mean the entire wing is changing position?"

"Nope. Just you and I. This is your reward for that—er—letter I believe you wrote. This mission will be the biggest thing to date. With this one on your record, you can write your own ticket. When we get back to England I'll see to it that you have your own squadron. How's that?"

BT concealed his dismay. "This is great news, General. I don't know how to thank you." You dumb bastard! he thought. This isn't going to be the piece of cake you seem to think. I have no burning desire to go along, and I *don't* want your damned squadron either.

Sprague wasted no time locating Colonel Deckard. "Eric," he boomed. "I want the best crew in the 866th. I'm leading White Two, the second wave, and I want your ace."

Deckard, relieved that he and Colonel Watson wouldn't be saddled with the wild-eyed Sprague in Red Lead, responded without hesitation.

"Captain Colyer, Sir. He's my new ops officer and the very best pilot in the squadron. Some tough missions under his belt—he'll get you there and back."

1415 Hours, 31 July 1943
Aboard the *Happy Hooker*

"My God, would you look at that?" Stan's voice, from the nose, was breathless with awe. Ross could spare only the most fleeting of glances. Every fiber of his mind and body was devoted to holding the *Happy Hooker* precisely in line with, and three hundred feet behind, his squadron lead. A scant fifty feet of atmosphere separated his ship and terra firma. Ahead and to both sides, 169 B-24 Liberator bombers, in addition to his own, formed a giant aluminum overcast.

Covering a five-mile front, the cumbersome formation fled the dusty maelstrom created by churning props and raced toward the familiar practice bomb range.

"And this is just a friggin' dress rehearsal!" Ross yelled at Norm without turning his head. "Don't see how combat can be any hairier than this." He thumbed the switch for his throat mike. "Mickey, how are our wingmen making out?"

"They're hanging in there, Captain," the tail gunner responded. "Close—too *damn* close for my liking."

Ross's smile was a brief flicker on his lips. "Just imagine that a half-dozen 109s are circling around out there looking for an opening," he replied. "Makes you feel better."

Upon their earlier arrival at Benghazi the 866th's crews weren't even given time to unload their gear. A harassed major had assembled Colonel Deckard and his lead pilots in front of their still cooling airplanes, handing out flimsies as he talked. "Practice mission in one hour, Colonel. Your squadron's position in the formation is indicated. Fill in your crew names and brief them from this ops order. Give a maintenance status to the duty officer as soon as you land. There's a Red Cross truck with coffee and doughnuts running around here someplace. Oh, yeah," he paused and flashed a smile before starting his jeep, "glad to have you with us. This is gonna be some goddamn show! And, something else—your crews will have to help the bomb handlers with loading. We're shorthanded as all hell around here this morning." The major then disappeared with a jaunty wave.

Ross gazed around the hectic scene, dazed by the scope of activity. Even with the heat of the day building, men trotted from one task to the next. A steady stream of jeeps, weapons carriers, and fuel trucks wove among each other, each seemingly on an errand of utmost urgency. Ross counted thirty-six B-24s parked wingtip to wingtip around the perimeter, saturating facilities intended for no more than a dozen aircraft. He watched Stan oversee the loading of a single hundred-pound bomb. His neck prickled; it was not a practice bomb. This would be a live drop.

"Colyer, over here." Deckard was waving the wandering, gawking aircraft commanders into a huddle in the shade offered by an overhanging wing.

"Okay, here's the scoop. You'll find your formation position, radio frequencies, and times on this flimsy." Continuing as the sheets of paper were distributed, he admonished, "Now, as you can see, this formation is line abreast by elements, something we haven't done before. This means that navigators and bombardiers in element leads will be on their own to locate and hit their assigned MPI. Wingmen will drop on their element lead, not the squadron lead. Your bombardiers are getting their specific targets and main points of impact over there. You have fifteen minutes to assemble and strap in before start-engines. There'll be a critique at nineteen-hundred. If there are no questions, I'll see you all after we land."

Ross's head buzzed. Questions? Hell, he had a dozen. A quick scan of the flimsy given him had produced an initial thrill: *Happy Hooker* would lead the third wave. But goddamn! What kind of join-up would this size formation use? When landing, would he stack up or down on his lead? His frame of mind wasn't improved by a question posed by Lieutenant Rowley: "You mean we're gonna be flying thirty-six airplanes wingtip to wingtip?"

Colonel Deckard chuckled. "You ain't seen nothing yet, Lieutenant. There'll be a hundred and seventy—three waves flying wingtip to wingtip." As jaws dropped, he added, "Now, it's going to be downright crowded out there. Just use your head during form-up and drop. And remember, this *is* a practice run; if you get totally confused and don't know what the hell else to do, break *up* and go straight ahead. Go to fifteen hundred and return alone. 'Course, you might want to just keep going north and drown yourself in the Mediterranean, because anyone flunking this one is slated for a cozy little heart-to-heart with me later on. Now, let's show this bunch what the Red Dogs can do. Good luck."

*   *   *

Without breaking his concentration on the desert terrain streaking beneath the *Happy Hooker,* Ross interrupted his mental replay of their arrival to listen to Stan.

"Our MPI is between three of those poles, Ross. Luckily, I think I remember it—kind of a lopsided triangle. Since we aren't on autopilot, I'll give you heading changes on the PDI. Oughtta be a piece of cake."

"Stan, I've been wondering. That bomb is going to hit flat. What's to keep the bastard from skipping right back at us?"

"Good question. They told us at the briefing that we're using a new fuse. We only have one safety; it's pulled when we release. That hundred-pounder is hot when it leaves the bomb bay. *Supposedly* it'll detonate on impact from any angle. Frankly, I think that's why we're flying this run. I don't believe those bastards *know* for sure. Okay, we're ten miles out. I'm opening bomb bay doors."

Ross flicked a look at the PDI, located on the lower left side of his instrument panel. When Stan took over on the bomb run, and they were not on autopilot, the pilot's job was to keep the little arrow centered.

Oblivious to the noonday heat and pounding, jolting vertical air currents, Ross drove the bellowing Liberator toward their gradually emerging target area. The PDI moved slightly. Ross, using willpower as much as physical prowess, eased his three ships slightly left.

Stan called, "I got the son of a bitch! Target dead ahead; drop in two minutes!"

Ross's vision blurred as sweat seeped into the corners of both eyes. Unable to remove either hand from the bucking wheel, he called, "Ham—my eyes. Give 'em a wipe, will ya? Can't see a damn thing!"

As the flight engineer obliged, Ross saw three metal-topped poles flash underneath. A split second later he felt concussion rock the controls. Then they were back over open desert.

They'd done it. They had found the target and hit it with live ordnance!

"Great job, Stan, Norm. The beer, if they have any, is on me."

The return trip, and sorting out into landing formations, seemed anticlimactic. Ross turned the task over to Norm and sat back in his seat, weary but exultant.

The 866th's crews, drained both emotionally and physically, had little time to recoup their energy. After a hasty shower with a heavenly adequate water supply, they barely had time to gulp down a trayful of lamb stew, tasteless gray bread, and boiled cabbage. Ross was ravenous and wolfed it down.

Norm, at his elbow, expressed a customary snide observation: "When the hell are we going to get something besides British rations? You could use the grease on this stuff for engine oil."

Then it was time for the critique. More than a hundred crew members straggled into a dilapidated hangar and perched on rough benches.

"Lot of goddamn MPs around for a training mission bitch session," Norm observed.

Before anyone could respond, a resounding "Ten-hut!" brought them to their feet. The group that took seats on the platform improvised from maintenance stands confirmed that the session might, indeed, be something more than a simple mission critique. Ross saw two stars on one collar, a half-dozen birds, and what could only be a British uniform.

Only Colonel Watson remained standing. His broad smile removed any apprehensions that someone was apt to catch hell.

"Take seats, men. The rundown on this afternoon's little demonstration won't take long. Briefly, we creamed that goddamn bomb range. I guarantee you that there isn't so much as a desert rat alive out there tonight. The boys who followed up with a recce overflight report that not a single marker pole is standing. Now, I believe General Flynt, commanding general of the Ninth Air Force, has a few words."

The lanky two-star wasted no time. "Sir Arthur Tedder, RAF commander for North Africa, and sitting here on my right, told me earlier, 'Enoch, that was the most impressive display of raw power I've seen in my entire career.' Now, you're asking, 'What do we do for an encore?' I'll tell you, gentlemen: We're going to give the Nazi war machine its most crippling blow to date."

The inevitable briefing map, cloth draped, was exposed. Only the faint rustle of jerboa mice, foraging in the corners, could be heard in the silence. A hundred pairs of eyes followed the familiar skein of red yarn as it skirted the Italian boot heel, crossed the Adriatic coast of Albania, angled across Yugoslavia and Bulgaria, then looped north.

"Where the hell is that?" Norm muttered.

General Flynt anticipated him. "Tomorrow, men, the biggest single air strike launched so far in this war will destroy the entire collection of oil refineries surrounding Ploesti, Romania. This complex is the source of approximately 30 percent of Germany's oil consumption. Within thirty days her reserves will be used up, and half of her tanks and warplanes will fall silent. Think of it: In one fell swoop this effort, code-named Tidal Wave, will move the end of this war forward by at least one year. It's a big undertaking, and to succeed it will require every ounce of skill and courage of every single crew member. I know none will falter. Now, Sir Arthur and I must move on. We have four other stops to make. Good hunting!"

Colonel Watson waited for the assembled crews to resume their seats after the pair of VIPs departed. In the hush that remained, he proceeded to give them an overview of Tidal Wave.

"This is a funny setup," he announced. "The refineries are mainly in a circle around the city of Ploesti. Just hitting the target area isn't going to do it. We could drop every damn bomb we get there with and still not hurt them badly. At every target there are cracking towers, powerhouses, and distilleries—*those* are your APs. It's why we have assigned specific aiming points down to individual elements in certain cases." He paused and looked over his audience.

"Now, the low-level aspect. For one thing, it improves accuracy. More important is the element of surprise it gives us. Defensively, it takes away half of a fighter's sphere of attack. They'll have to come from above and they'll have to break early to avoid flying into the ground. Another big plus—it removes the threat of their big guns, the eighty-eights, which can't track high-speed, low-level targets."

"It also takes away half of our ability to take evasive action," Kevin muttered sotto voce. "I don't like low-level flying one damn bit."

"We'll add to the element of surprise by coming in on a northwest to southeast axis," Watson continued, drawing a line with a pointer. "At the IP, a place called Floresti, we swing into line abreast and follow this railroad right into the heart of the target area. One sweep, that's all. Two minutes to take out every target. We reassemble straight ahead and head for home. That's the big picture. You'll have a detailed briefing in the morning. Now, Colonel Livingston will handle the intelligence side."

"This is going to be interesting," Stan noted. "These intelligence guys give me a pain in the ass. I'll bet our target photos will be something taken by a little white-haired woman in 1935."

"Gentlemen," the corpulent colonel said, speaking briskly and with authority, "we're counting on the element of surprise to keep losses to a minimum. Reliable sources tell us that Ploesti is defended by no more than a hundred guns, from eighty-eights to 20mm. But they're grouped to the south and northeast—that's the logical direction from which to expect an attack. So," he added with a smug smile, "we circle and come in from the northwest. We'll catch them with their drawers definitely down.

"Fighters. We know of four squadrons of 109s. Only one of these has German pilots, however. Probably inexperienced, since you can bet that Goering isn't going to strip his northern defenses. The other three squadrons are manned by Romanian pilots. Romanians are excellent fliers, but they mostly come from aristocracy and live the good life. By the time they dress for the occasion and get their act together, you'll be gone. Crossing Bulgaria you may see some of their fighters. Again, they fly a Czech-made Avia 534 that has a top speed barely in excess of yours.

"You'll hit the deck as soon as you cross the mountains to avoid early electronic detection. The Germans have a device called 'Wurzburg' that can detect metallic objects, like airplanes, for about a hundred miles. The English have a similar version they call 'radar.' We don't even know that the Germans have allocated any of these scarce sets to their neighbors, but stay down, just in case. You'll be well under their coverage in any event.

"If you go down inside Romania, you'll find the native Romanians, in general, to be friendly. Walking out could be tricky. There's no organized underground to help, and Russia, to the east, is our only ally. Just now Russia is on the run, however. Get south into Syria if you can. That means crossing Turkey, which is neutral. You'll be safe, but interned. While internment in a neutral country may appear to be an attractive alternative to fighting your way home in a crippled plane, rest assured you will face an abort board upon your return to U.S. jurisdiction. Your reasons for landing in a neutral state will be considered in a most critical light—which leads to General Flynt's message on the subject of capture. The general instructed me to remind each crew member of the executive order restricting information given the enemy to name, rank, serial number, and date of birth. Associated provisions include an obligation to attempt escape if captured and never to surrender so long as you have the means to resist.

"Now, we've made a movie that you'll find helpful, and in the hut next door you'll be able to see a three-dimensional table model of your targets. That's all for tonight. Get some sleep and I'll see you again tomorrow morning."

Sagging with fatigue, Ross, Norm, Stan, and Kevin stumbled toward their assigned tent. "Well, whatta you think, Ross?" Norm asked.

"If this afternoon's mission is any indication, it should go pretty much as briefed," Ross responded.

Stan, the news hawk of the crew, snorted. "I say we just got handed a plateful of unadulterated camel shit. If this target is such a cream puff, why don't we just stroll in there at about twenty grand and use Mister Norden's old reliable? Huh? I overheard the crew sitting next to me. They're old-timers, from the Ninth. It seems that this General Flynt, our leader, was just assigned to the run yesterday. It was supposed to be another general named Brereton. Plus, the guys who worked up the whole mission *also* got pulled this afternoon. Like I say, these troops are experienced, and I sure as hell didn't see any big smiles. Anyway, Ross, I got something I'd like to talk to you and Ham about. Can we go past the airplane?"

"Sure." Ross allowed himself to be steered to the *Happy Hooker*'s Plexiglas nose. "What's on your mind?"

Stan's eyes were bright with excitement. "Some of the crews across the field, they're rigging two *fixed* fifties to fire straight ahead out of the nose section. They figure that at the altitude we'll be flying, they can just strafe the hell out of anything directly in front. It isn't much of a job. They're just removing one Plexiglas panel and bolting the gun mounts to the bombsight supports. We won't carry the Norden and it won't interfere with that Woolworth job I'm supposed to use at low altitude. I think it's a helluva good idea. Whatta you say?"

Ross removed his cap and rubbed his sweaty, itching scalp. He laughed. "Well, I can see that it would give us more firepower in the nose. Any of these crews actually fired such a rig?"

"This bombardier I talked with claims he has. Says it really chews things up out in front."

"We don't have a lot of time," Ross mused. "It'll be a dark wake-up call."

"I've already talked with Ham. With him helping, I figure we can be in bed by ten at the latest."

"Well, okay. Can't see that it'll hurt anything. But don't stay up all night. Tomorrow's apt to take all we've got."

"Hey, thanks, Ross. Now, here's one other idea I have."

"Oh, oh." Ross said, grinning. "I should have known. What's this one? You plan to install a bar up there or something?"

"I hadn't thought about it, but I like the idea," Stan quipped. "No, it's like this. There's a wrecked Me 109 in one corner of that big hangar. Some Jerry pilot bellied it in while the British were here. It still has the guns installed—they weren't damaged. I want to pull that 20mm cannon and, instead of twin-fifties, put *that* beauty up there—just leave the fifties where they are."

Ross laughed at length. Ham, who had strolled up behind them, joined him. "Come on, Stan," Ross said. "A 20mm? You don't know the first thing about operating one. Besides, where will you get the ammo?"

"Aha, you forgot that bombardiers have a course in armament. An orientation on all German and Jap guns was included. And the ammo is still right there, belted and everything. Someone just pulled it and put it in a steel drum. You can bet that with this dry desert air, it's as good as the day it was manufactured."

Ham Phillips was getting excited about the idea. "You know, Skipper, I think it can be done. And, man, will *that* son of a bitch make a mess out of the landscape up front!"

Ross finally agreed, after giving it some thought. Ham and Stan walked away, talking and gesturing like a couple of schoolboys.

"We're gonna give 'em hell," Ross whispered aloud.

Chapter Twenty-four

0200 Hours, 1 August 1943
Benghazi

A half-dozen trucks, headlights turning night to day, horns blaring, invaded the transient crew quarters area, circling the big tents like marauding savages. Bullhorns thundered the message: "Okay, up and at 'em! Chow in thirty minutes; briefing at oh-three-hundred. Up and at 'em!"

Ross groaned and peered at the luminous dial of his watch: It was 0200. He lay silently, waiting for a recurrence of the stabbing abdominal pain that had awakened him earlier. His gut remained benign, but a trace of nausea lingered. The thought of breakfast almost sent him racing out of his tent again. He had made the trip twice, around midnight. When he reached the latrine area, he discovered a long waiting line. Ross placed a tentative foot on the floor and waited for the dizziness to recede. Three sleeping bags away Kevin groaned.

"Oh, Christ, I don't think I can make it, guys."

"Let's give it a go, troops," Ross ordered with more enthusiasm than he actually felt.

Dysentery. Of all the goddamn times for it to hit. Half the group must have been outside most of the night, moaning with excruciating stomach cramps as the contents of their stomachs and bowels erupted. Norm, the bastard, had escaped the scourge completely.

Standing and stretching, Norm taunted the navigator. "I take it all back, Kevin boy, you are *not* full of shit. You want me to keep the nose-wheel door open for you today?"

"Norm, I hope to hell you take a 20mm out there, right through your stupid fucking mouth," said Kevin.

Ross tried to obtain a condition report from the enlisted crewmen before entering the mess tent. A wan Ham Phillips reported that all except Reed and himself had spent a miserable night. They were all on their feet, however.

The disabling bacteria had missed very few. Would the mission be scrubbed? Three temporary tables erected at the entrance of the mess tent provided the answer. Each was manned by a brusque flight surgeon who first offered each airman a paper cup filled with a vile, chalky-tasting brown liquid, then asked sharply, "Any blood in your stool? Any fever? Sick call is in progress, but anyone with a temperature of less than a hundred flies. Next."

Ross walked away with a small bottle of the liquid antidote and an extra issue of the in-flight combat ration, "desert chocolate." It was said that the stuff could constipate a goose.

Ross concentrated on the briefing with difficulty, his bland breakfast of boiled eggs and toast sitting heavy in his stomach. The cooks deserved medals for coming up with this heretofore unheard-of menu. He had never felt so weak and listless. As the various staff officers droned on about the weather, intelligence estimates, formation procedures, and recognition codes, he grew more anxious to get on with it.

The squadron commanders, Eric Deckard among them, ended the briefing by calling for a quick meeting with their respective aircraft commanders. Deckard gave a concise pep talk, then said, "Colyer, would you step over here a minute?"

Leading Ross to one side, Deckard placed a hand on his shoulder. "You won't be flying with the Red Dogs today, Ross."

"What?"

"There's been a bit of last-minute shuffling around. General Sprague is leading the second wave—White Two. He asked me for the best crew I could put up; you're it. His aide, Templeton, will be your copilot. The general will stay on the flight deck. Your regular copilot will sit this one out."

"But—but, Colonel," Ross spluttered. "Jesus Christ, Sir, Stan and Kevin are briefed for Red Target. There—there isn't time for them to make that big of a change."

"There is, but I'll arrange for you to fly with the pair originally scheduled for White Two Lead, if you like. Look, Ross, I'm sorry as hell to lay this load of shit on you at the eleventh hour, but you're the only man I know who can pull it off."

Ross hesitated. To switch targets at this point was potentially catastrophic. He recalled the grinning Stan and Phillips, however, as they'd described the modifications they had made to accommodate the 20mm gun.

"No, damnit, I'll go with the crew I know. Stan is good; he'll handle it. Hanson—well, this is Kevin's twenty-fifth. I'd hate to put him up with an entirely strange crew." He shook his head. "I'm getting a bad feeling about this thing, Colonel."

Deckard tightened his grip on Ross's shoulder. "Don't feel like the Lone Ranger. But remember this: As long as you're in that left seat, you're in command of the airplane. Don't let the fact that you have a general on the flight deck throw you. He can tell you *where* to go, but the *how* and *when* are up to you. Don't forget that little fact. Things might get hairy out there today."

The desert wind came up early that morning. Driven by six-hundred-plus flailing propellers, a miniature dust-laden typhoon swept the bleak landscape. A green flare from the mobile control tower set 175 ungainly, overloaded Liberators trundling down the tarmac. The noise of their engines awoke a British coastal gun crew five miles away. "Wot on earth are the bleedin' Yanks up to now?" a sleepy Tommy had complained. The mind-numbing roar of protracted takeoff runs at the five closely bunched airfields continued for a full two hours.

The desert environment claimed a victim almost immediately. Ross watched, stunned, as a desert-camouflaged machine from another group lost an engine seconds after becoming airborne. Blinded by dust, unable to climb, the hapless pilot attempted to turn back to the field. His wingtip struck a fifteen-foot concrete pole supporting a power line. The predawn gloom flared to life as an orange fireball illuminated the eerie landscape with a ghastly flame.

Ross's crew had taken their change in assignment in stride. Stan and Kevin had undergone a hurried target briefing and, although Kevin was worried and upset, Ross knew that he would cope. Stan merely grinned and quipped, "Just another damn oil well, Skipper. We'll cream it."

The confrontation Ross had been dreading, however, went surprisingly smoothly. General Sprague and BT arrived a scant thirty minutes before time to start engines. Sprague didn't mention the training-flight incident. He was vastly impressed with the lash-up nose-gun arrangement.

Slapping Ross on the back, he chortled, "Now that, by God, is the type of thing I like to see. Some good old Yankee ingenuity."

BT slid into the right seat with a wry, "Well, déjà-goddamn-vu. Think you can keep this thing airborne this time?"

Norm seemed unable to believe his good luck. Not even waiting for transportation, he hustled back to his cot.

Guided by a clench-jawed crew, the *Happy Hooker* used all but a scant hundred feet of runway before lifting into the choking cloud of prop-blown sand. Nursing sluggish airspeed and straining engines, Ross released his pent-up breath as the altimeter crossed one thousand feet. A gradual climb established, Ross scanned the engine instruments for any sign of less-than-perfect performance. He gave the control console an affectionate pat and remarked to Ham, "I really think the old girl *likes* to fly overloaded."

The flight engineer, expressing the innate pessimism of his trade, shook his head dolefully. "As much sand as we sucked up just now, I'll be surprised if the engines make the whole trip, Cap'n. Look, the oil pressure on number two's already fluctuating."

Ross eyed the barely discernible movement of the offending instrument and chuckled. "Instrument error, Ham. We're going the distance—I can feel it.

"Ham, as soon as I start to orbit, start firing yellow-green flares. Mickey, keep us informed on how the group is joining up." Ross glanced out the windshield and shook his head. "Would you get a load of that mess up there?"

The entire crew—with the exception of Mickey in the tail turret—took in the panorama ahead, speechless with awe. Above a violet haze concealing the Mediterranean, a weaving swarm of black objects barely recognizable as airplanes made lazy circles as if lashed to an invisible carousel. From the left end of the horizon to the right, straggling streams of B-24s resembled five hives of bees seeking to unite with their queens. From the nucleus of their shapeless, wheeling masses an occasional magnesium Very flare identified the various slowly building formations.

The White One formation, which the *Happy Hooker* would follow, was to use red-yellow flares.

"Okay, at eleven o'clock, Ross. There's mother," BT announced. Ross altered course slightly and started a sweeping join-up turn to place them five miles behind.

Finally, with the stream of neatly stacked ships in their assigned berths, the foremost Liberator fired a double green flare and heeled into a turn northward.

Tidal Wave, the mightiest air armada to invade enemy airspace to date, started its long march toward Winston Churchill's "soft underbelly of the Axis" as a rising sun cast distorted shadows on the water below.

Major General Enoch Flynt, at the extreme tip of the deadly arrow, recalled President Franklin D. Roosevelt's words the day following Pearl Harbor: "And this is a day that shall reside in infamy. . . ."

It was a prophetic thought.

☆ ☆ ☆

THE HEARING

DAY FOUR

5 December 1945
Hearing Room B, Building 1048, War Department

"Colonel Timmerman, you were assigned to Ninth Air Force head-quarters during the summer of 1943, were you not?"

"That is correct." The officer's lean, sun-browned features beneath a receding hairline reflected alert concentration. A long, prominent nose, slightly bent out of shape by what Janet guessed was an old sports-inflicted injury, marred what would otherwise have been a handsome face.

"In what capacity?" Colonel Blankenship closed the file folder before him and resumed pacing a twelve-foot stretch of floor in front of the board members.

"I was briefing officer for the Directorate of Combat Operations."

"In line with your duties, were you briefed on all aspects of the Tidal Wave project?"

"As far as I know, yes, Sir."

"You are an experienced combat pilot, I believe?"

"I flew twenty-five missions as an aircraft commander during the battle for North Africa."

"I see. Based on your experience, Colonel, how did you rate the risk factor of Tidal Wave compared to that of, say, your own missions?"

Timmerman's eyes narrowed, filled with a wary light. He responded in measured tones. "I don't believe you could make a comparison. For one thing, the distance to and from the target was far greater than any

mission previously attempted: twenty-three hundred miles. Then there
was the low-altitude aspect—dropping from fifty feet or less from a
four-engine bomber. Well, there just wasn't any precedent."

"Yes, you're probably correct. Let me put it this way: What would
your feeling have been if you had been scheduled to fly the mission?"

"I requested permission to go," the colonel replied curtly. "My
request was refused."

"I see." Blankenship's voice dropped. His face wore a thoughtful
expression.

Janet fought an urge to speak out. Why? Why would you volunteer
to fly on what you had to have known was a highly dangerous undertaking? You'd already finished your own combat tour.

As if reading her thoughts, Blankenship added a quiet, "Why?"

"Why was I turned down? Because I hadn't flown the low-level
training syllabus."

"No, why did you volunteer?"

Timmerman's response was immediate. "Because I felt I had something to offer. Some of the aircraft commanders had no combat experience. The success of this mission was vital. I believed my presence
could possibly make a difference."

"That's commendable." Blankenship's dry rejoinder carried an implied,
if you can be believed.

Sensing the slur, Timmerman snapped, "I wasn't the only one.
Combat Ops volunteered to the man—even the enlisted clerks."

Blankenship avoided a confrontation by returning to his file folder.
Without looking up he asked, "What was your reaction when you
learned that General Brereton, along with the lead navigator and
bombardier, had been removed from the mission?"

"I was astonished. Tidal Wave was the general's baby. He had worked
night and day for months putting it together."

"Were you told the reason they were removed?"

A slight hesitation. "I was in General Flynt's office that afternoon,
when he received the TWX. It was signed by General Arnold, but the
feeling was voiced that it was at General Eisenhower's request. The
three of them—Brereton, Reddick, and Carson—were in possession
of highly classified information. That they could be captured and
tortured by the enemy was a risk the general wasn't prepared to take."

General Blake interrupted with one of his infrequent, quiet questions.
"I find this extremely interesting, Colonel. Were not both General

Arnold and General Eisenhower aware that Brereton planned to lead the mission from the very beginning?"

"I—I can't say, General. But General Flynt indicated that he believed they knew."

"What was Enoch's reaction?" Blake's voice had overtones of amusement.

"He seemed upset. Extremely so."

"I'll just bet he was." Blake's remark, sotto voce, promoted the first spontaneous chuckle Janet had heard the quintet utter.

Blankenship smoothly resumed control of the questioning. "Let's go back for a moment to something you told the board earlier, Colonel— that you requested a crew position on the mission. Did news that General Brereton had been removed and that General Flynt—who had opposed the low-level concept from the beginning—would lead alter your feelings?"

"Not at all. But, first, I would like to set the record straight on General Flynt's role. The general had expressed his views when asked for them by General Brereton. Thereafter, he accepted the Air Staff's decision and was slated to be a task-force commander from the mission's inception. He had not, however, planned to fly in the lead airplane. *That* was the only change in plans—that he would fly in the pathfinder position."

"Do you believe that change was responsible for General Flynt turning on the wrong IP?"

"I don't know, Colonel," Timmerman snapped. "I wasn't there. And neither were you."

Nausea enveloped Janet like a wet cloud. For a moment she feared she would have to rush from the room. A flash of recollection. A letter from BT, after he had left England. Inside, an envelope with instructions for her to hand-carry the missive, without delay, to his father. There were implications in his letter to her that something was afoot that he highly disapproved of. Could BT, via his father, have been instrumental in that last-minute change? Good God, no! Not BT. Not the casual, cynical man she had married. Why? In God's name, why?

Blankenship's final question to the witness was meaningless babble. Her mind made up, Janet gathered her purse and gloves and tiptoed from the room. She would miss the afternoon session. Her jaw set in stubborn determination, she was already forming questions to ask Senator Broderick Templeton II.

Chapter Twenty-five

General Alfred Gerstenberg, always an early riser, even on Sundays, scanned the papers that his aide, Maj. Hans Deitz, placed before him.

"The strength report and condition of readiness, *Herr* General."

The general noted with satisfaction that Battery Eight, Sixth Antiaircraft Artillery Battalion, had been restored to fully operational status. He was also pleased to see that the *nachtjagdgeschwader* at Zilistea carried seventeen of the new twin-engine Me 110 night fighters as combat ready. He tossed the document to one side and turned to another report of brawling between Romanian and German aircrews.

The readiness report that Gerstenberg tossed aside so casually would have been a source of shock and dismay to Maj. Gen. Enoch Flynt as his Tidal Wave strike force assembled after nearly two hours of circling off the coast of North Africa. Under the heading "Antiaircraft Guns, Operational" was the figure 237—almost three times the number that Allied intelligence had estimated. The "Four squadrons of fighter craft with partially trained crews" that Allied officers had guessed were in the area were actually four *wings* of deadly Me 109s, more than half of which were manned by crack *Luftwaffe* pilots. Other assorted groups guarded the outer approaches of what the general had designated *Festung* Ploesti.

Gerstenberg pushed back from his desk. "I'm giving the family an outing today, Hans. Away from that infernal heat of Bucharest. I don't anticipate an attack for several days; the Amis are still assembling their strike force. You may tell the combat control duty officer where I can be reached."

Yes, he was ready, Gerstenberg mused, as a hovering waiter replenished his coffee. It had been touch and go that day in Hermann Goering's lavishly appointed office. Only his close association with the *reichsmarschall* during World War I had emboldened him to speak as he did.

Now, almost half a year later, he had reason to be in high spirits. Over a period of months his chief had stripped units on every front and funneled them to the impatient commander of *Festung* Ploesti. Let the enemy come—in force. He was prepared.

But today Gerstenberg intended to put his cares aside. He would play a few sets of tennis with his daughter, Eva, followed by a swim in the spa's heated pool, then he would lounge poolside, sipping chilled wine. He could feel the tension slipping from his shoulder and back muscles already.

The weighty duties of high office were not long in reasserting themselves, however. The general had just delivered a sizzling ace to his nubile opponent when a black-tied hotel clerk approached.

"Telephone, *Herr* General. The caller insists that the message is urgent."

Gerstenberg tucked a towel around his perspiring neck and followed the minion to a discreetly located booth. "Gerstenberg here," he barked into the mouthpiece.

"So sorry to disturb your holiday, *Herr* General. This is Major Woldenga. I'm calling from the command bunker. Our listening post at Athens has intercepted a message that indicates a large force of American bombers is assembling off the coast of North Africa. I thought you would want to know."

"Of course. But don't tell me that the fools are using their radios?"

"*Nein, Herr* General. Their headquarters at Benghazi issued an alert to Allied forces in the seas around Sicily. They are advised to expect a large formation to pass overhead on a northeasterly heading. A precaution to prevent inadvertent attack. The code used is known to us."

"I see." The general frowned. "What targets are vulnerable?"

"Sofia, Wiener-Neustadt, and Ploesti, *Herr* General."

"The Liberators in North Africa haven't the range for Ploesti, Bernhard."
A pause.

"A faint possibility, I agree, *Herr* General, but our eyes on the North African waterfront report a large shipment of aircraft fuel tanks in the past month. And the move from Egypt to Libya brought the devils two hundred miles closer."

"Hmmm. What is your assessment, Major?"

"I suggest that we wait until the force makes landfall in Sector 24. I will issue a general preparedness warning but await a report on their direction after they pass Corfu. A massive training exercise is always a possibility."

"Good, keep me informed."

Enoch Flynt's advantage of surprise had evaporated even as his huge force left the assembly area.

Gerstenberg returned to his match. To her surprise, his daughter beat him easily 6-3, 6-2.

0835 Hours, 1 August 1943
Aboard the *Happy Hooker*
6,000 Feet Above the Mediterranean

The massive Tidal Wave formation droned northward. BT was holding the *Happy Hooker* in precise position five miles behind the White One formation. Dust-free air and the relatively cool temperature soothed nerves worn raw by the desert wind, sand, and heat. Ross, his feet propped atop the rudder bars, studied their newly assigned target information.

Stan was singing, off-key, "Give me land, lots of land . . ."

Their serenity was shattered by the drumroll of every .50-caliber machine gun on board firing in unison. Ross sat bolt upright, prevented only by his seat belt from leaping to his feet. BT's flinch was magnified by the control surfaces into a carnival ride deviation from course. Ross threw a wild glance over his shoulder and saw Phillips, a broad grin on his face, regarding him from the upper turret.

"Time to test-fire the guns, Cap'n," he yelled.

It was an old trick. The gunners, acting on a prearranged signal, simultaneously test-fired their guns without notice. If the stunt had

a name, it would be something like "Scare hell out of the officers."
It usually worked.

Ross frowned. Horseplay was one thing, but with the wing commander on board he had expected a more professional atmosphere to
prevail. He shot a quick glance to where Sprague perched on a stool
in a corner of the flight deck. The general's answering smirk reassured
him. Phillips had had enough sense to let the old man in on the stunt.

Ross resumed his reclining position with a rueful admission that
the life of a B-24 gunner was not just a bunch of grins. Endless hours
of riding in an uninsulated aluminum tube; noise; excessive heat or
cold; no constructive duty to perform; then an interlude of stark terror
as the bomber underwent attack from flak and fighters. This was
followed by the equally long trip home, again devoid of useful activity.
Ross knew there was an ongoing contest among the gunners to come
up with the most outrageous practical joke.

And he had heard of some pretty raunchy ones, he chuckled to
himself. He thought about the two waist gunners, with only each other
for company. Once, with the plane at altitude and oxygen masks
required, one of them had strolled to his buddy's auto-mix regulator—
the device that automatically produced the correct mix of pure oxygen
and rarified outside air—and, standing in the proper position, expelled
a huge fart into the regulator. The noxious odor passed into his buddy's
oxygen mask—which he hadn't dared to remove.

Ross chuckled again, but his reverie was interrupted as Kevin's angry
voice sounded over the intercom.

"Goddamnit, Phillips. Let's knock off the kid stuff. *Some* of us have
a bad case of dysentery."

It was a harsh reminder of reality. Ross polled the crew to get some
idea of the severity of the affliction. Other than Kevin, all stated that
while feeling "wrung out," they were having no real problems.

Stan, feigning hurt feelings, announced, "Okay, guys, but I wish you
would have let me add this 20mm to the gag. Now stand by while I
see if 'Big Bertha' up here is going to work."

The intercom went silent. Then, with jarring concussions that seemed
to loosen every rivet in the airplane, the 20mm nose gun announced
its presence. "Jesus Christ," Stan whispered. "Did you see *that?* A two-
second burst—this thing is mean! A thousand yards, just like a goddamn
fire hose."

Sprague was ecstatic. "What a weapon. I'm going to recommend that we put one in every plane in the wing when we get back. Let Jerry make a head-on pass into *that*."

Comment from the others was broken off when Kevin interjected, "Navigator to pilot, landfall in thirty minutes. We're scheduled to commence our climb to eleven thousand any minute now."

Ross thumbed his throat-mike switch. "Roger, Nav. Mickey, how does the formation behind us look?"

"I've lost the Blue bunch, Skipper. They kept dropping behind and now I can't spot 'em anywhere. White Three is still right behind us, though."

"Well, shit." Ross glanced at BT. "What the hell is Blue Leader doing? If we get hit by fighters, we're going to have our rear end hanging out. I don't relish being spread all over the place on this one. Remember Frankfurt?"

"Bet he's flying constant airspeed," BT observed. "There was talk about which method used less fuel: constant power setting or holding constant true airspeed. The White groups are from Ninth Air Force. If you notice, we're flying constant power setting. Our true airspeed builds as we burn off fuel."

"I expect you're right, BT," Ross replied. "Well, I just hope they get into position by the time we cross the mountains. Tell the general what's going on. Now listen up, everybody. Once we make landfall we'll be over occupied territory. You can expect enemy action. It's not anticipated immediately, but it's not impossible."

His transmission was interrupted by Stan.

"Bombardier to pilot. Surface ships, eleven o'clock. I can count a half-dozen. At least one cruiser and smaller stuff—destroyers maybe."

Ross peered through the haze; there they were, all right. He detected a blinking light from the larger lead vessel. "Leckie," he snapped, "we're getting Morse code from the big one. He's probably requesting a recognition code. What's it read?"

The radio operator scuttled to a window. A pause, then, "I read it as 'Go Blue,' Captain."

As Ross's face split into a grin, Kevin came on. "Hey, I don't have any code word like that."

"Where did you go to school, Kevin?"

"Arizona, why?"

"That explains it. That's a friendly down there, guys, believe me. Skippered, I'd say, by an alumnus of the University of Michigan. Okay, back to business. After we make landfall, you can shed life jackets. Keep the intercom clear of chatter. And, above all, keep those eyeballs on swivels."

As the tranquil Mediterranean disappeared behind them, even the sky seemed to lose its benign, friendly appearance. "We're starting to climb," BT announced briefly.

Ross lightly shook the control column. "Okay, I'll take it for a while, BT. It's your turn for a break. Give me another 100 RPM; see if that's enough to let us keep up."

A barely perceptible increase in crew diligence could be detected as the throaty roar of their four engines deepened fractionally. Ross concentrated on holding position on White One, five miles ahead.

Sprague, switching to intercom, snarled, "Any sign of Blue Group, tail?"

"Not a trace, Sir. It's getting sort of hazy back there, though."

"Well, it ain't gonna get any better," Ross observed. "We're passing through ten thousand right now. Look up there."

Ahead, hanging over the mountain range, towering cumulus clouds lay like a lace cap. Beneath the sun-painted tops, however, their bases were a sullen blue-gray. "Ain't no way we're gonna top that stuff at eleven. It looks like we'll be doing a frontal penetration. Let's go over the procedure again. Kevin, Stan, everybody. I want you to track BT and me through the whole maneuver.

"I'll lead the group into a big circle. Our three-ship elements will break off at two-minute intervals. Once on the original heading, wingmen will make a forty-five-degree turn away from their lead, hold it for forty-five seconds, then return to course. Everybody holds altitude, course, and penetration airspeed until we break out on the other side. And that is a by-God must. Anyone who doesn't fly this by the book is going to blunder into a midair. From the looks of that stuff, we're going to get bounced around something awful. Okay. Everyone get into your takeoff-and-landing positions. After penetration, lead will go into another orbit while we join up again. Keep your eyes peeled up front."

"Ross, look," BT broke in. "White One is still climbing. He's going over instead of through. See, way up there, he's above eleven right now."

"I'll be damned," Ross muttered. "Pilot to crew. Looks like Lead is going on top of this stuff. I'd guess we'll be going to about fifteen. You'd better go on oxygen now."

"Damn," an anonymous voice muttered. "It's getting colder than a bitch back here already. We didn't bring jackets and stuff. Can we have some heat?"

Ham Phillips nodded to Ross that he would see to the heat while Ross fumed about the two tardy groups to their rear.

The clouds, resembling piles of white cotton, dissipated rapidly. White One could be seen scooting down the reverse mountain slopes toward green terrain visible through a patchy lower deck.

"I make us less than two hours out, Ross," Kevin advised. "We must have picked up a real tail wind up there. We're indicating almost two hundred; I'd say you're about twenty minutes ahead of flight plan."

"Oh, great," Ross muttered. "If Blue and Red Groups take time to do a frontal penetration, we're going to meet them on our way home."

His concern was short-lived as the intercom crackled. "Bandits! Four o'clock level."

"What the hell," BT rapped. "Mickey, are you sure?"

"Dead sure, Cap'n. Two groups of about a dozen each. They're quite a ways out, but they're heading our way."

"Okay," Ross responded, "they'll be Bulgarian. Now, how did the bastards spot us? Keep calling their position, Mickey. And that," he sighed, "shoots hell out of our fat intelligence colonel's dream about 'total surprise.' Wonder if White Lead saw them?"

"I don't see how, Skipper. They came up from behind," Reed advised. "But they don't seem to be gaining much."

Ross glanced at their airspeed: two hundred and edging higher. "If those are the Bulgarians, their top speed is only about twenty or thirty miles an hour greater than ours. Maybe White One did see 'em. He's sure pouring on the coal."

"They're breaking off, Skipper." Relief was evident in the big tail gunner's voice. Ross realized that he was holding the wheel in a death grip.

"How about taking her for a while, BT?" Ross shook cramped fingers. "Looks like White One is taking us all the way to the deck. Let's spread out just a bit. He'll be going like a bat out of hell. Try not to lose our wingmen." Ross peered to his left rear to see how Standish and *Indy Annie* were faring. Standish was one of the new aircraft commanders on his first mission. His position wasn't perfect, but it wasn't bad either, Ross decided.

0920 Hours, 1 August 1943
Auto Route 5
Central Romania

Siren wailing, pennants fluttering from front fenders, Gen. Alfred Gerstenberg's Mercedes raced toward Bucharest. The peasantry dove for roadside ditches and urged ox-drawn carts to one side as the black banshee shrieked past. An errant white goose was unable to escape; white down and feathers created an unseasonable snowstorm. On spotting a roadside sign that read "PLOESTI" pointing to the left, the general tapped his driver's shoulder.

"Turn there, driver. That's where the action is going to be. I'll work out of the command post there."

There was little question in Gerstenberg's mind of the intent of the air armada bearing down on the Wallachian plain. The Wurzburg near Sofia had provided the final clue. "Many wings, heading zero-three-zero degrees."

The general, still in civilian clothing, swept into the command post, waving aside a belated *"Achtung!"*

Major Woldenga, with his head and one arm raised heavenward in supplication, was shouting into a telephone mouthpiece. "Colonel, I do not care if you, personally, find it necessary to search every gathering site your crews frequent—brothels included. I am telling you to man your planes for immediate launch. How's that? Sunday? Of course I know it is Sunday. Tell that to the *verdammt* Americans. Tell *them* that Sunday is a day to play instead of fight. I await your readiness report." Turning, he saw Gerstenberg.

"Herr General," he said in greeting. "It's those damned gypsies. They regard this whole defense posture as a joke. The squadron I was just talking to can muster a total of five aircraft for runway alert. The whereabouts of the remainder of the squadron are unknown; it is Sunday, you see. The commander's greatest concern? One of his pilots was reported passing over a sailboat at mast-height altitude. The boat capsized. Aboard were King Michael and his royal party. Thank God the pilot was Romanian instead of German.

"Now, *Herr* General, the situation." They turned toward a panel of clear Plexiglas that dominated one wall. Facing it, seated before a console adorned with telephones, were a dozen uniformed *Luftnachrichtenhelfeinnen*. Each of the women held an ordinary flashlight whose lens was masked to display a narrow arrowhead. As a plane position was reported, the beam was aimed at the reported coordinates. Other airmen marked the spot with crayon. Red indicated the enemy; white, Axis aircraft. Gerstenberg's eyes widened with surprise at the number of red marks in Sector 24, the extreme southwest sector of his zone.

"Your estimate of numbers, Bernhard?"

"Possibly as many as one hundred, *Herr* General. The Amis are coming in force. They have now passed Sofia and are far off course for Wiener-Neustadt. Bucharest and Ploesti are at risk."

"Not Bucharest, Bernhard. Here." Gerstenberg stabbed a stubby forefinger at the floor. "I relieve you. I suggest that you visit the mess hall and eat an early lunch. Arrange for the others to do likewise. It promises to be a long day."

The general assumed his customary brisk demeanor and seated himself at the command console. Placing one of their many previously rehearsed battle plans into action, he made his first phone call.

"Carl-Otto, General Gerstenberg here. Carl-Otto, it appears you will see action today. I project that American bombers will arrive here within two hours. Launch your fighters by eleven-hundred hours. Orbit in the northeast sector above the middle clouds. The axis of approach will be from the southwest. You will be positioned to attack head-on. As soon as our defense radar is effective, I will provide direction. Destroy them, Otto. Let us make Ploesti too expensive for them to come again, ever."

Another call assigned the Romanians to defend Bucharest. Keep the playboys out of the way, Gerstenberg thought. He verified that all gun emplacements were on full alert, then ordered the *Flakwagen* into position. Finally, displaying a grim smile, the confident general settled back, very much like a hungry cat waiting patiently for the mouse to emerge.

He jerked bolt upright in his chair. An airman was erasing the profusion of red marks. *"Was ist los?"* Gerstenberg called sharply.

"The direction-finding station reports that the enemy forces have disappeared from his display, *Herr* General." Gerstenberg scooped a phone from its cradle.

"Get me the senior officer at Mount Chernin," he snapped, then waited impatiently while he sorted through possible explanations. The bomber force had reversed course? No, a change in direction would have been spotted. Equipment malfunction? Most likely. This wondrous new device was prone to do this. But, of all times—its first test in other than mock battle. "Captain," he barked. "What has happened?"

"We do not know, *Herr* General. The devils have vanished!"

"Is your machine working properly?"

"Our technicians have checked and double-checked, *Herr* General. We still receive images of friendly aircraft."

A puzzled commander replaced the handset.

"Do you have reports from our ground observers?" he asked the line of young women manning the telephones.

"*Jawohl, Herr* General. Most are active, but they report no targets."

The general leaned back in his chair and placed his right index finger under his chin. How, he wondered, do you order an attack on enemy aircraft that have vanished from the skies in midair?

1050 Hours, 1 August 1943
Aboard the *Happy Hooker*

They were well below all of the cloud cover now, the fertile Danube plain visible beneath them. Dirkson moaned, "Look at that, guys. Green corn and grain. Ain't that beautiful? Looks just like Texas."

"Well, Texas it ain't, Milt." Kevin's voice reflected increasing tension. "You'd get your butt shot off down there. We're coming up on our first initial point, Ross. That was the Danube we just crossed. ETA for the second IP, Targoviste, is at oh-niner. Final IP, Floresti, at two-two."

"Roger, Nav. I got it, BT. Watch White Lead for a green flare when he turns at the IP."

Minutes ticked away as every eye scanned the terrain below and the skies above. But danger seemed remote. It was turning out to be a milk run after all, wasn't it? The sobering fact that they were deep into enemy-held territory failed to dispel the carnival atmosphere that had marked the trip thus far.

"Some of those goddamn people are actually waving at us. Can you believe it?" Stan observed. "I'm going back to the bomb bay and pull the pins, Ross."

"Okay, Stan. I'll be glad when we're rid of those babies—"

He stopped short as BT called, "Green flare; Lead is turning at the IP."

A startled oath from Kevin. "He's *what?* Ross, it can't be. We're still thirty miles from Floresti! Good God, he's turning at the second IP, Targoviste! And there goes his whole formation right behind him!"

"Oh, for Christ's sake," Ross groaned. "Kevin, are you sure?"

"Absolutely. I've double-checked everything. Those damn lead crew substitutions—the guys up there aren't the ones who planned this thing. They just got screwed up."

Ross motioned for General Sprague to switch to intercom. "General, White Lead and his entire wave have turned at the second IP, Targoviste, instead of going on to Floresti. If they hold the briefed heading, they'll miss the target by twenty—maybe thirty miles. Shall we follow or keep to the original flight plan?"

Sprague bounded into position between the two pilots' seats and peered forward. His jaw clenched; then, to Ross's surprise, a self-satisfied smile spread across his features. "Navigator, this is General Sprague."

"Yes, Sir?"

"Are you sure, are you *damn sure,* that this is the wrong turning point?"

Kevin hesitated as he thought about the enormity of his decision, then issued a firm declaration. "Dead certain, General. There's no double-track railroad leading south, for one thing. That was to be our final confirmation."

Sprague snatched the map from BT's lap. Ross pointed to their present location and the broad grease-pencil line indicating the planned flight path.

"Shall I break radio silence, Sir? There's still time for them to get back on the correct course."

Sprague didn't use the intercom. Putting his mouth close to Ross's ear, he ordered: "Never in hell. The dumb-ass is on his way to bomb Bucharest! Stay off the fucking radio and continue on course."

Ross's involuntary "But, Sir—" was broken off as Sprague whipped the dark glasses from his face. His narrowed eyes bored into Ross's like flaming lances.

Still off the intercom, the general snarled for Ross's ears only: "I tried to tell Brereton that Flynt was the wrong man for this job. Now maybe he'll believe me. As of now, we're flying mission lead."

Stunned at Sprague's decision not to break radio silence, Ross could only grunt in response.

As a clearly elated Sprague changed his comm selector back to the VHF monitor position, Kevin come on the intercom.

"Whatta we do, Ross? Follow them or stay on course?"

"We follow the flight plan, Kevin. For your information we're now leading the entire goddamn bomber stream. As for you being 'dead' certain, it could be a prophecy. If you're wrong, Hanson, then I have a strong feeling that you're gonna get killed. You get that, Stan?"

Stan, sounding as if Ross had given him nothing more significant than the correct time, responded, "Gotcha, Skipper. But if Lead discovers his mistake and makes a run on Ploesti from south to north—well, I just hope they've got traffic lights in this hick town. There's gonna be the biggest fucking traffic jam you ever saw up there if that happens."

The element of surprise had evaporated when the bomber stream was sighted by the Bulgarians. What, in Christ's name, was Sprague thinking of? Ross wondered. Thirty airplanes would miss their assigned targets. Or, if Stan had figured correctly, the first and second waves would cross the target on collision courses at an altitude of fifty feet. The very idea caused him to turn pale. And only he would ever know the real reason. That unguarded expression of glee that only Ross had been privy to: Brig. Gen. Elliott Sprague aspired to be man of the hour, the one who salvaged the mission. It was front-page hero stuff. A feat that in all probability would result in Sprague's promotion and Flynt's disgrace. It could also lead to a wholesale massacre if the two formations of thirty airplanes each met head-on over the target.

What the hell do I do? Ross thought. I can disobey orders and still alert Lead that they're off course. As he wrestled with his conscience, Kevin announced, "Over Targoviste. IP in ten minutes."

While Ross was sorting out the implications of Lead's mistake, the sacrosanct radio silence was broken with a terse, "Wrong turn, White Lead! Wrong turn!"

Ross half-turned to see Sprague's reaction. A rock-hard stare told him all he needed to know. There was no acknowledgment by White Lead. Ross responded to BT's "What the fuck's going on, Amigo?" with a blank expression—the dark glasses masked the torment in his eyes.

Sick with guilt and apprehension, Ross returned his concentration to the countryside rushing beneath the thundering Liberator. He'd get the mission over with and then work out the right and wrong of things.

The niggling thought that he should have been the one to make that radio call wouldn't go away, however.

Kevin, his voice tight, announced, "Turn onto target heading in two minutes. Fire a double green flare, engineer."

Stan brought them back to earth with a droll, "Okay, anybody don't want their booze ration tonight—I'll take it!"

Chapter Twenty-six

1112 Hours, 1 August 1943
Luftwaffe **Command Center**
Ploesti, Romania

"There they are, General." Major Woldenga touched Gerstenberg's arm and pointed. "They've reappeared—and close!"

Pugnacious jaw outthrust, the stocky commander glared at the offending wall display. Airmen were marking red slashes a scant thirty miles northwest. "Why didn't our artillery radars pick them up before now?"

"They are quite low, *Herr* General," the nervous major explained. "Those are reports from our Ground Observation Corps. We still do not have radar contact. They are reported to be possibly too low for our radar."

"Low?"

"*Jawohl, Herr* General. Our observers estimate no more than ten meters."

"*Ten meters? Mein Gott!* What kind of aircraft?"

Major Woldenga interrupted. "A report of engagement, *Herr* General. Just in, from a battery in the outer ring. They are Consolidated Liberators. And, please note, their flight path will carry them west of Ploesti. They are on a direct course for Bucharest."

"Liberators? Ten meters? Bucharest? It makes no sense whatever. No matter, engage them at once—the fighters Carl-Otto holds ready to the northeast, the Romanian squadrons at Bucharest, all flak batteries go to red alert. Order the railroad *Flakwagen* to proceed north on the Ploesti-Floresti line at full speed."

Sightings and reports of engagements inundated the overworked controllers. Woldenga and Gerstenberg made lightning-swift decisions as they sifted through the mass of information: "The machines are too low for our heavy guns to track." "Cut fuses to zero; fire in front so they must pass through it." "Bulgarian fighters reported that a huge formation of enemy bombers passed more than an hour ago." "What in heaven's name took so long for them to report?" "The leader's radio was inoperative. He was forced to return to base and report by telephone." "More sightings in the vicinity of Floresti. They are turning on a course for Ploesti." "The force headed for Bucharest is a diversion. Tell Carl-Otto's fighters to attack the second group at once!"

"*Herr* General, the Romanian pilots have our radio frequencies completely saturated. We are unable to talk with the fighters from Mizil. They orbit at six thousand meters—above the broken cloud deck. They cannot see the enemy."

"Wurzburg at Mount Chernin reports additional wings, *Herr* General, on a heading of zero-three-zero."

1115 Hours, 1 August 1943
Aboard the *Happy Hooker*
Approaching Floresti, Romania

"Okay, Ross," Kevin announced, "we're coming up on the double-track railroad that runs straight into Ploesti. Our aiming point is a powerhouse inside the Colombia complex. As you saw, it's on the southwest corner of the city. We'll fly over the city itself. White One was supposed to take the left side of the tracks; we were to take the right. I'll hand off to Stan at the railroad junction north of town."

"Roger," Ross acknowledged. "Turning now, crew. Remember the barrage balloons over the target. Supposedly we can snap the mooring cables, but I'd rather not try, so call out any you see that we can avoid. And no strafing over the city proper—shoot only when we're being shot at."

"What a ride!" Dirkson exulted from the waist. "Goddamn, if you don't believe we're causing some excitement down there, just look. People running every which way."

Even the normally closemouthed Leckie was moved to remark, "Look at that train! I'll bet that engineer's crapping in his pants trying to get the hell outta the way. Wait a minute—wha-a-a . . .? The goddamn sides are falling off the boxcars! My God, that train's loaded with *guns*. Shit—the bastards are shooting at us. Clobber 'em, everybody!"

Ross, stunned by the surprise attack, concentrated on holding a steady course toward the target. He could observe the fusillade of arcing orange balls only from the corner of his eye.

"Give me 2,500 RPM and forty inches on all engines, BT. I'm hitting the deck." Ross pushed the nose down and watched the airspeed build to 225 mph. He pulled up sharply to miss a grove of trees. "Kevin, get down beside Stan and handle that 20mm. Leckie, man the .50 caliber down there." Ross observed Sprague crouched between him and BT, barking into the VHF set.

On the intercom Ross could hear the excited crew over the continuous pounding of their guns: "They got one behind us! Over in the low box—he's on fire!" "Mickey, pour it into that last car—he's got us square in his sights." "We just took a hit!" "You okay back there? One o'clock—big stuff—Christ, they're using eighty-eights!" A series of blue-white muzzle blasts, followed by a jarring concussion, confirmed the analysis. "Three o'clock, that fucking haystack is a gun—get on him, Dutch." "Goddamn, they hit the number two—fuck, he just blew up in midair!"

Then it was over.

Mickey announced from the tail turret that the train, caught in a cross fire between two racing formations, was a smoking ruin, its locomotive having exploded in a ball of white steam.

Numb with shock, Ross counted five B-24s reported lost. And they still had, what, ten to fifteen minutes to target? Now they were being pounded by the 88s.

"Shoot for the gun *crews,* damnit," Ross heard himself order. "Not the *guns,* the crews." Small-caliber stuff, 37mm and 20mm, was already raking the lead ships. Ross, crouched behind the wheel of the thundering *Happy Hooker,* was about to be introduced to the gunners of Gerstenberg's "inner ring."

1120 Hours, 1 August 1943
***Luftwaffe* Artillery Battery Nine**
Southwest of Ploesti

Startled by the red-alert signal's rising moan, the two somnolent draft horses hitched to the battery's mess cart raised their heads—

nostrils flared in alarm. The dozen uniformed soldiers grouped around the mess cart immediately set up a plaintive grumble. "Sunday. Lunchtime. Why must the *verdammt* generals always pick times like these to play war?"

Pietre Somolovitch, the driver of the horse-drawn van, didn't share the casual unconcern demonstrated by the practice-weary gunners. A Russian POW, he served—as did all loaders for the huge 88mm guns— under threat of brutal beatings or worse, not from any feelings of loyalty. The old campaigner had heard that gut-chilling wail before. Perhaps it *was* a practice, perhaps not. At any rate, sitting inside a ring of antiaircraft guns during an air raid was not to his liking. Urging the lagging soldiers to hurry, the terrified driver applied the whip, fleeing the danger zone in a jangling rattle of pots and pans without further delay.

Werner Steinmann was one of the more dedicated members of Battery Nine. The twenty-year-old corporal prided himself on his unbeaten record of having his quad-mount 20mm gun operational in less than eighteen seconds. He had equaled that time just a few minutes earlier. Seated in the "saddle"—left hand on the elevator wheel, right hand on the azimuth control, and right foot on the firing pedal—he watched his gunner's mate activate the electric sighting device. Two POW loaders stood by. Smiling in satisfaction, Steinmann looked about to see that their performance was observed, and appreciated, by either *Oberleutnant* Hecht, the battery commander, or *Feldwebel* Raust.

Neither was to be seen. *Oberleutnant* Hecht had immediately departed via his motorcycle to inspect the thirty-six other guns—an assortment of 88mm, 37mm, and 20mm weapons—making up Battery Nine. Sprawled in a rough semicircle on the southwestern outskirts of Ploesti, they formed a part of Gerstenberg's vaunted "inner ring" of defense. Hecht was proud of his deployment techniques. The 88s, their bulk impossible to conceal, sat inside earthen walls a full six feet tall. The smaller guns, however, were cleverly concealed in barns with collapsible fronts, on platforms covered with hay, atop factory buildings; even a church steeple served as a flak tower.

Feldwebel Raust, on the other hand, had a problem. Upon arrival at his group of four 88s following the initial warning, he was greeted by a worried corporal shouting, "Sergeant, *Trudi* is out of operation!" *Trudi,* a gun imported from the north, was the pride of Battery Nine. Five white stripes painted around its barrel attested to that number of planes shot down over Paris. The mechanism that elevated the eight-ton, fifteen-foot barrel was jammed.

The alarmed NCO dashed to the electric control panel. He was allowed four minutes to report his guns operational to the control center. The red ready light remained dark. "'Nutti," he screamed. "Get your worthless Bolshevik ass over here!"

The POW dubbed 'Nutti, his Russian name impossible to pronounce, straightened from where he lounged against a stack of shell cases. Still stuffing lunch into his mouth, his Slavic features impassive, he strolled to where Raust was practically dancing up and down in his agitation.

"Fix this thing—now!" the sergeant roared.

'Nutti was the battery's secret weapon. An electrician in his home-town of Minsk, the Russian was largely responsible for Battery Nine's near perfect in-commission rate. And 'Nutti was not unaware of his worth. Despite frequent threats to ship him to the Bulgarians, noto-riously cruel to prisoners of war, his transgressions were invariably overlooked. He was even provided an occasional clandestine ration of *tuscia,* the fiery Romanian brandy.

He carefully emptied his metal bowl of the last of a watery cabbage soup and set the container carefully to one side. *Feldwebel* Raust and the rest of the anxious gun crew gathered in a circle behind him as he commenced to remove screws from the electrical control panel. Their concern for the punitive measures *Oberleutnant* Hecht might impose for a less than perfect in-commission status was far greater than any fear they had of an actual enemy attack.

1126 Hours, 1 August 1943
Aboard the *Happy Hooker*
Approaching Ploesti

"What the hell's going on?" BT shouted into Ross's ear. "This was supposed to be a goddamn milk run."

Ross shrugged helplessly. "Beats the hell outta me, BT. I count five down out of thirty-six—and we haven't even seen fighters yet. Now I know how Custer must have felt," he added. "Keep your eyes glued on those instruments. If we take a hit in an engine, don't wait for me to call it; feather the son of a bitch before she torches."

Stan's voice crackled over the intercom. "Eleven o'clock, Skipper. There's a flak tower on top of that concrete building. He's giving the boys on our left a fit. If you can turn left about five degrees, I'd like to try out this nose cannon."

Executing a careful, shallow turn, Ross pointed the ungainly bomber directly at the building. Sure enough, at least four streams of tracers were pouring from a concealed battery. It appeared to be 37mm stuff—punishing firepower. Even prepared for the multiple recoil of the nose-mounted 20mm gun, the flight-deck crew was shaken by its shuddering clatter. General Sprague uttered a yelp of satisfaction. With one three-second burst Kevin had obliterated the German gun position.

Stan's exultant "Way to go!" was quickly followed by "We're turning on the bomb run. Bomb bay doors coming open. Follow the PDI, Skipper. Bombs away in a minute and thirty seconds. Take her up just a bit—I'll have to drop inside some blast walls."

Stan's voice had all the emotion of a mortician's as he calmly assumed control. His aplomb cracked slightly, however, as Kevin called excitedly, "B-24s, pilot. Two o'clock, our altitude. Good God—they're on a collision course!"

Ross picked up the hurtling shapes but, probably for the best, had no time to take evasive action. Six stacked elements of three ships each crossed at a thirty-degree deflection. He glimpsed a huge shadow zipping past barely overhead. Then, like a shuttle passing through a loom, the two formations parted on divergent courses.

Before Ross could recover from the shock of the numerous blurred images, so close he felt he could have reached out and touched them, Stan's anguished cry proclaimed, "My target! Those bastards bombed my target! I can't see a thing through the smoke."

Ross made a swift appraisal: The group that had flown by on a collision course had to be White One. They had discovered their navigational error, turned toward Ploesti, and dropped on the first thing that resembled an oil refinery. He could see Sprague shuttling from one side of the flight deck to the other, temple veins distended with rage, yelling into the VHF set. So much for radio silence.

"Do the best you can, Stan," he snapped. "Get rid of those fucking things and let's haul ass. This is a monumental fuckup."

The words were no more than out of his mouth when Stan screamed, "Stacks—dead ahead. Take her up!"

Ross hauled back on the wheel, hoping that his wingmen could stay with him. As he did so, Stan called out, "I got it! Bombs away!"

The *Happy Hooker* cleared three smokestacks by inches, lunging even higher as her cargo of five-hundred-pound bombs dropped free.

1130 Hours, 1 August 1943
Luftwaffe Command Center
Ploesti

General Gerstenberg stood, legs apart, following developments on the wall map, listening above the din of war outside to information relayed by telephone and radio. The air battle was like none he had envisioned. Small-caliber antiaircraft guns had been deployed to counter fighter-bombers—if and when the Allies occupied Italy. Fighter aircraft and the 88s were to deal with big, high-altitude bombers. That an enemy planner had the cunning to reverse roles and employ the huge Liberators in this fashion earned Gerstenberg's grudging admiration.

The air in the noisy, smoke-filled command post was closing in. He had to get outside, *see* the battle, get the feel of it. Waving to Major Woldenga, the general indicated he was going outside and proceeded up the echoing concrete steps.

Gerstenberg stepped into an unreal world of half-light filtered through billowing clouds of acrid black smoke. A steeple clock across the square struck the half hour. It was nearly noon, but visibility could be measured in meters. There was, at the same time, a background of sirens, hoarse shouts, and the bellowing exhausts of racing vehicles. Rumbling crumps of sound in the distance resembled a mischievous giant dropping stacks of lumber. Those were bombs, he knew—bombs with time delay fuses to prevent the low-flying aircraft from passing through their own blast debris. In addition, the diabolical devices greatly discouraged damage control crews.

One moment the sky above was empty, the next it was filled as far as the eye could see with green and tan objects the size of moving vans. The aircraft skimmed over rooftops, the roar of their engines assaulting eardrums with physically discernible force.

Gerstenberg stared upward, fascinated by this quick glimpse into hell. One of the monsters passed directly above him. Its open bomb bay doors revealed ugly, finned cylinders poised to invoke death and destruction. Framed in an oversized window, a cloth-helmeted figure crouched behind a silent machine gun. Gerstenberg imagined that the pair of them exchanged glances. The general realized that, for fleeting seconds, his own life teetered on a fulcrum. A single three-second burst could tip the balance between life and death. Feeling remote from the scene, he wondered idly why the anonymous gunner held his fire.

It was then that he detected an intricate ballet taking place. Separated by inches, the racing behemoths were flying an intricate crossover pattern. He watched in awe. The skill, the daring! Simply to order such a maneuver required as much courage as executing it. Gerstenberg was moved to pay tribute to this audacious demonstration. He raised his arm in a salute to the brave men in the planes racing past him— changing it at the last minute from the stiff-armed Nazi salute to the more conventional fingertips-to-eyebrow type he had observed in American movies.

Reality returned as he speculated on the treatment the ships passing overhead would receive at the hands of his waiting fighters. The second wave! Rushing down the steps, he shouted to Major Woldenga, "The fighters—recall them at once. To destroy machines that have already delivered their bombs is of little consequence. The fighters must be rearmed and refueled in time to deal with the next attack!"

1133 Hours, 1 August 1943
22,000 Feet Above and Northeast of Ploesti

Kurt strained to hear the garbled radio transmission. A line of blue-black thunderstorms to the north, tongues of lightning flickering in their depths, created a harsh background of crackling static. Excited by the scramble, he quickly reverted to the icy remoteness that the oft-rehearsed routine of a combat patrol evoked. The aging 109 vibrated and gave off disconcerting noises. He frowned. Provisional *Jagdgeschwader* 99 hadn't received the new, up-to-date machines promised, so Kurt exercised his prerogative as squadron leader and selected the best of the lot. Also, although Major Eckert had grumbled, he had insisted on having his old markings added: black and silver spiral stripes on the prop spinner and the pale blue falcon, poised for a diving attack.

To concentrate on the task at hand required every ounce of that professionalism of which Kurt was so proud. He must keep the contents of that awful letter buried in a remote corner of his mind. He wasn't carrying it today—he didn't dare. Its very presence next to his body would dull his senses.

Gretta dead! It defied comprehension. Her existence was just something to be taken for granted; she *was* there—always had been and always would be. But the cryptic words scrawled on the half sheet of wartime gray stationery said otherwise.

Her aunt had been thoughtful enough to assume the unwelcome burden of contacting him. Gretta and her parents, foolishly ignoring the spreading destruction to their country, had boarded a train bound for Berlin. At Frankfurt the train was halted by air-raid warnings. The American bombers made their appearance at noon. Frankfurt's railroad marshalling yard was their main point of impact. Once again the Norden bombsight performed flawlessly. The remains of Gretta and her family were still there someplace, beneath the tons of debris.

Kurt reduced power to the minimum to conserve precious fuel. He watched the *schwarm* of thirty Me 109s follow him in a lazy elliptical orbit. It was his favorite position—on the perch. Twenty-two thousand feet should place him well above the approaching bombers.

Where the hell were they? The familiar outline of a bomber stream should be easily visible against the cottony cloud tops below. He switched to the frequency used by fighter control at Otopenii and thumbed the transmit button. "*Kampfhahn,* this is *Falke Eins.* What is the situation?"

A sudden break in the electrical disturbance allowed him to hear clearly. "*Falke Eins,* this is *Kampfhahn.* We have temporarily lost contact with the aggressor force. What is your position?"

He recognized Eckert's voice and replied, "Still parked in orbit in the northeast sector, *Herr Oberstleutnant.*"

Strain made his commander's voice harsher than Kurt remembered ever hearing.

"This is not an exercise, *Falke Eins.* Stay alert. Immediately report any sighting."

Kurt scowled behind his confining oxygen mask and switched to the common fighter frequency. He straightened at the sound of the Romanians' excited jabbering. They sounded as if they were engaged. Damnit! Why didn't they have a German interpreter? He attempted to break into the conversation in case a German-speaking pilot was among them. Futile. He switched back to his own control.

"*Kampfhahn,* this is *Falke Eins.* Are the Romanians engaged?"

The reply was broken, choked with static. It sounded like ". . . north . . . Bucharest . . . very deep . . ." Deep? The top of the broken cloud deck beneath was no more than five or six thousand feet. Big bombers "deeper" than that? Beneath the clouds? Unlikely. Anyway,

Bucharest was outside his zone. But he worried, nevertheless. Something was not right. Kurt rolled to the right, still holding in orbit, thinking furiously. Then, as the nose swung onto a new heading, he saw huge plumes of black smoke billowing above the snow-white cloud tops. Near Ploesti. It *was* Ploesti!

Through a break in the lower cloud deck he glimpsed the unmistakable shape of three American Liberators in a loose vee formation, streaking south. The canny devils had sneaked in *beneath* the cloud cover! He thumbed the transmit button.

"*Kampfhahn, Falke Eins.* I have the enemy in sight. I'm attacking!"

Without waiting for a reply, Kurt pumped a clenched fist above his head to signal the attack and rolled into a split-S dive. This would be more than just an objective, impersonal engagement of inanimate machines, he thought. The person more dear to him than life itself lay dead because of the American bombers. Today he would at least extract some small measure of revenge.

Aboard the *Happy Hooker,* that embattled bomber crew's elation was dampened by a terse announcement from the rear.

"Waist to pilot. *Indy Annie*'s hit. Looks like her Tokyo tank's on fire. They're breaking off—up and right. Looks like they're trying to get enough altitude to bail out."

As the *Happy Hooker* plunged into sunlight, the carnage of Ploesti behind them, Ross took stock of their situation. He spotted the high element leader, with a single wingman, streaking southwest. A lone straggler chased after him. My God, thought Ross, is this all that's left of the squadron? Where had they come from? Jesus Christ, he had been indicating more than 200 mph; these other ships had been *behind* him. They must all have had their throttles to the firewall. A quick glance ahead made reassembling their remaining numbers imperative. The decimated and disorganized formation ahead was enveloped in a swirl of black dots.

"Fighters, many, twelve o'clock," Ross announced wearily.

Chapter Twenty-seven

1136 Hours, 1 August 1943
Luftwaffe **Artillery Battery Nine**
Southwest of Ploesti

The late morning sun beat through a thin, high overcast, undiminished by any hint of breeze. Sweat trickled from *Obergefreiter* Steinmann's armpits, forming dark rings on his uniform coveralls. He no longer sat with hands on the controls; they were growing too hot to touch. The smell of hot metal, gun oil, and body odor made him regret the heavy meal he had just consumed. But he continued to scan the heat-hazed sky, determined to be the first to spot the familiar, lumbering Ju 52 target plane. He would then declare a kill and add to his unblemished record.

His aimer, wiping moisture from his eyepiece, grumbled, "This is about enough. How long are they going to keep us here?"

Obergefreiter Steinmann didn't have an opportunity to respond. A white-faced communications runner pounded up and yelled, "This is not a practice! Enemy planes are approaching!"

The alert gunner, feeling his upset stomach churn, snapped, "What kind? From what direction?"

"How the hell should I know? I'm only telling you what they told me."

As a disgusted and thoroughly frightened *Obergefreiter* Steinmann and crew renewed their vigilance with wide-eyed concentration, *Feldwebel* Raust, a scant mile distant, received additional information.

"They are very low," his controller screamed. "They are four-engine bombers. Big. Depress your guns as low as they will go. Cut fuses to zero and lay your barrage in front of the formation."

Raust, confused with this turn of events, paced in circles and railed at 'Nutti. "Hurry, you fool, we are under attack! Can't you understand?" Where the hell was Lieutenant Hecht? he wondered.

'Nutti, who didn't understand a great deal of German, ignored him and methodically checked each of *Trudi*'s several electrical circuits. That the mess cart had trundled off before he was issued his ration of black bread was of far more concern than the frantic, screaming exhortations of *Feldwebel* Raust.

Then the faulty connection, loose and covered with corrosion, revealed itself. It took him thirty seconds to scrape and tighten the errant component. He was rewarded with the glow of the elusive ready light. Looking around him to reassure the fuming sergeant, his eyes bulged. Level with the horizon and rapidly growing in size was the biggest airplane he had ever seen. 'Nutti yelled a pair of Russian oaths and dove for cover.

1138 Hours, 1 August 1943
Aboard the *Happy Hooker*
Southwest of Ploesti

The course line of Ross's oversized gyrocompass read 234 degrees—in the direction to home and safety. It also led directly into the heart of General Gerstenberg's inspired defense. From cunningly disguised emplacements, sweating Russian POWs fed shells into smoking guns as fast as the gunners could locate a target and fire. The blackened carcasses of shattered Liberators dotting the landscape testified to their skill.

Ahead, Ross saw three crippled planes claw for bailout altitude. Five chutes blossomed from one aircraft. An entire tail section, severed by a direct hit, spun into the wind, emitting winking reflections of sunlight with each revolution.

Ross, intent on achieving the relative safety of a box formation, called, "Let's have a condition report. Anyone hurt? Any bad hits?"

"Waist and tail okay, Captain," Corporal Dirkson responded, his voice tight with strain. "Sir, can you get us the hell out of this mess? We're just getting the holy shit shot out of us."

"We're going to get out of it, but we're going to have to fight our way out. Now, how about ammo?"

"We're down to less than five hundred rounds for the nose fifty," Kevin replied. " 'Bout a hundred 20mm shells."

"Okay, bring a couple of belts up front, Dutch. Then—"

Ross never finished his instructions. The *Happy Hooker* had flown directly into the sights of *Obergefreiter* Steinmann's quad-mounted 20mm cannon.

1138 Hours, 1 August 1943
Luftwaffe Artillery Battery Nine

A sweating, cursing *Feldwebel* Raust was having only slightly better results with his six closely bunched 88s. The idiot gun layers couldn't adapt to the idea of shooting *ahead* of and level with their swiftly moving targets. The sight of airborne shapes the size of railroad cars had left them stunned and motionless at first. They were accustomed to firing blind at objects they could barely see with the naked eye. Then there was the problem of being fired *at*. Having a target return their fire was most disconcerting. The first man to die after being hit by a burst of .50-caliber fire came very close to causing wholesale desertion.

Feldwebel Raust, rushing from gun to gun, shouting directions, backed by threats of physical mayhem, was finally rewarded with the sight of one of the monsters emerging from a barrage of black bursts trailing smoke and flame. But the battery was beginning to pay a price. Flying almost level with the gun emplacements, airborne gunners were raking the exposed crews with vicious streams of sparkling tracers.

Raust observed one gun fall silent. It was *Trudi*. He couldn't allow this to happen. Of all the guns operated by Battery Nine, *Trudi* must remain active. Dashing inside her revetment he discovered the entire crew sprawled in the unnatural positions of violent death. One surviving Russian POW cowered against the protective earthen wall. Raust didn't hesitate. Racing to the immobilized weapon, he threw open the breech and signaled the terrified loader to bring him a shell.

A formation of three bombers loomed into view, barely clearing the treetops. Sighting through the open barrel, Raust waited until he could see the lead airplane. Stepping over the lifeless gun captain, the sweating POW heaved a fifty-pound projectile into the gaping breech. Raust slammed it shut and pulled the firing lanyard in one motion.

The onrushing Liberator, bearing the whimsical name *Lonesome Lil,* disintegrated in a burst of flame.

"Links, links—und feuer! Feuer!"

Obergefreiter Steinmann froze, unable to follow his frantic aimer's instructions. They had practiced this drill a hundred times. Always before, he had spun the wheels and hit the firing pedal exactly as directed. They had chewed up an endless number of cloth sleeves towed by Ju 52s and old Heinkels, but Steinmann had never fired the deadly four-barreled weapon at a target taking evasive action.

The attacker had materialized as if by magic. Although forewarned that the bombers were low, he searched several degrees above the indistinct horizon. The hurtling shape blended into a line of trees not a hundred yards distant. It looked harmless, just as the practice targets had always looked.

Steinmann gulped and bit his lower lip as the aimer screamed, "He's gone. We could have had him! Why didn't you shoot?"

"I'll get the next one," Steinmann said, gritting his teeth.

The next one was upon them before he could complete his excuses. Now he could hear it—the menacing thunder of its huge engines a deafening bellow. He heard, *"Recht—und auf. Feuer!"*

Steinmann pressed the firing pedal and watched the magnesium-loaded tracers arcing harmlessly several meters below and behind the green and dun shape, now directly in front of them. Ears still ringing from the multiple detonations of his own guns, he could only stare in surprise at the sudden disintegration of the wooden platform supporting the emplacement. Splinters flew in every direction. The gun mount trembled as invisible projectiles struck sparks from its parts.

Turning to express astonishment to his aimer, he confronted a flopping, headless rag doll floundering in a widening pool of blood. It registered then. That innocent-looking apparition had shot at him!

Astonishment turned to savage anger. The bastards had killed his friend—had almost killed *him*. To hell with an aimer; he would shoot the next one freehand—just like pointing a garden hose.

He didn't have long to wait. This time there were three of the huge planes, nearly wingtip to wingtip. He selected the nearest one, mashed the firing pedal, and moved the tracer stream toward the onrushing target, leading it ever so slightly. A hit!

As the tracers brushed the nose and an outboard engine, he saw a burp of black smoke followed by a tongue of orange flame. The damaged plane, which bore a painting of a scantily clad woman on the nose, swept overhead. He realized that his guns had stopped firing. The breeches were empty. Steinmann wheeled to order the loaders to replenish his ammo cans. The position his loading crew normally occupied alongside their neatly stacked crates was empty. The unwilling POWs had fled during the early seconds of the attack.

Steinmann swore in frustrated anger. He neither saw nor heard the storm of .50-caliber slugs dispatched by the departing Liberator's tail turret.

Obergefreiter Werner Steinmann died instantly.

Aboard the *Happy Hooker,* an exploding 20mm round spewed destructive fragments in all directions. The rounded Plexiglas nose evaporated. Shrieking wind swirled loose gear like confetti. A single fragment penetrated the fragile covering of 2d Lt. Stan Cryhowski's cranial cavity. Another fragment, passing through the nose compartment without exploding, buried itself deep into number four engine.

"Anybody hurt down there?" Ross called out. He wrestled with a violent yaw set up by the dead engine. No responding transmission was forthcoming.

"Number four feathered, rotation stopped," BT called. "I had to pull the fire extinguisher. Fire's out."

"Ham, check the nose." Ross's voice was showing the effects of their ordeal. As Phillips scrambled from the upper turret, Kevin appeared at Ross's side on the flight deck. Bright red blood saturated his flying suit. His eyes, their whites contrasting with his blood-smeared features, were wide with terror.

"Stan," he babbled, "Stan's dead."

"Oh, my God," Ross moaned. He retained self-control with difficulty. "How bad are you hit, Kevin? What about you, Leckie?" he added as the radio operator appeared.

"We're not hurt—not bad, anyway, I think," Hanson whimpered. "This is Stan's blood; we've got Stan's blood all over us. I gotta change clothes."

"Kevin, listen, are the guns still working?"

"I dunno, Ross. I don't care if the fucking guns are working or not. Stan's dead, damnit! Can't you understand? He doesn't have a *head.* He's just layin' there—looks okay, but his fucking head, it's *gone!*"

Jaws clenched, Ross issued orders. "BT, set max continuous rated power on all three engines. We simply have to hold formation." He turned to the hysterical navigator. "Now, Kevin, snap out of it. Keep those guns going. Get below and get with it—you too, Leckie!"

"No!" Kevin's voice was shrill with panic. "I won't do it, Ross. I won't go back down there. Look, take up a heading of one-three-five. That'll take us to Turkey. I'd already plotted the course before I lost all my charts. We can land there. We'll be safe. Then I can take a bath." The young navigator was sobbing openly.

A garbled sound caused Ross to throw a startled look to his right. General Sprague, his .45 pistol drawn, white-faced with rage, was screaming.

"Navigator, damn you. Get your ass down there and get on those guns. Do you hear? You too, Corporal. Otherwise I'll shoot you cowardly bastards where you stand!"

The harassed aircraft commander could feel their situation slipping completely out of control. In subdued but precise, icy tones, Ross ordered, "General, put that fucking gun away. You aren't going to shoot anybody. *I* am in command of this airplane and responsible for the lives of everyone in it. Now, holster that thing or I'll place you under arrest.

"BT, watch those cylinder-head temperatures. Let me know if they go above two hundred and thirty-two degrees. Ham, help Lieutenant Hanson and Leckie get the nose compartment in working order. We're going to be mixing it up with that bunch of 109s up there in just a few more minutes. Guenther, goddamnit, where's that spare ammo?"

Ross turned back to the front, watching Sprague's reaction from the corner of his eye. It'd be just like that crazy bastard to shoot me, he thought flittingly.

Sprague stood, stunned, his jaw muscles bunched in white knots. He returned the automatic to its shoulder holster—an angry thrust that reflected his outrage—but not before the yawning muzzle bore swung in Ross's direction. Ross felt the back of his neck prickle.

Crossing to the pilot's console, Sprague raised his voice above the unnerving shriek of wind through the shattered nose. "I'm relieving you of command, Captain. Get out of that seat."

"Sir, under the Articles of War, an officer in command of a vessel or, in this case, an airplane, serves by direction of the president. You have authority to direct the air battle, but not to interfere in the operation of this airplane."

Ross drew a deep breath and held it. He believed he was right; he'd damn well better be.

Sprague stood wordless for long moments. "You may continue as pilot, Colyer," he said curtly, "but the moment we get on the ground, consider yourself charged with failure to obey a lawful order."

"Yes, Sir." Ross felt sick. What the hell had he done? Disgust at Sprague's decision not to alert White One of his error, the unexpected ferocity of the German defense, Stan's violent death—things had just suddenly boiled over. They were locked in a struggle to survive.

Okay, first things first, Colyer, Ross thought. How in the hell do you intend to get this crippled bird home? Then it hit him. Christ, he was responsible for getting the other aircraft home as well!

He thumbed the intercom. "General Sprague, I suggest we enter an orbit and try to reassemble the formation. We're facing what looks like half the goddamned *Luftwaffe* up ahead. If we try to get through as singles, we'll get picked off like flushed quail."

Sprague, however furious, was still a professional. The situation called for decisive command. To circle and attempt to regroup would expose them to the maurading fighters for additional, crucial minutes. But Colyer was quite correct in his assessment. Most of the bombers in sight were damaged in varying degrees. With their limited firepower condensed, they at least stood a chance.

"Commence our rally orbit, pilot. I'll announce our intentions by radio. Engineer, start firing yellow-green flares."

Order, of a sort, restored, Ross climbed to three hundred feet and entered a gentle, circling pattern. It became apparent that those with all four engines turning had no intention of doing anything other than creating distance between them and Ploesti.

Ross slowed to 150 mph to permit the battered survivors to stagger into position. Dirkson reported that four had joined and two others were laboring to catch up. Looking ahead, Ross estimated that they had five, possibly ten minutes before they would be in the midst of the massed fighter force.

BT took advantage of the respite to lean across and, off intercom, ask in mocking tones, "Sort of stepped on your dork that time, didn't you, Colyer?"

Ross, preoccupied with the ordeal they faced, responded with a terse, "I'll live with it. Instead of gloating, why don't you give us a reading on our chances of reaching Benghazi on three engines with what fuel we have remaining."

"I don't even have to get out my pencil," BT replied. "Chances are zero to none. We pulled takeoff power for damn near an hour. Do you think that pansy navigator can find Turkey? Or maybe Cyprus?"

"Stay off Hanson's back, BT," Ross snapped. "He had twenty-four rough ones before today. He'll get us home if it's possible. Now get me some specific calculations. I'm not interested in your bullshit guesses."

BT's eyes held a sardonic glint. "Sure. By the way, old buddy, just how did *you* enjoy looking down a fucking gun barrel?"

Ross was spared the need to respond as a circling group of fighters swooped earthward like sharks encountering blood in the water.

"Here they come," said Kevin. Ross was startled at Hanson's calm speaking voice. The guy had guts when the chips were down, he observed.

"Okay," Ross said, forcing his tone to be as devoid of emotion as Kevin's. "I'm taking her back down on the deck. Don't waste any shots. One last effort and we'll be shitting cotton. Next stop Benghazi."

The wretched grouping of battle-weary planes worked its way west toward safety. The broad, muddy reaches of the Danube slid into view. They were a big step closer to home.

Kurt paced impatiently at the edge of the hardstand, chain-smoking cigarettes in short, nervous puffs. The Romanian ground crew seemed to be taking forever to refuel and rearm his parked Me 109. He had lead his *schwarm* into the base at Otopenii after they had expended their fuel and ammo. Although it was sixty miles closer to the battle scene than Mizil, he began to regret his decision. The Romanians still hadn't absorbed the urgency of the situation.

At last, the mechanics, standing idly by with two-handled starting cranks in hand, moved to start engines for the impatient German pilots. With puffs of blue exhaust smoke and stuttering surges of power, the little armada waddled to the grass takeoff strip, Kurt in the lead.

"Proceed to the area of Craiova," the controller directed. "Intercept the second bomber stream approaching from Sector 24."

Kurt leveled his loosely knit formation at three thousand feet, eyes sweeping the areas between rapidly developing rain showers to the north. The low-flying bastards would be difficult to spot in this weather, he thought. He recognized the urban sprawl of Craiova and wheeled into orbit, searching for the elusive green and tan shapes aimed at the still-blazing, exploding oil fields.

"*Amerikanisch* bombers, four o'clock, very low," his earphones crackled.

Kurt swiveled his head. There they were. But wait—a disorganized gaggle of twin-tailed shapes was heading southwest—*away* from the target. It registered then: He had stumbled onto the first stream of American bombers leaving their target zone.

What to do?

"Ignore the ones who have already bombed; stop the approaching ones." His controller's directions were logical, but no approaching planes were visible. Those beneath him were escaping to their lair. They would return. Long-range strategy prevailed—kill the wolf at any opportunity. Protect tomorrow's lamb crop, logic told him.

Who are you kidding?

Emotion prevailed. Kill the murdering bastards any way, any time you can! Did they give Gretta an even chance?

Kurt pumped his clenched fist above his head: Attack! Now!

Target selection became confusing. The bombers had no semblance of a formation, just ones and twos flying in random patterns. A group of three circled—firing yellow-green flares. That had to be the mission leader! He was attempting to re-form the force for an organized withdrawal. That nucleus would be Kurt's target. He checked to see that his wingman, *Kadett-Feldwebel* Kruze, was tucked in, then he dove to the attack.

Closing on the scattered invaders, Kurt could see the damage that flak and his own fighters had inflicted. Scarcely a single Liberator was intact; he could see none with all four engines functioning. Headed for what he assumed to be the lead ship, he passed up an easy target— a limping, smoking hulk, trailing wires from its tail assembly. Good God, those had to be guy wires from a refinery smokestack! He pressed on, turning to make a tail-to-nose pass on the only four-ship formation visible. From the corner of his eye, he saw the Danube flash beneath them. The battle would take place over Yugoslavian soil. No matter. The rearmost bomber was in his sights. He rolled and aimed, drawing closer and closer. Kurt could see the tail gunner now as tracers flitted past his canopy. Closer, closer—now! His aim had been less than perfect. Large chunks of the Liberator's tail section had broken off, but the lumbering bomber still held its position. Angrily, Kurt hauled back on the stick and whirled to make another pass.

In the act of passing the pathetic, fleeing huddle, Kurt glanced at the nose of the lead ship. It couldn't be! But it was. There was no mistaking that audacious, provocative figure, clad only in bra and panties. He didn't have to see the name, *Happy Hooker,* to know that it was his old adversary from the north. With one prop feathered into the screaming slipstream, a gaping hole in the nose, and missing parts from the tail, the gallant lady of the evening was attempting to lead her flock to safety.

Not today, Kurt told himself with a grim smile. Today, my dear girl, I shall prove to you who is the braver, better airman. He raced ahead to turn and execute his favored head-on attack. A glance to his rear and right. Damn. He'd lost his wingman. Standard operating procedure demanded that he break off and reunite with the junior pilot. Not yet, he thought. The opportunity to destroy his personal enemy might never recur. He made another turn, barely clearing the rising, mountainous terrain west of the Danube, rolled out on a reverse course. There!

Dead ahead sat four fat, cross-shaped targets.

"About a dozen fighters, closing from seven o'clock." Dirkson's voice cracked slightly. "They're after our number three wingman."

Ross tensed, waiting for the fusillade of covering fire from the *Happy Hooker.* Only a few sporadic rounds broke the strained silence.

In the waist compartment, Guenther and Dirkson crouched over their flexible .50s. The 150-mph slipstream screamed past open windows framing gun barrels still too hot to touch. Milt shifted his stare from the hostile outside environment to inventory their remaining ammo. It wasn't reassuring. He saw Dutch turn. The gaze from behind the goggles that his buddy wore as protection against the howling blast of air seemed to plead for a release from this insane situation. Milt stepped backward and shouted into his ear, "You got a cigarette, Dutch?"

Guenther's glare conveyed eloquent expression of his opinion of Milt's attempt at levity. Dirkson forced a wide grin and returned to his search for the enemy. Funny, he thought, how much better having someone else with you makes you feel. Mickey, on the other hand, seemed to prefer the isolation of his tail turret, some fifteen feet to the rear. Milt could see him as only a dim, partial silhouette through the tunnel formed by the round yellow oxygen tanks lining the fuselage walls and the ammo track feeding Reed's tail guns.

As if prompted by Milt's stare, Mickey's voice filled his headset. "Here they come. Two of 'em. Seven o'clock level."

Milt swiveled his gun to its extreme rearward limit and strained his eyes. He was permitted only a fleeting glimpse. Two shadows flitted across the dappled landscape a scant fifty feet beneath them and were gone before he could obtain a sight picture. A dozen *pfitt—pfitt—pfitt*s behind him marked their passage. That and a half-heard "Goddamn— I'm hit, guys."

It had to be Mickey. Milt turned to see Guenther scrambling toward the rear. "Get the hell back here, Dutch," he screamed. "Don't leave your gun." If the pudgy gunner heard him, he ignored the order.

"Where'd he get you, Mickey?" Guenther yelled as he crouched behind the writhing tail gunner.

Reed turned powder-blackened features, contorted with pain, toward him. "The fucking ankle. I can't move it. Can't use the pedal to rotate the turret."

"Okay." Guenther, confused, hesitated. The tail turret was crucial. He considered calling Captain Colyer for instructions. He didn't have his headset plugged in. He made up his mind, although he had the feeling he'd probably get his ass chewed for it.

"I'm gonna drag you forward into the waist, Mickey. Maybe I can do something for you, then I'll take over back here. I know enough about the turret to at least shoot back. Now, undo your safety belt and turn—just a little more. . . ."

Reed bit back screams of pain as Dutch dragged him across the uneven, vibrating floor into the waist. He watched Guenther bend and examine the blood-soaked flying boot. "How bad is it?"

Guenther swallowed bitter-tasting vomit. The foot and ankle were a mangled crimson mess. Reed was losing blood at an alarming rate. "Uh—it don't look too good, Mickey. I'm gonna try to stop the bleeding."

His words were cut off by the big tail gunner's scream as he sat up and regarded the brutalized foot, turned at a forty-five-degree angle to its mate.

"My ankle! The miserable cocksuckers. They ruined my ankle. I'll *never* play pro ball with that thing. It'll heal stiff, sure as hell. The bastards. I'll get even if it's the last thing I do." Tears streaming from his eyes, he grated, "Drag me over to your gun, Dutch. I can kneel and see out. Just show me that fucker one more time. I'll make him wish his Kraut bitch of a mother had drowned him when he was born."

"Aw, Mickey, come on now. Lay back and take it easy. We're almost out of this shit. We'll have a doctor for you before you know it. Please Mick. Don't try to move; you're gonna bleed to death if you try that. I don't want that, you big bastard." The anguished waist gunner blinked rapidly to halt his own scalding tears.

Pain and loss of blood thwarted Reed's determined efforts. Deep in shock, he slumped to a prone position, unconscious and blessedly removed from the raging hell about him. Dirkson, loosing a clattering burst at an out-of-range target, turned to yell, "You can't take care of him now, Dutch. We got our hands full. Give him a shot of morphine and get back to those tail guns."

"Fuck you, Dirkson," Guenther mouthed silently. In a flash of inspiration he fashioned a crude tourniquet with the strap from a near-by Mae West life jacket. Ripping open the first-aid kit on Mickey's parachute harness, he fumbled out one of the three morphine Syrettes inside. Goddamnit, he cursed under his breath. He'd practiced injecting a grapefruit in first-aid training; why couldn't he remember how it was done?

Finally, he managed to crush the thin glass tube protecting the needle and jammed the needle through the flight suit covering Reed's thigh.

Only then did the dazed but resolute Guenther make his way to the empty tail turret on hands and knees. His flight suit became coated with the rapidly congealing blood marking Reed's path to the waist section. Drying rapidly, the stains were soon indistinguishable from one created by a mashed and melting Hershey bar in Dutch's breast pocket.

Then came a smothered oath from Ham Phillips.

"I'll be damned, Cap'n. Do you know what I just saw? Remember that Jerry fighter who got Lieutenant Tyson and we saw a couple of other times over Germany? The one with the black and silver spinner— and that damn bird painted on his nose? Well, he just went past us like a big streak of shit."

Ross jerked to attention. "The hell you say? You're sure?"

"The same one, Cap'n. It's that bastard who likes to come at us head-on. Sure enough. There he is up ahead, turning."

"Kevin?"

"Yeah, Ross?"

"It's our old friend from Germany, the one with the black and silver spinner. He's up ahead and looks like he's making a pass. You okay?"

"If you mean have I gotten used to standing here, ankle deep in blood and empty shell casings, with Stan's body rolling all over and a big goddamn hole in the nose—yeah, I'm okay. I've only puked twice."

Ross winced at the bitter overtones in the navigator's voice. "Here's what we're gonna do, Kevin. This guy likes to come at us from head-on. When he does, I'm going to raise the nose and fly right at him. Empty that goddamn 20mm at him. Can you do it?"

"I'm not yellow, Skipper. I probably want to get out of this fucking mess worse than anyone on this plane. I'll stick this son of a bitch right up his nostrils."

Kurt concentrated on setting up his attack. Stay down—don't get within that deadly upper turret's field of fire. The cunning devil was himself below fifty feet. Very well, I'll get lower.

Treetops brushed the 109's underside.

He was closing at breakneck speed—no chance to break down and underneath. He'd fire at extreme range with his cannon, well outside the reach of the Liberator's nose-mounted .50-caliber machine guns, then break straight up. The Plexiglas nose, its upper portion a jagged, irregular wound, filled his reflective gunsight. Kurt's finger tightened on the red firing trip built into the control stick.

His eyes rounded with shocked surprise and his hand froze on the controls before he could carry out the slight movement required to send a hail of explosive 20mm projectiles into the hapless bomber. A stream of fire had erupted from his oncoming prey.

Time stood suspended. Kurt could almost count the individual golf ball–sized tracers as they crept in slow motion toward the 109's whirling propeller.

The unpardonable mistakes he had committed marched past his mind's eye in an orderly parade: He had ignored his controller's order to seek out the approaching bomber stream. He had allowed a personal vendetta to divert him from the attack procedures he had himself preached on so many occasions. He had lost his wingman and committed himself to an unprotected attack. He had waited too long to fire.

Even as the first rounds from the *Happy Hooker*'s improvised, forward-firing 20mm cannon impacted, Kurt's conditioned reflexes hauled the stick into his gut and the mottled gray-green fighter lurched straight up.

Still, with seemingly unlimited time at his disposal, he felt overcome by weary resignation. Old falcons, like old tigers, become lazy and complacent with age.

Where in hell had that bomber acquired a weapon equal to his own? he wondered.

Chapter Twenty-eight

1217 Hours, 1 August 1943
Aboard the *Happy Hooker*
Over Southern Romania

Ross listened to Ham's and Leckie's elated shouts without comment. "Great shooting, Lieutenant Hanson!" "You got the bastard! Look at that, he's breaking up—he's on fire, by God." Ross saw the sleek 109 in a brief, flat spin trailing flame and smoke. With barely fifty feet of altitude the pilot would have no chance, even if he hadn't been killed by that prolonged burst of cannon fire.

The German fighter passed from view without him actually seeing it crash, however.

Feeling strangely unmoved, Ross automatically issued a warning, "Okay crew. He was only one. Don't let another one slip in on us— keep those guns moving."

With so damn much going on, he couldn't truly savor a victory over their most dangerous enemy. The attack had seemingly been broken off. The *Happy Hooker*'s guns were silent. Fighting sagging weariness, Ross asked, "What's the situation in the rear? Any substantial damage?"

There was a pause, then Dirkson's subdued voice. "Mickey's been hit. His foot and ankle. He's lost a lot of blood. We have him stretched out on the floor of the waist compartment. Dutch's in the tail turret. I dunno. Mick's unconscious and don't look so good."

Ross gnawed his lower lip. Decision time. He indicated to General Sprague that he wished to speak to him off intercom. Facing the senior

338

officer's piercing gaze, Ross said: "Sir, we haven't enough fuel to reach North Africa on three engines. If we could fly directly over the Balkan Mountains, we could possibly reach Syria. It would mean overflying neutral Turkey, though. I'm not sure we can climb high enough to fly direct. If we keep to low ground and follow the Danube Plain to the Black Sea, we can make it no farther than Turkey. The alternative is to try to return across Yugoslavia and ditch as close to that navy task force we saw as we can—if we can find them."

Sprague's expression remained cold and impassive. "What is *your* recommendation, Captain?"

Ross swallowed. "First, Sir, I suggest we advise the formation— what's left of it—of our fuel situation. Give them an option of re- forming and selecting their own destination or staying with us."

"And do what?"

Ross's features were drawn with strain. "Try to make it across the Balkans, Sir. Stay in the valleys if necessary and attempt to reach Syria. If we fail, we land in Turkey and submit to internment."

"I'm the task-force commander, Captain. Are you suggesting that I abandon my command responsibility?"

"There's no way we can lead a formation through those mountain passes, General. You'll end up losing most of the aircraft. To stay over low ground is to concede ahead of time that we're leading them to Turkey and internment—something they may be able to avoid on their own. They should be given an opportunity to make their own decision. Some may have enough fuel to get home. There's another consideration. If we reverse course now to follow the Danube, we're going to have Bulgarian fighters on our ass for the next two hundred miles.

"We're not in shape to withstand a sustained attack, even from the slower Bulgarian planes. We're low on ammo. Our tail gunner is wounded—it sounds bad. God knows how much concealed mechanical damage we have. If we lose another engine we won't even reach Turkey.

"To be blunt, Sir, your task force is without a flagship. My respon- sibility now is to do everything possible to save the lives of my crew. In about two minutes I'm turning south. What you order your formation to do is up to you."

Sprague's face turned white. Speaking between clenched teeth, he grated, "Colyer, you insolent, insubordinate son of a bitch, I'm going along with you. Do you know why? I want to keep both of us alive long enough to attend your court-martial. I'll advise the formation of our situation."

Ross released pent-up breath. "Sir, I strongly advise against announcing our intentions in the clear. Crippled planes draw fighters like flies. Just now, they appear to be back there engaged with our Red and Blue formations. Let's let them stay there. Have Corporal Leckie relay your message by signal lamp. He can use the tail turret."

BT leaned over to shout above the sound of wind screaming through the stricken ship. "Don't be stupid, Colyer. Those mountains are going to be a nest of afternoon thunderstorms. You're going to pile us up sure as hell, blundering around down there. Stay on the deck and follow the low terrain. Turkey is our only hope."

Ross's jaw set. "We're not voting on this, BT. We have better than a fifty-fifty chance of making it back to Allied territory. What you're talking about is surrender while we still have the capability to fight."

"It isn't surrendering to the enemy, goddamnit," BT retorted angrily. "There's nothing dishonorable about internment. You're going to wipe out a plane and the entire crew with your pigheadedness. General," he turned to Sprague, "don't you agree?"

Sprague had listened to the exchange between Ross and BT without changing expression. "It's Colyer's decision," he replied. "He hasn't asked for my advice and I doubt that he will. Besides, I happen to share his opinion about giving up before you're whipped."

Sprague thumbed his intercom switch. "Down there in the nose. This is General Sprague. Send the radio operator to the flight deck. We have a message to get off."

Ross allowed himself a brief, private smile. It was quickly erased as he grappled with the task ahead.

"Kevin, take one of those oiled-silk maps from your escape kit and give me an initial heading for Syria. Work up a flight plan as best you can and get a reading on our fuel situation from the engineer. Ham, go to the performance charts and give me our service ceiling with three engines, taking our battle damage into consideration. BT, go to the waist and make a damage assessment. Do whatever you can for Reed."

Ross prepared for the ordeal ahead with a crisp decisiveness that was far from representing his true emotions. BT's admonition had come too close to his own reservations for comfort.

With Leckie in the tail relaying Sprague's revised withdrawal order, Ross eased the *Happy Hooker* onto an east by south course, her guns silent, number four engine feathered, gaping wounds in the nose and tail compartments. Six-plus hours of tension-laden flight exacted its toll. Adrenaline-charged bodies sagged as imminent danger receded. Kevin relayed his new flight plan details in a weary, resigned monotone.

Only three of the *Happy Hooker*'s seven alive and conscious occupants refused to succumb to the aftermath of their nightmare. Ross struggled to keep the stricken craft flying. Ham Phillips perused performance charts and searched for unreported system malfunctions. Sprague prowled the flight deck, his face a frozen mask of rage.

BT returned to the cockpit and slid into the right seat, pale and tight-lipped. "We have two control cables parted and a chunk of rudder shot away on the left side," he announced. "The tail turret is operational but won't rotate to the stops to the left. If we get into turbulence, don't get too heavy on the controls—the backup cables are all you have. I doubt that Reed will make it. Guenther rigged a tourniquet and gave him a shot of morphine. He's out of it right now, but judging from the amount of blood back there, he has to be in a bad way. I put him on 100 percent oxygen. He probably won't recover from shock when the dope wears off." BT shrugged and regarded blood smears on his tailored flight suit with a fastidious scowl.

Ham Phillips appeared between them. "We got a main system hydraulic leak in the bomb bay, Cap'n. Just don't turn on the auxiliary pump until we're ready to put the gear down. There should be enough in the system for that and brakes. There's flak holes everywhere you look, but other than that the old girl seems to be in good shape. I figure that if we pull no more than 1,900 RPM and thirty-three inches of manifold pressure, we have three hours and ten minutes of fuel remaining. That'll keep the cylinder-head temperatures at the red line, but that's our max endurance. And stay as low as you can—the charts say our three-engine cruise ceiling is eleven thousand. Subtract the drag that nose and tail damage gives us and call it nine."

Ross sorted through the depressing facts. God, he was tired. "Kevin, will you come up to the flight deck for a minute?" Ross forced calm authority into his voice.

When Hanson made his appearance, Ross surveyed the blood-spattered figure closely. Weary, drained, and despondent, the navigator's eyes were steady and his look determined. He'll be okay, Ross told himself—just keep him busy.

"Well, where do we go from here, Prince Henry?"

Hanson ignored the feeble sally and opened the silk map from his escape kit across the control pedestal.

"We're here," he said, pointing to a penciled cross. "Up here," he paused as his finger traced a penciled path, "we turn south to a heading of one-four-five. We'll be in the foothills then and the terrain rises gradually to about four thousand. The main range we have to cross is about a hundred miles south and the lowest pass I can find is marked seven thousand feet; we'll have peaks between nine and ten on either side. After that, it'll be clear going."

"Looks good, Kevin. Now, the big question: What's our estimated time en route for Syria?"

Hanson's brows furrowed: Worry lines formed crow's-feet around his eyes. "Well, I don't have a winds aloft to go on, but assuming a prevailing southerly wind component I'd say three hours at our present airspeed."

Ross threw BT, who had been following the conversation, a tight smile. "How about that, Sport? Exactly enough juice in the tanks to get there and taxi to the parking ramp."

"Oh, shit," BT snapped, snorting in disgust. "You're out of your goddamn mind. We can't make Syria and you know it. Use your fucking head. We can follow the low ground and make Turkey with no sweat. But go ahead. I plan to sit here and let you bust our butts without lifting a finger."

"Wrong." Ross's voice was cold, without expression. "You'll do your part. I want you to go down there with Kevin and help with the pilotage. We'll need two sets of eyes to negotiate some of those tight spots."

BT's glare was poisonous. He opened his mouth, but no sound came out. The furious copilot wordlessly unsnapped his seat belt and followed Hanson forward.

Ross altered course and surveyed the distant jumble of forested landscape jutting skyward. His arms and legs felt as if they were made of lead. With a hundred questions churning through his mind, he had difficulty keeping the plane on course and trimmed to keep drag to a minimum. The temptation to close his eyes, just for one brief moment, required superhuman effort to resist.

Ham Phillips appeared at his side. "Sir, those broken control cables. You know, there's a repair kit back there. It's in a little bag attached to the fuselage. It has two cables with clamps and a stretcher handle. All I gotta do is clamp the broken ends together and tighten 'em with the ratchet handle. You like for me to go back and see if I can rig a fix?"

Ross emerged from his fatigue-induced lethargy. "Good thinking, Ham. I should have remembered that. By all means, give it a try. But I need you up here. Can Dutch and Milt do it?"

"I—I suppose so," Phillips replied hesitantly.

"Okay. Go show them what to do, then come back up here. Just be damn sure they don't get mixed up and attach the elevator cable to the rudder cable."

The flight engineer flashed a weak grin and disappeared into the bomb bay, treading the catwalk with careful steps.

"Tail to pilot." The silent intercom came to life. "Sir, we have one plane still with us. He has one engine feathered and he's trailing smoke from another. Can't see any markings but he's hanging about a hundred yards behind. The others broke off and looked to me to be headed west. Guess they're going for home."

Ross frowned. If they had a wingman, however far out of position, he still had a responsibility to lead it to safety. The situation couldn't be helped, but it cut down the options he would have if the situation worsened.

"Okay, let me know if he starts dropping back. After we get a bit farther south, I'll try to raise him on the short-range command radio. Hey, Leckie?"

"Yes, Sir."

"I'm going to assume that we're out of immediate danger from fighters. Come back to your station and see if there's a high-frequency ground station in Syria. Should be one at their airfield at Aleppo. In about a half hour try to raise them. Maybe we can get them to give us a QDM. Radio direction steers would sure as hell help later on."

"Yes, Sir!"

Ross smiled to himself. The radio operator would be only too glad to get out of that charnel house that was the nose compartment. It must be hellish down there, especially with Cryhowski's body never out of sight. Ross looked around in surprise as General Sprague slid into the right seat.

"You look like you could stand to take a break, Captain," he said.

Ross hesitated. It was essential that they maintain the most efficient attitude and power settings possible to conserve fuel. Sprague sensed his reluctance. A dry "Don't worry, Colyer; I *am,* after all, a command pilot, and current in the B-24" brought a sheepish grin to Ross's face. "In fact, it's even possible I could show *you* a few tricks about flying crippled airplanes."

Ross relinquished the controls. He lit a cigarette and leaned back.

"We're to follow this river valley south," he said, looking at Sprague. "The chart shows a gradual climb to about four thousand. We ended up with a wingman, by the way. Tail says he's about a hundred yards back. Corporal Guenther will keep an eye on him. We may have to reduce speed to let him stay with us. Dutch says he has one mill shut down and another one smoking."

"I've been following the intercom talk. You probably don't know how glad I am to have this stint at the controls. I hope to hell that someday *you* have to stand by and let someone else do the actual flying on a mission."

Wary of becoming involved in a conversation with the acerbic senior officer, Ross leaned his head back and closed eyes that were burning and gritty from strain. He couldn't resist, however, an occasional surreptitious observation of the general's flying technique. He paid grudging respect to the deft touch that Sprague demonstrated. The general coddled the lumbering bomber seemingly without effort.

They began encountering increasing turbulence as the wind swirled fitfully down the slopes of the approaching mountain range. The gyrocompass appeared nailed to its course line, though, and the altimeter reading varied only fractionally.

Ross acknowledged Dirkson's proud "We got the cables repaired, Sir" with warm praise. A guilty feeling that he should be providing encouragement to the battered crew was overridden by exhaustion. He dozed.

Ross awoke with a start. A hand he realized was Sprague's was shaking his shoulder. The general's voice penetrated his sleep-fogged brain.

"Time to get with it, Captain. Looks like problems ahead."

Rubbing filmed eyes, Ross became aware that the lowering sun was now partially obscured by high clouds. He glanced at his watch and noted he'd been out for a good thirty minutes. The altimeter revealed that Sprague had nursed the plane to four thousand feet. They were still skimming a bare five hundred feet above broken terrain bordering a twisting stream. To their left, a range of hills rose a good thousand feet higher than their cruising altitude.

What jarred Ross wide awake was the view dead ahead. The sawtooth outline of peaks was no longer visible. The irregular skyline had been replaced with the solid gray of rain clouds.

Ross pressed the intercom button. "What happened to our weather?"

"Things went to hell in a hurry, Captain," said Hanson. He sounded worried. "We're gonna have to climb. Can't skirt those peaks in that stuff."

"How high?" Ross snapped, now alert and fully awake.

"I won't be comfortable under twelve thousand indicated. We don't have a current altimeter setting; we're bound to be entering a low-pressure area—give a possible altimeter error of a thousand feet. The map shows about fifty miles of peaks running between nine and ten thousand—if the thing is dependable. There'll be some hellacious vertical currents, you know."

Mind racing, Ross queried, "Ham, can we make twelve?"

Phillips, already peering at performance charts, face puckered with concern, responded slowly. "We'll have to carry close to max continuous power, Cap'n. The engines can take it, but it's gonna shoot our endurance square in the ass."

"What if we were a thousand pounds lighter?"

"That'd sure help, Sir. Two thousand would be better, though."

Ross's reaction was immediate. "Pilot to crew. Start jettisoning anything not essential to flight safety. Guns, ammo, even the tail turret, if you can get to the mounting bolts. I mean *everything*. Coffee jugs, life rafts, the works.

"Sir," Ross turned to Sprague in the right seat, "I'm giving you 2,200 RPM and thirty-five inches. See if you can coax a five-hundred-feet-per-minute climb out of that setting. We have about twenty minutes to get to twelve thousand."

Sprague gave him a nod of understanding and reached for the elevator trim wheel.

Ross reached for the mixture control levers, then hesitated. "Watch the cylinder-head temperatures, if you will. If necessary, I'll go to auto-rich mixture, but let's hold off as long as possible."

Again a nod of agreement. Then Sprague asked calmly, "What about our wingman?"

"I'm breaking radio silence, Sir. We're not going to see any fighters in that stuff ahead. First though, what is Reed's condition, waist?"

A pause, then Dirkson spoke up. "He's still out cold, Captain. He's

still breathing and the bleeding has pretty well stopped. But, Sir, if
we don't get that tourniquet off pretty soon—well, he's gonna lose
that leg, Sir."

"I know, Milt. Do the best you can." He switched his radio selector
to VHF. "Tidal Wave aircraft following White Two Lead south. If you
read me, come in."

He was about to repeat the call when he heard, "White Two Lead,
I think this is the airplane you're calling. Rock your wings, please."

Sprague obliged and a relieved voice responded, "Yeah, we have
you in sight. This is Anvil Seven, out of White One. You're looking
awfully good up there."

"Roger, Anvil Seven. What's your condition?"

"Uh, not real good. We can just barely keep up with you. We got
one shut down and can get only about thirty inches out of number three.
Where we headed?"

"Aleppo," Ross responded. "How're you fixed for fuel?"

"If we can get our Tokyo tank to feed, about two-plus hours.
Otherwise we're hurting. We're working on it, though."

"I see. Can you climb to twelve?"

"No way." The response came without hesitation.

"Well, here's the picture," Ross said, his voice firm. "We figure
twelve's the minimum safe altitude over these mountains. We're throwing
everything that's loose overboard. Is your navigator okay?"

"Roger. Chewing his nails, but okay."

"Well, we're starting our climb, Anvil Seven. I'll stand by this
frequency. Do the best you can, and good luck."

"Roger, White Two Lead." The pilot's voice belied his confident
words. "We'll make it. See you on the ground in Aleppo."

Ross switched back to intercom and glanced at Sprague. The general's
jaw was set as he returned Ross's gaze. "They won't make it," he stated
flatly.

Ross said nothing. What would he do if he were back there? he
wondered. It was too late to turn back and follow the Danube. Find
a level place and crash land? The Bulgarians were reported to be
unmerciful to POWs. No, he would do exactly what this guy was doing.
Press the plane to its limits, pick a dead-reckoning course between
the highest peaks, and hope for the best.

Ross watched the altimeter wind upward with agonizing slowness,
the rate-of-climb indicator pegged on five hundred feet per minute.

The turbulence grew more pronounced as they entered the wind spill effect of the mountain's downwind slope. He could hear and feel the thuds and vibrations as the crew labored to discard unwanted weight. Above the nerve-grating screech of wind through the shattered nose he heard a yell as they wrestled the two-hundred-pound 20mm cannon through the open Plexiglas. He dared not lower the gear to permit use of the nose escape hatch. A look behind him revealed Leckie, hunched over his console desperately tapping out call signs with his Morse key. Radio contact wasn't likely, given the weather ahead, but . . .

BT leaned between the two pilots' seats. He was breathing heavily. "We're rid of everything that was loose. Except one thing, Ross." BT wore a hard, challenging expression. "Your dead bombardier. He weighs almost two hundred pounds. . . ." He let his words trail off.

"Jesus Christ, BT! Are you suggesting that we jettison Stan? If so, forget it."

"Think about it, Colyer. This thing is gonna be touch and go. Eight— seven very shortly—of us and one of him. His weight could make the difference. If you're too squeamish, take a vote. We all have a stake in this, you know."

Ross kept balled fists in his lap with effort. "BT, you make me sick," he snapped. "If I hear another word about this, so help me God I will throw *you* out the goddamn bomb bay with my bare hands. Now get out of my sight."

BT, unperturbed by Ross's outburst, shrugged and returned to the nose compartment. Still shaking with rage, Ross glanced at Sprague, now flying by instruments as the first wisps of cloud whipped past the cockpit windows. The general's face bore a mocking smirk. The son of a bitch had overheard the exchange. He was actually *enjoying* Ross's discomfiture.

The embittered aircraft commander grabbed his control wheel and snarled, "Okay, I'll take it."

Sprague wordlessly relinquished the controls and stripped cellophane from a fresh cigar.

"Pilot to crew," Ross announced. "Okay, we're going to get shaken up very shortly. Everyone hang onto something. Do what you can in the waist to keep Reed secured. Kevin, give me a best heading to punch through this stuff."

Ross pressed the RPM increase switches. As the Pratt & Whitneys surged to 2,550 RPM, he crammed the mixture control levers to auto-rich and set forty inches of manifold pressure with the supercharger controls. Piss on asking BT to perform what were his normal duties. I'll bring this plane home by myself, by God, Ross muttered to himself.

Scattered drops of rain blurred the windshield. Then, without warning, the *Happy Hooker* entered a deluge. Ross could hear the pounding thunder of water striking exposed surfaces above the laboring engine roar. He anxiously surveyed the instrument panel. Almost eleven thousand feet. As he watched, however, the rate of climb plummeted to a thousand-feet-per-minute descent. The altimeter unwound with sickening speed, losing in seconds the precious altitude they had gained over a five-minute climb. Ross gritted his teeth. Don't chase the rate of climb, he recalled. Keep the nose level and airspeed constant. Every downdraft is followed by an updraft—if you don't encounter a mountain peak before that happens, he reminded himself.

Ross watched the instruments as the big plane bucked and lurched crazily. He heard and sensed Kevin and BT emerge from the nose compartment.

"Jesus Christ, the water is coming in that hole up front in buckets!" Kevin clutched their sole remaining pilotage chart in a death grip. "You got two big ones coming up on your left, Ross," he yelled. "Take about five degrees right."

Taking up a position between Ross and Sprague, Kevin spread the limp, waterlogged map on the throttle quadrant and stared helplessly at the opaque windshield.

The thought of the brutal punishment dealt the Liberator's airframe by flak and machine-gun fire flitted through Ross's mind. Hang together, old girl—just a little while longer, he thought. We're gaining back some of that lost altitude—good. All the pressures and temperatures in the green, that's good. Airspeed down to one-thirty-five—gotta watch that. A stall now and forget it.

The sound of pouring rain began abating somewhat. Was the sky ahead growing lighter? It was! They were almost through the worst of it. Then Ross heard a strangled croak from Hanson on his right. He glanced in that direction and saw the navigator's mouth formed in a round O, like a carp's. His finger was pointing to the left.

Ross sneaked a quick look. Through his rain-streaked side window, he could see the tops of several towering pine trees drift past, not quite obscured by the gray mist. A fleeting glimpse, then the gut-wrenching sight was replaced by inky nothingness. A sweeping look at the others, peering intently forward, told Ross that only he and Kevin had been privileged to experience that peek at near oblivion. With icy sweat trickling down his back, Ross gave the shaken navigator a level look and slowly shook his head. Another brush with death behind them. The time for recitation—cold drink in hand, feet propped up—would come later. Hanson gulped and forced a sickly grin.

Suddenly they broke into bright, blinding sunlight. The horizon ahead was still marred with cloud tops, but of the benign sort. Kevin's lightning-quick survey of the terrain was followed by, "We're on the south slope, guys. It's downhill from here on."

Another boost was provided by Leckie's triumphant, "Hey, I've raised Aleppo. They're standing by to give us a steer."

Intercom chatter resumed as spirits soared. Ross selected the VHF transmitter. "Anvil Seven, this is White Two Lead. What is your position?"

A disembodied voice, dripping with tension, responded. "We don't rightly know, White Two. We're in clouds at nine thousand. Our dead-reckoning position puts us about in the middle of the range. Number three is running hot and vibrating—I give it about another fifteen minutes. I've told the crew they can bail out if we lose it."

"Hang in there, Anvil Seven. We're in the clear. You shouldn't have more than another fifteen minutes to go. White Two Lead, standing by."

Ross didn't have the heart to tell him of their own near miss.

"Roger, roger, White Two Lead. Much thanks for your help." The voice regained a measure of its former cockiness. "Have ten double scotches lined up for us. We're gonna be there."

Ross grinned, then, sobering, spoke the words that he knew would silence the crew's ebullience. "Ham, read the fuel tanks. Kevin, give me an ETA for Aleppo."

The answer was a foregone conclusion. That hour at high boost had made fatal inroads on their dwindling fuel supply.

Ross turned to Sprague and quietly asked, "Would you prefer Istanbul or Ankara, Sir?"

Chapter Twenty-nine

1604 Hours, 1 August 1943
Aboard the *Happy Hooker*
Over Bulgaria

Ross thumbed the intercom switch. He tried to hide the weariness and disappointment he felt.

"Pilot to crew. Okay, troops, it looks like Turkey. We just don't have enough fuel to reach friendly territory. I'm sorry. We gave it our best shot. I'll say this, though, if I had it all to do over, I wouldn't want to do it with any other crew. You earned your pay today. Now," his tone sharpened, "our destination is Ankara and we'll be interned by the Turks when we land. That means spending the rest of the war there. It'll be better than being a POW, but we can look forward to a long stay away from home."

There was silence while the crew considered his words. "What's this internment mean, Captain?" asked Dirkson. "And why? We aren't at war with them. Why can't they just send us back to the States?"

"Being neutral means not helping either side," Ross replied. "If they release us, the Germans would see it as taking our side and might declare war. We have to be careful. I have no idea what kind of treatment we'll get. You hear stories of crews interned in Switzerland living the good life: staying in good hotels, eating in good restaurants, chasing girls—really living it up. I don't know if that's true, but one thing I do know: The Turks are different. They can be mean mothers. Don't look forward to a warm welcome. Keep your mouths shut until we get the lay of the land. Above all, stay away from their women. You can get your balls cut off by just looking cross-eyed at one.

"Listen up. I want anyone carrying a side arm to pitch it overboard—now. No guns. No knives, either, but don't discard your escape knives just yet. We still might have to bail out. Put them in a sack of some kind just before we land and I'll turn them over to the police."

Turning to Sprague, Ross said, "You, too, General."

Sprague withdrew a silver-plated service automatic from his shoulder holster. It was the same weapon that he had drawn against Hanson only hours earlier. He fondly regarded its engraved barrel and ivory grips.

"This was presented to me at the Point, Colyer. I was captain of the pistol team. I'm not throwing it away."

The two men regarded each other, eyes hard and unyielding.

"That's an order, General," Ross stated flatly.

"Piss on your order, Captain," Sprague responded in deceptively pleasant tones. He rolled the now-dead cigar to one corner of his mouth. "I call your bluff. I have no intention of going in there unarmed, meek, and defeated. We represent the strongest nation in the world today. We negotiate our situation. We are *not* surrendering to a superior force. And," a wicked grin creased his face, "don't forget—once we land *I* am the senior officer."

Ross accepted defeat. "Your decision, General. I just hope you don't get shot when you go waving that thing around."

Sprague's laconic "I'll just bet you do" was interrupted by an excited Hanson.

"Hey, looky there, P-40s."

Ross and the general, locked in bitter argument, had failed to notice that they had been joined by two mottled brown and green aircraft. They sat just off each of the *Happy Hooker*'s wings. The pilot on Ross's side had lowered his landing gear and was tapping his helmet.

"I'll be damned," Ross muttered. Hanson's aircraft identification was absolutely correct; there could be no mistaking that shark-nosed shape. The star and crescent insignia looked out of place on the American-built fighter, but it was a P-40, all right.

"Looks like the Turkish air force has joined us, gentlemen," Ross announced. He punched channel D, the international distress frequency, and listened.

"American bomber, you have entered Turkish airspace illegally. You will follow me and land immediately."

Ross nodded vigorously and responded, "Ankara. Land Ankara." He took the gargled response, which sounded like "Gah," as an affirmative reply.

Hanson scrambled into position and watched silently as the unlikely three-ship formation set up a descending eastward path. "We're about thirty minutes out, Ross," he said softly. "It's been a bitch of a day, hasn't it?"

"A real bitch, Kevin. And it ain't over yet."

Ham joined them. "Cap'n, what's going to happen to our airplane?" he asked.

"Well, I assume it will be impounded," Ross replied slowly. "I don't know what the procedure is, but I'd guess we've seen the last of her."

"Aw, no, Cap'n. Not the *Happy Hooker*. Hell, she's part of the crew. I'm not gonna see some goddamn foreigner messing around with her." Ham's voice rose in indignation.

"She's been good to us, all right." Ross's gaze took in the familiar cockpit: the battered ashtray and coffee cup holder Ham had fabricated for him; the deep scar across his control wheel, left by an errant piece of flak over Germany; the throttle and mixture levers, paint chipped away in places and shiny from use; the smell of fear, sweat, and gasoline that permeated the canvas seat fabric. With a pang of remorse he realized that in roughly thirty minutes they would be without what had become a second home.

Kevin broke the somber silence in the ship. Even the wind shrieking through her wounds seemed subdued. "Ross," he said, clearing his throat, "I gotta tell you this. Don't laugh at me. You remember that mountain back there?"

Ross nodded, a grim smile on his face.

"That heading I gave you. You were damn near ten degrees off—to the right."

Ross stared at the navigator. "So?"

"Well," Hanson said, avoiding his gaze, "I watched you turn exactly *on* that heading. Between then and the time we missed that peak, this goddamn airplane turned herself enough to miss it."

The astonished pilot opened his mouth to make a scoffing rejoinder. He closed it. The three stared at each other in awe—Ham just beginning to understand. Ross muttered a subdued, "I'll be goddamned."

Switching to channel C he called into the mike, "Anvil Seven, White Two Lead here. Do you read me?"

"You're weak but clear, White Two Lead. We're over the coastline and in the clear. We'll try Istanbul. Number three packed it in, so we're down to two engines. What's your position?"

"About a half hour out of Ankara, Anvil Seven—with a Turkish escort. Looks like we have it made, but we won't have that drink waiting for you. Good to hear your voice. I expect we'll be seeing each other in the next year or so."

"Yeah, I expect so. When we do—well, let's just say I owe you, guy."

Ross switched off with a feeling of relief. The trip across Ploesti seemed eons in the past. He switched to intercom. "Pilot to crew. Prepare for landing. Standing by for before-landing checklist."

Sprague, who had given no indication of relinquishing his seat to BT, reached for the checklist. "Nose compartment clear?"

A silence. Then Hanson's hesitant voice. "What about Stan, Captain? Should we, uh—"

"Is he secured?" Ross's voice cut him off without emotion.

"Uh—yeah. We tied him down with his parachute harness."

"Very well. Waist, is Reed secured?"

"Yes, Sir. We lashed him to a gun mount during all that turbulence back there."

"Okay. Next item, General."

"Aux hydraulic pump?"

Ham spoke up. "I suggest we just turn it on for the brake pressure check, then back off, Cap'n. We don't know how many lines are broken in the bomb bay."

"Roger." Sprague reached for the toggle switch at Ross's nodded assent. After a brief wait he responded, "Brake pressure holding at 1,050 psi, pilot. Aux pump returned to off. Autopilot is off. Cowl flaps, closed. Mixtures set to auto-rich. Intercooler shutters open. Fuel booster pumps on. Landing gear lever. Shall we make the kick-out pressure check?"

"Let's pass on that," Ross answered. "We're going to land whether we have three down or not. When we get on final I'll call for the aux hydraulic pump and gear down—then we'll see what happens."

An airfield on the outskirts of a sizable city entered Ross's field of vision. Their escort swung to one side but remained in sight.

"Very well," said Sprague, working with cool detachment. "Call for flaps when you want them after we have hydraulic pressure. I'm setting

the turbosuperchargers in case you do have to go around. Props, high
RPM. Standing by gear and flaps."

Milt Dirkson watched a sprawl of dun-colored buildings take shape
against an equally dun-colored landscape.

God, what a desolate-looking place, he thought. Leaning against the
open waist window, Dirkson let the cooling slipstream tear at his
smoke-grimed, blood-smeared features. Interned. For the duration.
How long was this damn war apt to last? What would life be like in
a strange country where he didn't speak the language, where the food
was probably lousy, and where the girls—the captain had sounded real
serious about staying clear of the women. Anyway, he thought, they
probably have every kind of VD known to man.

But Dirkson's mind was filled by a torment that had nothing to do
with the unhappy fate that had befallen the *Happy Hooker*. Money could
make any ordeal more bearable. He had none, but he knew where more
than a thousand dollars was stashed. Mickey Reed carried it in a slim
money belt under his blood-soaked flight suit. That last night in
Benghazi Mickey had slipped into his cot next to Milt's, the jubilant
winner of a late-night crap game. He wasn't going to trust anyone,
not even the chaplain, to hold it for him, he had confided.

Milt stared thoughtfully at Reed's inert form. Captain Templeton
seemed sure that Mickey wouldn't survive—he'd lost too much blood.
But Mickey would be taken to a hospital as soon as they landed. The
damn Turks would find the belt, and it wasn't hard to figure out where
the money would end up. He owed it to Mickey to hold it for him,
in the event the big tail gunner survived.

He moved to Guenther's side and yelled, "Hey, Dutch, the captain
wants you to go back to the tail and double-check those cable clamps.
He sure as hell doesn't want 'em to come loose on final approach.
I'm gonna loosen Mickey's tourniquet one more time."

Dutch nodded and scrambled toward the tail compartment. Milt
unzipped Reed's flight suit. In one motion he severed the soft leather
belt with his escape knife. Seconds later it was concealed inside his
own baggy coverall. You're stealing, Dirkson, he told himself guiltily.
You don't intend to tell anyone, just in case Mickey doesn't make it.
He brushed the thought away. There comes a time when it's every man
for himself.

Ross eased the elevator trim back a fraction. It required effort not to slap the wheel forward and get the landing over with. A runway had never looked so good. His concentration was helped by Ham's cryptic announcement as they had rolled onto final.

"Sir, better turn that aux hydraulic pump off. We're losing fluid like crazy back in the bomb bay. Turn it on again on the runway for brakes. Also, I smell av-gas. Must have a small leak—we ain't reading anything on the sight gauges."

The *Happy Hooker* settled to earth with the drawn-out squeaking sound of a perfect touchdown. Ross let the rumbling bomber roll to the end of the runway and allowed momentum to carry it into a turn onto the perimeter taxiway. His knees were trembling and almost too weak to apply brakes. It was obvious that they would go no farther. Vehicles formed a solid barrier. Fire trucks, an ambulance, jeeps, panel trucks, even a sleek Cadillac limousine. The halted array was disgorging a small army.

"Shut 'em down, General. This is as far as we go." Ross slurred his words like a drunk. He rested his head on arms crossed on the control column.

Sprague, extracting himself from the copilot's seat, shook the slumped figure. "Not yet, Colyer. I have a hunch your day is far from over. From this point on, I'm in charge. Let me deal with the locals. You look after your crew. I see what looks to be an American civilian and a navy officer getting out of the Caddy. At least we'll have the embassy to run interference for us. I also see a whole damn regiment of Turkish uniforms. Put on your best front, Captain. Let's join the party."

Ross recovered enough to issue his last order for the day. "Pilot to crew. General Sprague and I will deplane and see what's going to happen. The rest of you stay on board until we make arrangements for someplace to go. Get Reed ready to move." He forced his legs to hold him upright and prepared to follow Sprague out the open bomb bay. BT was standing on the catwalk. "'The rest of you' means you, too, BT. Don't, for Christ's sake, make a scene at this point," Ross snapped.

"I rank you, Colyer. We're on the ground now. We'll settle things later, but we'll settle them. I guaran-damn-tee you that."

Ross didn't respond. He dropped to the ground and joined Sprague to confront five disparate figures. A Caucasian wearing a seersucker suit was first to approach.

"I'm Chet Henderson, gentlemen, first secretary at the American embassy." He stuck out a hand. "Good to see you on the ground. We'll talk about your ordeal later. Ambassador Stevens couldn't be here; he's on the TWX to State trying to get some instructions. I'm assuming you're off the raid on Ploesti—details are just starting to come in over the wire. What are your immediate needs?"

Sprague grasped Henderson's hand. "Brigadier General Elliott Sprague, Chet."

Ross saw Henderson's eyebrows, and those of the khaki-uniformed navy commander standing behind him, rise slightly.

"We have a seriously injured man on board and one dead," continued Sprague. "If you could arrange for them first. The rest of the crew are okay—just tired, dirty, and hungry. Captain Colyer here is the aircraft commander. He'll fill you in. In the meantime, I would like to go to the embassy and prepare a flash report for army authorities."

Henderson hesitated slightly before smoothly answering, "Of course, General. If we could take just a moment, however, I would like to introduce you to Commander Hoskins, our military attache; Major Kuprilli of Internal Security—the police, in other words; and Colonel Fizal, of the Turkish army."

As handshakes were exchanged, Henderson continued, "And this is Abdul, our interpreter. He will stay with you until you are settled. Now," he rubbed his hands together briskly, "to the business at hand. Major Kuprilli is required to place you under arrest for entering Turkey without papers. I assume you carry no identification?"

At Sprague's affirming nod, he continued. "A formality, I assure you. We will issue temporary documents making you American citizens and assume responsibility for you until your hearing."

Abdul was providing a running translation for the Turks. Ross was far from convinced that Henderson's scenario was a part of their thinking. For one thing, a quick survey showed that gun-toting soldiers had formed a ring around the parked airplane. The cordon included a jeep-mounted machine gun with a scowling soldier lounging at the breech. Major Kuprilli's swarthy features were impassive, but a slight frown flickered across his forehead.

Picking up on Henderson's last words, Ross addressed the American naval officer. "Commander, could you lean on them to get our injured tail gunner to a hospital?"

"It's already being taken care of," the blond, middle-aged commander assured him. Ross turned to see two white-uniformed medics

helping Dutch and Milt wrestle a stretcher through the waist window.
"He'll get the best treatment they have," Hoskins continued. "They
do have a top-notch hospital here."

Guenther was making urgent signals from the waist. Ross moved
closer. "I wanta go with Mickey," Dutch called.

Ross glanced at Hoskins, who slowly shook his head. "I wouldn't
advise it," he replied cryptically. "I'll explain later."

They turned from a forlorn-looking Guenther and rejoined the welcoming party, where an effusive Colonel Fizal had preempted Abdul's
services and was expounding on something to Sprague. The American
was putting forth his best parade-ground manner—steely-eyed, jaw
outthrust, and, Ross noted with amusement, the butt of his holstered
.45 plainly visible.

Hoskins spoke to Ross from the corner of his mouth. "You've thrown
the entire Turkish military into a tizzy—landing with a general officer
on board. Five'll get you ten that in less than ten minutes a Turk
general—or at least someone wearing a general's insignia—will come
driving up. Bad form, you know, meeting another military man with
an officer of inferior rank."

"Commander," Ross said, "the first secretary mentioned a hearing.
What was he talking about?"

"Well, you see, the Turks don't have any real procedure, or law,
for that matter, for handling people like yourself—combatants who
drop in unannounced. Whenever they're faced with a situation like this
they just put everything in front of a judge—passing the buck, so to
speak. The judge will decide what to do about you, for the time being.
The real issues will be discussed over coffee. You'll be treated okay,
don't worry.

"Three of your bombers limped in here about a year ago. The crews
were given the run of the place and eventually about half of them
escaped. The government was embarrassed and the German ambassador raised hell. They'll be more careful this time—on the surface
at least."

Ross decided he liked the big, lumpy-faced commander. The guy
radiated efficiency. His pale blue eyes missed very little. And, a
welcome trait, he had a sense of humor.

Feeling himself growing unsteady on his feet, Ross said, "Commander, I have a crew of men in there who are out on their feet. I know
this formal stuff has to get done, but can you help get them someplace

to clean up, get a hot meal, and a place to sack out? It's not been an easy day, I assure you."

"I know it hasn't been. Frankly, I'm dying of curiosity. From what we're picking up I gather it was a bad show. Henderson's doing the best he can. He's smooth. We'll have you in a hotel as fast as is humanly possible, believe me. Besides, we're expecting more. Birds are coming down all over the place. Syria, Cyprus—there's supposed to be one right behind you. We'll probably have to do this all over again before long."

A half hour later, Ross was able to tell the jaded crew members, "Okay, guys. There's a bus out here. We'll go to a hotel for the night and pick up the pieces tomorrow. Come on now, move."

The slack-faced crew, slumped in hard, bench-type seats, watched soldiers clad in mustard brown uniforms swarm over the now-deserted *Happy Hooker.*

Ham, his eyes glistening wetly, growled, "Look at those bastards. They'll take everything that ain't welded down. I wish we'd torched her the minute she stopped rolling. She don't deserve to be raped."

Ross watched the scene through eyes dulled by fatigue. By God, she looked good, sitting there square and straight on her tricycle gear, as if she was ready to take to the air. Number four engine wore her feathered prop like a cockade above an oil-drenched nacelle. As he watched, the shattered nose took on the appearance of a battle wound, worn proudly like a saber scar.

"Yeah," he spoke softly, "we should've done that. They shoot crippled horses. It would've been the decent thing to do."

Chapter Thirty

2 August 1943
The Chancery, U.S. Embassy
Ankara, Turkey

Chet Henderson sipped coffee and listened to General Sprague provide a sanitized version of the previous day's mission. Commander Hoskins was an attentive, if slightly skeptical-looking, listener as well.

"So," Sprague concluded, "as I indicated in my report to Washington last night, the B-24 is not a viable low-level bomber. I was opposed to the concept from the beginning, you know."

Ross smiled. Bullshit, General, he thought. You were wetting your pants to get a place in Tidal Wave. It looked like a glory ride from back there in Benghazi. Ross scanned the rest of the crew, seated around the huge oval table wolfing down eggs, ham, buttered toast, and slices of cold melon. Everyone except Reed, that is. Ross's first question to Henderson had been a query regarding the tail gunner's condition. The news was sobering. Mickey's leg would have to be removed. Surgery was scheduled for later that morning.

Ross hardly recognized the crew in civilian clothes. There had been howls of laughter earlier when Henderson had shown up at the hotel with slacks, shirts, underwear, and shoes. None of the crew members had seen their buddies in civvies before. Ross barely remembered someone taking down sizes the night before. In fact, the previous night was a void in his memory. He recalled reaching the hotel, sitting down at a table in a private dining room, and having food and drink set before him. After that, oblivion.

Henderson was talking, Ross realized.

". . . not the best of times for you to arrive, I'm sorry to say. You see, the Turkish government is pretty well evenly divided—half pro-Allied and half pro-Axis. Just now sentiment is tilted toward the Germans. Franz von Papen, the German ambassador, is a master at playing on their emotions. Just recently he convinced them that the United States was preparing to sell Turkey to the Russians if the Allies win. To a Turk, being ruled by their enemy of two thousand years is something unthinkable. They don't know who to trust. Now, you may have noticed a guard in your hotel corridor this morning. You can expect to see him for some time to come; the civil police are a suspicious lot.

"I have ID cards for each of you. Your hearing is scheduled for about an hour from now. It won't be necessary for you to appear. I'll represent you. In the manner of doing things here, Ambassador Stevens met with the minister of the interior this morning and arrived at an understanding. If each of you gives your parole and agrees not to attempt escape, you will be free to live in a hotel of your choice and otherwise have the run of the city. You will continue to draw your military pay through the embassy, so it shouldn't be a terribly adverse life."

"And if we refuse to give our parole?" Sprague inquired.

"In that case you will be placed in a camp outside the city with a dozen or so other internees—eight Russians and four South Africans. It's an unused school building, actually, located on a model farm that didn't work out."

"Prisoners of war, in other words," Sprague observed.

"Not really. There is a token guard force, but passes into town are issued without question."

"No parole," Sprague snapped. "It's contrary to army regs."

BT stirred in his seat. "Uh—Sir, could we maybe discuss this a moment? . . ."

"No."

Ross grinned. BT was hatching a scheme—he recognized the indicators. He addressed Henderson. "Sir, I would like very much to be at the hospital when our man undergoes surgery—maybe see him beforehand."

"I believe that can be arranged," Henderson agreed. "I'll have Abdul go with you. His presence will keep the Turks happy and you'll need a translator in any event."

Milt Dirkson's face bore a stricken look. "I—I'd like to go, too," he stammered.

"And me," said Guenther.

Henderson shook his head. "I'm sorry. Let's not crowd things. A few days and you can go pretty much anyplace you please. But for today, I'm afraid it's back to the hotel. Or, if you like, you can use the reading room here."

"I'd like to go now, then." Ross pushed his chair back and stood.

"I'll drive him, Chet," Hoskins said, rising to his feet as well.

"That would be even better, Cory. See if there's anything further the embassy can do. While you're there, I—ah," Henderson looked uncomfortable as he glanced at the glum-faced gathering, "I will see to arrangements about sending the lieutenant's remains to the States."

As Ross, thoroughly depressed, followed Commander Hoskins from the room, Dirkson stood and called out, "Sir. Hey, Sir, could I see you a moment before you go?"

"Later, Milt. I'll see you all after we get back." Ross saw Dirkson slump in his chair.

6 August 1943
Embassy Row
Ankara

Brigadier General Elliott Sprague, back straight, walked at the head of the little column of airmen clad in civilian clothing. A catafalque, drawn by four black horses, preceded the pathetic little cortege. American flags, covering the cargo of two coffins—Corporal Reed hadn't survived the radical surgery to remove his leg—provided the only visible splash of color. No roll of drums marked their passage, no fanfare— only the clatter of iron-shod wheels, a muted clopping of horses' hooves, and the muffled scuff of marching feet.

Tears streamed down the cheeks of Dirkson, Guenther, and Hanson, but they stared straight ahead, marching at attention. All eyes flickered to the left, however, as they passed the red and black bunting–draped German embassy.

At a barked command the seven Turkish soldiers serving as their escort each pumped three rounds skyward. The blank cartridges made flat, hollow reports. Appropriate, Ross told himself. The whole damn show was an empty expression of respect and grief. Ambassador Stevens had insisted on a ceremony with full honors. The foreign community would expect it, he had explained.

The *Happy Hooker*'s entire crew, serving as pallbearers, hefted the coffins containing the earthly remains of 2d Lt. Stanislaw Cryhowski and Cpl. Mickey Reed aboard a Swiss airliner. Ross did an about-face, saluted Sprague, and formed the crew for the brisk march back to the two embassy limos.

A festive air slowly replaced the somber atmosphere that had prevailed earlier in the embassy ballroom. The funeral party had adjourned here to, in Henderson's words, "accept the condolences of the diplomatic community."

Ross's crew made frequent trips to the well-stocked bar. Bourbon and scotch, they had already discovered, were not easily obtained in the Ankara bars. BT, effusing debonair charm, strolled among the throng of lesser diplomats and, Ross noticed, conducted a discreet inventory of the better-looking women. But the bastard had to be up to something besides bedding the first willing female, he thought.

Ross had prepared himself for a showdown on the matter of who would be acting camp commandant when Sprague had accepted the ambassador's offer to live inside the embassy compound. But BT apparently didn't want the job and had accepted the terms of their internment.

Don't believe it, Ross told himself. BT was roaming the city on his own, declining to join the others on evening sojourns to Papa Karpic's. The restaurant, reputed to be Ankara's best, was an exclusive watering hole for Allied sympathizers. The occasional German who wandered in was apt to be insulted. BT had closeted himself with Sprague and, on the third day of their internment, the ambassador himself.

The wires were probably humming to Papa's senate office, Ross guessed. But to what end?

Ross took up a position at Commander Hoskins's elbow and listened politely as Colonel Fizal made an emphatic point. The conversation was in Turkish. Hoskins turned. "Oh, hi there, Colyer," he said. "Colonel Fizal was just telling me that the Germans are denying that American bombers ever reached Ploesti. They were all destroyed before reaching their target."

Ross formed a tight smile. "Ask them to sell you a quart of oil labeled 'Made in Ploesti.' "

Hoskins translated the comment and the big Turk shook with laughter. He departed to tell his boss, General Mustafa, this latest American joke. Mustafa, true to Hoskins's prediction, had adopted Sprague, was clinking glasses with him even now. Ross had heard, through BT, that Sprague had been the guest of honor at a full-dress dinner party at Mustafa's elegant home. The Turkish government might be divided, but there was little doubt where the army's sympathies lay.

"How's life in the little red schoolhouse, Captain?" the commander inquired.

"Not bad, not bad at all," Ross replied evenly. "We eat good, we're getting used to these Turkish mattresses, and that swimming pool was an unexpected bonus. In fact, things may be too good."

"Oh?" Hoskins raised his eyebrows.

"Yeah. The men are already bored. Not one of them can beat the Russians at chess or the South Africans in our daily swim meets. Frankly, some of them are drinking too much and little quarrels are breaking out."

"Yes," Hoskins frowned into his drink, "confinement, even in a gilded cage, will do that. It happens to the people working in the embassy, in fact."

"I've been trying to think of a way to keep them busy," Ross said. "I think I've come up with something, but I need your help."

"I'll do anything I can."

"Okay. We were greatly attached to that airplane. She was the only one we flew in combat and she always came through like a champ. The crew is convinced that she saved our lives crossing the mountains, in fact. We were in clouds, could climb no higher, and saw a peak go past not a wingtip's length away. The navigator swore she turned herself to the right just before that."

"I can appreciate what you're saying. I've served on ships that we developed a love affair with."

"Well, we left her in a helluva condition. Big holes, an engine out, and blood everyplace. Some of the crew damn near cried when we drove away from her that afternoon. I'd like to have permission to go out there and spruce her up a bit—patch those holes. Maybe we could even overhaul that bad engine."

Hoskins pursed his full lips. "That may be easier than you think," he replied with a slight smile. "You see, the army is fascinated with that big, four-engine bomber. They'd give their eyeteeth to own her. I have no doubt that schemes are being hatched right now to get their hands on her, legally. I'll talk to General Mustafa about the project."

"Hey, great! Oh, and while you're at it, Commander, you might explain that on a big airplane like that, it's important to run the engines every day and taxi her around the field to keep from getting flat spots on the tires."

A mask dropped over Hoskins's normally cheerful expression. He gave Ross a fishy, skeptical look. "It won't work, Colyer. Believe me, you'll never pull it off."

Ross shrugged. "A project to keep the men busy, Commander. Let's just take it one day at a time."

Hoskins sighed. "I'll talk to the general for you. Henderson and the ambassador won't like it, but I can't help you there. Now, a few things you need to know. For one, this place is swarming with espionage agents. They'll know you're repairing the ship. Even your favorite restaurant, Karpic's, has its share of spies. Come up with some damn good reason why you're doing this and hope none of your crew leaks the real one. Major Kuprilli's probably your biggest problem. The major is as pro-German as Mustafa is pro-American. In addition to the German spies, the Italian spies, the English spies, and those of God knows how many other nations, you have police spies. Always remember, if a man is caught attempting to escape, Kuprilli has full say as to how he will be guarded in the future. Don't rule out prison. Don't count on us, or General Mustafa, to prevent it. In many ways Kuprilli is a stronger man in government than any army general."

Ross picked the following morning to broach his plan. He wrestled with the matter of whom to include in his "work party." BT. He neither liked nor trusted the man, but he was, technically, one of the crew. General Sprague. Okay, not in the first discussions, but later, after—if—they decided to make the try. His personal preference would be to confide only in Ham, but that wouldn't be fair to the others. He sighed.

As the crew members strolled from breakfast toward the exercise compound, Ross passed the word. Crew meeting in the far corner before exercise. No Russians or South Africans.

"Okay, troops," he said as he faced the circle of quizzical looks, "how many of you would like to bust outta dis joint?"

There were surprised looks and a few halfhearted chuckles as they digested his words.

"Whatcha got in mind, Skipper?" asked Hanson, his eyes narrowed to slits.

"First, I must know who wants to go. Sorry, but there can't be the slightest leak of our plans. Any who want to stay, just say so. You won't be given any details, so you can't be forced to give information if the rest of us are caught. This isn't any kind of an order and nothing will ever be said if you elect not to take the risk."

"What risks we talking about, Captain?" asked Leckie, the ever cautious one.

"Frankly, I'm not sure. If we're caught in the act, possibly an 'accidental' shooting. If not that, I'm told that we can expect this police major, Kuprilli, to slap us in one of their prisons."

"Whew," Dirkson exclaimed. "From what I hear that's about the same as getting shot. How good do you put our chances?"

"I think they're good enough to be worth the effort. Otherwise I wouldn't be giving it serious thought."

A silence, then BT spoke softly. "What does the general say, Ross?"

"I haven't told him yet, BT. Didn't figure there was any use if we decide not to try it. If we do, I'll see what he has to say."

"And if he says no?"

"Well," Ross drew a deep breath, "we'll just have to cross that bridge when we get to it."

"You mean you would disobey his orders?"

"Now, BT, let's not anticipate that he's going to say no. As a matter of fact I think he'll be in favor of it."

"Well, I say we consult him *before* we go any further on some nutty scheme of yours that could get us killed or tossed into one of these cesspools the Turks call a jail. He *is* my boss, after all. I insist that he be told the whole plan before I have any part of it."

Ross's offhand response gave no clue to the anger he felt. "Okay, BT, I take it from that you're not in. Just as well, perhaps. How about the rest of you?"

"Count me in, Cap'n." Ham Phillips's Tennessee drawl left no question as to his feelings.

"Goddamnit, I finished my missions." Hanson's tone was bitter.

"Now I'm looking at another year, maybe more, stuck over here. I got nothing to lose. I'll go."

Dirkson, Guenther, and Leckie exchanged anxious glances. "Captain," Dirkson said, his voice sounding miserable, "I guess I'll just have to take some time to think about it, you know?"

Guenther and Leckie nodded their heads vigorously in agreement.

"I was sure that you would want some time. It's a big step. What say we get together again after evening chow? Right here, same place. I don't want any eavesdroppers."

Ross faced a livid BT as the others drifted off. "Goddamnit, I didn't say I refused," BT snarled. "You left the others with the impression that I wasn't to be trusted."

"Maybe I *don't* trust you, BT."

"What the hell is that supposed to mean?"

"It means that I included you in the plan because we're all in this together. It means that I would be just as happy if you *did* decide to stay behind. It means that I would be more comfortable if you didn't know of the plan."

With the heat of the day past and a cool evening breeze stirring dust around the softball backstop, the escape committee, as Ross now called it, reassembled. Guenther, Leckie, and Dirkson looked uncomfortable. What rationale prompted them to join? Ross wondered. BT was absent. Ross's expression was intended to radiate confidence—he hoped that it did.

"Glad to see you all here. Captain Templeton, well, I'm just sorry to see him make whatever decision he has made. One thing I must impress on you, however, is not to confide what we're about to do to anyone. No one. Is that clear?"

Serious nods prompted Ross to continue. "Okay, here's what we're going to do. We're going to patch up the *Happy Hooker* and fly her out of here."

A stunned silence was followed by an outburst of enthusiasm. "Hot damn, what an idea," exclaimed Ham Phillips. "Hey, that's cute, real cute. Right from under their fucking noses."

Wide grins indicated hearty approval by the others. As the ebullient mood faded, the crucial question was voiced by Leckie. "How we gonna do this, Captain?"

Ham sobered to ask, "What about number four engine?"

"Well," Ross resumed, "we take things one step at a time. Commander Hoskins thinks the Turk general will okay our going out there and working on her. Hoskins says the general has an eye toward keeping her when we leave. I'm using the story that if the engines aren't run every day and she isn't taxied around the perimeter, she'll soon be a scrapheap. When they get used to seeing her moving around the field—bingo! One morning we just pull onto the runway and pour the coal to 'er."

"They gonna *believe* that shit?" Hanson hooted.

"They'd better," Ross replied grimly. "The whole scheme hangs on them believing exactly that. We just have to put on a damn good act.

BT slammed his drink on the table in disgust. That imbecile! That moron! Who else but Colyer could screw up things in such royal fashion. The deal was as good as made.

"There's a problem," he snarled at the beetle-browed man facing him.

"Problem?" Obsidian eyes narrowed in the brown face, bearing evidence of Mongolian ancestors. "I was led to believe that everything was arranged at your end."

"It was, damnit. The entire five thousand is in a Swiss bank. As soon as I cable the under-secretary that I'm in friendly territory, it's yours."

"The minister's," his companion corrected him.

"Okay, whatever." BT picked up his drink, then set it down again. Vodka and orange juice, for Christ's sake. Would he *ever* be glad to be back in civilization. He looked around the dark, smoke-laden tavern. Customers could have come from the same mold. Everyone wore hats. Dark, light colored, wide brimmed, narrow brimmed—they seemed to be afraid the headgear would be stolen if removed. Not an idle precaution, BT observed grimly. Chronically half-smoked cigarettes drooped from full lips. Highly polished shoes displayed a discreet length of usually yellow silk socks. BT couldn't recall having heard laughter in the half-dozen times he had met with the man he knew as Kemal.

"The problem," his companion reminded him gently.

"Right," said BT. "This jackass, Colyer, called the crew together today and announced that *he* has an escape plan."

"And?"

"Don't you see? Whatever he has come up with is bound to fail—he's talking in terms of the entire crew going at once. When they get caught, all hell is going to break loose. Henderson is going to develop amnesia where I'm concerned. Major Kuprilli will have us signing in every hour on the hour."

"What is this plan your Captain Colyer proposes?"

BT scowled and gulped a measure of the loathsome cocktail. "I don't know," he rasped.

"But surely you can find out?"

"I—I'm not sure. There was an argument. I am no longer in their confidence."

"On the surface, a foolish act, Captain Templeton." Kemal's voice was as flat as his gaze.

"Well, you're just going to have to move faster. God only knows what this fool has in mind, but it could happen anytime."

"In good time, Captain, in good time. These arrangements, if they are successful, are not made overnight. In the meantime, I suggest that you attempt to discover the method that the others plan to use. It could influence our plan."

The dapper little Turk rose and added, "I believe that I would start with your Mister Henderson." He strode toward the door, leaving BT, as usual, to pay the check.

BT gazed at the departing Turk, fighting to keep his temper. The arrogant son of a bitch. For a guy selling out his own country he had a lot of nerve. Don't blow it, BT admonished himself. The man was situated in the right place, the interior ministry, to get him the necessary papers and transportation out of there.

Money—and a politically influential father—opened many doors, he observed.

Chapter Thirty-one

11 August 1943

Ankara

Ross felt his throat constrict slightly as the battered open army truck clattered to a halt in front of the parked *Happy Hooker.* The entire crew sat, stunned, unable to dismount. She seemed to regard her former masters with the reproof of a dowager confronting ne'er-do-well sons who deserted her.

The Turks had towed her to a remote corner of an area reserved for derelicts. Two American-made P-40s with Turkish markings sagged on flat tires nearby. A German Heinkel He 111 minus one engine, the wreckage of assorted light planes, and an unidentifiable heap of rusting junk lent an air of despair to the setting.

For the first time, Ross felt doubt. Good God, he thought, it would take a month in a fully equipped maintenance hangar to even begin to restore her. Their ambitious plans, discussed so optimistically, returned to mock him, as did the celebration following Hanson's solution to their stickiest problem: how to convince the Turks to help them without giving away their purpose.

"Well," Kevin had observed with a frown of concentration, "if this General Mustafa wants her so badly, let's offer to restore her, then *give* the damn thing to him as an expression of appreciation for our treatment here."

That proved to be the touch that brought General Sprague into the conspiracy. Ross's first discussion with the general hadn't gone well.

369

"You're tampering with international politics, Colyer—a subject about which you know nothing. If you make the Turks look foolish, the Allied cause will suffer. Ambassador Stevens will veto the project, I assure you."

"But, Sir," Ross had pleaded, "we have an *obligation* to attempt to escape. This isn't too far removed from being a POW. We didn't give our parole; we live under armed guard. Why does the ambassador have to know what we have in mind?"

"These people aren't stupid, Captain. Don't you think they will make the connection between your 'restoration' project and the presence of Syria, less than three hours' flying time distant?"

In the end, Sprague had relented enough to say, "I won't oppose your efforts, but neither will I be a part of them. You're asking me to dupe a man who has befriended me. I've been a guest in General Mustafa's home, met his family. He is a friend of the United States: That is of more potential benefit than the return of one aircrew to the roster of combat crews."

Ross spoke without thinking. "He's a 'friend' whose sole objective is to get his hands on that four-engine bomber, General. He wants that airplane legally. He sees you as a means to an end."

Sprague leaped to his feet, his face a thundercloud of anger. "That's quite enough of that kind of talk, Captain. I don't need you to instruct *me* on conduct. This interview is terminated. I will forget that you ever made that remark."

Ross apologized and departed, abject at his failure. But the thought that he'd seen a flash of confused doubt in the fiery general's last outburst gave him a glimmer of hope.

He stopped by Commander Hoskins's office. "The thing looks like a bust, Commander."

"Oh, I wouldn't say that," Hoskins said, tapping his lower teeth with a pipe stem. "I mentioned the idea to Mustafa. *He* seemed quite receptive. Kuprilli will still be your biggest stumbling block. Like I said before, you have to come up with some angle to satisfy him."

Sprague agreed to visit the schoolhouse camp and listen to Ross's embellishments to his original plan. Seated on spectator benches behind the backstop, the crew watched intently as Ross explained Hanson's suggestion. The general heard Ross out, then his wooden face cracked into a wintry grin.

"You bastards are really something. That is a mean, dirty trick—but it will work. I like it. And the ambassador will not be told. That includes Henderson."

Ross walked to the car with Sprague. Stopping short, the general turned and asked, "I noticed Captain Templeton wasn't with you. Is there a reason?"

"Sir, BT has severed any relationship with the crew. He was asked to join an escape plan and declined. He has no knowledge of our plan, and I would hope it remains that way."

Sprague made a *hmmpf*. "You two young fools need to work together. You're like a couple of yearling bulls facing each other and pawing the earth."

Ross hesitated. "Uh—General, there's more to it than that, really. To be blunt I have a feeling that BT is working on some scheme of his own, and it doesn't include the rest of us."

The general slid into the embassy car's rear seat. "That's what I was talking about," he said as the driver placed the car in motion.

Ross tried to force enthusiasm into his voice as he announced, "Okay, troops, up and at it. We got work to do."

As the disheartened crew gathered around the nose, Hanson voiced their disillusionment. "My God, where do we begin?"

Ham Phillips was the first to respond. "Okay, let's open her up and take a look inside. I want to see if the thieving bastards left my tool kit—or much of anything else."

There being no hydraulic pressure to open the bomb bay doors, they trooped to the tail section, where Ham tripped the rear hatch and swung himself aboard. A scant minute elapsed before he jumped to the ground. His face was pale. "Uh—Cap'n, it's pretty bad in there."

"The blood?"

"Yeah. It's dried, but the smell is real bad. And the heat and the flies—it's been closed up all this time, you know."

"Okay, Abdul," Ross said, turning to the young interpreter, "you and Phillips take the truck and go see if you can locate a water truck and a pressure pump. You may as well see about a power unit and a maintenance stand while you're at it, Ham. The general promised help; let's see if he can deliver."

The crew of the *Happy Hooker,* freshly showered and reflecting a more cheerful attitude, gathered in Ross's room before evening chow. "Well," their aircraft commander said brightly, "today was a start. It may be a bigger job than we first thought, but it'll get done. Just getting her hosed out inside is a big help."

"Yeah," Ham muttered wearily, "I wish I had that oil all cleaned off the number four nacelle. I got a pretty good look at the engine. I'm afraid she's a write-off, Cap'n. The oil was coming from a scavenge return line; a piece of flak had cut her right in two. That's easy to fix, but it also went right through the number seven cylinder. There ain't no repairing that."

"I was afraid of something like that," Ross admitted. "Well, it *is* possible to make a three-engine takeoff; doesn't leave much margin for error, though. Mustafa isn't going to be too happy to learn he's getting a three-engine airplane, but we can string him along for a while. Well, let's eat. Get back at it bright and early tomorrow."

Abdul proved to be an invaluable asset. Mustafa's young, energetic aide was a born scrounger. Sent after a power unit to recharge the batteries, he'd returned thirty minutes later with one bearing the blue Lufthansa logo on its side.

"Abdul, that's the goddamn *German* airline!" Ross shouted.

"Oh, that—well, it was just sitting there, not being used," the young Turk replied innocently.

Abdul was on hand the day Major Kuprilli showed up with their guard. Kuprilli, through his own interpreter, announced that the airport was a security area. The Americans, therefore, could continue their task only under the supervision of one of his men.

Ross shrugged. It would be days, possibly weeks, before the man could create a problem.

Abdul, standing beside Ross, watched the major depart. A man in a business suit had remained inside the rear compartment. Abdul stared hard as the sedan passed them, then spat in the dust. "A bad one, that."

"Major Kuprilli?" Ross asked.

"No—well, the major is a right bastard, but I mean the one with him. His name is Kemal."

"Who is he?"

"He is the minister of the interior's personal assistant. He is also Major Kuprilli's snoop. He buys and sells information to everybody—

German, Allied—it makes no difference. The jails are full of men who owe their fate to Kemal, my brother included."

Ross's response was cut short by a gleaming sedan and its motor-cycle escort entering the compound gate, red lights flashing and sirens wailing. General Mustafa was paying his respects. The jovial army chief requested a tour of the bomber. He and the junior officer with him examined each instrument and control, asking endless questions.

As they prepared to leave, Mustafa introduced the young man as his personal pilot. He was also one of the P-40 pilots who had escorted the *Happy Hooker* over Turkish territory.

Disgustedly, Ross watched the convoy race out of sight. When the hell was he ever going to get any work done? The day was almost shot and all he'd managed was to play tour guide. Some thing told him that the general would be a regular spectator. This was okay—it would keep his enthusiasm at a fever pitch. The fact that a fully qualified pilot would be watching bothered Colyer, however. Some of the things he had in mind wouldn't fool the greenest aviation cadet.

Ham interrupted his task of replacing missing Plexiglas panels in the shattered nose section with scraps of salvaged aluminum skin. "Cap'n, I've dipped all the main tanks and I figure we don't have more'n a hundred—maybe a hundred and fifty gallons left. Figuring that you can trap damn near that much in a nose-up or nose-down attitude in flight, that don't leave enough to go very far. How much flying time did you say it was to someplace friendly?"

"Kevin figures the trip to Syria at about five hundred miles if we take the shortest route out of Turkey and turn back east when we're over international waters. At a hundred and fifty-five indicated—about all we can expect on three engines—that makes three hours plus.

"Damn, we're talking about at least another thousand gallons, Cap'n."

"Yeah. Well, here's what we'll have to do. We ask Mustafa for three hundred gallons to test run the engines and do a taxi run. We shouldn't need a fraction of that, but we'll ask for another three or four hundred gallons after that. Then, a few days later, some more. We'll just have to rathole a little bit at a time."

Phillips wiped sweat from an already grimy brow. "I suggest we hide it in the Tokyo tank, Sir. When we was showing that general and his pilot through the flight deck, they were real interested in how the sight fuel gauges worked. Well, what little we got now don't even show on the gauges. But I have a hunch they'll be back and sure as hell they're gonna notice we're squirreling it away."

"Hey, good thinking, old buddy. We're going to make a crook out of you yet, Ham." Ross grinned. "Now, you think we can try those engines tomorrow?"

"Reckon so. We got a hot battery and enough gas to at least start 'em up. I have that broken hydraulic line tied off so we'll have brakes—could use some more fluid in the main reservoir, though."

"Good enough. Tell you what I'll do. Before we leave tonight, I'll go over to the army fuel dump and try to get our first transfusion tomorrow."

Abdul spread his hands and shook his head. "He says no petrol, Captain Colyer. It is not authorized. Petrol is very expensive."

"Did you tell him that the petrol is for General Mustafa?"

"I did. He says he must have written authorization."

"Oh, shit." Ross—hot, tired, and disgusted—did not try to conceal his irritation. The Turkish noncom, seated behind a desk laden with soiled papers and the greasy parts of some mysterious machine, appeared unimpressed. "Okay, Abdul, let's go. This ape wants General Mustafa's authorization, he'll get it. I'll stuff it down his goddamn throat."

Abdul was forced to a near trot to keep up with Ross's angry strides. "Captain," he said breathlessly, "something is not right back there."

"That's for damn sure," Ross snapped.

"General Mustafa issued orders to give you full cooperation. I heard him myself."

"So what is that shithead sergeant trying to pull?" Ross asked as he slowed his pace.

Abdul's face assumed a pained expression. "Sir, you Americans have trouble understanding how the Turkish government works. You see, General Mustafa has full authority in matters of fighting a war. With affairs of state security, however, the Directorate of Internal Security has the final say. The sergeant has orders from Major Kuprilli to withhold the petrol. I would wager a month's pay this is true."

Ross came to a halt. "You're saying that Kuprilli can override the general's order to give me fuel?"

"Yes, Sir. If he considers that you are planning to use the petrol to escape internment, he could withhold approval."

Ross's jaw dropped. "If wh-a-t?"

Abdul's face wore a sickly grin. "Yes, Sir, I have thought from the beginning that such was your intention. Also, I believe that is Major Kuprilli's opinion."

Ross resumed walking, but at a reduced pace. After a few moments of thought he chuckled and said, "Abdul, my lad, methinks you have hidden depths."

"I don't understand, Sir."

"Never mind. Tell me, *if* such were the case, how would you get your hands on a thousand gallons of one hundred octane aviation fuel?"

Abdul walked in silence as he considered the question. Finally, "One could arrange to have that amount stolen, I believe, Sir."

"Nix on that idea, Abdul. So far, nothing in our plan violates Turkish law. We get caught stealing gas and Kuprilli will bury us in the deepest jail in Turkey."

"Very probably," Abdul responded matter-of-factly. "One could always *purchase* the petrol."

"From whom? And with what?"

"The foreign airlines, Sir. Would not the embassy approve such an expenditure?"

"Hardly." Ross barked a short laugh. "But, just for discussion, how much does av-gas go for here?"

"I—I would have no knowledge of that, Captain," the young man replied evasively. "But, under the security conditions that exist, a premium would have to be paid, of that I'm sure. Possibly the price could be as much as two dollars, American, per gallon."

Ross let out a low whistle. "Wow. We aren't apt to come up with that kind of cash. Still, ask around. See if you can find some airline that would be willing to part with that much fuel—and an idea of what they would ask, okay?"

He smiled to himself as they approached the compound gates. The gas was available—and for two bucks a gallon. On that he would stake his reputation. Abdul was indeed a resourceful lad. So where in the hell could he raise two thousand dollars?

They were met by a grinning Ham Phillips. "Cap'n." He was talking even before they came to a stop in front of the airplane. "You ain't gonna believe this."

"I've just gone through one unbelievable predicament, Ham. I hope to hell yours is *good* news."

"An engine, Cap'n. I found an R-2800 Pratt and Whitney in perfect condition. It's in the army hangar, back in one corner. It's off a B-24 that crash landed here about a year ago—one of the Halpro group."

"I'll be goddamned." A wide smile spread across Ross's features. "What do you know about that? You sure that it's in running condition? Can we have it? Shit, where would we get the stands, A frame, tools, and so forth to hang a new engine?"

"We don't need the entire engine, Cap'n. Just the number seven jug. Those cylinders are mounted with bolts. I'll just take the damaged one off and replace it."

"Won't even have to remove the engine," Ross mused. "But wait a minute. Ham, with that hunk knocked out of the cylinder, the piston would have shed every ring on it. And she must have ingested a handful of metal particles."

"A good chance you're right, Cap'n. We'll just have to wait and see about the rings, but even if they're gone, we don't need any one cylinder for power. We just pull a plug and let 'er run free. As for the metal, I can get most of it out by draining and flushing a few times. Even if we lose a cylinder later on, we still have four for takeoff."

Ross turned to Abdul. The young Turk's eyes were sparkling with excitement. "Abdul, is Major Kuprilli going to go along with this?"

"I would think that the repair will be completed before the major is consulted, Sir. If the captain has fifty dollars, the part you require will be removed and placed inside your airplane tonight."

Ross opened his mouth to speak, then closed it. Some things were best left unsaid. "You'll have your money as soon as we return to the camp, Abdul."

Ross sipped his bourbon and water and wandered disconsolately to the patio railing, away from the chattering group that made up the ambassador's cocktail party. The job of replacing the cylinder on number four was only half finished. Leckie, Guenther, and Dirkson were behind schedule with their skin repair. Pieces of salvaged aluminum had to be fitted and riveted in place with hand tools.

The invitation, more like an order, to attend the Sunday afternoon affair couldn't be ignored. The old man thinks he's being good to us, Ross reflected. Oh, well, just hope that one of the crew doesn't get a load on and blab something he shouldn't.

Commander Hoskins interrupted Ross's distracted examination of the lush lawn area stretching downhill from the patio. "You don't appear to have the party spirit, Colyer. Something bothering you?" A sardonic cast in his eyes betrayed the navy officer's concern.

"Guess I'm just not a social animal, Commander. It all seems so, I don't know, out of sync. Here we are having a party while a few miles away there's a war going on—men getting killed and all that."

"There is that aspect," Hoskins observed. "But, hard as you may find it to believe, wars—battles, anyway—are won and lost at affairs such as these. Over there," he gestured toward the crowd milling about the bar and pool, "are at least four, probably more, men who are hard at work. They're in the business of not only collecting information, but spreading false stories made to appear factual. But, enough shop talk. How's the restoration coming?"

"Oh, as well as could be expected. We have one hang-up, though. I was going to ask if you could talk to General Mustafa about it."

"What's that?"

"Fuel. We don't have enough on board to do a daily run-up and taxi check. The army refuses to give us more. Could you convince the general to sign a chit or something?"

"Why don't you ask your General Sprague? The two of them are on close terms—especially since Sprague convinced him that he could authorize the transfer of a four-engine bomber to a foreign power. That took guts, Colyer, sheer guts." He chuckled.

"I did ask Sprague. Mustafa was evasive. What I'm led to believe is that Major Kuprilli has revoked Mustafa's okay."

"Hmm, anything is possible around here. I'll check it out. I understand that Captain Templeton is not involved in your restoration project."

"BT and I had some words. He refused to help."

"I see. Well, what I was leading up to is that your friend's social life could lead to problems. Some of his drinking companions, for example, have questionable pedigrees. And he has been seen visiting a place called Ali Bey's. The place is nothing more than a clearinghouse for espionage, smuggled goods, you name it. You might give him a gentle hint."

"I doubt that he would listen. Frankly, Sir, I think BT is dealing on his own—possibly with the connivance of your Mister Henderson— maybe even the ambassador. You see, BT's father is a senator."

"Do tell," said Hoskins, noncommittally. "Well, over there is one example of what I was referring to. See that Turkish civilian Templeton is talking with?"

Following the commander's gaze, Ross located BT. Templeton's handsome features were set in angry lines. He was speaking rapidly. The Turk was listening with seemingly bland indifference. Where had he seen that man before?

As Ross searched his memory, Hoskins continued. "The man's name is Kemal. He's strictly bad news."

"I don't believe I know him," said Ross.

"If you ever meet him and shake hands, count your fingers when you leave."

Chapter Thirty-two

17 August 1943
Ankara

"Clear number four." Ross, finger on the starter toggle, surveyed the crowd of onlookers who had come to observe the first engine start since the *Happy Hooker* limped to a landing almost three weeks before.

"Number four clear," Ham Phillips called, his face pinched with worry. He had just secured the last bit of cowling on the damaged power plant moments before. Would that replacement cylinder hold?

"Turning four," Ross called above the building whine of the inertial starter. General Mustafa, on hand for the big day, stood spraddle legged, arms folded, beaming confidence. Already he could see himself in the cockpit as the starting routine was carried out by his own troops.

Then, as Ross engaged the starter, its high-pitched whine changed to a deeper note and the prop blades commenced a sluggish rotation. The onlookers collectively held their breath as first one cylinder fired—providing a jerky reaction—then another, and still another. A cloud of blue smoke erupting from her exhaust, the plane shuddered as the explosions blended into a stuttering roar and the prop blades became a blur of movement.

Cheers could be heard even above the building roar at his right elbow. Ross felt tears brim in his eyes. You beautiful bitch, you did it again, he thought. Okay, we're going to get you out of this boneyard—get you home where you belong.

*   *   *

Papa Karpic's reverberated with the sounds of revelry—a good portion of it generated by the crew of the *Happy Hooker*. Ham Phillips, his eyes growing slightly out of focus from endless champagne toasts, seemed to have a permanent lopsided grin plastered on his face as a stream of well-wishers pounded his back. He was the hero of the hour. Only his slavish dedication to "his" airplane had brought them to this point.

Karpic himself stood beaming alongside Ross, explaining that the caviar and champagne were on the house. The paunchy White-Russian émigré extolled the virtues of the American bomber crewmen, referring to their part in the Ploesti raid as "courage without equal."

Several patrons left, their faces contorted in disgust. "Nazis," Karpic sneered. "They'll be back. Papa Karpic serves the best food and drink in all of Ankara."

Ross wished he could enter into the carnival mood of the others, but the more sparkling white wine he consumed, the more he brooded over their predicament. They still were without a legitimate source of fuel. No one had been able to budge Kuprilli's embargo on Turkish army gasoline. But Abdul had fulfilled his promise: He could arrange a surreptitious transfer of one thousand gallons of high octane from an unnamed source for two thousand dollars.

Ross had consulted Sprague, asking if, as a last resort, they should ask Ambassador Stevens for the funds.

"Stevens will not only turn you down, he'll expose the hoax," Sprague had told him.

Meanwhile, Leckie, displaying hidden talents, had typed up an impressive document, full of admirable officialese that obligated the U.S. Army to pay the bearer the sum of two thousand dollars, plus 6 percent interest, upon presentation after hostilities. His Spencerian signature—"by and for the President of the United States of America, Franklin Delano Roosevelt"—was embossed with an undecipherable seal and two ribbons. Ross laughed with the others, but he kept the document safely tucked away. Stranger things have happened, he thought. It might even work, if all else failed.

"Look, everybody wire home and ask for a loan," Hanson had suggested. Hoskins quickly squashed that idea. Infusions of foreign currency into the local economy were closely scrutinized by the Internal Security Directorate. They would forward a discreet inquiry to the embassy. How could Ross explain an urgent need for two thousand dollars?

That brought him to the second matter he couldn't ignore: BT. The damn fool was playing a game that had rules he didn't understand. Ross could shrug off the hazards where BT himself was concerned, but the bastard was the one person who could arrange, through his father, for an interbank transfer of funds to a foreign airline.

Glancing at his watch, Ross made his decision. It was ten o'clock. BT had curtly refused to join the celebration. Could he be found at Ali Bey's place? Ross's pass was good until midnight. He put his mouth close to Hanson's ear.

"Look, Kevin, I'm pooped. I'm going to run along. See you all back at the camp."

The taxi driver, ignoring the fact that Ross spoke no Turkish, talked nonstop as the battered '34 Ford carried them deeper and deeper into the old part of town.

Cobblestone streets grew narrower; the buildings, set behind stuccoed walls, were smaller. They soon left behind what passed for nightlife in the Turkish capital. Street lamps, often at least two blocks apart, shed dim cones of light on ancient stones. The night air wafted a thick cargo of stale cooking odors mixed with the fetid stench of rotting garbage.

Just as Ross was thinking of abandoning his mission and returning to the party, the taxi drew to a stop.

"Ali Bey," the driver said, gesturing toward an iron gate and a blank wall fronting a building looking much like all the others in this neighborhood.

Ross hesitated. With no sign displayed, no lights visible, he was unsure of what to do. Was it the right place? Would the driver wait until he could check to see if BT was inside? A look at the frowning, gesticulating man told him that prospect was not likely.

As soon as Ross counted out the fare into the driver's hand, the aging Ford sped off, trailing a cloud of oily exhaust smoke. A foraging mongrel dog was sole witness to his arrival. The mangy canine inspected Ross briefly, decided he had nothing to offer, and slunk away.

How the hell am I supposed to get home? Ross wondered as he approached the ornately scrolled wrought-iron gate. It was unlocked and opened silently to his touch. He walked through a tiled courtyard. To his immense relief muttered conversation filtered through a background of flute and some kind of string music coming from the back of the building.

A heavy, solid door loomed ahead at the far end of the path. He turned its crudely fashioned L-shaped handle and stood in the open doorway. The place appeared to be a tavern, although the music he had heard seemed to have come from outdoors, at the rear. A fog of harsh tobacco smoke layered the low ceiling like blue batting. A short bar—two planks attached to the wall displaying a half-dozen bottles and an old-fashioned beer "pump"—was presided over by a fez-capped gnome with an outsized handlebar mustache.

Ross's entrance did nothing to alter the subdued level of conversation, but every eye in the place was turned in his direction. He crossed to the minuscule bar and asked, "You speak English?"

The swarthy bartender shrugged. "Some—a little. You want beer, vodka, brandy?"

"Uh—a beer, please." Ross watched as the man selected a dingy glass mug from beneath the bar, wiped it on his soiled apron, and drew a foaming measure of dark brew. "Does another American, tall, dark, come here?" Ross asked, placing a Turkish pound on the bar.

The bartender counted out change, gave him a blank look, and ignored his question. Apparently his English was limited to orders for drinks.

Ross, feeling uncomfortably exposed, strolled toward open French doors. Beyond was a postage-stamp courtyard with four tables. The patio was dimly lit by a fly-specked overhead bulb. The single occupant at the one table in use lounged in a straight-back chair and regarded him with a lazy smile.

"Well, as I live and breathe, if it isn't our gallant leader." BT raised his glass in mock salute. "Ross, my lad, you do astonish me. I shouldn't ask—I'm not sure I even want to know—but just how in the hell did you find me?"

Ross slid uninvited into the chair opposite BT. "Elementary, Captain. I just asked around for directions to the place where all the crooks, thieves, and blackmailers hang out. They all said, 'Try the Ali Bey.' And, behold, here you are."

A flush deepened BT's already sun-darkened features. Muscles bunched at his jawline. "Someday, Colyer, you're going to shoot off your smart mouth once too often. Now, I'm not going to waste time on pleasantries. You aren't welcome here. I'm not going to ask you to join me for a drink. We have no business to transact, so why don't you just get back to your precious crew and play with your airplane."

Ross sipped the bitter, watery beer. "BT, I don't know what it is with us—we just seem to piss each other off. But we're in a situation where we have to put our personal differences aside and work together."

"Give me one good reason."

"Well," Ross paused to light a cigarette, "for openers there's the matter of returning an airplane and crew to active combat status." He exhaled a plume of smoke and continued. "I'm not waving the flag, BT, nor am I going to lecture you on the responsibilities of rank and command. But they play a part. Basically, it's just that we're paid to do a job. We owe it to the people who pay us to do the best we know how. Our job, maudlin patriotism aside, is to win a war."

"Very prettily said." BT had recovered his composure and reverted to his old, sneering, arrogant self. "A speech worthy of my esteemed father. 'But' I ask myself, 'why, at this particular time, do you track me down waving an olive branch?'"

"Because you have something we, the crew, need."

"How flattering, Colyer. When I think of how much of that stiff-necked, stubborn, midwest pride you had to swallow to come to me for help, I'm impressed."

"I'll concede it did take a bit."

BT barked a short laugh. "So much, in fact, that I'm curious to hear what it is you want from me. Shoot."

Ross stubbed out his cigarette and leaned across the table. "BT, we have the *Happy Hooker* flyable. Syria is roughly three hours' flying time from here. Major Kuprilli refuses to issue fuel for us to even run the engines up every day. But we've located a civilian source that will sell us av-gas. We need two thousand dollars. Two grand, BT, and we're home safe and sound. You're the only one who can arrange, through your father, for an interbank transfer. What do you say?" Ross leaned back and fished another cigarette from his crumpled pack.

BT's response was blunt. "I say go get fucked, Colyer. I've known from the beginning that your wild-eyed scheme didn't stand a chance. At one time I could have—would have—cut a deal that would have gotten us all out of here. But no, you had to play hero. 'Old BT isn't to be trusted,' you said. Well, you can rot here—you and your entire bunch of grubby little hero worshippers. I'll send you a postcard from Miami Beach. Now, I'm to meet someone here. I'd rather he not see you—catch my drift?"

Ross refrained from issuing an angry retort and sipped his beer. "BT, listen to reason. Look, you consider yourself a smart poker player. Okay, I'll grant you that. But you've taken cards in a game where, if you win, you get your goddamn hand chopped off at the wrist when you reach for the pot. You should be smart enough to see that. I don't know the details of whatever deal you're making, but you're making it with a gang of cutthroats." He made a shrewd guess. "Take this guy, Kemal, who you're trusting to get you out. He's on everybody's payroll in town—those he hasn't double-crossed. You're going to give him some money and he's going to deliver you right into the hands of the police—if he doesn't spill your guts on the street first. Christ, he's on Kuprilli's payroll!"

BT's involuntary start and the widening of his eyes told Ross that the thrust had hit home. "Get smart, Templeton, not only are you in a game you can't win, but when you get taken, it queers any chance *we* might have."

"You make me sick, Colyer. You're always the one with the answers. 'Colyer's the best pilot in the outfit.' " BT's voice became a mimicking falsetto. " 'Colyer's crew has the best everything.' 'If you want to know how to fly combat, talk to Colyer.' Even Janet. 'Lieutenant Colyer was the only one brave enough to try to save an airplane that day at Hickam.' Oh, she never said so, but she found out about that gun-pointing business. Don't think I don't know that I was her second choice for a husband.

"No, Colyer, you've been a pain in the ass ever since I first met you. Now, sit back and watch. I have the down payment on a ticket home right here." He fished a heavy, bulging manila envelope from inside his loose sport shirt. "One thousand dollars. For that I get taken to a fishing boat—the balance due when I reach Allied territory. So you just—" BT stopped in midsentence. His eyes, looking over Ross's shoulder, narrowed.

"Oh, for Christ's sake, here comes my man now. There's a gate into the alley in that corner. Go! Goddamnit. I'll arrange for your money after I get home. I guess I owe you that much."

Ross, bitter and disappointed, stood in a little vine-covered arbor and watched as Kemal approached his just-vacated chair. BT's face appeared sallow in the dim light. The guy's scared shitless, Ross thought. He almost failed to notice the small, dark sedan ghosting down the alley, engine idling and lights extinguished. Ross shrank into the shadow cast by the overhanging vines and watched the car stop alongside the Ali Bey's walled rear courtyard.

A lithe, small man scrambled to the auto's roof and peered over the wall. A half-dozen whispered words and the driver passed him a cylindrical object roughly two feet long. The man standing on top unwound what appeared to be wires and shielded a cigarette lighter's flame. The "wire" sputtered as it shed a stream of sparks. In one motion he lobbed the contraption into the tiny courtyard and swung himself through the car's open side door. With a roar of its surprisingly powerful engine, the vehicle disappeared down the narrow alley.

Ross, horrified, watched what looked like his mother's rolling pin turn end over end, shedding sparks and smoke. Shaking with numb incredulity, he screamed, "Jesus Christ, BT—get down! There's a goddamn bomb!"

Sheltered by the heavy wall surrounding the courtyard, Ross was spared the brunt of the blast. The device erupted with a sheet of white flame. The concussion was preceded by a searing hot wind rushing past him as he crouched, arms over his head. Debris—broken tables and chairs, chunks from a tired palm tree gracing the little enclosure, and bits of tile flooring rained down around him.

Ears ringing, Ross rushed into the enclosure. Although the overhead bulb had been a casualty, he could see through the swirling dust and smoke by light reflected from inside the bar. Chaos. A body, clothing smoldering, lay sprawled alongside the wall.

Ross recognized the sport shirt and dark trousers BT was wearing. Kneeling, he gently turned the body face up. It was BT all right. His right arm was missing just above the elbow; dark blood spurted from its stump. His face was black and minus hair and eyebrows. BT's eyes flickered open as Ross cinched his belt around the stump of his arm. The bleeding slowed but continued to saturate the dusty ground.

"Wha—what the hell happened, Ross?" BT croaked.

"A bomb, BT. Some bastards drove by and tossed it over the wall. You'll be okay, though. We'll have you in a hospital in no time." Remembering Kemal, Ross glanced around the courtyard. The big Turk's body lay grotesquely askew several feet away.

BT's eyes fluttered closed. "You're shitting me, Colyer. I'm not walking away from this one. The double-crossing . . ." His voice faded away as a few frightened patrons emerged from the interior of the tavern.

In the distance the *hee-haw-hee-ah* of sirens shattered the stillness. With superhuman effort, BT raised his head and shoulders. Though groggy, his voice was clear and steady. "You're okay, Colyer, it's just your damned efficiency and being right all the time I couldn't stand. I was wrong—again. Look, take that envelope inside my shirt. Use the money to buy gas and get the hell out of here. Tell your crew that it was ol' BT's last—"

His head dropped. BT gasped, then expelled a rattling exhalation as his body slumped lifeless to the cobbled bricks of the courtyard.

The party at Karpic's was winding down when Ross dragged an empty chair alongside Hanson and Ham Phillips. Keeping his voice steady, he muttered, "Get everybody back to camp. I mean now! All hell's broken loose. Get black coffee into everyone. We may be taking off by dawn. I'll explain later. Abdul, come with me. We've got an errand to run."

Twenty minutes later, Ross faced a rapidly sobering crew in the dim light of the overhead bulb in his room. "We have problems. First off, Captain Templeton was killed just an hour or so ago by a bomb thrown into a restaurant. The problem is this: The police are going to find out I was there—too many people saw me. Major Kuprilli has been waiting for some pretext to make life miserable for us. He's bound to take away the freedom we've had, and you can bet that the engine run-ups and taxi checks will be forbidden. So much for a flyaway. If we go, it has to be tonight—before the police start putting two and two together."

The others stood silently. The shock of Ross's words drove the last vestiges of alcohol fog from their brains. Ham recovered enough to ask, "How about fuel, Cap'n? We ain't going *nowhere* without some."

Ross's lips tightened. "There's more about BT's death than I have time to go into just now, but, just before he died, he gave me a thousand dollars. Abdul is on his way to the airport to purchase as much gasoline as he can with it. I figure that if we can't make Syria, we'll go to Cyprus. There's fighting going on down there and it'll be a toss of the coin whether we can tell who'll be in charge of the airfield. We may even have to find a Royal Navy ship offshore and ditch alongside. As always, anyone who wants to stay here—well, nothing will ever be said."

He paused while the crew members exchanged glances.

"We're ready, Sir," Dirkson assured him.

"Very well, I suggest you try to get some sleep. I have to go to the embassy, but we'll plan to arrive at the airport just at dawn. Tell the truck driver and the guards that we want to get our work finished tomorrow before it gets too damn hot."

Ross faced a grim gathering that included First Secretary Henderson, Ambassador Stevens, and Commander Hoskins. General Sprague sat to one side, silent but alert. An ornate, porcelain-faced clock struck midnight.

". . . so that's about it, gentlemen. The police and ambulances—and reporters—were there in less than ten minutes. I slipped into a cab that one of the newsmen used to get there and got the hell out. There was nothing I could do for BT. He was still conscious when I got to him, but he didn't live more than a few minutes." Ross sipped from a cup of coffee and stared at the floor.

Henderson cleared his throat. "How do you see it, Cory? Who— and why, for God's sake—would want to assassinate Templeton?"

Commander Hoskins tamped coarse tobacco into his pipe. Before lighting it he observed, "It wasn't Templeton they were after. This Kemal he was meeting was the target. I'd wager he pulled some kind of swindle on the wrong people. This drive-by-and-toss-a-bomb technique is one of the favorite ways to express displeasure in this part of the world."

The ambassador's eyebrows almost touched as he frowned. "Are you telling us that Templeton's death was nothing more than a mistake, for God's sake—an accident?"

"It looks that way, Sir."

"Outrageous. Senseless and barbaric," Stevens muttered. "Very well, I suppose we had best prepare to meet with the press. Chet, would you draft me a statement? And, as soon as we have official confirmation, there's Senator Templeton to notify. I'd best handle that."

After muttered acknowledgments, and a clatter of coffee cups and saucers being returned to the tray, the little assemblage prepared to adjourn.

"Mister Ambassador," said Ross, "there is one thing that hasn't been discussed."

"Yes, Captain Colyer?"

"I think it highly probable that I will be arrested, possibly yet tonight."

"Whatever for?" Stevens asked, returning to his chair.

"You see, Sir, BT—Captain Templeton, that is—was planning to escape from detention. I don't know the details, but this man, Kemal, was to make the arrangements. BT was going to give him a down payment at the Ali Bey tonight."

The absence of surprised exclamations told Ross that they knew BT was trying to buy his way out. The bastards.

Henderson's face took on a closed look. Stevens peered at Ross and said sharply, "I hope you had nothing to do with it."

"No, *I* didn't," Ross replied pointedly. "But Major Kuprilli doesn't know that. It can easily be established that I was at the scene, however. The major will be only too happy to find a charge, any charge, that will let him place us under arrest. Kemal was on his payroll as an informer, so Kuprilli has a personal interest in this."

"Oh, for heaven's sake. This could get sticky. Chet, what do you think? Is Colyer in danger of being arrested?"

The first secretary shifted in his chair. "It's possible," he conceded.

Ross dropped his bombshell. "I think it best, Sir, if my crew and I disappeared—tonight."

Stevens's jaw dropped. "*Disappear?* Where, pray tell, do you plan to hide?"

"Not hide, Mister Ambassador, depart. Look, we've repaired the *Happy Hooker.* She's flyable—we ran up the engines and did a taxi check today."

"My God in heaven." Stevens removed steel-rimmed glasses and rubbed the bridge of his nose. "I knew of the restoration project, but I had no idea that there was any intention to make the plane *flyable.* Chet, did you know any of this?"

Ross skewered the sweating Henderson with a direct gaze. You'd better hang with me, his look said.

"In general terms, Sir. I wasn't aware of the extent of their progress; I—I planned to brief you if and when a possibility to use the craft for—er—escape materialized."

Sprague broke into the confused silence. "Colyer is right, Mister Ambassador. A great deal of embarrassment could be avoided all around if your internees, all of us, were to disappear."

Ross shot the general a surprised look. He received a wolfish smile in return. Stevens looked thoughtful. "But how on earth do you plan to get to the plane, get it started, and off the ground without being stopped? There are guards both at the airport and at the school."

"We've taken that into consideration," Ross responded enigmatically. Hoskins was regarding him with a quizzical look. "We need your help in only one aspect. We don't have enough fuel to reach Syria. We can buy the stuff from one of the civilian airlines—Kuprilli controls access to army stores—but we need a thousand dollars." A glance showed that Hoskins could no longer conceal his grin of admiration.

Stevens's face paled. "No—no, I will not place the embassy in a compromising situation. I will turn a blind eye to all of this, but I will not risk losing credibility with the Turkish government."

Ross stood. "Very well, Sir. I'll be going now. There's a great deal to do." He turned to Sprague. "If you're going to join us, General, I suggest you come now. I have a cab waiting outside."

Sprague leaped to his feet. "Give me five minutes to throw a few things together." He turned to a dazed Stevens and Henderson. "We're going to win this war, gentlemen. We'll win it because we have two things going for us. We have more guns, tanks, and airplanes than the enemy; more important than that, we have guys with ingenuity and guts." He turned on his heel and departed in his best parade-ground manner.

Hoskins rose to his feet and knocked out his pipe. "I believe I'd better drive them back to the schoolhouse in a limo, Chet. It's after their curfew, you know."

"Oh, yes, of course, Cory. By all means do that," Henderson replied absently.

Ross and Hoskins found Abdul in the entry hallway chatting with the marine guard. Ross drew him to one side. "How did it go?"

"Like silk, Captain. You'll have a truck standing by when you get there. But be at the gate right at the crack of dawn. They want to be out of there before it gets too light."

Ross sagged with relief. The last roadblock had been hurdled. "Don't worry," he said, slapping Abdul's shoulder with a tight grin, "so do I."

The Chrysler limo purred through deserted streets, its passengers each preoccupied with private thoughts. Finally Hoskins cleared his throat. "In a way, I wish I were going with you. That was a pretty shitty demonstration back there. If you guys crash on Cyprus because you don't have enough fuel for Aleppo—well . . ."

"We'll make it," Ross said with more confidence than he felt. He turned to Sprague. "What made you change *your* mind, Sir?"

"Say it was a whim. After listening to that pair give you the run-around, I decided I couldn't stomach a year or more around them. Colyer, we've had our differences, but you're solid—I always know where you stand. I infinitely prefer your company to theirs." The general paused, then he chuckled. "Shit, I have to be honest. I can't pass up excitement. Abdul, can you talk our way past that airport guard?"

"With you aboard, Sir? It'll be easy."

Sprague grunted. "I look forward to it—but I keep thinking that nothing has been 'easy' since we left Benghazi."

The old school building was dark and quiet as they drew to a stop in front. Hoskins shook hands all around. "I wish there was more I could do. This war won't last forever, you know. We'll get together for some serious drinking when it's over. Now, go with God."

As the trio crossed the front porch, a figure stirred in a chair situated in a far corner.

"Skipper, Captain Colyer, Sir, I have to talk to you."

Startled, Ross snapped, "Who's out here?"

"Dirkson, Sir. I really have to talk to you."

"Okay, Dirkson, what is it?" Ross asked, slumping into an adjacent chair as the others went inside.

"Sir, I've had something on my mind ever since we got here, and I just can't stand it anymore." Ross, bone weary, waited silently for Dirkson to continue. "I stole some money, Captain. I don't know what got into me, but I took Mickey Reed's money belt while he was unconscious."

"You *what?*" Ross snapped upright.

"I—I took his money belt. I was the only one who knew he had it. He won the money in a crap game the night before the mission."

"Why, Milt? What did you plan to do with the money?"

"Like I said, Sir, I don't really know. It's just that, well—things were all confused. You told us we wouldn't be going home. I didn't have any money. Captain Templeton had said that Mickey was a goner. I didn't think Mickey would mind. I could have given it back to him if he'd lived. Did you get to talk to Mickey before he died, Sir?"

"Yes," Ross replied slowly. "He was still pretty well doped up, but, yes, we talked until they came to prep him for surgery."

It was a conversation he would not soon forget, Ross told himself.

"They're gonna take my leg off, Skipper."

"Yes, Mickey. It's the only way they can save your life. You see, you had that tourniquet on so long that the leg didn't get enough blood."

"Don't let 'em do it, Sir, I beg of you."

"There just isn't any other way, Mickey, believe me."

"Then let me die. I'll be a freak. I'll never play ball ever again. Stop them." Tears streamed down the big tail gunner's cheeks.

"I can't, Mickey. The doctors won't listen to me. They know what's best—you'll feel different when you're back home."

Two attendants came then and indicated they were wheeling their patient into surgery. When Reed protested, they gently placed a broad leather strap across his chest.

Mickey Reed's last words on earth were, "Goddamn you to hell. You're too big a coward to let me die a whole man. I just hope that when *your* time comes, you ask someone to shoot you to get you out of your misery, and he refuses. You'll know then."

Ross shook off the memory of Reed's emotional plea and told Dirkson, "It was a day when a lot of us did things we can't understand now. When we get home, why don't you look up Reed's next of kin. Give them the money and explain how Mickey died a hero. Don't let it eat at your conscience."

Dirkson sat quietly. "Captain," he finally asked, "do we need a thousand dollars to buy gas?"

Ross sat bolt upright. "Yes, but why do you ask?"

"'Cause that's how much Mickey said he had—maybe even a few dollars more."

"Mother of God." Ross had trouble making his numb lips form words. Would Reed want the money used for the benefit of the crew? Recalling those last, bitter words, he somehow doubted it. "What do you think, Milt? Would he want us to use it or would he want his family to have it?"

"I don't really know, Sir." Dirkson's voice carried a thoughtful note. "You see, Mickey didn't have a family, so far as I know. His mom and dad were dead. There may have been a sister or something, but he didn't hardly ever get mail."

"Have you talked to the others about the money?"

"No, Sir. I was ashamed to. Guenther especially would be mad—
he and Mickey were pretty close toward the end. No, I've thought about
it a lot. It comes down to this—there's a right and a wrong thing to
do. I want to do what's right. I just don't know what 'right' is in this
case. Mickey was so damn big and strong. Next to you, he was about
the bravest man on the crew. If he was here, I think he'd say, Hell,
yes, go ahead and take it. Then again, I don't know. Do you suppose
we should ask the general?"

"No, Milt. Deciding this is my job. As you said, there's a right thing
to do and a wrong thing to do—and Mickey isn't here to tell us which
is which. We'll spend the money for fuel. I vow that I'll look up his
next of kin when we get home and make reimbursement. If this is wrong,
then this whole cockeyed war is wrong. Only history can sort out which
courses of action were the proper ones and which ones were blunders."

The distant range of barren mountains was framed in the gray-pink
flush of dawn. Ross sat beside the truck driver, straining to understand
the conversation between Abdul and the gate guard. He told himself
that the tendency for his teeth to chatter and knees to tremble resulted
from the early morning desert chill.

The indistinct shape of a fuel bowser lurked to their left. The
occasional glow of a cigarette attested to the driver's patience. The
first rays of light revealed the *Happy Hooker,* looking as if she were
already straining forward for takeoff. Ross felt a slight catch in his
throat. Could a machine have feelings? The thought was heresy, perhaps,
but he'd like to present the affirmative side in a debate.

General Sprague had joined the pair at the locked compound gate.
Ramrod straight, he issued orders via Abdul. The confused guard
saluted and began fumbling with his keys. Ross released breath he
hadn't realized he was holding.

"Okay, troops, get cracking." Ross swung into the accelerated predeparture routine they had rehearsed the day before. Dirkson and
Guenther clambered onto a wing to help the fuel truck driver wrestle
thick hoses to open tank-filler caps. Leckie and Hanson tugged each
prop nine blades in reverse to free any fluids collected in the bottom
cylinders. Ross and Ham raced through their preflight—Pitot-head
cover removed, landing gear pins removed, chocks—to hell with them.
There was no ground crew to pull them after engine start anyway.

In the cockpit, General Sprague was setting controls and switches to start-engines positions. Their army truck driver and the gate guard watched this unaccustomed flurry of activity with looks bordering on awe.

Ross was fastening his seat belt as he heard the fuel truck's engine rumble to life. Ham swung up from the bomb bay catwalk, calling, "We got fourteen hunnert gallons in the mains, Sir. Ready to start engines." A ragged cheer sounded from the waist compartment.

Force of habit made Ross shout, "Clear three!"

To Ross's amazement, Sprague's response from the right seat was a roar of laughter. Hanson joined in, then Ham. Following Sprague's pointing finger, Ross saw the departing fuel truck. As the vehicle paused at the gate, he saw Abdul hand the driver a small packet. Then he saw why his crewmen were laughing. The sun, now fully risen, illuminated the tanker's white broadside. The dark blue Lufthansa logo made the whole trip worthwhile, Ross decided.

"Start number three," he called out crisply. "We're going home."

Epilogue

☆ ☆ ☆

THE HEARING

DAY FIVE

6 December 1945
Hearing Room B, Building 1048, War Department

Janet inspected the day's first witness with extreme interest. The pale, lantern-jawed man was seated stiffly erect, feet planted firmly on the floor and seemingly oblivious to his surroundings. He leafed through a small notebook, removed from the breast pocket of his gray wool suit. A German. The enemy. He was the first German she had ever seen up close, she realized with surprise—the first whom she knew to be a German, at least.

He hardly resembled the blond, blue-eyed, Teutonic prototype she had come to associate with the race. This one had black hair, brown eyes—he didn't even have a saber scar on his cheek. He did, however, have an artificial left leg. He also spoke flawless English.

General Woods was conferring with Colonel Blankenship prior to opening the day's session. The recorder nodded and seated himself behind his file-laden table.

Woods departed from routine and initiated the questioning himself. "Your name is Klaus Weber?"

"It is." Weber's voice was calm, measured.

"You are a native of Germany?"

"I am."

"You were formerly an officer in the German army? The rank of colonel, I believe?"

"That is correct."

"What were your major duties and assignment during the summer of 1943?"

"I was assigned to the Military Assistance Group in Bucharest, Romania, as Speer's representative to coordinate oil production and delivery."

"Yes," Woods said, consulting his notes. "*Herr* Weber, I see here that you are scheduled to give testimony before the War Crimes Commission. I wish to assure you there will be no attempt by this board to establish your guilt or innocence of any charges preferred by that body. We are concerned only with establishing the defensive capability in place around Ploesti prior to the bombing raid of 1 August 1943. Do you understand that?"

"Yes, Sir."

"Very well. For the record I will state that the commander of the Romanian Defense Forces, Maj. Gen. Alfred Gerstenberg, is not available. It is believed that the general was captured by the Red Army when it overran Bucharest in 1944 and is presumed dead. Can you confirm that?"

A shadow flitted across the man's prematurely aged features. "I'm sorry, I cannot. I was evacuated from Bucharest after I was injured during the August 1944 raid." He lightly slapped his left leg. "The official reports I had access to in 1944 state that the general was captured, however."

"Thank you. Colonel Blankenship, will you continue the questioning?"

"Yes, Sir." The lanky officer remained seated as he asked, "*Herr* Weber, the German order of battle as we have reconstructed it was, on that day, roughly four wings of fighter aircraft and forty antiaircraft batteries. I realize that your duties were not essentially military in nature, but do you agree with that estimate?"

"From my observation, I believe that those numbers sound correct."

"Can you tell us of other defensive measures General Gerstenberg developed?"

"The general's most effective passive defense was a pipeline erected on the town's perimeter and connecting the major refineries. Its purpose was to divert supplies of oil from bomb-damaged facilities to those still functional."

Janet wished for a cigarette. The German was interesting, but his dry voice and dull testimony grated on her nerves. She would hear nothing she sought in the way of answers from this man.

Her thoughts turned to Ross Colyer. He had phoned to tell her that he would not be called by the board after all, and would be returning to his home in Kansas City the day after next. She had agreed to meet him for lunch. A mental picture of their dates in Hawaii, what seemed eons ago, brought a pang of nostalgia.

She returned her attention to the hearing.

". . . the blast walls surrounding key production facilities—power-houses, cracking plants, and the like—were particularly effective. Although these walls were originally constructed to contain explosions and fires of normal origin, any bomb dropped outside of them caused minimal damage. The later, high-altitude attacks did not have the pinpoint accuracy to drop inside them."

"Yes." Blankenship had risen and resumed his customary pacing while asking questions. "Much has been said about the low-level-delivery aspect of the mission. You indicate that, in your opinion, the bombing was more effective than later high-level raids, am I correct?"

"If the mission had been flown as planned, the results would have been devastating. Consider that less than half of the bomb tonnage departing North Africa was actually dropped on critical targets."

"Interesting. Accuracy and surprise were considered key elements," Blankenship mused.

"Surprise?" Weber raised his eyebrows. "The command post alerted us at oh-nine-hundred hours that a large task force of American bombers had assembled off North Africa and was headed in our direction. Confusion resulted when they approached at low altitude, but they were expected."

Weber's words produced expressions of astonishment. General Blake's normally pallid complexion was marked with two red spots, resembling rouge, on each cheek. "Just a minute, *Herr* Weber. You say your defense forces knew when Tidal Wave left Benghazi?"

"Oh, yes. The leading formations were tracked from over Corfu, across Albania and Bulgaria—yes, the defenses were all in position, but prepared for an attack from high altitude."

A silence ensued during which the board members rapidly scribbled notes.

Blankenship resumed his questioning. "*Herr* Weber, what was the net result of the mission, in terms of curtailed production?"

The stolid German pursed his lips. "In the short-range view, negligible." He heard sharply in-drawn breaths from the board members and turned to face them.

"Consider that the Ploesti complex was operating at about 80 percent capacity before the raid. Damage estimates placed initial destruction of key production units at between 20 and 30 percent. Within five days the perimeter pipeline arrangement allowed undamaged plants to pick up that loss by going to full capacity.

"In the long-range view, however, those lost facilities were irreplaceable. The steel and skilled manpower required for reconstruction simply wasn't available. Therefore, production curtailment was immediate after the massive high-level raids of 1944 began."

General Woods interrupted. "Colonel Blankenship, we are approaching the noon hour. How much longer will you require to obtain *Herr* Weber's testimony?"

"At least two more hours, General."

"Very well. Let's recess until thirteen-hundred hours. Will you see that *Herr* Weber is accommodated?" Woods tapped his gavel and the group rose, stretched, and commenced discussing lunch arrangements.

Janet had dressed with unusual care that morning. She wore her last pair of new silk stockings, a moss green suit, white silk blouse with a touch of lace gracing the high neckline, and pumps with heels higher than she was accustomed to wearing.

Showered, standing nude in front of the open lingerie drawer, impulse had prompted her to select the sexiest bra and panties she owned. You idiot, she scolded herself, whatever do you think can happen on a one-hour luncheon date? Nevertheless, she took extra time to pile her hair into the upswept swirl that Ross had once admired.

Ross had captured a table and stood as the maitre d' ushered Janet to the secluded corner. Ross had selected a waterfront seafood grotto.

"I'm trying to wipe out the cherrystone clam inventory before I go back to Kansas," he explained.

Janet extended both white-gloved hands. "Oh, Ross. God, it's good to see you."

Clasping her hands, Ross bestowed a chaste peck on her upturned cheek. "I'd forgotten how elegantly beautiful you are, Janet." He grinned. "Don't look around, but I'm getting envious looks from every man in the house."

Janet chuckled as he seated her at the white linen–draped table.

"Well, Major Colyer, at least the war has taught you how to turn a nice bit of flattery. I can remember when it was 'Hi, red on the head. I'm starved, let's eat.'"

Ross smiled, but let the remark pass as he folded his lanky frame into the chair facing her. "A martini?" he asked, raising an eyebrow.

"Why not?" Janet responded.

Ross beckoned a waitress. "First of all, my sincere condolences. I don't express my emotions well in writing, but I know it was a bad time for you."

Janet twisted the wedding set she still wore and sobered. "Thank you, Ross. And your letter was beautiful; I still have it. I'm still not sure I understand what happened—or why."

"It was all so damn senseless, bizarre . . . ," Ross responded.

Janet held up her hand for him to stop talking. She waited until the waitress deposited their drinks, then said, "Ross, before you start explaining, I want you to know something. I am not good at putting up pretenses—mouthing emotions I don't feel."

She sipped the chilled martini and nodded with approval. "About BT," she resumed. "Our marriage was a mistake. He knew it and I knew it. We talked about it before he went overseas. We agreed to wait until after the war and try to start over. Maybe things would have worked out—I don't know. You see, I didn't know the man I married. Of course, I was devastated by that telegram from the War Department—I was truly fond of BT. But after the shock wore off I realized that I had no deep sense of grief or loss." She raised her eyes and met Ross's level stare.

"I—I had no idea, Janet. I'm sorry. I—"

"Don't apologize, Ross," she said, cutting him off. "I've only recently faced up to the situation—been truly honest with myself. Attending the hearing has helped, although I've learned nothing I had hoped to find out. You see, I felt frustrated. I was angry. I'd been cheated, I told myself. Cheated out of a little house on the edge of town, of bearing children, of attending the PTA, of going to the seashore on vacations—all because of a goddamned war. I'm afraid I blamed BT for something he had absolutely no control over." Janet paused as the waitress returned.

"You folks ready to order?" she asked cheerily. "Another cocktail?"

"Uh—" Ross tore his attention from Janet's discourse with difficulty. "You ready to order, Janet?"

They ordered cherrystone clams, with stuffed crab to follow, and a dry Rhine wine.

Janet gave a shaky laugh. "Oh, Ross. Forgive me. Here we are—haven't seen each other for ages and I'm pouring my heart out like a teenager. I haven't heard a word about what you're doing—haven't given you a chance. Tell me about your tour in the Pacific. Did you get back to Honolulu?"

"Yeah," Ross laughed. "You wouldn't know the place. I don't think I like the new Hawaii. All hustle-bustle—the old lazy life has disappeared."

"And the airplane," Janet queried, "the *Happy Hooker*. What eventually happened to her?"

Ross grinned happily. "We brought her home, you know. She was declared war-weary and was headed for the scrapyard. The crew wanted to steal her—same as we did in Turkey—and head for the States. Anyway, a reporter from some paper in New York became interested and ran a feature article. The brass couldn't stand the heat and allowed us to ferry her to our old base, Mountain Home, Idaho. She was still there being used to train new pilots at the end of the war. It was like losing one of the family—that day we walked away."

Janet nodded understandingly. "Then?" she asked. "I know you went to the Pacific with a fighter squadron. How did that happen? Wasn't one combat tour enough?"

Ross chuckled. "When I came back from Turkey, my Christmas present was a set of orders sending me to B-29 training. That was okay—it's a great airplane. But the training was to be en route to a new group being formed. A group to be assigned to the Twentieth Air Force. And guess who got orders to serve as one of their new wing COs?"

Janet laughed. "From your tone, it could be none other than—"

"None other," Ross admitted with a rueful grin. "Brigadier General Elliott Sprague. I just couldn't go through another combat tour under that guy. I'd been in touch with my old CO at Thunderbird Field—Major Wilson. Remember him? His wife was a cousin or something to BT."

Janet nodded.

"After his heart attack, he was grounded and ended up in air force headquarters as a personnel officer. I did something I vowed never to do. I asked him as a personal favor to get me off that damned assignment. He did, and I ended up flying P-51s out of Iwo Jima.

"The Templeton family was finished with me, though. I applied for a regular commission, but the senator blocked it. I had enough points for discharge after V-E Day, so I said to hell with it and took a release from active duty. Kept my reserve commission, as you can see, however."

"So what are you doing now?" Janet queried.

"Going broke," Ross replied bluntly. "I teamed up with a discharged flight engineer and we bought a couple of war surplus C-47s—DC-3 in civilian talk—and an old Nordung Norseman and went into the air charter business.

"Well, first thing, a pilot we hired pranged one of the gooneybirds— lost an engine on takeoff and couldn't handle it. That almost wiped out our operating capital. I'll clear more money from my travel voucher to show up here for the hearing than we made last month."

He shook his head. "That's the end of the saga of Ross Colyer," he said. "Now I want *you* to finish. You said you learned something at the hearings, but not what you went there for. I'm confused."

Janet finished her drink. "How awful. I know you had your heart set on an army career—then to have that happen. But," she faced him with a wry grin, "back to your question.

"I wanted to know *why,* Ross. *Why* do men do this? Would it have made any difference if we had just shrugged our shoulders and said, 'Okay, Tojo, you can have that goddamn island. It really isn't good for much anyway'? Or maybe, 'Okay, *Herr* Hitler, do whatever you like with Europe. Stay on your side of the Atlantic and we'll stay on our side—raise our kids, make our automobiles and refrigerators—only don't *bother* us.'"

"Janet—" Ross, shaken by what he was hearing, reached across and imprisoned both her hands in his. "Janet, it isn't like that—not like that at all."

She freed one hand and reached for her empty martini glass. Ross pushed his own barely touched drink in front of her and continued.

"What they were doing was evil. It wouldn't have ended in Honolulu or London. *We* would have been next. No little houses on the edge of town, no PTA, no new cars. It would have been concentration camps, forced labor, and churches turned into office space for bureaucrats here, too. Can't you see?"

The cherrystone clams sat in their melting bed of ice, ignored. Janet finished half of Ross's drink as he continued.

"We *had* to fight back. It's always been like this—ever since the cavemen decided they couldn't live with the mammoths and saber-toothed tigers sitting outside."

Janet smiled bitterly as she ordered, "Eat your clams, Ross. I know what you're saying. It's what I learned during these past five days; it's something I learned when our neighbor's boy wrecked my play-house."

Ross dipped a clam in tomato sauce laced with horseradish and grinned. "What did you do?"

Janet speared the last clam and waved it playfully in front of him. "I had a new pair of roller skates. I asked that little bastard over to have some lemonade and cookies. While he was drinking his lemonade I went behind him and cold-cocked him with one of my new skates." She swabbed the clam with hot sauce and devoured it. "It caused quite a fuss," she concluded.

Ross roared with laughter, causing heads to turn. Wiping his eyes, he said, "I rest my case."

Janet adjusted her napkin as the waitress slid platters of crabs bulging with aromatic dressing before them. "Don't be smug, Major. I haven't finished. The 'Big Truth' I learned is that there is no one answer. All men react differently to war. Some, like General Sprague"—she made the name sound like an epithet—"revel in it. Some—my father is one—treat the business of killing other people like an eight-to-five job. BT saw war as a great big poker game. Then there are the cowards—the ones who throw down their guns and run. Those I can understand. Others, like yourself, regard war as a distasteful duty—like changing a dirty diaper. It takes a fortitude you didn't know you had, but you do it. But I still don't know *why*. And don't try to tell me that you're all slavish robots willing to lay down your lives just because someone orders you to. I may never know—can *you* explain it? Do *you* know what I'm asking?"

They put down their eating utensils alongside their unfinished lunch. Ross regarded the tense face only an arm's length away.

"Yeah, I know what you mean. Why do crews pass up a perfectly sound reason to not go on a mission? Mechanical problems, you're running a temperature, weather—but you know that the other crews are going with the same problems. You get sidelong looks and veiled questions in the club. So you go. You tell yourself that the absence of one plane in a formation can make a difference."

"What about Ploesti, Ross?" Janet was back to twisting the platinum and diamond wedding set. "This board of inquiry was called to determine if the losses were justified. Were they? Was Ploesti *that* important?"

Ross summoned the waitress and ordered brandy alexanders. Not until they were served did he answer.

"I don't know, Janet. You could go nuts trying to answer that. You see, there were lots of Ploestis. We didn't have a Jomini to extol the beauty of classically executed battle plans. We just went out there toe-to-toe and slugged it out. Mistakes were made, sure. But we won the damn thing. I guess it all comes down to this: Is war itself a barbaric, anachronistic way of settling disputes? Most people will say yes, but I'll bet my money, marbles, and chalk that this won't be the last one. Likewise, I'll bet that a lot of people around the world, the Jews for instance, would say that the war was necessary and worthwhile."

Janet sipped her drink as she considered his words. "I just wish I knew what it was like up there. I'd like, for instance, to have you describe a mission. From beginning to end—how you felt, what you said, what other people said and did."

"I'd like to tell you about it—some of it, at least." Ross drew a deep breath. "Janet, it would mean that you'd have to come back to Kansas City with me. The explaining may take some time—a long time."

"I have the time."

Ross regarded her at some length before responding. She met his level gaze, her lips forming a faint smile, pulse fluttering in her throat.

"Then let's not waste any of it. My place or yours?" he asked softly.

Janet flashed an impish grin. "Neither, for the time being. Ross, do you remember what we did four years ago today?"

He looked blank.

"It's December the sixth. Four years ago today you took me to the Hickam base theater to see Bob Hope and Dorothy Lamour in *Road to Morocco*. It's playing here, in one of those theaters that show nothing but old movies. I'm not going back to the hearing—there are no answers there. For a couple of hours I'd like to put the war behind me. Later, we'll talk about Kansas City—among other things."

With those words the years between them dwindled away, faded out. All the bad times, the distance, their separate journeys, the people they had once known receded into the background with one tender, lingering look. None of it was as important as the moment they now shared, a moment that seemed, somehow, in the silence, eternal.

"Yes," Ross said softly, "we'll do that."

Book Two in Ray Rosenbaum's
Wings of War

☆ ☆ ☆

HAWKS

Continuing the saga of the United States Air Force as
you follow Ross Colyer through World War II in the
Pacific and beyond.

From the Book:

"Are you calling me a coward?" Ross asked, his eyes blazing.

"No way. You've flown a combat tour in bombers—looked death
and destruction straight in the eye and didn't blink. Given time to apply
logic in a dogfight, you'd still come up with the right answer. But right
answers have to come instantaneously, a reflex; in other words, instinctively. It's no discredit. You're a brave officer and a great pilot, but
with your attitude you won't last five missions in a fighter."

Ross leaped to his feet. "That's bullshit, Major! Put me up against
the best damn pilot you have in the squadron—the group. I'll prove
you're wrong."

Cipolla studied Ross's white-lipped expression for a moment, then said, "That's me, Colyer. Get into your flying gear. Takeoff's in thirty minutes. I'll whip your ass."

Ross spurred his Mustang into the air with harsh, punishing movements. Within minutes his throbbing rage changed to icy, detached composure. Stick and rudder became an extension of taut motor nerves —his every thought transmitted to control surfaces without conscious effort.

A coin toss had designated Cipolla the aggressor. Where, when, and from what quarter would his attack come? Ross wondered. Ross's first reaction was to climb, take up a position at about thirty-five thousand feet, close to the '51's operational ceiling eliminating the possibility of a high-angle attack out of the sun. No, he was no match for the experienced combat ace upstairs. Ross smiled grimly and decided to do just the opposite. He nosed over and, leveling off at a hundred feet, took up a heading for sector five—the area reserved for simulated air-to-air combat.

Okay, he muttered to himself, streaking across the desolate terrain, come on down and mix it up. I can see you coming. By halving the sphere of the aggressor's attack, he could concentrate on the intensely blue sky, with only a few puffy cumuli to provide scanty, inadequate concealment. He reached the sector's northern boundary and reversed course—wondering as he did what the cunning veteran was up to.

Tight-lipped, Ross systematically scanned the pristine dome of desert sky. There, almost on the horizon; a flash of sunlight reflecting off glass or metal. He lost it—then suddenly he was staring a spinning prop directly in the face. Jesus Christ! The racing airplane was coming at him *head on.* Not only head on, but slightly lower than Ross's own jackrabbit-scattering altitude.

About to haul the stick into his gut and break straight up, Ross hesitated. No—that's exactly what the son of a bitch wants me to do, he thought. Cipolla would use his superior speed—he must have his ship past the redline—to loop above Ross and dive from behind for a shot a child couldn't miss.

At the last minute Ross stood the Mustang on one wing without climbing. Its wingtip brushing cactus, Ross crammed on war-emergency power, then pulled the protesting craft into a gut-wrenching climbing turn. He clawed for altitude, searching ahead for his attacker. There!

By God, he was above the other fighter. Hold the altitude advantage, he told himself, all the way to forty thousand if necessary. He felt the oxygen auto-mix regulator start feeding its dry, biting gas.

Ross watched the altimeter wind steadily upward, the powerful Rolls-Royce/Packard Merlin screaming at max continuous-rated power—its supercharger at high boost. Cipolla's ship was still below the horizon. Ross's altitude advantage had dwindled, however—a thousand, perhaps two thousand feet; not much. The altimeter's short hand, the one measuring tens-of-thousands of feet, edged toward the four. He was entering altitudes well above student restrictions. The rarified atmosphere dictated a change in breathing: Instead of inhaling, he let the regulator feed his lungs with pressurized oxygen, then forcibly expelled it. To hell with it, he thought. He was in a sudden-death struggle; there'd be no second chance.

Then he saw his adversary level off and turn away. All right! Ross turned to take up the chase. At last he could use that slim altitude advantage. The distance between the two aircraft narrowed. Ross frowned. Watch that sneaky bastard, he told himself. Not even the greenest novice would turn tail and flee in straight and level flight. What did his elusive quarry have in mind? It came to him in a flash—a long-ago description of a maneuver the Russians used with their slower P-39s against the superior Messerschmitts.

Ross focused his attention on the dark plume of exhaust smoke pouring from Cipolla's engine. Suddenly it disappeared. Now. He hauled his own throttle to full idle and raised the nose. There it was: a snap roll. Had Ross remained straight and level at full power, he would have gone screaming past, unable to fire, and Cipolla would have neatly reversed their roles.

Calmly, coldly, Ross moved into position for a classic firing pass from above and to one side. He started the gun camera running before the squadron commander's ship entered his sight picture. Then he held the target centered for a full three seconds.

Ross swooped away in a victory roll and pressed the mike button. "Tallyho, Red Aggressor," he called cheerfully.